50690010: W9-APM-734
Alwyn, Cy...
Scent of murder /

NOV 0 5 2001

11-6-01

SCENT OF MURDER

CYNTHIA G. ALWYN

THOMAS DUNNE BOOKS / ST. MARTIN'S MINOTAUR ≈ NEW YORK

THOMAS DUNNE BOOKS.
An imprint of St. Martin's Press.

www.minotaurbooks.com

Designed by Lorelle Graffeo

Library of Congress Cataloging-in-Publication Data

Alwyn, Cynthia G.
  Scent of murder / Cynthia G. Alwyn.–1st ed.
    p. cm.
  ISBN 0-312-26559-X
  1. Women volunteers in social service–Fiction. 2. Search and rescue operations–Fiction. 3. Sacramento (Calif.)–Fiction. 4. Women dog owners–Fiction 5. Serial murders–Fiction. 6. Search dogs–Fiction. 7. Kidnapping–Fiction. I. Title.

PS3601.L88 S38 2001
813'.6–dc 21

                            2001019271

10 9 8 7 6 5 4 3 2

For "The Girls." Always remembered:

Chance Independence

Vonshore's Tallee Ho

CH. Woodbine Madrone Ledge Keely

ACKNOWLEDGMENTS

To Anne Hawkins, my agent and true friend: thank you for the surprise telephone call and your unwavering support.

To Ruth Cavin, an exceptional editor: thank you for your encouragement.

Special thanks to Lori Bailey, Media Coordinator, Federal Bureau of Investigation, Dallas, Texas, and Sabino Vasquez, Arson/Bomb Investigator, Fort Worth Fire Department, Fort Worth, Texas, for their patience, time, and wise counsel.

SCENT OF MURDER

"ARE WE LOST?" Jett asked.

Lightning dissolved the night.

"Wow." Brenna squinted and shifted her gaze to the dark floorboard. "That made my eyes ache."

Thunder boomed, deep and heavy. The rain's raps on the Suburban turned into a drumroll. "Chattanooga Choo Choo" blared from the radio, the peppy beat syncopating with the swipe of the windshield wipers. From the cargo area of the truck came a softer thumping, out of sync.

"Can you see the street sign?" Jett asked.

She wiped a peephole in the fogged window and peered out. "No, I can't see anything."

"Neither can I."

Even at high speed, the windshield wipers couldn't open a visibility hole.

Lightning blinded her again; thunder bellowed. A flash of yellow skidded sideways in front of them. Jett jerked the steering wheel to avoid hitting the other car, but the Suburban continued forward instead of turning.

Brenna braced herself against the dashboard, held her breath, and glanced at Jett. He sat rigid, his hands fused to the steering wheel.

The two vehicles sped past each other without touching.

She exhaled a shaky breath and then realized she was sweating. With a sticky hand, she turned off the radio.

"Jett . . ." she said, softly.

"I know."

A few moments later, he veered into a dry cleaner's parking lot. She watched him peel his fingers off the steering wheel and then grimace, as if they ached. Only then did she notice the marks of her fingernails in her own palms.

Jett leaned back, sighed, and rubbed his eyes.

The rain blasted the truck in waves.

He turned toward her and smiled. "Don't worry, Irish. This downpour won't last long."

She looked at the green digits on the dashboard clock: 1:43.

The worst of the storm had passed through Seattle and its suburbs twenty minutes earlier, leaving downed tree branches and scattered power outages. Emergency crews were already out, their yellow lights flashing in the night. But this sudden deluge had sent even those brave souls dashing for cover.

When lightning flashed again, Brenna glanced at the bruised, swollen clouds. "This is the wrong night for a little girl to run away from home."

"If it keeps raining, you may not have to look far." He twisted and set his right foot on the hump between the front floorboards. "Okay, Miss Navigator, do you know where we are?"

Brenna smiled at her boss. During high school, twenty-odd years ago, she and Jett had been friends. Then he moved to California, and she ended up as a schoolteacher in Texas, taking care of her grandmother. Years later, she began working with a renowned dog trainer. When Aaron told her a private investigator was arriving one afternoon to pick up two dogs to work narcotics detection for his new business, she was amazed to find the man was Jett. They renewed their friendship. After both her grandmother and Aaron died, Jett offered her a job as his administrative assistant. She'd needed a change and accepted.

"The next time somebody wakes you up in the middle of the night to give you directions, print."

"Very funny."

He tried to hide a grin, but she saw it. Good-natured teasing peppered their relationship, easing the tension and slowing the adrenaline that a callout raised.

"Let me see those directions," he said. "Maybe I can decipher them." He turned on the interior lamp, highlighting his neatly trimmed reddish-blond hair, ruddy complexion, and moss green eyes. Right now those eyes were squinting at the words.

"Want to borrow my reading glasses?" Brenna asked.

"I don't need them," he said, holding the paper to the light.

She laughed and handed them over. "Here, Mr. Magoo."

He sighed and slipped the glasses on without looking at her. "You know, this has to be our little secret."

"It'll cost you."

Brenna's black-and-tan German Shepherd hung her head over the seat and gently bumped Brenna's jaw with her long muzzle.

"Take it easy, Brie," Brenna said. "We're almost there."

Sabrina's long tail thumped against a red backpack. She leaned over to Jett and licked his ear.

Brenna laughed and stroked the dog's muzzle. "Leave him alone, Funny Face. Come pester me, if you must."

Jett peered through the windshield. "I think I see a McDonald's farther down." He glanced at her. "We're on the right street."

"I hope the kid holes up somewhere until the rain stops."

"We got an early call on this one," he said. "There's a good chance we'll find her."

As quickly as the torrent began, it stopped. Jett drove out of the parking lot, and, two turns later, found Stanford Circle.

Brenna didn't need to double-check the address: two police cars and a sheriff's unit sat in front of a one-story redbrick ranch with white shutters and a deep front porch.

The entire neighborhood was dark; no streetlights or yard lamps glowed.

"The power's out in this section," she said.

Jett parked on the street behind the sheriff's cruiser. "I'll start the report," he said. "Meet me on the porch." He cut across the yard to the house.

Brenna scratched the dog's ears and patted her nose. "Are you ready?" Brie wagged her tail and perked her ears.

Raindrops freckled the windshield. Thunder grumbled. As Brenna opened the passenger door, the sprinkles became a shower, dumping another wash on the saturated ground. She slammed the passenger door and glanced at her watch.

Brie nudged her and rested her head on Brenna's shoulder.

She patted the dog's head. "Me, too."

Three minutes later, the rain hitched a ride on the wind and drifted east. As Brenna opened the door, a police car drove past. Tires hissed on wet pavement. Water coursed in rivulets along curbs and gurgled into storm drains.

Brenna got out of the truck and walked to the back; Brie was pawing at the tailgate. This dog lived to search. When she found her "victims"—those searched for—she wiggled all over and tickled them with doggy kisses.

"Do you want out, Funny Face?"

The dog stretched her neck and bumped her nose against Brenna's chin.

Brenna lowered the tailgate; Brie stepped forward, anxious but awaiting her owner's command. When it came, she jumped to the ground and began sniffing for an appropriate place to relieve herself. Meanwhile Brenna studied the neighborhood.

Spots of light dotted the darkness between houses and in an open space where the street curved out of sight. At least a few people were out with flashlights.

Most of the older brick homes had yard lampposts and trimmed lawns. The police cars sat in front of a ranch house with limp daffodils and tulips in the front flower bed.

A tall black man stepped between the sheriff's car and the Suburban. Without his law-enforcement equipment belt, he always reminded her of a ruler, straight up and down.

"Is that you, String Bean?" she asked.

"Rob Garrett at your service, ma'am." He placed a huge, scarred hand on the side of her face and planted a kiss on her forehead. "Jett said you were out here."

"Hey, big guy." She slipped her arm around his waist and gave him a hug. "I expected to see you this afternoon."

"I'd planned to come, but Yvonne had a honey-do list with my name on it."

"How's the family?"

"Reggie's great; Yvonne and I have our good days and bad days." He stepped back and glanced at the street. "Who else is coming?"

"Adam is flying up Marco and Connie."

Garrett shook his head. "The ex-cop brigade. Adam and Jett."

"And you."

"Not quite the same," he said. "Now Adam is a big financier with his own plane, and Jett runs his own company."

Brie trotted over to them; Garrett squatted and spread open his arms. "Come here, you beautiful girl." He hugged the dog and then gently rubbed her ears. "Are you still digging in the garbage?"

"Yes, she is," Brenna said. "If I don't watch her, she pulls everything out of the trash and sets it in a line across the kitchen floor. Then she wags her tail and perks her ears. I think she expects a reward."

Garrett laughed and hugged the dog again. "I sure have missed you."

"I've got a second dog now, named Feather. A Bouvier des Flandres."

"She look like a Giant Schnauzer? That kind?"

She nodded. "Stockier, though. A longer coat. From a distance, she reminds me of a bear." Brenna smiled. "You should see the two of them. She and Brie play tag and Catch the Paw and a dozen other games. They're so funny."

"Why didn't you bring her?"

"She pulled a leg muscle. Better for her to stay home this time."

When Brenna clapped her hands, Brie tore away from Garrett, jumped into the Suburban, and lay down.

"I thought you were working for Seattle PD," she said.

"Being a sheriff's deputy for King County keeps me plenty busy."

"Is this place under county jurisdiction?"

"The city limit is just over there." He pointed toward the end of the street. "City and county work together when it's this close to the line. You'll like these guys, Bren. They're easy to work with."

She nodded toward the house. "What's the story? I know the little girl ran away."

"Four years old."

"Why did she leave?"

He shrugged. "No one knows."

"There has to be a reason." Brenna glanced toward the house. "Isn't four a little young to run away?"

"The family has a new baby. I suspect sibling rivalry played a big part in Zoe's decision to take a hike."

"Zoe." The name created an image in her mind: short, dark hair, fair skin, dark eyes. She wondered if the mental picture would resemble the child. "Did they have an argument?"

"Dad says no."

"Both parents here?"

"Yep."

"How long has she been gone?"

"Best we can tell, about half an hour or so. A big clap of thunder woke everyone up just after one."

Brenna glanced at her watch: 1:47

"Mr. Hendricks went to check on Zoe and found her gone," Garrett said. "Would you talk to him?"

"Jett's taking the preliminary report."

"But your first impressions of people have been dead-on. I'd like to know what you think of this guy."

"Why?"

He grinned. "Humor me. I'll have Evan stay with Brie."

Garrett spoke into his radio; Brenna took the opportunity to kiss Brie on the nose.

A sandy-haired young man came out of the house, carrying a lit hurricane lamp. He set it on the wicker porch table. Then he removed a pink towel from around his neck, draped it over the arm of the wooden porch swing, and jogged toward Garrett.

"He's soaked to the skin," she said. "Been out in the rain?"

"He fell in the creek."

"What creek?" She turned and scanned the area.

Garrett pointed past the houses. "Over there, behind the park."

Evan stopped in front of Garrett. "Yes, sir?"

Brenna thought Evan looked young, maybe twenty-two: a babe compared with her thirty-nine years. He stood rigid, ready for action.

"Stay with Brie until we get back," Garrett said, indicating the dog.

Evan glanced at the truck. "But—it's a dog, sir."

"A very special dog," Garrett said.

The young deputy snapped to attention. "Yes, sir."

Brenna started toward the house.

"Uh, ma'am . . . shouldn't I put the tailgate up to keep the dog in the truck?"

"No need; she'll stay right where I left her." Brenna smiled. "Brie won't bite, Deputy. Give her a pat."

As Brenna and Garrett walked up the driveway toward the house, she touched the hood of the black Seville parked in front of the garage. It felt hot.

A police officer came onto the porch and held the front door open for them. Brenna paused in the foyer. Hurricane lamps burned in every room; another police officer bent over a map spread on top of the table in the dining room to her right; a short brunette paced the hallway, a crying baby in her arms.

Garrett directed Brenna into the living room.

"Brenna Scott," Jett said, rising from a white couch. "This is Tom Hendricks, Zoe's father." A dark-haired man in a wet gray jogging suit extended his hand.

She noticed his long fingers, manicured nails, and soft skin. These were not a workingman's hands. But he looked like the average guy. Medium height. Medium weight. Silver-framed glasses resting on a narrow nose. Dark eyes that alternated between dazed stares and frantic blinking.

"And this is Gary Brown," Jett said.

The other man in the room, wearing jeans and a red golf shirt, nodded.

Jett handed her the clipboard and his small flashlight. "I think we have all the information we need to get you started on a hasty search."

Tom Hendricks's hands opened and closed as if he were doing finger exercises. "Can your dog find my little girl?"

"We'll try," she said.

"Try?"

"I never make promises," she said. "I can't."

"Don't you have more than one dog?" Gary Brown stood. "Zoe could have gone anywhere."

"The rest of our team will be here soon." She smiled at him. "Are you part of the family, Mr. Brown?"

"No," Tom Hendricks said. "Gary works with me and lives close by, and I called him to help me look for Zoe."

"How close?" she asked.

"Ten minutes."

She turned to Tom Hendricks. "May I bring my search dog into the house?"

"We've looked everywhere," he said. "She isn't in the house and her Pooh Bear is gone . . . Winnie-the-Pooh. I looked outside, ran up and down the—" His voice broke. He cleared his throat and started again. "Gary drove all the streets in the neighborhood."

She turned to Gary Brown. "Do you have children? Might Zoe head for your house?"

He wilted and shook his head. "We hadn't thought of that."

Tom Hendricks said to Jett, "When you asked if Zoe had a

favorite place or if she had a special friend, I never thought of Gary's Amy. Our families spend a lot of time together, but I–I didn't think about the girls as friends."

"How old is Amy?" Jett asked.

"Five."

"May I bring in my dog?" Brenna asked again.

"Of course." Tom Hendricks hurried toward his wife in the hallway. "Honey, she might be on her way to Amy's."

Brenna returned to the Suburban and found Evan sitting on the tailgate, his arm looped around Brie's neck. The dog pawed his leg, demanding another pat.

When Evan saw Brenna, he jumped to his feet. "Sorry, ma'am."

"Fine with me," she said. "Brie loves attention."

"Friendly dog," he said. "Are you going to breed her?"

"No, she's got flat feet."

She scooted onto the tailgate, flipped on the rear overhead light, and scanned the information Jett had written on the Missing Persons form. Physical description, personality, fears. Zoe's father had discovered her missing shortly after one o'clock. She'd gone to bed at nine-thirty. Last seen wearing Tigger pajamas. On no medication–

"This license tag says California," Evan said. "How'd you get here so fast?"

Brenna glanced up. "I was in town anyway. We gave a presentation on search dogs to the Emergency Management Conference in Seattle this afternoon."

She looked at the report again. The family had eaten dinner around seven . . . except for the usual reluctance to go to bed, the little girl–

The truck says "Culpepper Investigations." Evan said. "What does a private investigator have to do with search dogs?"

"He works base camp for us. Communications, maps. Jett's dispatcher answers the telephone for our volunteer group twenty-four hours a day." She flipped the page and read as she talked. "We use his office as our callout number."

Brie wiggled her head under Brenna's arm, laid her chin on her owner's leg, and sighed.

"Then how did he get involved with your group?" Evan asked.

"When Jett offered me a job as his administrative assistant, the six years of search work I'd done in Texas came with me. Now, a number of Jett's employees are on our volunteer search team." She smiled. "I run the team, and he goes to presentations with me to help with the slide show and make new contacts for his business."

Brie sat up, her ears perked. She looked at Brenna, stretching her neck forward the way she always did when something unusual interested her.

Brenna followed the dog's gaze. In the darkness, something moved. A few seconds later, the form took the shape of a man sloshing across a front yard several houses down.

"Do you recognize that guy?" she asked.

He watched the figure a few seconds. "Looks like Mosser. He said his flashlight was on the blink." When Evan called out, the man waved.

"Brenna," Garrett called, "you ready?"

She slid off the tailgate, stepped onto the curb, and waved at him. Then she tied her shoulder-length dark hair into a ponytail, smiled at Evan, and clipped a leash onto Brie's collar. "Come on, girl."

The dog jumped out of the truck, moved to Brenna's left side, and trotted beside her to the front porch. When they reached the foyer, Tom Hendricks picked up a hurricane lamp and led them to Zoe's bedroom.

"WE'LL START HERE," Brenna said, "and then go through every room in the house."

"I told you, she's not inside."

"It won't take long to search your home. Sometimes we find kids sound asleep under a pile of clothes or inside a large box in the basement." She scanned the dark room. "May I use one of Zoe's shoes as a scent article?"

"What does that mean?"

"This dog is both an air-scenter and a scent discriminator. She'll find every human in a given area, or she can search for one particular person. She'll get Zoe's scent from the inside of her shoe. If the rain hasn't washed away your daughter's trail, Brie should be able to follow her."

"Could she confuse Zoe with someone else?"

"Everyone has his or her own specific scent, just like a fingerprint. Letting Brie smell a scent article is like showing you a photograph of my friend. If you saw her, you'd recognize her."

"But . . . if you find her, will the dog–"

"Brie is very gentle and she loves children." Brenna patted his shoulder. "Try not to worry." She stepped around a doll's house to the closet and chose a red-and-white tennis shoe. "Does this still fit her?"

He nodded. "She wore it yesterday."

She held it for the dog to sniff. "Brie, mark it." The dog nosed it and wagged her tail.

"Find her, Brie. Find Zoe."

The dog circled the room, stopped at the bed for a second, and then returned to Brenna. As they started to leave, the lights came on.

"Finally," Tom Hendricks said.

Brenna paused for her eyes to adjust. Then she studied the child's room: celery green walls, white wooden headboard, blue-and-green paisley comforter. Built-in bookshelves filled with dolls, stuffed animals, storybooks, puzzles. A book, *The Velveteen Rabbit,* lay on the floor beside the white nightstand. Black clumps and streaks formed a path on the beige carpet.

"Where did this mud come from?" she asked.

He looked at his crusted tennis shoes. "From me, I guess. When I couldn't find her outside, I searched the house again."

In the light, Brenna saw Hendricks clearly—a pale, frightened, thirtysomething man. His wife moved behind him, gently jogging her whimpering son.

Brenna pointed at the raised window beside the child's bed. "Do you always leave the window open at night?"

"It's only up two inches," he snapped. Then he softened. "Lori thinks . . . we think fresh air is good for her. It isn't too cold this time of year . . . is it?"

Brenna wondered how long it would be before he cracked. A framed photograph was lying facedown on the carpet near the door. She picked it up and studied the four faces smiling at the camera. Zoe had hazel eyes and deep dimples; her copper hair was held in place by a huge green bow. Not quite the image she'd imagined.

"I must have knocked that off the wall in the dark," Tom Hendricks said. He took the picture from her, stared at it a few moments, and then hugged it.

"Irish!" Jett called. "What'd you pick?"

She stepped into the hallway and showed him the shoe.

"Have you checked to see if any of her clothes are missing? A jacket, maybe?" Brenna asked.

"I did," Tom Hendricks said, "but without the light, I . . ."

"Would you look now, please?"

He rifled through the closet with a trembling hand, still hugging the picture with the other. "She has a coat and a jacket. They're both here."

"We're ready to search the other rooms," Brenna said. "Do you have a basement or attic?" When he nodded, she said, "We'll save those till last."

As Brie checked every room in the house, Brenna asked questions, both to obtain information and to keep Tom Hendricks from panicking. Zoe wanted a pet, a bunny if she couldn't have a cat or a dog, but she was allergic to animal dander; Tom Hendricks worked as a computer analyst; his wife, Lori, had quit her part-time job as a beauty consultant for Lady Lillian Cosmetics three weeks before Zachary was born. Zoe loved franks and beans, and waffles with cheese instead of syrup. Until the new baby came, she'd gone to day care three days a week. During the past two months, Lori had kept her daughter at home.

"Does Zoe have a temper?" Brenna asked.

"I guess," he said. "What do you mean?"

"What does Zoe do if she doesn't get her way?"

"She pouts a little, but she gets over it pretty quick."

"Has she ever said no to you or yelled at you?"

He looked horrified. "Of course not. We've taught Zoe to be respectful to all adults."

Brenna bit her tongue. Anything she said now might send Tom Hendricks into a tailspin, but once Zoe was found, she planned to have a little talk with him about teaching his child the basics of Stranger Danger.

They had reached the pink-walled living room; no Zoe. Brenna turned to Hendricks. "Does Zoe usually wake up during the night?"

"No, she's a very sound sleeper. I've carried her from the family room to her bed many times and she never stirred."

Searching the house had taken less than five minutes, but Brenna still felt a sense of urgency. She stopped in the foyer again. One of the front door's security bolts shifted up into a bracket above the door frame; the adjacent alarm panel showed a green light, indicating it stood disarmed.

"Mr. Hendricks," she said, "which exits are connected to your alarm system?"

"The doors."

She forced a smile and glanced at the floors. Except in the bedrooms and hallway, the house had hardwood floors with area rugs. Muddy footprints covered the foyer and led into the living and dining rooms. There had been tracks in the hallway and Zoe's room, but the other bedrooms' carpets hadn't shown smears. If Tom Hendricks had searched . . .

"Ready?" Jett stopped beside her and nodded toward the officer in charge, a uniformed man hunched over the table in the blue-and-white dining room. "The sergeant has had officers out looking for the last twenty minutes. He wants you to check the park and the creek area."

Still hugging the picture, Tom Hendricks stepped forward. "She wouldn't go there. Zoe's afraid of water, and we decided she's on her way to see Amy. Didn't we say that? Don't you think that's what happened?"

"Mr. Hendricks," Brenna said, "how did Zoe get out of the house?"

"I . . . I don't know."

"When you ran outside to look for her," she said, "how did you get out of the house?"

He stood there, blinking. "What?"

"How did you leave the house?"

He squinted as he looked past her, as if he were trying to remember.

Garrett and the police sergeant moved beside Jett.

"Irish?" Jett said.

"Mr. Hendricks," she said, "did you go out the back door?"

The sergeant shook his head. "I unlocked the patio door and checked the backyard. No sign she went that way."

"Did you go out the garage door?" she asked.

He began panting. "I–I don't know. I threw on some clothes and ran outside."

"Did you unlock any door?" she asked.

"I don't remember. Why?"

Hesitant to speak her concern aloud, Brenna glanced at Brie. Then she looked at Zoe's father. "If we knew which way Zoe left, it would give the dog a place to start, a spot where we can pick up her trail."

"I don't know," he said.

One of the officers guided Tom Hendricks into the living room. Brenna said, "Down," to Brie beside the front door and followed the sergeant into the dining room.

Garrett hooked his thumbs into his back pockets. "So, what do you think?"

The sergeant looked from Garrett to Brenna.

"I don't think he knows where she is," she said, "but I'd bet he's hiding something." She turned to the sergeant. "What did the mother say?"

He shrugged. "Nothing. She's been busy with the baby; Mr. Hendricks answered all my questions. Mrs. Hendricks asked if I wanted coffee." He looked from her to Jett. "Is there a problem?"

"If one parent is too quiet," she said, "we sometimes–"

The sergeant interrupted her. "Do you see a problem, Culpepper?"

The good-old-boy network was thrumming on overtime. Once again, she'd been dismissed for whatever reason the sergeant deemed important. Because she was a woman? A dog handler? Who knew? Anyway, he preferred talking to Jett.

"Could be," Jett said. "If she hasn't said anything about Zoe, she might be afraid to talk to you in front of her husband. It's happened before." He turned to Brenna. "You and Brie get started. Garrett and the sergeant can visit with the parents while you're out looking for Zoe."

"We've searched everywhere around here," the sergeant said, "but you can walk over to the park."

"Show me on the map," she said.

"You don't need a map," he said. "It's right across the street."

"I understand that, but it helps if I know—"

"Just go where I tell you to," the sergeant said.

She glanced at Garrett, inhaled a deep breath, and counted to ten, by twos, before she spoke again. "Sergeant, if I'm to conduct an efficient search, I need to have a sense of the entire area. I will gladly clear any park, alley, easement, or sewer you wish, but it makes my job easier if I know how this neighborhood connects to the area around it."

"There's nothing for you—"

"I need to know what the entire area looks like."

The sergeant tugged on his equipment belt the way large-bellied men hitch up their pants. "We're here," he said. "The park is over there." He extended his arm and pointed across the street. "It doesn't take a rocket scientist to find it."

She struggled to keep her voice even. "Have you ever worked with dogs, Sergeant?"

"Not directly, but—"

"Let me educate you, quickly. Well-trained dogs can follow a person's trail for miles, find someone hiding under piles of leaves or debris that most people walk past, locate drowning victims from a boat, find people buried under feet of snow or tons of debris, and tell their handlers if those people are unharmed, injured, or dead. Now, if we're going to work together—"

"I didn't call you for this search," he said. "Garrett did."

"Fine." She marched to the front door, called Brie, and then jogged down the driveway.

As she reached the truck, Jett called, "Irish, wait."

She whirled toward him. "Scott is not an Irish name!"

"Brenna is," he said, softly. "Now, calm down." He sat on the tailgate next to Brie and watched Brenna pace beside the truck. "You hit irritable pretty quick on this one."

"I hate being first on scene; it takes too long." She reached past him for her navy windbreaker, but he grasped her arm. Brie thumped her tail and nuzzled Brenna's hand.

"We've gotten a lot of information in"—he glanced at his watch—"thirteen minutes."

"Feels like longer."

"First on scene has to gather information and do the initial search of the house. We're not far behind her."

She straightened and stared into his eyes. "How do you know? Mr. Hendricks found her gone around one o'clock; what if she left at twelve or eleven-thirty?"

He watched her a moment. "What else is nagging at you, besides the sergeant being a jackass?"

"I want to know how Zoe got out of the house," she said. "Did you look at the front door? That security lock pushes up into a bracket. How could a four-year-old reach that high? And if she went out through the garage, wouldn't the noise of the garage door opening wake her parents? Their bedroom is right next to it."

"Maybe she stood on a chair."

"And then put it back? What about the alarm?"

"Hendricks said it doesn't monitor the open windows."

"If she went out a window, wouldn't it still be raised?" She shook her head. "A child doesn't run away for no reason, and this storm's been brewing since before she went to bed." Brenna looked at the house. "The window."

Before he could ask what that meant, she was on the way to the side of the house.

He followed. "Where are you going?"

When she neared the window of the child's bedroom, she saw that the screen lay propped against the brick instead of fastened over the glass. The ground sloped toward the backyard, placing the windowsill a good four feet off the ground. Brenna flashed her light at the earth. Whatever tracks might have been visible earlier were now small puddles; the ridges and prints made by shoe soles had been beaten down by the rain. Still, she studied them.

Jett squatted beside her. "Looks like somebody has walked all over this." With the back of his hand, he raked standing water away from some of the indentations. "If someone made me guess, I'd say this looks like a toe of a tennis shoe, and this one"—he pointed—"might be the heel of a boot." He took her flashlight and bent over. "This could be a trace of a lugged sole."

"They've trashed whatever might have been here."

Standing, he said, "You can't blame them, Irish, everyone was looking for her. Six guys probably walked by here, and most law-enforcement academies don't preach track preservation except in crime scenes."

Garrett called to them from the driveway. "What are you doing?"

She looked over her shoulder at him. "Staring at footprints."

"Whose?"

"Everybody's."

"I've got the map," he said.

"Meet us at the truck," Jett said. Then he turned to her. "What's done is done, Irish. We're here to help find this child, nothing more. Don't let details and questions drive you crazy. When Zoe is found, we'll have the answers."

She stood. "You're right. I shouldn't worry so much about the little ones; they can be very creative."

He smiled as he nudged her toward the truck. "Remember Eli? He crawled into a ditch, covered himself with leaves to stay warm, and had a good night's sleep. Except for a few mosquito bites, there wasn't a scratch on him."

She laughed. "When we found him, he wanted to know if we'd brought breakfast."

Garrett had spread the map on the tailgate. "We're here," he said. "Gary Brown lives here." He pointed to another development.

"What's this open space behind these streets?" Brenna asked.

"County land. Most of this part is still undeveloped, but there are a few farmhouses. The creek that runs through the park across the street eventually joins the river . . . here."

Brenna studied the two housing developments. "If Zoe really was going to see Amy, might she cross this open stretch as a shortcut?"

"There aren't many roads on farmland. And unless someone had taken her that way before, how would she know—"

"She wouldn't, I guess."

Garrett stepped back and smiled. "I have more news. When the sergeant quizzed the parents again, the truth came out. The baby's been fussy, parents arguing, not much sleep the last few days. Zoe went to bed tonight without her usual hot chocolate and bedtime story."

"That answers a big question," Jett said.

"Why didn't he just say so?" Brenna asked.

"He didn't want to look like a neglectful parent," Garrett said.

Things were beginning to make sense. Jett was right; details did chew Brenna up. And the most important thing right now was finding Zoe.

Evan leaned on the truck. "Can I do anything?"

"You can pull out that red backpack," she said.

Evan patted Brie and crawled into the cargo section of the truck to grab the item.

"Get that blue shirt, too," Garrett said.

A blue long-sleeved shirt was under Brie's paws. When Evan tugged it, the dog growled. He jumped back.

"What's wrong with her? I just petted her a minute ago."

"Don't touch her shirt," Jett said.

"*Her* shirt?" Evan asked.

Brenna slipped on her navy windbreaker. "It was mine once," she said. "The vet kept Brie a couple of days after she was spayed and I left the shirt with her so she'd know I was coming back. It's been hers ever since."

"Kinda like a security blanket?" Evan asked.

"I guess. She drags it everywhere." Brenna opened the backpack and pulled out her hiking boots.

Jett turned to Garrett. "Do you have an extra radio? Marco and Connie have ours."

He nodded. "Evan, give him yours."

"It's out, sir—it went dead after I fell in the creek. But I can go back to the office and get a new one."

"Go ask the sergeant if we can borrow one of his," Garrett said. Evan trotted toward the porch.

Jett studied the map. "I'd like to make a copy of this so we can mark where the dogs search."

Garrett nodded. "There's a convenience store back at the main intersection. It's open twenty-four hours and has a copy machine." He sent Jett off with one of his officers.

Garrett sat down beside Brenna and looped his arm around Brie's neck. The dog wagged her tail.

"Are you still making stained-glass windows?" he asked.

Brenna looked up from lacing her hiking boot.

"Not very often. I don't have time." She pulled on her other boot and then stood and stamped her feet to make sure she'd laced the boots tight enough. "How's your own sideline going? The carpentry?"

"I don't have much time, either, but I do get a few jobs here and there."

She slipped the lanyard with the whistle around her neck, then pulled a pair of gaiters out of the backpack, wrapped them around her calves, and zipped them up. They weren't great protection from snakebite, but they kept burrs and mud from crawling inside her jeans.

"Still wearing those pink gaiters," Garrett said. "I thought you hated pink."

"I do."

"Hate" was too mild a word. She detested pink, but these gaiters were special. Aaron, her mentor with the dogs and the closest thing she'd ever had to a grandfather, had presented them to her the same day he'd given her a cock-eared pup named Sabrina. Brie, for short. Every time she wore them, she felt Aaron with her.

She was fastening her fanny pack around her waist when Evan returned. "The sergeant said he'd rather not lend her a radio just yet. Patrol spotted a child on the swings at Sandy Park. By the time they got out of the car, the kid was gone. The sergeant thinks it might be Zoe."

"Where's Sandy Park?" Brenna asked.

"About halfway between here and Amy's house." Garrett shook his head. "Guess you can take off your gear."

"Well, I'm ready; I might as well look around."

"Does this kind of thing happen often?" Evan asked.

"Sometimes," she said. "It's better to be called out early on a false alarm than be called out late on the real thing."

A police unit turned at the corner and stopped beside the Suburban. Jett climbed out.

"Did you hear?" Garrett asked.

He nodded. "Let me return this map to the sergeant; I'll be right back."

Brenna leaned into the truck and pulled out a three-foot dowel.

"Why do you have a dowel?" Evan asked.

"I use it as a tracking stick."

He looked at Garrett.

"Bren puts the toe of the child's shoe at the tip of the dowel and measures the foot," Garrett said. "Look, she's marking it with a rubber band. Then she measures the width of the shoe and marks it with another rubber band. If she finds a print, she'll know if it matches Zoe's shoe size."

"Why not take the shoe?"

"The tracking stick is easier to carry," she said, "and I don't have to worry about losing the shoe." She laughed at Evan's expression. He'd had a hard day. "Come on, Evan. You can be my flanker."

He looked at Garrett.

"Her partner." The sheriff turned to Brenna. "Where do you plan to start?"

"I'll try to pick up her trail, check the storm drains."

"You think there's a trail after all that rain?" Garrett asked.

"Probably not," she said. "And to please that pigheaded sergeant, I'll clear the park, just to make sure she isn't hiding over there."

"Stay away from the creek," Garrett said. "That bank is so saturated, it crumbled under Evan's feet. If I hadn't been there, we might have lost a promising rookie."

Evan blushed.

"Come on, promising rookie," she said.

"But," Evan objected, "they think they spotted her."

"Until someone has hold of her," Garrett said, "she's still officially missing."

"Brie, ready to work?" Brenna asked.

The dog bounded out of the truck and leaped into the air one, two, three times.

Brenna held the small tennis shoe for Brie to smell. "Mark it. Now, find Zoe. Find her."

They followed Brie onto the front lawn, along the side of the house, and into the backyard. The dog circled several times, paused at the patio, and then sniffed the privacy fence at the rear of the property.

"Why is she back there?" Evan asked.

"Zoe's scent would be around her home. With this sloping lot, the water must have washed the scent to the fence. It's probably clinging to the wood."

"How can scent cling?"

Brenna called the dog and directed her to the street.

"A person's body sheds thousands of skin cells a minute, and the cells carry proteins and bacteria that make a person's scent. Some of the cells float in the air and some fall to the ground. That's what the dog smells."

When they reached the street, Brie sniffed the storm drains.

"Why is she doing that?" Evan asked.

"In case Zoe lost her balance and fell into a drain."

"Has that ever happened?" he asked.

She nodded. "If a child gets stuck in a drain, its scent will follow the flow of water. If Brie finds it, she'll tell me."

"Is this Zoe's trail?"

"No, Brie's air-scenting now. I suspect Zoe's trail washed away."

As they passed the park, an officer walked out of the shadows. The man waved at them and headed toward the Hendrickses' house.

Five blocks down, at the curve of the street, a concrete bridge crossed the rushing stream.

"Is this the creek?" she asked. "It must be twelve feet wide." She glanced at Evan. "How deep is the water?"

"Usually only a couple of feet, but it's running six or seven feet now. With all the rain here and farther north, it's riding high."

The creek that had turned into a river rumbled three feet below the bottom of the bridge. Water foamed in places: debris was trapped somewhere below sight level. A tire, plastic bottles, paper cups, and a rusted metal barrel were caught in the current, rushing past. Chunks of Styrofoam rode the swift water next to the carcass of a rabbit.

"Oh," Brenna said, "poor baby."

"Guess it drowned," Evan said. "Happens a lot, when there's a big storm."

In places where the channel narrowed, collected debris formed loose dams that shifted each time a new piece of junk hit the snag.

"Ready to go back?" Evan asked.

"Is this where county jurisdiction starts?"

He nodded. "Why?"

"Look." She tapped her tracking stick on a worn path that lay parallel to the creek.

"How can you see without your flashlight?"

"Practice."

"Why not use a flashlight?"

"When you get away from the city lights, there are different shades of dark. Most of the time, we don't need lights unless we're looking for tracks or tromping through heavy woods." She smiled. "Besides, if a runaway sees us coming, she'll keep running." She stared into the woods. "I wonder how far back that goes."

"Does it matter? They spotted Zoe in the opposite direction."

She knelt, studied the ground. "Someone's been through here. See that print holding water?"

"Is it Zoe's?"

"No, a man's shoe. Walking in but not walking out."

"The city boys have been all through here. Probably one of them."

She trotted across the bridge, Brie on her heels, and then studied the other side. A similar path ran parallel to the stream. "Jogging trails."

"Are you ready?" Evan called.

"Do these trails curve around, come out somewhere else?"

He shrugged. "I don't know. You coming?"

"You go on," she said. "I'm going to wander around a bit."

"Why?"

She needed to walk off her resentment of the jackass sergeant who didn't take her ability or experience seriously. If there was one thing she did well, it was searching. And searching was the one accomplishment that gave her a sense of pride.

"Restless," she said. "Brie and I need to work off the adrenaline rush of starting a search."

After a moment, Evan stuck his hands in his pockets and turned toward the neighborhood.

Jett wouldn't approve of her searching alone, but he'd get over it. Anyway, the officer on patrol probably *had* spotted Zoe; it made sense the little girl would head in that direction.

"Come on, Funny Face. Let's take a walk down Jogger's Lane."

BRIE BOUNDED AHEAD of Brenna. Fir, spruce, and red cedar lined the path as though someone had planted them for decoration. Night shadows darkened the woods. The terrain was beautiful but rugged: thick trees, rocky slopes, thorny vines. Only the lane lay clear and smooth.

Instead of enjoying the walk, Brenna reviewed the past twenty minutes. She'd gotten too worked up over this missing child. Searching was a job, nothing more.

On her first few searches with Aaron, each outing had been a personal quest, a race to beat death to the victim. Then Aaron had talked her through the emotional roller coaster of finding and losing. She'd finally learned calm acceptance of whatever lay at the end of the trail. But echoes of those original feelings still lingered.

Time to clear her head, gain perspective. She could almost hear Aaron's voice: *We always hope to find someone alive. If death has already come, at least the family won't have to wonder what happened, where their loved one is.*

Brie trotted back to her and then whirled and darted off again. Brenna smiled. The dog reminded her of a horizontal yo-yo. No matter how far Brie ran ahead, she made sure her owner was always in sight. That little habit had come in handy one night on a rural search when Brenna decided to check a small cave Brie had bypassed. A bobcat didn't appreciate the interruption, and if Brie hadn't barreled back to her owner's side, growling and barking, Brenna might have been bitten and badly scratched. The episode had reinforced one of Aaron's primary lessons: *Always trust your dog.*

Ahead of her, Brie sat on the path. Brenna turned on her light and discovered a small building, like a three-sided carport. A covered bench. A few yards farther down, a wooden footbridge crossed the creek. Several boards had come loose and dangled from the structure; a smile with missing teeth.

She turned her flashlight to locate the path, which continued through the woods, and then switched off her beam.

"I wonder if there's another bridge down there."

The dog wagged her tail.

"We should go back," she said, "but if there is another bridge, we can cross and come up on the other side." She glanced at her watch. "We'll give it five minutes. If we haven't found a way to cross over by then, we'll come back."

As Brenna took a step forward, Brie popped up and trotted in front of her. They followed the path through the timber and emerged into an open stretch where the trees angled away from the stream. On the far bank, the woods were still thick. Then she saw another footbridge in the distance. A stand of cedars obstructed her course, and as they walked through and came out the other side, she realized they'd passed their destination.

"Too far, Funny Face, we missed our turn. Come on." Brenna pivoted and walked back into the trees, angling toward the creek.

Brie trotted to catch up, and as she passed Brenna, her ears perked. Then she stopped and looked over her shoulder at her owner.

Was someone else out here? The wind had been at their backs on this side of the creek, but now it blew into their faces. When Brie's ear leaned all the way over her head, Brenna knew they had company.

She backtracked until she found where the path led to the bridge. As she and Brie left the darker shadows and went toward the bridge, the dog stopped and wagged her tail. Then her head lowered and her ears flattened against her skull. The wagging stopped and Brenna heard the dog growl.

A man lumbered across the bridge, a bundle in his arms. A Pooh Bear snuggled between his arm and his ribs.

Before Brenna could react, he saw her.

"No light," he said. "Take her!"

He pitched his bundle over the railing, keeping hold of one corner of its wrapping. The material unfurled. A child shrieked, tumbled into the river.

Shocked, Brenna heard her own voice: "Brie, swim!"

The dog jumped into the water. Zoe splashed and screamed.

Brenna raced along the bank, her mind spinning.

No radio. If Brie caught up with Zoe, could she keep the child afloat? Maybe.

They needed help, fast.

She slipped on mud, stumbled into a patch of vines. The whistle around her neck caught on thorns. Whistle! Even before she'd regained her balance, the whistle was in her mouth, shrilling.

She scanned the river. Brie had caught Zoe. The child clung to the dog's neck so tightly, she was pushing Brie under. No way they'd both stay afloat.

If there was another bridge . . .

She looked ahead. The creek narrowed.

Just as Brenna was getting ahead of them, mud caked her boots. Cedar blocked her path. She tore through a mass of brush. The shrubs grabbed at her legs. Stumbling onto the bank, she realized Brie and Zoe were caught in the current.

Still running, she unbuckled her fanny pack, dropped it, and plunged into the water.

Cold. Strong. It sucked her under, stole her breath. When she surfaced, Brie and Zoe were a few yards behind her.

"Come on, girl!"

She fought to swim upstream, narrow the space between them. As they neared, Brenna stretched for Zoe. She caught the pair in a one-arm hug.

The river carried them along like a speeding roller coaster. They dipped and bobbed. Every time they sank and then popped up again, Zoe screamed.

Then something lodged below the surface snagged Brenna's leg like a bear trap, jerked her horizontal. Zoe and Brie broke free. Water rushed over her with frightening speed and weight, pushing her down, down, down.

Caught.

Below the surface, the world lay silent. Still, except for the water's force pulling her straight. The current kept her arms extended. She couldn't bend her knees, fight her way to the object holding her leg captive.

Wiggle. Wiggle your foot. Kick.

Her chest ached. One breath. Just one breath.

Kick!

She broke free. Arms flailed. She reached the surface, gulped air, and choked.

Riding the current, she caught her breath. Then she saw Brie and Zoe floundering in a heap of branches and junk. Every time Brie pawed at it, tried to climb on top of it, the debris collapsed, and she splashed back into the river. Zoe clung to a branch with one arm, the other curled around the dog's neck.

As Brenna neared, the snag separated into jagged sections. Zoe screamed, let go of the branch, and clung to Brie. The dog went under.

Brenna swam as fast as she could.

"Zoe, grab the branch! Grab it!"

The child screamed, screamed, screamed.

"Zoe!"

She disappeared into the surge.

Brenna lurched forward, stretched so hard her fingers ached. Her hand closed around a fistful of hair.

Yank!

When the child bobbed up, Brenna hooked an arm around her. "Hug me, Zoe. Hug tight."

"Daddy." She choked, coughed. "Daddy!"

A few feet ahead of her, Brie's head poked through the surface. "Brie, here!"

The dog's ear tilted back toward her. Brie toiled against the current, her head bobbing at each stroke of her paws.

"Come on, Brie, come on."

When the dog was within reach, Brenna grabbed a handful of neck ruff and pulled her closer.

Then Brenna struggled to pull up her feet, stretch them in front of her to float. She wiggled Zoe's legs around her waist and used her body like a raft for the little girl. Then she tugged at Brie until the dog could wrap her paws around one of Brenna's legs.

Zoe's screams turned to sobs.

"It's all right, Zoe. We've got you."

"Dad-dy!"

Brie wrapped her paws around Brenna with all her strength. The dog alternated between panting and gagging. She watched Brenna with soft brown eyes.

Darlin' Brie. Hold on, Funny Face. We'll get out of this.

The river widened and dipped, forming a section of rapids that cascaded through the channel. Then it narrowed again and threw them into a whirlpool with thorny branches and plastic bottles, turning them around and around. After a few swirls, Brenna kicked free and the surge pushed them toward the bank.

She grabbed for a limb protruding between two rocks; it broke. A patch of green pulled out in her hand. She clawed for solid ground, but the river turned into a frightening sluice ride. Then she spotted a twisted root jutting out from the mud a few feet ahead of them.

"Hold tight, Zoe."

As they neared, Brenna swiped at the root. It held, yanked them to the edge of the current, and swung them into the bank. Zoe screamed again. Brie lost her hold on Brenna's leg and frantically pawed the water.

Brenna kept hold of Brie's collar, fought to maneuver her leg under the dog again. But a floating tangle of branches, lawn chairs, and tires knocked into them. It shoved them into the bank, smashed Brenna and Zoe's faces into the mud. Trapped them in a cage of sharp twigs.

She felt the bank with her knee. With all her strength, she pushed her back against the snag. It shifted. Moved. Caught the current. Wrenched Brie from Brenna's grasp.

The dog yipped, wildly fighting the water and the limbs keeping her prisoner.

"Brie!" She grabbed for the dog, but the water swept her out of reach.

Brie bucked against the tangle of debris, tried to shake it off her. Then soft brown eyes stared at Brenna, begging, pleading. A surge carried Brie and the snag downstream. She barked . . . once.

"Swim, Brie!" Brenna yelled. "Swim, Funny—"

She couldn't see her anymore.

Zoe hugged her tighter. Only then did Brenna realize she still held Brie's collar in her hand.

The water kept pushing and shoving, throwing debris against them. She looked up. The slope to the top was higher here. No way she could boost Zoe up and get her on solid ground. But the root was strong. Maybe they had a little time.

She strained to see downstream. *Swim, Funny Face.*

Zoe shivered.

The cold water and the struggle to stay afloat had drained body heat. If Brenna wasn't careful, she could still lose Zoe to hypothermia.

She felt the bank with her feet, slowly inching them up until her knees were folded between her and the mud. Then she slipped Zoe into the curve of her body. Maybe her body heat would slow the numbing effect of the river.

"You okay?" Brenna asked.

Zoe sniffed. "I want my daddy."

"I know." She shifted her hold on the child. "I'm going to blow this whistle. It's going to be loud, but it will bring help. Ready?"

Brenna put the whistle between her teeth. The water flowed away from the housing development, but the riverbed would act like a tunnel. When she didn't come back, someone would come looking for her and, eventually, they'd hear the whistle. All she had to do was blow and blow and blow.

JETT CULPEPPER SAT on the front steps of the Hendrickses' house. Occasionally he missed being a police officer, but most of the time he enjoyed his job. He still had to evaluate people on first impressions . . . when he remembered to pay attention. It had taken Bren to catch Mr. Hendricks's Swiss cheese story.

You're slipping, Culpepper.

The neighborhood had taken on a new feel since the electricity had returned. Yard lights glowed in front of well-kept houses. This was no transient area; the people who lived on this street were putting down roots. They'd probably be neighbors most of their lives. A person's house and surroundings told a story. The Hendricks appeared to be upper-middle-class folks, but they hadn't squandered their money on a fancy new house they probably couldn't afford just to impress his coworkers. And they'd waited to have their children. Pictures of a young couple gradually growing older decorated every room. He'd guess the Hendrickses had planned their family.

Sergeant Clark groaned as he plopped down beside him.

"Well," Clark said, "that kid Patrol saw was a boy. Sneaked out when the baby-sitter went to sleep. I guess our little girl is still missing."

"Are you planning an all-out search?" Jett asked.

He nodded. "When will the rest of your team be here?"

"A little under two hours."

"Is what that woman said true? Can dogs do all those things?"

"Yes, they can," Jett said. "But they aren't miracle workers. When you have this kind of on-and-off-again rainstorm, there's not much trail left to follow. Brenna calls them gullywashers."

"She's about right. Hell, it rains nine months of the year. Sometimes I think I'm half duck." He glanced at Jett and smiled. "I'm not sure there's much point waking everybody up to do a door-to-door. Be a whole lot easier to find her once it gets light, but . . ."

"Duty calls?"

He nodded. "I hate it when kids go missing. They don't understand how dangerous the world is these days."

"Unless they're in a job like ours . . . yours," Jett said, "most adults don't understand, either."

"Why'd you quit the force?"

"Three kids and an expensive wife. Ex-wife, now."

Clark nodded. "Better money?"

"The first couple of years were hard, but I've been lucky." Jett smiled. "If you move to Sacramento and want a job, give me a call."

Clark laughed. "Sounds good to me." He rubbed his forehead and sighed. "I don't know where I'm going find extra officers to help search. With all the power outages, most of our guys have three calls waiting already."

"I'm not official," Jett said, "but if you'll lend me a radio, I'll–"

A sheriff's cruiser fishtailed as it slid to a stop in front of the house. Garrett opened the driver's door and hollered.

"There's a whistle blowing."

Jett jumped up. "Where?"

"South, somewhere by the creek."

Clark stood. "What does a whistle mean?"

"Trouble." Jett sprinted across the wet lawn and then turned back toward him. "We may need help. Can you–"

"Right away," Clark said. He yanked the radio from his belt and spoke into it.

Jett climbed into Garrett's car. "Where are they?"

"Evan's at the bridge." He pulled into a driveway, backed out, and then sped along the street.

"They aren't together?"

Garrett shook his head. "Evan headed back to the house while Brenna checked out a jogging trail."

"Damn her. Going out without a radio, without backup."

"Her?" The car slid sideways at the bridge. "I told Evan to stay with her. Instead, he lets her go off on a wild-goose chase alone, and then he meets Baker, and they take a ten-minute coffee break. As he's moseying back toward the house, he sees me and asks if a whistle blowing means anything."

Both men jumped out of the car and paused at the guardrail.

Evan faced Jett. "I–I'm sorry–"

"Hush," Garrett snapped.

The shrilling of a whistle floated in the distance.

"Where'd you see her last?" Jett asked.

Evan pointed toward the far side of the bridge. "I think she went down there, but she might have come back and–"

"I'll take the right," Jett said. "What's downstream?"

"Not much," Garrett said. "Woods and farmland."

Two police units stopped behind Garrett's cruiser. When three officers got out, he motioned for one to come with Jett and him, and the others to go with Evan.

Jett ran to the right side of the bridge and found the path with his flashlight. Most of the tracks were muddled. Several yards down, he spotted a paw print and a trace of lug-soled boots heading downstream. Garrett and an officer caught up with him.

As they ran deeper into the woods, Jett slipped and slid in the mud. But the whistle's shrill fed his determination, his panic. The blasts grew shorter and farther apart.

Bren was in trouble.

He should have paid more attention to her intuition, played

mother hen the way she did with the other members of the team. First on scene, last to leave, she always knew where everyone was, even when she was in the field. He'd been too busy remembering old times.

Damn fool.

As they ran past a footbridge, Garrett slowed and then stopped. He bent and grabbed something from the brush beside the bridge.

"Look." He held up Pooh Bear. "Think Bren found Zoe?"

Jett didn't know whether to hope yes or no.

Brenna rested her head against Zoe's. The child was quiet now. Too quiet. Brenna hoped she had felt a little safer and had fallen asleep, but she suspected mind-numbing hypothermia had accompanied the sandman. Both of them were trembling, and Brenna couldn't feel her legs. Cramps plagued her fingers, and she ached to flex them. But she didn't dare let go. The water still tugged at them, threatening to rip them away from the bank and send them into the flux of the raging stream. Trash pushed against her, and every few minutes she struggled to knock it away with her shoulder.

She blew the whistle one more time.

Could Brie hear it? Maybe she'd gotten out, maybe she'd found a shoal and was lying on it, too tired to climb the bank. As long as Brenna blew the whistle, Brie would know she was close by. She'd come to her when she could.

Memories clouded reality. Thoughts faded. When she realized her mind was drifting, she shook her head, vigorously.

Stay awake; keep Zoe awake.

"Z-Zoe." Her teeth chattered. "Zoe, wake up. Can you count for me?" Brenna nudged the little girl's head. "Z-Zoe, count."

No response. She blew the whistle again.

"Zoe," she said louder. "Say 'One.' "

The child whimpered.

"S-say 'One.' Zoe." She concentrated to stop stuttering. Then she used the I-mean-business tone she'd mastered when teaching high school English. "Say 'One.' "

"One."

"Good, Zoe. Let's try two. Say 'Two.' "

"Tooo," she whined.

"One, two, buckle my shoe."

"One, two . . . shoe." Her head lolled against Brenna's arm.

Blow the whistle. Blow.

"Three, four, open the door." She waited, but the little girl didn't mimic her. "Z-Zoe, say 'Three.' "

Nothing.

"Zoe! Three, four . . ."

"Brenna!"

"Bren!" A different voice.

"Here, over here!" another yelled. "Garrett!"

She twisted until she could see the opposite bank. Was that Evan . . . pointing at them?

A moment later, three men towered above her. Jett. Garrett. A man in blue.

"Hang on, Bren," Garrett said.

Jett lay on his stomach and reached toward the water. "Can you boost her up?"

Her arms felt too weak. "No."

"Garrett, hold my belt." He stretched, shifted, and then leaned over the bank. His fingers closed around the child's upper arms. He lifted her, dragged her across the slope of the bank. Mud sloshed down the slope and into Brenna's face. Zoe kicked her jaw as the child dangled from his grasp. Then another pair of hands grabbed the little girl. They plucked her over the rim and out of sight.

Jett leaned down the bank again. "Come on, Irish. Take my hand. Take it."

With all her strength, she raised her arm. Fingers closed around her wrist. As Jett tugged her up, Garrett grabbed her belt. Together, they hauled her to solid ground.

"Are you all right?" Jett asked. He shed his windbreaker and wrapped it around her shoulders.

"Z-Z-Zoe?" she stuttered.

"He's taking her to the hospital," Garrett said.

He? Oh, the other officer.

"What happened?" Jett asked. "Where's your shoe?"

She looked at her feet. One boot was gone, as well as her windbreaker and one of her gaiters. Aaron's gaiters. The water must have sucked them off.

"A man . . . a m-man had Zoe."

Garrett knelt beside her. "What man?"

When she tried to talk, she spat her words instead of saying them.

"He had her in a blanket, with the bear. Threw her into the river."

"When?"

When? When. She couldn't think.

"I–I don't know. At a bridge."

The men looked at each other.

"He could still be here," Garrett said, pulling out his radio. Jett hugged her.

She pushed back and gazed into his eyes. "Brie . . . Brie's still in the water. I couldn't hold her. I . . ." Something jingled in her trembling hand. Metal tags. She still clutched Brie's collar. "I . . . couldn't hold . . ."

"We'll find her," Jett said.

Garrett took Brenna's hand. "Tell me about this guy, Bren. What did he look like, how was he dressed, did you see which way he went?" She stared at him. "We need to catch him before he takes another little girl."

She shivered; her legs cramped.

"Bren, you've got to remember."

Zoe was safe. Brie was still missing.

"How tall was he?" Garrett asked. He grasped her shoulders, gently. "Bren, you must help me before it's too late."

"I . . . I only saw him for a second."

"Think," Garrett said.

Closing her eyes, Brenna tried to picture the man, but all she could see was Brie pawing the branches, trying to swim back to her.

"Irish . . ."

She tried again. "Dark jacket. Jeans . . . boots. A dark cap."

Garrett repeated the information into his radio. "How tall?"

"I don't know."

"Can you guess?"

"He stood on the bridge. Maybe if I saw it again."

"Can you stand up?" Jett asked.

When she tried, her legs buckled. Jett braced her, and after a few moments the stiffness and trembling eased.

She turned to him. "Brie . . . I have to find Brie."

"We have to find this guy," Garrett said. "What if he takes another little girl?"

Everything inside her pulsed to find Brie, but could she live with herself if she failed to give Garrett information that might save another child?

"Bren . . ." Garrett said.

"You go with Garrett," Jett said. "I'll search for Brie, and I won't stop until I find her."

With Garrett's help, Brenna staggered back to the footbridge where she'd surprised the stranger.

"We were upwind," she said. "I don't think Brie knew he was here until just before I did." She pointed to the opposite bank. "Single tracks over there. I thought they belonged to an officer looking for Zoe. I guess they didn't."

When they reached the bridge, Garrett found a green wool blanket caught on vines in the woods. Beside it lay a small plastic container filled with orange liquid.

He had Brenna stand where she thought she'd been when she saw the man.

"Can you tell?" he asked. "How tall, what kind of build?"

"I don't know." She noticed Winnie-the-Pooh in Garrett's hand. "Put the bear under your arm and stand on the bridge."

He did, but there was too much distance between the top of the bridge's railing and the bear. Then Evan took his turn and, finally, the officers with him. The last one seemed about right. She thought she could remember that when the bear was under the stranger's arm, it looked as if it was sitting on the railing.

"That one is closest," she said, "but your guy's too stocky."

Garrett spoke to the officer and then relayed the information. Evan dashed toward the main road. He returned with a blanket, which he wrapped around her, and he offered her a pair of wool socks and worn tennis shoes.

"I'm sure they won't fit," he said, "but if you lace them up tight, you might be able to walk in them."

"Thank you, Evan. At least my feet will be dry."

After talking to Garrett, Evan disappeared again. Garrett turned to her. "The paramedics want to check you for—"

"No, I have to find Brie."

Sirens *wow-wow*ed in the distance. Flashing red and blue lights reflected off the stream near the housing development.

"Reinforcements?" she asked.

He nodded. "It's not likely, but that guy might still be hanging around. We've pulled county and city cops to try to catch him. If he brought Zoe in this direction, he had to be going somewhere."

"What are you going to do?"

He smiled and tightened the blanket around her shoulders. "Go with you."

She stared downstream.

Hang on, Funny Face.

JETT FOLLOWED THE curve of the stream, flashing his light on both shores and every heap of floating rubbish. Maybe Brie'd gotten out. Maybe the current had washed her toward shallow water as it careened around a curve. If the dog found something sturdy, she could cling to it until help came. Brie was a trooper, a fighter, just like Brenna.

He caught a movement on the other side of the river. Stepping into the night shadows of a spruce, he turned off his light and remained still.

"Jett? You around here?"

Evan, with another man wearing a deputy's uniform.

"Here," he called. As he neared the water, the ground fell away from his foot. He grabbed a sapling; it bent and then toppled, its roots reaching toward the sky. Instinctively, he twisted as he fell to the ground.

"You all right?" Evan called.

Stupid move. The unstable bank couldn't support his weight after all this rain. Even the path felt spongy.

"Fine." He belly-crawled to solid soil and then stood. Mud covered his chest and stomach like squishy armor. He slung it off his arms and found his flashlight. At least it hadn't fallen into the water.

As he tested the beam, the light flickered across some pale objects against the dark mud and vines near the trees. He moved closer and discovered four cigarette butts beside a clear print of a man's boot. Moisture had seeped only halfway up the butts, darkening the filter with a tan line. These were fresh.

Had someone stood in the shadows, watching as Brenna and Zoe struggled to survive? The man who'd snatched Zoe, had he stuck around to watch the show? Bastard.

He remained crouched a few seconds, listening. Might the abductor still be hanging around?

Suspecting the man had run off when he'd heard everyone yelling for Brenna, Jett tied his handkerchief to a stick, stuck it into the ground to mark the find, and then stood.

"Does your radio work?" Jett called.

Evan shouted back, "Affirmative."

"Notify Garrett I found a clear print next to cigarette butts. Tell him to bring a first-aid gauze pad and a Baggie."

"Tell him to bring what?"

"He'll understand," Jett said.

Another deputy spoke into his radio, handed it to Evan, and headed upstream. Since Garrett had worked with Brenna and the dogs before, he'd know to open the packets of sterile gauze and lay them on the print. After a few minutes, the gauze patches would soak up the scent of whoever had been standing there. Then Garrett could seal it in the plastic bag. If this guy made a habit of snatching little girls, Garrett might need the scent patch for evidence somewhere down the line.

With Evan on one side of the river and him on the other, they continued to search for Brie. Fifteen minutes later, he flashed his beam on a tangle of branches, twigs, and lawn chairs banked against another large snag at a narrow spot in the channel. Then he moved the light and spotted a tan paw caught in the debris.

He squatted, turned off his light, and passed a muddy hand over his eyes. This would break Brenna's heart. Didn't do much for his, either.

"Is there another bridge around here?"

Evan stared at the snag. "I-I never would have left Brenna and the dog if I'd thought . . ."

"Bridge?" Jett repeated.

He pointed farther downstream. "A train trestle, about half a mile down."

"That'll do. Stay right there and wait for me."

He picked his way through thickets and vines. This was the real reason he'd left the force: too much loss. He'd spent most of his time as an officer dealing with humanity's slimiest creations. It didn't take long for his help-make-this-world-a-better-place idealism to splinter. Then he'd decided to strike out on his own. He still dealt with loss and sadness, but less. He could make choices now. Death wasn't thrown into his face every day. Just some days.

He picked his way across the bridge, then trotted upstream. Brenna wouldn't leave without Brie, and he didn't want her to see the dog trapped in the snag.

When he neared Evan, he asked, "Has all that stuff moved?"

"No, it's stuck." Evan shook his head. "It's forming a dam. This whole area will flood soon."

Jett stared at the river. "How are we going to get her out of there?"

Evan held up an orange sack. "Garrett told me to bring a rope."

Thank you, Garrett.

He looked at Evan. "Tie one end to a tree—a big tree, several feet away from the bank." Then he dug into the sack. Five three-foot-long strips of flat red webbing were bound together with a short piece of rope. They reminded him of thick nylon dog leashes. He'd tie one into a harness, hitch it to the rope, and feel secure going into the water.

The purple-and-yellow rope was deceptively thin; the same type of rope the team used in high-angle training, it could hold three times his weight. One foot at a time, he lowered himself into the surge. The water knocked him against the bank and then into the makeshift dam. Little by little, he shifted debris until he could latch on to Brie. With one arm around her torso, he kicked at tangled branches until he'd tugged her free. Then he draped her across his shoulder and motioned for Evan to pull him up.

When he reached the top, he gently laid the dog on the bank. Then he stroked her head and ran his hand down her neck. "You did a good job, Brie. A real good job."

Lights filtered through the darkness. Then he saw Garrett and Brenna.

When she saw Jett, she stopped. "Did you . . ."

He stepped back. "I'm sorry, Irish."

"Brie . . ."

Brenna approached slowly, sat in the mud, pulled Brie's head into her lap, and hugged her. Then she tugged the blanket from her shoulders and wrapped it around the dog. Every few seconds, she flicked away tears and whispered in the dog's ear.

Jett untied the rope and harness and let them drop to the ground. "She was a working dog, Irish. This isn't your fault."

"Maybe." She caught several quick breaths.

"She saved Zoe." Garrett knelt beside Brenna, his hand on her shoulder, while she slowly rocked with her partner. After a few minutes, he said, "We need to go back, Bren. You're still trembling. Are you ready?"

She hesitated and then got to her knees, slipping her arms around Brie's chest and back legs.

"Bren," Garrett said.

"I won't leave her," she said.

Jett squatted beside her. "Let me take her."

"No," Garrett said, "let me. I'd be honored."

Garrett picked up Brie and Brenna tucked the blanket around her. He and Evan led the way back to the neighborhood. Jett walked beside Brenna.

He wanted to put his arm around her, but that gesture might make her go to pieces. He'd seen her angry, frustrated, and occasionally melancholy, but never distraught. He suspected she and grief would share a private moment later on.

"Brie was a funny girl," he said.

"Funny Face," she whispered.

"Remember that time you ran into that flock of chickens?"

Garrett turned around. "I do." He laughed. "The air was filled with fowl. Looked like a tornado of white plumes."

Brenna smiled. "But she didn't hurt them. She just had this fascination with chickens, as if they were playmates."

"That farmer didn't think they were playing," Jett said. "He threatened to sue."

She smiled and patted his arm.

Several officers passed them going in the opposite direction, their flashlights picking out the path. When they reached the footbridge, Brenna paused and glanced at the river.

"Remember anything else?" Jett asked.

She shook her head.

A few minutes later, they passed a covered bench set a hundred feet back from the river. Two men in blue bent over the ground, one picking up something with tweezers.

Brenna stopped and looked across the river.

"What is it?" Jett asked.

"I passed one of these on the other side."

One officer turned toward them. "It's farther up, closer to the houses."

Brenna's forehead wrinkled. "Did you find something here?"

The officer nodded. "Footprints and a dozen cigarette butts. Someone waited out the storm in this shelter."

"Can I see it?" she asked.

"The butts?" he asked.

"No, the footprint."

As she knelt, Jett looked over her shoulder. "What?"

"Wavy sole. Slight curve on the inside of the heel." She glanced up at him. "I think this is like the one I saw near the main road."

"Are you a tracker?" the officer asked.

Jett glanced at Brenna and then answered for her: "Not tonight." He studied the print. "Looks like the one I found."

"Where?" Brenna asked.

"On the other side," he said.

"Show me."

"Irish, you can barely stand up. This part is Garrett's job. Let him do it."

She stared at him a moment and then nodded.

"Why is this shelter back in the trees?" Jett asked. "The other is almost at the water's edge."

The officer shrugged.

She turned to Jett. "That's why no one saw him. And he didn't see us because I wasn't using the flashlight."

The officer looked at Brenna. "After you get cleaned up, do you want to help us track this guy?"

"No, thanks," Jett answered for her again.

Better get Brenna back to the hotel. A hot bath and a warm bed were what she needed most.

As they walked along Stanford Circle behind Garrett and Evan, he saw the neighborhood had awakened. Porch lights glowed. Neighbors clad in bathrobes clustered around officers in the middle of the street. When they passed one group, he heard part of a conversation.

". . . to the hospital. They don't know for certain, but they think she'll be all right." Several people spoke at once. Then the officer said, "Yes, ma'am. We have people out looking. I doubt he's still around here, but if you see anything suspicious, please call the police."

When Garrett reached the Suburban, he turned to her.

"Bren, what are your plans?"

"Take her home," she said.

"To Smoke Rise?" Garrett asked.

Jett sighed. He should have known Brenna would have the dog cremated. She lived in a rented duplex now, and he knew her too well to think she'd bury Brie and then have to leave the dog behind when she moved.

"That's a long drive," Garrett said. "My vet is a good man; he'll take care of her like she was his own. Let him make the arrangements for cremation. We'll get her back to you as soon as possible."

"No, I–"

"Yes," Jett said. He didn't want Brenna to watch rigor mortis take her beloved partner during the drive home. "That's a smart move, Irish. We'll get some sleep, leave tomorrow."

She nodded, and gently stroked Brie's ear. Garrett carried the dog to his cruiser. Jett closed the Suburban's tailgate and opened the passenger door for Bren.

As he waved to Garrett, the deputy motioned for him to come to the car.

"After you get Brenna settled," Garrett said, "are you interested in coming back?"

"Why?"

"I don't think our kidnapper chose the creek area by accident," Garrett said. "He had to have a destination in mind. Since it's county property, I'll be directly involved in the investigation. Want to tag along?"

Tempting. As much as he hated to admit it, he was much like Brenna. Missing pieces drove him crazy, too.

"Sure. Give me an hour. Where will you be?"

"Look for Evan at the bridge. Maybe by the time you get back, we'll have some kind of lead."

At the hotel, Jett slipped the key card into the lock and escorted Brenna into her room. Still wrapped in the green blanket, she took a few steps and leaned against the wall beside the bathroom door.

"Irish, you'd better get out of those wet clothes."

She just stood there, leaning against the wall and staring at the room, Brie's collar in her hand.

He guided her to the blue club chair and ottoman. "Sit here. I'll be right back."

"I'm all right, Jett." She shook off the blanket. "You go to bed, or whatever. I'm going to soak in the tub until I can feel my feet again, and then I'll get some sleep."

Even though she sounded rational, she looked dazed. He suspected she'd sit where she was until sunrise unless he forced her to move.

"I'll start filling the tub," he said. He turned on the taps, then hurried to his own room next door and found the mild sleeping pills his doctor had given him for those nights he tossed and turned. When he returned to Brenna's room, she was sitting right where he'd left her.

"Take this—you need to sleep." He handed her a tablet.

"I don't want it."

"I don't care. You need it. I expect you to share the driving tomorrow," he lied, "and I don't want you falling asleep behind the wheel." He pushed a glass of water into her hand. "Take it."

After she grudgingly swallowed the pill, he pulled her to her feet and gently pushed her to the bathroom.

"I've left the tap dribbling on hot," he said. "After you get in the tub, let the water warm slowly."

"I know the procedure."

He grabbed the hotel's white terry-cloth robe and draped it over her shoulder. "Put this on so you won't chill."

"Yes, Mother." She took the robe and then closed the door in his face.

As much as he wanted to rush back to Garrett, he didn't dare leave Brenna alone until she was resting in bed. While he waited for her to finish the bath, he folded the blanket and then packed Brie's rawhide bone and her other belongings into the gym bag Brenna used for the dog's hotel trips. Finally, he collapsed the wire crate and leaned it against the wall in the cubbyhole closet.

Then he knocked on the bathroom door. "You okay?"

"Fine, go away."

He could hear the water still running. "Don't drown."

As soon as the words hit the air, he cringed. What a stupid thing to say.

Sitting on the gold bedspread, he studied the room, which was identical to his own. Odd: it felt empty without Brie. How could that be? This was only their second night in this hotel; surely a room couldn't take on a personality, a feeling of a person's or an animal's presence, in so short a time.

Maybe his sense of helplessness made the room seem huge and

cold. Brenna had fought showing her grief, but he knew it would come, and he'd never known quite how to comfort a sobbing woman. Not even his daughters. When they were small, he'd hug them and whisper he loved them. Somehow, he got through it and the girls always said he'd made them feel better.

When the bathroom door opened, he stood. Brenna walked out, clad in the robe, a white towel around her hair.

"Get a good look, Jett." She held her arms to the side, Brie's collar dangling from one hand, and slowly turned in a circle. "I'm fine; everything works." She yawned and then smiled. "You can go now."

"Are you going to bed?"

"After I dry my hair." She stepped back into the bathroom.

He moved to the doorway, watched her pick up the hair dryer in the same hand as the collar, and wondered if she realized she was still holding it. Then he moved the desk chair into the bathroom.

"Sit, let me." He gently pulled the brush and dryer from her hands.

"No . . ."

"I'm an old hand at this. When my daughters were little, this was my job."

In a few moments, she folded her arms on the counter and rested her head on her wrists. Then she started crying, soft and quiet, as if she were trying to hide it from him.

"Irish . . ." He put down the dryer and gently turned her until he could hug her. "It's all right to grieve over Brie."

"But . . . Zoe . . ."

"I know. We're happy Zoe is safe, but that doesn't mean you can't cry for Brie. She was a part of our lives."

As he held her, he realized how much Brenna had become a part of *his* life. More than an employee, she was the person he trusted most with his worries and celebrations. Now, for the first time during their friendship, he had found a crack in her independence; she needed and accepted his comfort.

After the grief eased, he put her to bed. It didn't take long for her to fall asleep. He tiptoed to the door, placed the "Do Not Disturb" sign on the knob, and glanced at his watch. If he hurried, he might find Evan still waiting for him.

When Jett returned to Stanford Circle, the neighborhood was quiet again. Most of the houses were dark, though all had their porch lights burning. The police and sheriff's cars were gone, leaving no sign of the commotion an hour before.

At the concrete bridge, he found Evan waiting for him.

"Where's Garrett?" he asked.

"Your truck got four-wheel drive?"

He nodded. "Why?"

"We're gonna need it."

He followed Evan's directions through the adjacent development and eventually turned onto a gravel road that bisected a rural area. Off to the right, a farmhouse and two outbuildings sat on a hill. When Jett spotted a glowing lantern at the edge of a strip of woods, Evan told him to veer left and use the lights as a guide.

The truck bumped and rocked over uneven ground, the tires spraying mud in their wake. The headlights' beams looked puny against the dark haze of the woods, making Jett feel that the darkness was a living thing closing in on them. A city boy, he'd never longed for country life. It was too quiet, too far from neighbors, cultural interests, and glittering gatherings.

Evan pointed. "There's the next one."

Lanterns lit the trail. He drove between huge trunks and over shrubs until he saw the flashing yellow lights of a sheriff's cruiser. Two police cars and a crime-scene van shone their lights on a small wooden building. The spotlight mounted on top of the van lit the entire area like a stage.

Jett stopped behind one of the police cars. "What is this place?"

"An old smokehouse," Evan said.

Jett climbed out of the truck and caught sight of Garrett knocking mud off his boots beside his cruiser. A man with a camera walked out of the small building, shaking his head.

"Garrett!" Jett called. He stepped over a pile of branches and stood beside the deputy. "What are we doing here?"

"You want the story blow by blow or the short version?" Garrett asked.

"Try something in the middle."

"All right." Garrett leaned against the car and crossed his arms. "With the footprint you found and the ones at the bench, it wasn't too hard to track this guy in the mud. Got tougher when he hit rocky ground, but after a few hits and misses, we ended up here. He's long gone, but there's no doubt this was his destination."

"Evan said this is a smokehouse."

"Was." He nodded toward a section of ground where a lone, stone chimney rose amid saplings and clumps of brush. "Looks like a farmhouse used to be over there. No telling how long the house has been gone, but the smokehouse is still standing. In fact, it's got a brand-new roof."

"Does it belong to those folks on the hill?"

Garrett shook his head. Then he spoke to an officer who'd just exited the wooden structure.

"Find anything, Sam?"

"Nothing you can't see with the naked eye."

Garrett turned to Jett. "Come on. We hung a light so you can get the full effect of this thing."

He led Jett to the door and then waited for the other men to step outside.

Jett couldn't believe the scene before him. A black potbellied stove with ventilation holes sat in the middle of the ten-by-ten room. Four or five inches of torn newspaper carpeted the dirt floor; on the right, a wooden crate lined in green satin held a small mattress and a white knit blanket. Green tapers in silver holders snuggled in the paper around the crate, and a large mug of orange liquid that looked like juice sat on a makeshift table of four red bricks.

"We blew out the candles," Garrett said.

"What is this?"

"We suspect it was intended to be Zoe's death chamber." He

pointed toward the crate. "When the candles burned down, the flames would have set the paper on fire. Sam found scraps of wadding—he thinks it's mattress stuffing—and dozens of charcoal briquettes crammed into the stove."

"Isn't charcoal smoke toxic?"

He nodded. "The wadding, too. Zoe would have died from inhaling the smoke before the fire touched her." He pointed to the side of the building. "All those cracks between the boards have been caulked, and the door had a brand-new bracket and padlock. This guy was extremely organized. If Brenna hadn't stumbled onto him, we might never have found that little girl."

"But, what was he after? There was no ransom demand."

"I don't know; none of us can figure this out."

"Is that why you called Crime Scene?"

"This was not an impulsive act. If he went to all this trouble, chances are we'll hear from him again. And if we do, evidence from this scene may help in the next case." He glanced at Jett. "We had more than our share of luck tonight. Gives me the shivers to think what might have happened if he'd gotten Zoe out here."

"Do you think he chose Zoe at random?"

"Do you?"

Jett shook his head. "On the surface, I'd say no. The child's room was green, her favorite color, and the satin in the crate is green. Don't ask me to prove it, but I'd say he's been watching her. He knew where her bedroom was, and he got in and out of the house without waking her parents."

Jett walked back to the Suburban and leaned against the fender. Brenna had been right in wondering how the child left home; he should have paid more attention. But, selfishly, he was glad the abduction hadn't happened in Sacramento. This was Garrett's problem now, and although he'd request a copy of the completed report for the search team records, he and Brenna could go home and leave the whole thing in Garrett's capable hands.

CHAPTER

6

THE TELEPHONE HAD been ringing all day, as usual for a Monday at the office of Culpepper Investigations in Sacramento. Brenna had grabbed lunch at her desk around one-thirty and still had half a chicken sandwich left at five-forty-five.

She glanced across the room at their client: a local attorney who was considering throwing his hat into the political ring. As Jett's administrative assistant, she knew the reason for his visit: he wanted Jett to run a background report on him to see what his opposition might find should he decide to become a contender. This type of job wasn't unusual. The company had completed similar investigations for other high-profile businessmen.

The man stood and began to pace in front of the fireplace, his gaze focused on his brown Italian shoes.

"Can I get something for you?" she asked. "I just made a fresh pot of coffee."

He stopped and glanced toward her, visibly surprised that she was still there. "No, thanks."

When Jett had first opened his business, he chose a Victorian house on a corner lot for his office, thinking the ambiance would make his clients feel more comfortable. Most people did seem to relax in the reception area that had once been the living and dining rooms. Painted in a soft taupe with white trim, the room felt soothing and restful. Ferns and rubber plants filled the corners and stood next to the blue-and-gray-striped sofa and chairs.

"How about a glass of wine?" she asked.

He shook his head. "How much longer before Mr. Culpepper can see me?"

"A few minutes. Your appointment is scheduled for six."

"I know. I thought he might be able to work me in earlier."

She pointed to the patio door leading to the adjacent glass-enclosed atrium. "If you enjoy gardening, we have a new pink-and-white variegated rose you might like to see."

"My wife gardens," he said. "I don't care much for flowers."

She went back to the computer, thinking this dark-haired, slightly built man didn't have the temperament for the political arena. A few moments later, Jett came out of his office with a woman in a gray suit. They shook hands; then he turned to the attorney.

"Sorry to keep you waiting." He glanced at Brenna. "Would you get Mr.—"

"Right here." She handed him the manila folder. Then she whispered, "Do you need me? Puppy class starts in fifteen minutes."

"Go on; he's my last appointment."

Brenna shut down the computer and scanned her calendar for the next day to make sure she hadn't forgotten anything for Jett's schedule or hers. When the telephone rang, she thought about letting Mike at the dispatch desk pick it up, but she couldn't ignore a ringing phone any more than she could ignore a yelping pup.

With the receiver tucked between her ear and shoulder, she forced a pleasant "Culpepper Investigations."

"Buddy check," a female voice said.

"Hey, Sparks." She eased into her desk chair, glad to hear her best friend's voice. Barbara Ann Sparkston's telephone conversations were always long on Sundays, but a midweek call usually signaled a problem. "Something wrong?"

"No, I just wanted to check on you. Are you okay?"

"Fair." She leaned back in her chair. "When we drove in from Seattle yesterday, the entire team was waiting for us. Thankfully, no one asked questions. I hold up pretty well if I don't have to say the words. They each gave me a hug and then went on their way."

"Makes me wish I lived in Sacramento instead of L.A.," Sparks said. "How's Feather taking it?"

"Slightly better than I am. After dinner, she went outside and came back with the blue shirt. I guess she's adopted it; she drags it around the way Brie did."

"Give her a hug for me," Sparks said. "Listen, I'm off tomorrow morning for the location shoot in Canada. We'll be out in the boonies, but I'll try to keep in touch. If we don't connect, check your e-mail."

"How many stars are you making beautiful this time?"

"I get to work on everybody but the big shots," she said. "What did Ryan say about Brie?"

"I haven't told him."

"Why not?"

"He's traveling again," she said. "Ever since his company bought out their competitor, he's holding down two sales jobs."

"Who'da thought the food business would be so time-consuming?"

"Not me," she said. "He was in town eight days last month. Sure makes it hard to have a relationship when your sweetheart's not around."

"You have to tell him, Bren." Sparks brightened. "Now, give yourself a break from that job, and if you get the house, leave a message on my machine. I'll check it at least once a week."

Brenna hung up and leaned back in her chair.

The house. She'd been saving since she moved to California to buy a place of her own, a home for her and the "girls" where they could put down roots. Only one girl now. Feather. Still, the stone cottage with diamond-paned windows and a large backyard that she'd been eyeing for nearly two years had finally come onto the market. Maybe getting this house would be a turning point in her life, a sign of better days.

The mantel clock chimed six.

Puppy class!

Brenna locked the front door and hurried down the hallway. Jett's office with its dark-wood shelves sat on the right, next to the one reserved for Connie, the firm's bookkeeper and a search team member. Marco's office lay at the end of the hallway. But Brenna turned left, through the green-and-white kitchen, around the breakfast counter, and into the former family room, which had become the break room. Jett had set a pool table in the open space between the round dining table with six rattan chairs, and the beige overstuffed furniture in front of the fireplace and media center.

As she passed the staircase that led to the four bedrooms upstairs, she glanced at her watch. She stopped at the entrance to the oversize two-car garage—the "workroom." The dispatcher kept tabs on everyone in the field from the brown desk and credenza, which formed a U-shaped command central next to the eight-by-ten closet Connie used as a darkroom.

"Hi, guys," Brenna said.

Mike, the dispatcher, covered the mouthpiece of the receiver. "How's your Spanish?" he whispered.

"Great," she said. "I can say yes, no, and '*Yo quiero Taco Bell.*'"

He frowned. "No help."

She placed papers on his desk. "Would you tape one of these schedules to Jett's bedroom door? I don't have time, and if he doesn't see it right before he goes to bed, he'll miss his breakfast meeting tomorrow morning."

On her left, two of the three computer stations squeezed between a supply closet and built-in cabinets were empty. Hatcher Smith, a bright young twenty-year-old studying to be a physical therapist, occupied the center station on a computer he'd named Emily. He was the computer geek in this office, if one could call a slender, handsome young black man a geek. His primary job consisted of running background checks for clients.

"Hard at work?" She flicked the brim of the faded royal blue Brooklyn Dodgers cap Hatch always wore, brim backward.

"Wait up," Hatch said. "You've got e-mail on the company's address."

"It wasn't there at three."

"It's here now."

She ducked into the darkroom and slipped out of her navy suit and into a white shirt and jeans. She perched on the edge of the dispatcher's desk to lace her tennis shoe.

"Who's it from?" she asked.

Hatch scrolled up the screen until he found the entry. "Somebody named Job Won."

"Never heard of him . . . her . . . whoever." She slipped her foot into the other shoe. "What does he want?"

"You want me to read it?"

"Yes." She gathered her clothes, purse, and backpack. "I'm so-o-o late. Did Marco leave on time?"

"Yep," Mike said, replacing the receiver. "Don't have a wreck driving over there. Marco will get the class started."

"Y'all have a good night."

As she yanked open the door into the parking lot, Hatch called to her.

"Brenna, what about your e-mail?"

When she'd first started working with Jett, she'd promised to answer all Culpepper Investigations e-mail on the day it arrived, if at all possible.

"What does he want?" she asked.

"He has a question."

"Do you know the answer?" When he nodded, she added, "Take care of it for me, will you? I don't have time to fool with it right now."

Brenna and Marco held puppy kindergarten in the parking lot of an office building. They had eight participants this session, all first-time dog owners. The class had two Golden Retrievers with huge feet, a black Lab, a bumbling black-and-white Great Dane with tape on his ears to make them stand straight, a white Poodle who still looked like a lamb, a Basset who tripped over his ears, and two mutts, one with a strong terrier influence.

When she arrived, Marco had already positioned the new owners and their pups in a large circle and was demonstrating the correct way to leash-break a bouncy little one. Brenna remained in her white Blazer for a moment, watching him. In his late forties, he had wavy black hair and a thick black mustache just showing signs of silver. Even though he stood only a shade over five eleven, he gave the impression of being taller. She often connected Marco to Theodore Roosevelt's line "Speak softly and carry a big stick." He didn't need the stick. But his demeanor changed when he dealt with the dogs. He was like a kid with his first pup, clapping and running and chattering in a high falsetto voice to get the little guys excited and playful.

Instead of getting out of the car, she leaned against the door. She didn't want to face these people; the loss of Brie was still too fresh, and she dreaded having to talk about it with this group. Owning a working dog was different from owning a pet. From the first day, a working-dog handler knew loss would come. Some hoped they'd lose the dogs on the job, a bittersweet validation that the dog died as it had lived, working to help someone. Others hoped the angels would take their partners during sleep—a kind, gentle journey into the next world. But Death had plans of his own, and no one was ever ready to say good-bye.

This group didn't need to think about that right now. They were in the first days of a new experience, not yet aware of the joy and unconditional love these little guys would give them.

Part of her wanted to drive away, let Marco finish the session. Another part remembered Aaron's words after he lost Beau. *If you can't take losing a dog, you're in the wrong business. Tough up, Bren; deal with it and move on. We still have a job to do.*

She had a job to do now. Puppy class.

As she joined the group, three of the women stopped watching Marco and went over to her.

The young blonde, Gayle, spoke first. "I'm so sorry about Brie."

The other women nodded as though Gayle spoke for all of them.

"Thank you," Brenna said. "Unfortunately, this moment comes for all of us. You just have to get through it."

One of the two men in the circle, a pudgy guy with short, spiked hair, wandered over, dragging his resisting black Lab puppy by the leash.

"I'm sorry, too," he said, "but the kid was more important. You can always get another dog."

She chose her words carefully.

"True," she said, "and please don't drag your pup. You want Diego to look forward to going out with you on a leash." She knelt and patted the dog. All feet, he stumbled around and tried to climb onto her knee.

"I meant to ask you about that group," Pudge said. "How much do you get paid?"

"Nothing, we're volunteers."

"Nothing? Why would you do it for nothing?"

She ran her fingers over the pup's body and then grazed her thumbs over its stubby face. Such big, dark eyes. Diego would have a real nose soon instead of a stubby little snout.

"At least you get your picture in the paper, don't you?" Pudge asked.

Brenna stood. "Not if I can help it."

"Then what do you do it for?"

She stared into his eyes. "Because." She turned and smiled at Gayle. "Everybody ready? Let's get to work."

As the class continued, she and Marco took turns instructing the owners on the basics of living with a dog. As the group walked around in a circle, she realized she knew the names of all the dogs but only one of the owners: Gayle. Petite, hair the color of straw; slender, with an hourglass figure. Every woman there avoided standing beside her. Of course, that made the two men happy; they sidled up to her every chance they got.

Gayle's pup was a Golden Retriever female named Visa. She had a sweet disposition and, a typical puppy, wanted to play with everyone. Brenna's only concern about the dog was her age. Visa had been taken away from her littermates at five weeks, too soon to suit Brenna. Now, at seven weeks, she had just started her puppy shots. There was so much disease lying in wait for unprotected little ones; Brenna worried Visa might catch something. But Donny, an officer in the Sacramento police crime-prevention unit, had asked Marco to make an exception for Gayle and Visa and admit them to class.

"Your turn," Marco called.

"Let's remember," she said to the group, "that you're smarter than your pup. Keep a few basics in mind, and training and house-breaking won't be a chore."

When the class ended, Marco walked Brenna to the Blazer. "We can mark Wilson off the invitation list."

"Who?" she asked.

"Diego's owner."

"Oh, Pudge. No, he's a hot dog; I don't want him anywhere near the team."

"What about Gayle?" Marco asked. "She asked me a dozen questions before you got here. I suspect Donny had an ulterior motive when he signed her up for this puppy class."

"Ah. Does she know about his scheme?"

"I don't think so, but he must think she'd be a team player. He knows how we work."

"Visa does look promising." She turned and spotted Gayle leaning against her car, watching them. "Did you tell her to wait?"

He smiled. "Actually, I'd like to invite her to search training Wednesday, but I wanted to clear it with you first."

"You don't have to do that, Marco. The team belongs to all of us."

He shrugged and smiled again.

"Fine with me. Tell her not to wear shorts."

As he walked toward Gayle, Brenna watched his almost stiff stride. Marco was an odd man, in his way. Obsessively loyal, he was very careful about boundaries and expected everyone else to hold the same view. He managed Jett's security division, hired and fired, and trained the drug dogs. No one disagreed with or contradicted him. But he felt the search team was Brenna's domain. She ruled, and he gracefully bowed to her judgment. As far as she was concerned, the five search team members were equal partners in this organization. If Gayle came on board, there would be six.

Rob Garrett returned to his desk at the end of his shift. Information was still filtering in about the little Hendricks girl's abduction, and with each lab report that ended up in his basket, his stomach twisted tighter. Most kidnappers dreamed of big-money ransoms; not this guy. Whoever snatched that child had a demon inside him, or no soul at all.

What if that had been his little girl, Reggie? The thought made the knot in his stomach throb.

"Ready to leave?" Evan stopped at Garrett's desk.

"Has anyone talked to Mr. Hendricks since Sunday morning at the hospital?"

"I don't know. Why?"

"I think we need to pay him a little visit."

Evan sat on the edge of the desk. "He didn't have anything to do with his daughter's disappearance."

Garrett leaned back in his chair. "You remember how nervous he was at the house when we asked him the initial questions?"

"Yeah, but so what?"

"Turns out, he hadn't told us about Zoe's going to bed angry or her not getting her bedtime story. When we talked to him at the hospital yesterday, that nervousness was worse. He should have been calm by then. Zoe was safe."

"So you think he's still hiding something?"

Garrett nodded. "I'd bet on it. Want to come with me?"

"I'll come, but . . ."

"What?"

"Zoe was found; isn't the case on the back burner now?"

"No, we haven't found the kidnapper yet. And there's a big chunk of something missing in this situation. I want to know what it is."

BRENNA WAS THE first to arrive for the training session on Wednesday. The search team trained two or three days a week, at various places; today's session was being held on a piece of county property she had nicknamed Puppy Park. It consisted of three tiers, each with varied terrain. The enormous top section, crescent shaped, paralleled the adjacent river. The spring grass was still short; wild shrubs framed the area, some with pink and white flowers. Two dozen red cedars and several oak trees dotted the plateau, providing generous shade and suitable hiding places for puppy runs. Someone had anchored a wooden picnic table within a triangle made by three great oaks. It was a good spot to take a break or fill out paperwork.

The second level, a wide strip filled with six-foot-high sunflowers and thick, high brush that obscured the ground, bordered the lower level, the rock-covered bank of the thirteen-foot-wide creek. On the other side of the water, animal trails cut through dense woods and led to both bluffs and ravines. It was a perfect place to introduce new dogs into the program.

Brenna stared at the area; instead of planning trails for the dogs to follow, she saw Brie there, wagging her long tail and jumping into the air the way she always did before her run.

Darling Brie. I'll see you every place I go.

Feather scraped the back of the driver's seat with her paw and barked.

"Okay, toots." Brenna climbed out of the truck and left the door open for the dog. Feather bounded out and raced across the park. When she reached the shrubs, she wheeled and charged back to Brenna.

One by one, the rest of the team arrived. Connie, a stocky dark-haired woman of Italian heritage, parked next to Brenna's Blazer. Her red Bloodhound, Margarita, jumped out of the car to join Feather in the race, her long ears flapping like skinny wings.

Marco parked next to Connie and unloaded his German Shepherd/Collie mix, Chelsa, and his new Jack Russell Terrier pup, Sophia. Harley Rusk drove his red Jeep around in circles before he stopped and let Brooklyn, a black Lab, join playtime with Feather and the others. Last, Gayle pulled in.

"Gayle," Brenna called. "Glad you made it."

The blonde kept Visa in her arms as she walked to the picnic table. Before she could put Visa down, everyone took turns holding the pup. Then each team member tied a thirty-foot leash around the trunk of a tree and clipped it to his or her dog's collar.

Once everyone was settled and all the dogs had full water bowls, the crew welcomed Gayle.

Connie, the other female on the team, started the introductions. "Oh, good, someone shorter than I am. Hi." She extended her hand. "I'm Connie, better known as Five Foot Four, Two Ton Tillie. The red Bloodhound is mine. Margarita. Feel free to tag along with us on a run anytime."

Brenna smiled. Two Ton Tillie, indeed. Connie might be big boned, but she didn't tote a smidgeon of fat. When Jett first hired her as his bookkeeper, Connie was quiet and shy. Different woman now. Even though she still shopped at the most fashionable stores in town, she'd developed a fascination for professional wrestling. A transformation from her former self.

Harley offered his hand next. "Just call me Grizzly," he said. The nickname fit. He shaved his head, but his mustache trailed down the sides of his mouth to his goatee. He worked as a firefighter and paramedic every third day, lifted weights in his spare time, and ran an after-school program for kids at his favorite gym. His muscles were so huge, his shirt was stretched skintight across his chest and arms.

Marco glanced at Brenna. "Puppy test?"

She looked at Gayle. "Bring Visa over here."

When Gayle joined her, she said, "This takes a whole lot longer to explain than it takes to do, so just bear with me."

"I read all the information Marco gave me," Gayle said. "Sounds really interesting. You think you can train Visa to do this kind of work?"

"All of us participate in a dog's training program and in yours."

"Mine?"

Brenna smiled. "Training the handlers is much more difficult than training the dogs."

"Great," Gayle said, "I'm game. What's first?"

"We test Visa."

Brenna squatted and placed the pup between her knees. Harley stepped forward, played with the dog, and then ran a C-shape pattern. While he was running, Brenna used an excited, whispery voice to ask, "Where's he going? Watch him. Where is he?"

When Harley stopped behind a tree trunk, Brenna turned the pup loose with the words, "Find him!"

Visa lumbered toward Harley, a ball of yellow fuzz stumbling across the grass, like someone running in clown shoes.

Each time the pup moved forward, Brenna followed. When Visa peeked around the tree behind which Harley was hiding, he squealed and clapped. Then he and Brenna played with Visa until the dog wiggled all over.

"I get it," Gayle said. "The dogs think it's a game."

"It is, in the beginning," Brenna said. "Visa did okay on her first run. She went after a stranger, and she kept going until she found her victim. That's a good sign."

"What's a victim?" Gayle asked.

"A search term that means the lost person or whoever we're looking for." Brenna glanced at Harley. "Let's do it again."

Harley played with the pup and then ran the pattern, stopping behind a different tree. This time, Visa struggled against Brenna's gentle hold. When she turned the dog loose, the pup jumped forward in baby leaps, stumbling over her feet at first; then she pushed herself up and continued the game. Harley squealed and clapped again. Then Connie squatted a few feet from the picnic table and clapped. Visa bounded in her direction.

"We'll let her rest and then do it again," Brenna said.

"Gosh," Gayle said. "Visa's training for search work and she hasn't been housebroken yet. Do you start all the dogs this early?"

"Our team does. Feather and Chelsa were older because we didn't get them as pups, but the others started training as soon as they'd had their puppy shots."

They watched Marco run behind Sophia, who was several weeks ahead of Visa in training. When the pup didn't find Harley where she'd expected him to be, he shook the bush that hid him and Sophia dashed to him, Marco close behind.

"Why did Harley shake the bush?" Gayle asked.

"He's teaching her to listen as well as look. Sometimes in the field, nature will give us clues if you pay attention. If several birds take flight at the same time, someone might have spooked them. Owls will often warn other animals if a predator is around, and if vultures are circling overhead, they're probably impatient for dinner, if you know what I mean."

Gayle nodded.

Patrick Holmes, running a little late, pulled into the parking area with Dorsey, his black German Shepherd. In his usual shy way, Patrick only nodded to Gayle; he tied Dorsey to a leash and set a water bowl beside him. Brenna smiled. Patrick was cute, with a wide smile that looked as though someone had drawn it on his face with a marker.

Gayle nodded at Patrick, put Visa inside her crate, and turned to Brenna. "When I read the packet Marco gave me, I couldn't believe some of the things this team does. Can you teach me to read maps and rappel off a cliff? I've never done that stuff before."

"It's part of the training program, and if I could learn to do it, so can you."

"How often have your searches meant life and death to somebody?" Gayle asked.

Brenna glanced at the tree Brie had chosen as her spot whenever the team trained at this park.

Life for Zoe; death for Brie.

"Hard to say," Brenna told her. "So much depends on weather, the person's physical condition, how soon we're called. I don't know that I can give you a definite answer or a success rate. We often get calls to clear an area, make sure whoever the police are searching for isn't hiding out." She went toward Feather, and Gayle tagged along. "I suppose that kind of search follows the premise that if you know where someone isn't, you're closer to figuring out where he is."

As Brenna neared, Feather barked, her front feet dancing. Brenna loved this dog's personality. "Say hello to Gayle."

Feather sat and raised her paw to shake, cocking her beautiful head. The flat, level skull between short pointed ears gently sloped down the top until it straightened along the muzzle. Even though Feather was female, she had the beard and "bangs" typical of Bouviers; they added a dignified flair to her intelligent expression.

"She's a big girl." Gayle jiggled the paw. "How much does she weigh?"

"Between eighty and ninety pounds."

"I bet she could take somebody down in a hurry," Gayle said. "Are all the dogs protection trained?"

"None," Brenna said. "In fact, we teach our dogs *not* to bite. We don't do criminal chase—we don't go after escaped . . . anybody. We aren't trained as law-enforcement officers, and we don't carry guns, so the task of finding criminals on the loose belongs to other people."

"That's a relief," Gayle said. "I wouldn't want to come face to face with a murderer. But I don't hear of many escapees around here."

"We get search requests from other states, as well as lower California. We go wherever they need us."

Feather barked.

"Yes, toots, I know what you want, but you have to wait." Brenna glanced at Gayle. "We let them play a running game before we all go home. You'll see."

Connie stopped beside them and smiled. "Even Margarita gets to run off leash in this game."

"Isn't she always off leash like the others?" Gayle asked.

"Hardly," Connie said. "If that Bloodhound gets a scent in her head, she won't stop for anything. I have to keep her on a long line, or I could spend two days looking for her."

After each dog had taken its turn finding that day's "victim," the handlers set up the last game. Wally, a young volunteer victim, crossed the river, climbed up on a rise, and disappeared into the woods. Then the handlers placed their dogs on a sit/stay command and removed the leashes.

When Wally blew the whistle, the dogs whined and looked at their owners, their front paws dancing as if to alert a deaf handler that someone was sending out a call for help. One by one, the handlers said, "Whistle, go!" The dogs dashed toward the sound.

"What's the game?" Gayle asked.

"The dogs must use their ears as well as their noses to find Wally," Brenna said. "When they reach him, he gives them a special treat of cooked liver."

"Why is a whistle so important?" Gayle asked.

"The blast of a whistle is our last-resort, emergency, need-help-fast signal," Brenna said. "A dog's sense of hearing is so much more acute than ours, it can hear pitches we can't. So we train them to tell us if they hear something we miss. We make it a game."

"It's the only time we let all our dogs work loose and together," Connie said.

"They run in packs on television," Gayle said.

"Some do," Connie said. "Ours don't."

"Each search dog team sets its own policies," Brenna said. "Most basic training for the dogs is the same: air-scent, trailing, disaster work, water work, cadaver recovery. Depending on local resources, a team might encourage Schutzhund or bite work. We don't."

Connie nodded toward the rise. "Come on. We've got to catch up to our four-legged friends."

Before the group left for home, every person patted and hugged each dog. In a way, every dog on the team belonged to all of them.

Gayle put Visa in her car and got ready to leave. "Are we meeting here Saturday morning?" she asked.

"Yes," Brenna said, "seven to ten, and then we're going to the lake for water work. We should finish about noon."

Gayle grinned. "I'm looking forward to it."

Brenna decided Marco had made a good move. Gayle had been interested but not too eager; she was observant, and she mixed well with the members. And she'd read the material about the whys and hows of the organization. Not bad for a visitor's first session. Maybe Gayle was just what this team needed.

Rob Garrett arrived at Jett's office shortly after two o'clock on Friday. He carried a manila folder and a wooden box with fleur-de-lis carved into the lid next to Brie's name. When Jett told him Brenna was giving a Hug-A-Tree presentation to a local first-grade class and planned to go home afterward, he asked if they could meet her at the school. He knew Bren would be anxious to have Brie home again, and he needed to talk to Jett away from the office, so no one would overhear.

By the time the assistant principal escorted them to the classroom, Brenna was at the end of the presentation. Clad in her search uniform of red shirt and khaki pants, she stood in front of the projection screen, a big black dog beside her. Someone wearing a costume representing an oak tree waited a few feet to her left. The children sat on mats, circling the slide projector perched in the center of the room.

"Is that hairy beast Feather?" Garrett whispered.

Jett nodded. "Stocky dog. She's worked great for Irish, specializes in cadaver recovery. As you can see, she's as gentle as Brie."

Garrett tightened his hold on the wooden box. "How has Brenna handled the loss?"

"Hard to say. She's pacing a lot, and I suspect she's taking it hard, but she won't let any of us see it. That's not her way."

Garrett turned his attention to the children and the classroom. Bright blue walls, bulletin boards with colorful pictures next to huge letters of the alphabet, posters that displayed numbers beside comic book or cartoon characters. Apparently someone had discovered how to make learning fun.

"Now," Brenna said, "what do you do if you get lost outside?"

"Hug a tree," the children said.

"What?" She held her fingers to her ear. "I can't hear you."

"Hug a tree!" the children yelled.

"Yes! Now, if you get lost in a store, who do you talk to?"

"The person who takes the money," they yelled.

"Yes!" She applauded the class and they clapped their hands, too.

Rob Garrett smiled. She'd conned him into wearing that tree costume more than once, but he'd never minded. Teaching a kid to stay in one place if he or she got lost was an important lesson. People were so much easier to find if they didn't move around.

He leaned to Jett. "Who'd she get to play the tree this time?"

"Looks like Donny," he said.

"From Crime Prevention? Right up his alley."

"Who wants to hug our tree?" Brenna asked.

Fifteen small hands each strained to reach higher than the others.

"Who wants to pet Feather?"

All the hands went up again.

"Okay," she said, "line up. Mrs. Coleman will give each of you a turn." She glanced toward the men and waved.

A few minutes later, the bell rang.

"Time for recess," Mrs. Coleman said. "Thank Miss Scott for visiting with us today."

High-pitched voices echoed thank-you's as the children filtered out the door toward the playground.

When everything was packed and loaded into her Blazer, Garrett stopped beside her in the parking lot. Since he didn't know what to say, he handed her the wooden box.

"Oh, Garrett . . . you made this for her." She glanced at him but then looked away. "Thank you, String Bean."

"My pleasure," he said. "And I have other news I had to deliver in person."

"About Zoe's abduction?" Jett asked.

He nodded. "When the Hendrickses got home from the hospital the next day, they found a big surprise."

BRENNA COULDN'T WAIT to hear what Garrett had uncovered. After she dropped Feather at her duplex, she joined them in a rear booth at the IHOP. No matter the hour, her boss craved pancakes; it was one of his few observable vices. After the waitress came and went, Garrett opened the manila folder and slid it in front of Jett and her.

"For your files," he said. "Pictures, lab results, copies of the official reports from the police and sheriff's departments."

"What pictures? What lab results?" she asked.

"Are you sneaking these to us?" Jett asked.

"Not exactly," Garrett said. "You sent us a copy of your report, so it seems only fair we should give you copies of ours."

"What lab results?" Brenna repeated.

Garrett looked at Jett. "Didn't you tell her?"

"Tell me what?"

The waitress returned with coffee for the men, a Coca-Cola for her. After the waitress left, Brenna tapped the table with her fork.

"Don't leave me in the dark." She turned to Jett. "What didn't you tell me, and why didn't you?"

"You were already overwhelmed," he said, "and I didn't think you could handle more. Besides, Zoe was safe. As far as we were concerned, that job was over."

"Then why did Garrett personally bring the reports to you?"

"Because I don't think it's over," Garrett said, "and even though the case is still open, no one is making it a priority except me. There are no new leads. I need to bounce ideas off somebody." He smiled. "I don't know why, but you two immediately came to mind."

String Bean Garrett. She'd enjoyed working with him. Calm, open-minded, he was always willing to learn something new, unlike some of the good old boys in his former department.

She pulled the file away from Jett and opened the folder. "What did I miss?"

"Take a look at the smokehouse pictures," Garrett said. Then he leaned toward Jett. "When the Hendrickses returned home from the hospital, they found a note from the kidnapper."

"He went back to the house?" Jett asked.

"No, we missed it."

Brenna looked up and leaned toward Garrett.

"What do you mean, we missed it?" she asked.

"It was on an eighteen-by-twenty-four piece of green construction paper in Zoe's bed."

"Where in her bed?" she asked.

"What did it say?" Jett asked.

"It was under the covers," Garrett said. "If the lights had been on, someone would have seen it, but, if you'll remember, the initial search of the house took place in the dark."

She leaned back against the blue booth. How could she have missed the note? Had she made other mistakes? Had her preoccupation with calming her resentment toward the sergeant blinded her to something that might have saved Zoe *and* Brie?

Garrett leafed through the pictures until he found the two he wanted. "Here. Front and back."

The two eight-by-tens were in color and very clear. On one side of the large note, the words "BEST SERVED COLD" were printed in huge capitals in the center of the page. In the upper left-hand corner, someone had written "01:03," and in the upper right-hand corner, "8 HOURS."

" 'Best served cold.' " She looked at Jett. "Does that sound familiar?"

"You taught English for ten years," he said. "Everything sounds familiar to you." Then he looked at Garrett. "What does that phrase mean? Their daughter will be returned to them after she's dead and cold?" He shook his head. "That's a horrible thought."

"What's this 'eight hours' thing?" Brenna asked.

"Look at the pictures of the smokehouse," Garrett said. "The lab says those eight-inch candles would've burned close to eight hours before setting the paper and charcoal on fire."

"He gave the parents eight hours to find their daughter before he killed her?" Jett asked. "What about the potbellied stove? Did he plan to stick around and light that thing at the end of their time limit?"

"I don't know."

The waitress set their plates in front of them. Instead of slathering his pancakes with butter and syrup, Jett pushed them aside. Brenna slid her salad next to the wall.

Garrett leaned over his club sandwich toward Jett. "Remember the orange juice we found? The lab report said it was loaded with Restoril."

"What's that?" Brenna asked.

"Prescription sleeping pills." He leaned back. "Enough to sedate her permanently."

"That doesn't make sense," Jett said. "He gives them eight hours to find her, but he plans to overdose her on Restoril before the time limit? What kind of plan is that?"

"Maybe he wanted to raise false hope," Garrett said. "And I finally did talk to Zoe. She doesn't remember much, but she said he gave her orange juice—"

"Laced with Restoril to keep her calm?" Jett put in.

Garrett nodded. "She did remember their waiting at the covered bench until the rain stopped, and he said he wouldn't take her near the water or hurt Pooh Bear if she stayed quiet."

"Could she describe him? Did she say how he got into her room or how they got out?" Jett asked.

"No. I'm surprised she remembers that much. She just turned four a couple of months ago."

Brenna studied the second photograph. The other side held a different message: "DON'T BET WHAT YOU CAN'T AFFORD TO LOSE."

"This sounds personal," she said. "Is Mr. Hendricks a gambler?"

"He said no when I interviewed him the first time. Little by little, his story changed until I think we finally have the whole picture." Garrett poured catsup onto his plate beside the french fries, but he didn't taste his food. "When he was in college ten years ago, he and a buddy named Miles Chaney took a trip to Vegas and lost a bundle. His aunt and uncle had already signed their house over to him as his inheritance, with the stipulation they would continue to live there and pay him a nominal sum in rent each month."

"Don't tell me," she said. "He bet the house."

Garrett nodded. "And lost it, plus a little more. The aunt and uncle cashed in an insurance policy to pay off his debt, but a year later, his uncle died in a car wreck. Hendricks borrowed money from a shark to pay for the funeral."

"What does this have to do with now?" Jett asked.

"Miles Chaney contacted him a couple of weeks ago. Wanted cash to keep a moose-size money collector off his back. When Hendricks refused, Miles threatened to call his employer, implicate him in his current gambling problems, and suggest his boss audit Hendricks's accounts."

"Has he been pilfering?" she asked.

"Hendricks says no, but I discovered the import/export company he works for has been fighting a takeover. He was terrified his boss might suspect him of cooperating with the enemy and fire him.

They just bought their house, and with the new baby, he couldn't take that chance."

"So Hendricks gave Chaney the money," she said.

"Borrowed it as a small home equity loan. Then, two days before Zoe's abduction, Miles hit him up again. Hendricks refused."

"Did he suspect Miles had taken Zoe?" she asked. "Why didn't he say something when the police arrived?"

"I don't think he wanted the police involved until he knew whether Zoe had really run away. His wife called nine-one-one the instant he went outside to look for Zoe. I think he half expected Chaney to ransom his daughter."

"Oh," Brenna said. "That's why she was so quiet. He must have been furious with her, and she with him."

"Makes old Miles look like the prime suspect, doesn't it? Have you talked to him?" Jett asked.

"Nope. Can't find him. He hasn't been home in the past couple of weeks, but I have the Louisville police watching for him."

"Kentucky?" Brenna leaned back. "It's a long way to Seattle just to take a child for money."

"But Chaney thought he had a hold on Hendricks," Jett said.

If Tom Hendricks hadn't been gambling recently, what was the point of the kidnapper's note?

Garrett laughed. "You two."

"What?" she asked

"You're staring into space, humming something, and Jett's staring into space, tapping his fork on the table."

"I was not humming," she said.

Jett smiled. "You do it all the time."

She ignored him and looked at Garrett. "Do you have a picture of Miles Chaney?"

"There's a copy of his driver's license photo in the folder."

Brenna studied the picture. Dark-haired, with a long face, he didn't look a bit familiar.

"Anything?" Jett asked.

"No. Maybe if I saw him again, something might click. Right

now, I'm no more help than Zoe." She shook her head. "I just didn't get a good look at that guy."

Jett turned to her. "What do you mean, if you saw him again? We're out of this thing, Irish."

"Maybe you are; I'm not." She knotted her hands on top of the table. "I missed the note. If we'd known Zoe had been abducted–"

"You wouldn't have been involved," Jett said. "We don't search for criminals, remember?"

She wanted to argue, but he was right. They didn't search for criminals. But if she'd found the note and they'd decided to search for Zoe anyway, things would have been different. She might not have assumed the footprint she'd found at the jogging trail belonged to a searcher. She wouldn't have walked the trail alone. If someone had been with her, an officer with a gun, the stranger might have been caught. He might not have thrown Zoe in the river, and even if he had, somebody would have been there to pull them out.

Jett looked at his plate of neglected pancakes, spread his napkin over it, and turned to Brenna. "There's nothing you can do, Irish. Let it go."

"I'm not sure I can," she said.

"You could be my sounding board," Garrett said. "That would help."

"Have there been similar abductions in your area?" Jett asked.

"Not that I can find," Garrett said.

"What about that National Crime computer thing?" Brenna asked.

"The NCIC?" Garrett shook his head. "I checked but didn't find anything." When the waitress returned, he nodded for her to refill his cup. "I sent queries to Idaho, Oregon, and British Columbia. Not one department had had any cases like this one, so I sent my report to VICAP for FBI analysis."

"What's VICAP?" she asked.

"The Violent Criminal Apprehension Program," he said.

"What did they say?"

"I haven't heard from them yet."

"If this abduction turns out to be an isolated incident," Jett said, "that sure reinforces the link to Chaney, doesn't it?"

"He's my best suspect, at the moment," Garrett said.

"Your only suspect," Brenna said. "Now, all you have to do is find him."

After Brenna left Jett and Garrett at the IHOP, she returned home. Feather greeted her at the door, tail wagging.

"Hi, toots. Have you been a good girl?"

She stashed her purse in the coat closet in the foyer, if one could call a six-by-eight rectangle of brown tile adjacent to the front door a foyer. Clutching the wooden box, she went into the daffodil yellow living room. A photograph of her with the two dogs, Brie and Feather, sat on the mantel over the fireplace. Those had been happy days. She skimmed her finger over Brie's image and hugged the box.

When Feather barked, Brenna set Brie's ashes on the mantel and followed the dog through the yellow-and-white kitchen. She slid open the patio door and let Feather romp into the backyard.

This splash of grass really was too small for big dogs like Feather and Brie to get much exercise, but they'd managed. An eight-inch dirt path paralleled the fence line. Now, Feather ran it alone.

While Feather was outside, Brenna gathered laundry and piled it on top of the washing machine. Towels, jeans, socks . . . the blue shirt.

Tough up, Bren.

She let Feather into the house, then rummaged through the clothes hamper, looking for more towels. When she returned to the washer, the blue shirt was gone.

Where? . . . Feather.

When she walked into the bedroom, Feather lay beside the bed, the blue shirt under her paws.

"Give me that shirt."

As she reached for it, the dog jumped up, grasped the shirt in her teeth, and trotted into the bathroom.

"Feather, give."

When she tried to grab the shirt, the dog trotted through the galley-style bath and circled into the living room. Then she dropped the shirt and barked.

"At least Brie let me wash it."

Feather barked again.

Suddenly weary, Brenna wilted. She understood the dog's refusal to let go of the shirt. Brie's scent was on it; Feather kept it close to keep Brie near. Some people said dogs didn't grieve. They were wrong.

"Okay, toots. You win this one."

She glanced at the carved box on the mantel. The laundry could wait. She hugged the box and eased onto the sofa. In a strange way, having Brie home made her feel whole again. Feather snuggled next to her feet, the blue shirt beneath her paws.

It was then that Brenna noticed the flashing red light on her answering machine.

"Sorry, Brenna," the female voice said. "They turned down your offer on the cottage, but don't give up. We'll find another house any day now."

She tightened her grip on Brie's box. They'd lost the cottage, but that didn't seem important at the moment. It wouldn't have been the way she'd imagined it, not without Brie.

Still hugging the box with one arm, she leaned down and ran her fingers through Feather's black coat.

She'd made mistakes on Zoe's search. Costly mistakes. She'd missed the note. That damn note. When they searched Zoe's room, Brie had stopped and sniffed the bed. Brenna thought she was taking scent. What if she'd been sniffing the note?

Why hadn't she checked? Dear, Lord, why hadn't she checked the bed when Brie stopped there?

"Oh, Brie . . ."

The tears came, and she didn't try to stop them. She remained on the sofa long after the sun disappeared and stars dotted the sky.

When Brenna finally rose, Feather followed her into the bedroom and stood beside her as she studied the bookcase opposite the bed. Four large photographs took center stage on the top shelf. One of her father, forever thirty-nine years old; one of her and Sparks together at the beach; and a double frame with Aaron and her, a cock-eared pup sitting between them on one side, a picture of Brie and her in a boat during a water recovery search outside Fresno on the other.

She placed the box in front of the double frame.

"Is this the right spot?" she asked the dog.

Feather sat, cocked her head, and then woofed, softly.

She laughed. "Sometimes I think you can read my mind."

Feather stood and barked, backing up with each woof. Then she swiped her paw through the air.

Brenna glanced at the clock. "We're way off schedule tonight. Why didn't you tell me?"

Feather wagged her bobbed tail, threw her head up, and howled. Then she looked at Brenna expectantly.

"Okay, toots. Supper time."

The dog sprinted from the bedroom into the kitchen.

Brenna ran her fingers over the photographs and the box. Then she turned and followed Feather into the kitchen.

CHAPTER

9

THE DAYS GREW longer as May became a memory and June blended into July. Brenna didn't mind the shorter nights; she'd had nightmares since Brie's death, and she'd begun to welcome the morning's alarm.

She heard Connie stash her belongings in her file cabinet and go into the reception area.

Connie glanced at her watch. "What time did you get here this morning?"

"Five," Brenna said.

Easing into a chair beside an ivy with trailers four feet long, Connie asked, "Why?"

"I'm transferring records to a new computer program, and—"

"You've been here by six every day for the last month," Connie said.

Brenna leaned back, and her desk chair squeaked. "I'm just trying to get ahead."

"What's wrong, Bren?"

"Nothing, why?"

"You look tired." Connie leaned forward. "Are you sleepwalking again?"

Surprised, Brenna glanced into Connie's dark eyes. "What makes you think I sleepwalk?"

"I've been with you on searches."

"What do you mean?"

"We've shared a hotel room," Connie said patiently. "Not only do you sleepwalk, you talk in your sleep."

"I do?"

"I've caught you sleepwalking once," Connie said, "when we were staying at the Grayson's in San Francisco during that conference. You took the dogs out, about three in the morning. But you talk in your sleep all the time, and you never remember our conversations."

Brenna hadn't realized her childhood trouble had returned. Ryan hadn't said anything. "Why haven't you mentioned this before?"

Connie smiled. "It doesn't change our friendship, and it's comforting to know you're human, just like the rest of us."

Stunned, Brenna leaned forward. "Connie, have I done something to make you feel—"

"No," Connie said. "You're always there for me, Bren. For all of us, but, just in case you don't know it, you're two different people."

"How?"

"Jett calls you a mother hen," she said, "and he's right. You remember everyone's birthday, take up the slack if somebody's out sick. All the good stuff. But when it comes to search work, you're so focused, you become intense. Sometimes I wonder if I meet your standards."

"Oh, Connie, I never meant—"

"You're missing the point," she said. "You've trained me well; I know I'm a good searcher. The point is that all of us have quirks; I'm glad to know you have some, too. It's hard to get close to you, Bren, and you've pulled away the last few weeks. What's bothering you?"

Brenna didn't know how to explain without sounding melodramatic or superstitious. Brie's loss, Zoe's abductor, missing the note in the little girl's bed, losing the cottage.

"Are you thinking about quitting the team?" Connie asked.

"Of course not. Why did you ask that?"

"You didn't come to water training last Saturday," Connie said, "and the time before that, you didn't go out in the boat. You've handed off puppy training to Marco, and when we got that search call last Friday, you sent Marco and me."

"The two of you were first response," Brenna said. "I would have come if you'd needed me, but you didn't. The callout was canceled even before you got there."

When Connie stared at her, Brenna squirmed in her seat. She suspected that her spur-of-the-moment explanation didn't sound convincing, especially since she usually dropped everything when a search arose . . . and everybody knew it.

"What's caused this change in you, Bren?"

She didn't have an answer.

"All right," Connie said. "Let's start at the beginning. Why did you become involved in search work?"

Angie's image flashed in her mind. Blond hair, brilliant blue eyes.

"A darling sixteen-year-old girl was murdered and we couldn't find her," Brenna said. "Angie had been a student in my English class, and her parents were my friends. Six months after she disappeared, Aaron moved into town and he and his Bloodhound eventually found her bones in a shallow grave we'd all walked past a hundred times." She shut down the vision and looked at Connie. "I never wanted to feel that helpless again, so I started training with Aaron."

"Is every search symbolic of Angie?" Connie asked. "Are you, somehow, trying to find her before it's too late or trying to save someone else the pain you experienced?"

Brenna rested her chin on her palm. "Where did you get all this insight?"

"I'm naturally clever," Connie said, smiling. "And my second husband was a psychologist. I must have gained some knowledge through osmosis at all those conferences I attended with him." She sat straight. "Am I right?"

"Sounds good to me."

"No, really. Does that make sense to you?"

"I haven't thought about it that way," Brenna said. "Aaron said searching gave him a sense of purpose, a feeling that he was doing something that might make a difference."

Connie nodded. "I find myself wondering about the victims, wanting to know what happens after we find them. Sometimes I wish I could call the family and ask questions."

"That's a very big no-no in this line of work. It clouds our objectivity."

Connie leaned back and crossed her arms. "Tell me you don't feel the same way."

Brenna smiled. "Only with the young and very old. Those people have no control over what happens to them. I remember the others, too, but the special ones stay with me like . . . characters from a favorite novel." She glanced at the duck-shaped crystal paperweight beside the computer, but what she saw was a little girl with copper hair and hazel eyes. "I wonder how Zoe's doing?"

"Why haven't we talked about this before?" Connie tilted her head. "Do you think it's maternal instinct that makes us curious about their lives? Since neither of us has children, maybe we're substituting strangers for family."

"Is that more psychologist talk?"

Connie shrugged. "Maybe. You never talk about your family, Bren. Do you have brothers or sisters?"

"Sparks is the only family I claim."

"Sparks!" Connie jumped up and disappeared into the hallway.

"What are you doing?" Brenna called.

Connie returned with a large package tied with a huge red bow. "Sparks made me promise to give this to you yesterday, but I forgot." She set it on the desk and then returned to her chair. "She wanted it to be a surprise, so she sent it to me. Why is she giving you a present?"

Brenna smiled and leaned back. "It's a birthday gift."

"Isn't your birthday on Christmas Eve?"

She nodded. "Sparks and I have a deal: I give her a gift on my birthday and she gives me one on her birthday."

"Why?"

"Sparks thinks I get cheated out of birthday presents because mine comes at Christmas. And this way, she gets two presents for the holidays."

"So yesterday was her birthday." Connie eyed the package. "Open it."

Brenna slipped the red ribbon off the box. Inside, she found a sparkling bright blue dress with short sleeves and a sweetheart neckline.

"Wow," Connie said. "You'll get noticed in that outfit." She touched the material. "I like it, and it'll look great on you."

Brenna laughed. "Sparks is cooking up a plot of some kind. This is not my style."

"Maybe it should be. You're a workaholic, Bren. Between work and the team, you never take time for yourself."

"Oh, really." She leaned forward and rested her chin on her palm. "I see Ryan whenever he's in town. Who have you been out with lately?"

Connie sat straighter. "I'll have you know I met a very handsome man last weekend at the grocery store. His name is Brad. I liked him immediately, so he'll probably turn out to be a real jerk. My first impressions are always wrong."

"Mine are usually right," Brenna said, "but I rarely listen to them if I'm romantically tempted by a charming man. That's when I get into real trouble."

"We should team up. You pick the good men and then I'll flirt with them." She pointed at the box. "You can wear your new dress."

"Actually, I did buy a new outfit last weekend for Ryan's company party, and last night I found out he isn't going to be here." She shrugged. "Maybe I'll find another place to wear it."

Brenna had found a longish, little black dress with a sexy slit that revealed a hint of thigh. The matching beaded jacket tapered to complement a shapely waist.

"Let's go out this weekend and you wear this blue one," Connie said. "When I was married, we were on the social 'A list' in San Francisco. That's where you belong. You like going to the ballet, symphony . . . all that stuff." She pointed to the box. "That dress might get you noticed by the right people."

Brenna smiled. "This is a jerk-bait dress, designed to attract men who want flash, fun, and flings."

"Then why did Sparks send it to you?"

"She loves flash, fun, and flings," Brenna said. "We are exact opposites and we've been friends for twenty-five years."

Jett came into the reception area. "Good morning, ladies."

"Where have you been?" Brenna asked. Then she realized she'd gotten there at five that morning, and if Jett was just now coming home . . . "Never mind," she said. "I don't want to know."

He flashed her a smile and strolled into his office.

Connie leaned forward and whispered, "Why don't you want to know? I'm curious about who he's seeing these days."

"I don't want to know because of Joanne."

"His ex-wife?"

Brenna nodded. "She divorced Jett so she could find herself, and now she wants to find herself his wife again. She calls me every day wanting to know where he is and if he's dating anyone in particular. As far as I'm concerned, Jett's personal life is private."

The intercom buzzed.

"Where are the vet records on the drug dogs?" Jett asked.

"In the kennel," Brenna said. "Do you need them?"

"Would you mind?" he asked.

"Right away," she said. "Do you want coffee?"

"Not if you made it," he said.

"Very funny." She replaced the receiver and glanced at Connie. "I'm off to the kennel. Will you watch the phone?"

"Sure, and I'll make a fresh pot of coffee."

"Is my coffee really that bad?"

Connie frowned and then smiled. "Let's say I have a bit more talent in the kitchen than you do."

"You're a woman of tact, Connie."

Two drug-dog handlers were loading the Culpepper Blazers with gear before heading out to their assignments. Brenna waved at them before she entered the kennel she'd helped design.

The entire back wall of the thousand-square-foot main room held cabinets, a water-heater closet, a raised bathtub, and a grooming stand that pulled out from the wall to form a T for easy brushing, trimming, and drying. Two large wire crates sprouted hair dryers so a dog could lie down and relax while drying if the groomer needed to work with another animal. Seven indoor/outdoor runs jutted from the building, all spotless. A desk and file cabinets filled one corner of the room.

After she found the files Jett wanted, she sat at the desk and thought about what Connie had said. Had she been different these past few weeks?

Not really. Avoiding water training wasn't that big a deal, was it? She and water had barely tolerated each other since she'd almost drowned at the age of nine; now, they weren't even on speaking terms. Aaron would have told her to deal with it. She would, later. At this point, she needed a break from creeks, rivers, and lakes.

Puppy training was different. Marco did a fine job with his little Sophia and Visa. Connie had nicknamed the newest pup their Golden Child. Even though Visa was progressing in search work, the pup's obedience did need attention. Maybe Connie would agree to spend a little extra time with Gayle.

Could Connie have picked up on Brenna's preoccupation with wanting to find the man who'd taken Zoe? She'd wanted to help identify the guy. But finding the kidnapper was Garrett's job and there wasn't anything she could do.

At least they'd have a break from search training the next weekend. Instead of working the dogs, the team had agreed to help fingerprint children during the Child Fair at the mall. Happy children, colorful balloons. Maybe the break in routine would restore her spirit.

Rob Garrett sat at his desk in a room with a half-dozen other desks and four deputies. Even though he'd sent his report to the FBI, he couldn't abandon this project and let someone else do all the research. Zoe had been kidnapped in his jurisdictional backyard, and he took that abduction personally.

Two of the remaining deputies filed their reports and left. One still typed on his keyboard, but he sat across the room. Maybe one guy wouldn't matter; they were far enough apart. Harrison wouldn't know what Garrett was doing when he fired up his computer, even if his snooping was against orders.

Last Friday, the sheriff had invited Garrett into his office and then closed the door.

"Drop this abduction case," he'd said. "That little girl is fine and I don't want you wasting any more time on it. The election's coming up, and I need you to work with me on that."

"But, sir," Garrett had said, "if we can find—"

"You're using my time and my department on something we can't change. Turn over everything you have to the FBI and get on with business here."

There hadn't been any talking to him. The sheriff, the main man, had ordered him to drop it.

If the sheriff or his captain caught him now, Garrett could lose his job. As if it mattered. Yvonne had taken their daughter, Reggie, and moved to Pennsylvania last week. A reconciliation seemed impossible at this point. She'd gone off with everything they owned, leaving him little for his new, bare apartment.

With no reason to rush home, he'd accelerated his research about the kidnapping. If Yvonne hadn't taken their computer, he could have searched the web from home, but she'd cleaned him out. Set a certain tone for the ensuing divorce. At least he didn't have much left for her to take.

Leaning back in his chair, he rubbed his eyes and thought of Reggie. What if someone took *her*? It would slash the heart out of him. Then he turned to his computer and typed "best served cold" in the "search" box. When the blue bar disappeared, he found his answer.

Revenge is a dish best served cold. A Klingon proverb.

My God, was this guy a Trekkie?

He searched on the complete quotation and dozens of results filled the screen. Each site dealt with getting even for an unintentional slight or calculated betrayal. It would take hours to sift through all the material.

So, this guy was out for revenge. Garrett just didn't know why.

CHAPTER 10

THE STORES AT the mall opened at ten o'clock, but the Sacramento police officers and the search team were ready for the crowds at nine-thirty. In the center of the highest-traffic area, they'd arranged long tables to form a large rectangle, where they'd set up six fingerprinting stations. The inside of the rectangle held tanks of helium, boxes of balloons, cartons of child record books, and puppets for entertaining those disgruntled children who didn't want anyone pressing their fingers onto a card.

Another set of tables sat in U-shaped formation at both ends of the rectangle. Parents could have their child measured and weighed before he or she was photographed, in the center of the "U." The completed record booklet included the child's age, height, weight, photograph, and fingerprints. Parents were responsible for keeping the information current—noting new scars, medical information, and changes in appearance.

Although no one wanted to contemplate the possibility of a child being abducted or running away from home, more and more parents were following crime-prevention suggestions to keep the child's personal information current. Everyone participating in the Child Fair understood the unspoken superstition: taking precautions might warn off the unthinkable. The last time they'd held a Child Fair Weekend, the group logged information on over seven hundred children.

Gayle Travis stood next to her dazzlingly blue-eyed boyfriend, Donny, in front of the Gap. Donny had had to stretch to make the minimum height requirement for the Sacramento police department, but he loved his job, and she suspected she was falling in love with him. Brenna had placed her in charge of blowing up and handing out balloons until someone's back gave out at one of the fingerprint stations. Then she'd get to hold little fingers in her hand and press them onto a card. Like all of those working today, she hoped no parent would ever have to hand over the booklet to an officer because a child was missing.

"How did you con the team into helping you this weekend?" she asked.

Donny smiled and slipped his arm around her waist, a major infraction of on-duty protocol. No officer was to display public affection while in uniform.

"They help us in July and on Halloween, and we help them with the Christmas tree lot."

"Halloween?"

"Trick-or-treating door to door isn't safe anymore, so the stores hand out candy and the mall holds a best-costume contest. Since everyone comes, it's a good time to offer the fingerprinting again."

"What Christmas tree lot?"

An officer paused in front of them long enough to hand them two foam cups filled with coffee.

"The team runs a Christmas tree lot every year," Donny said, "to pay for equipment and travel expenses. People can only spend so much out-of-pocket. The owner of the hardware store was planning to cancel his order for trees one year, but the team volunteered to take over running the sale if he'd split the profit with them. So he orders the trees and takes over if a search comes up, but the team prepares the lot, puts up the fence and tents, unloads the trees, keeps them watered, and sells them."

"Sounds like you've taken a turn at the lot," she said.

He nodded. "We get repeat customers each year. Harley and I have about convinced some of those kids we're Santa's nephews. The minute their parents let them out of the car, they start yelling for us."

Brenna and Marco came over to them and Brenna handed Gayle a whistle on a red lanyard.

"We usually try to make this presentation a bit more formal," Brenna said, "but since we're fingerprinting today, you get the short version."

"Consider this an official welcome to the team," Marco added.

"Thank you." Gayle smiled and slipped the lanyard over her head. When Harley, Connie, and Patrick, behind the tables, showed her thumbs-up signs, she waved back.

"Ready?" Brenna asked. "We've got about fifteen minutes."

As Brenna walked away, Donny hugged Gayle.

"Congratulations," he said. "You've passed your probation."

"What?"

"Look at your whistle. Is your name engraved on it?"

She turned it over; her name was etched into the silver.

"You've made second level," he said.

"How come you know about this and I don't?"

"It's simple," he said. "After you visited training and got a feel for what they do, did you sign a letter of intent?"

"Yes. So?"

"That put you on level one," he said. "While you learned about the team, they evaluated you. They didn't just consider whether your dog seemed suitable, they studied you. Did everyone like you, were you a team player, did you make an effort to learn how things work and why they operate in a specific manner, did you have an ulterior motive for wanting to join the squad?"

"What kind of ulterior motive?"

"All kinds of people have been interested in that group for all kinds of reasons," he said. "Some want to learn all they can and then break off and start their own team, for profit. Some undesirables have petitioned to join to learn how the dogs work so they can figure out how to fool them."

"You're kidding."

"I'm not. The whistle means you've moved up from potential member to trainee," Donny said.

"Why a whistle?" she asked.

"It's a symbol of teamwork."

Donny pulled his arm from her waist. It amused her that he couldn't talk without gesturing with his hands.

"It was my first search with the team," he said, "and I'd been paired with Brenna. This fourteen-year-old kid's pals had dared him to hike through Weisman's Gulch. You know, that chunk of land donated three years ago as a wilderness preserve."

She knew about the property. The newspaper had run a big article about how the owner of those several thousand acres had willed the spread to the city as a wilderness park, though it was nowhere near the city limits. The city didn't know what to do with it, so it had been closed to the public until decisions could be made.

"Anyway," Donny said, "this kid had been dared to sneak out of the house and spend the weekend alone at the Gulch, but he never came back. Since that land officially belonged to the city, the chief called the search team and sent us out there with them." He motioned with his hands. "You should see this place. It's got woods, cliffs, rocks the size of Delaware, caves. And a river winds right through the middle."

"What happened?"

"About ten hours into the search," he said, "Harley found the kid on a cliff overlooking the river. But the kid panicked and slipped off the edge. Harley caught his wrist, but he couldn't let go to get to his radio, so he used his chin to push his whistle into his mouth."

"He didn't have a flanker?" she asked.

"We didn't have enough extra people," he said. "When that whistle started blowing, Brie started barking, completely changed her direction, and raced through the trees. Brenna jerked out her roll of red flag tape and tied one end to a branch to mark where we'd stopped. Then she slipped the roll over a twig and let it unwind as she ran after the dog. I didn't know what was happening, but when she started running, I did, too."

"If Harley couldn't use the radio," she said, "how did they know where to start looking?"

"We followed Brie while base camp called everyone on the radio to see who didn't answer, and Harley was the only one. They had the teams' sectors marked on a map.

"We came out of the trees at the river," he went on. "You should have seen it. Dogs and people were coming out of those woods at a dead run. Some were running upstream, some down. Several guys from base camp were hauling ass along the bank."

"What happened to the boy?" she asked.

"The high-angle team got him down," Donny said. "He was all right."

Gayle looked at the silver whistle in her hand. Just holding it made her feel warm inside. "Who'd have thought I'd be so excited about getting a whistle?" Then she looked into Donny's blue eyes. "You did this on purpose, didn't you?"

"What?"

"Sign me up for that puppy class. You knew I'd get interested in the team and probably want to join." She slapped his sleeve. "You plotted against me, didn't you?"

He smiled. "You're a stubborn woman, Gayle. If I'd mentioned the team and told you what they did, you would have thought I was trying to control you."

"So you let me discover it on my own."

He shrugged. "I hoped you'd get hooked and finally understand my commitment to my job. Remember when we first met?"

"I almost didn't go out with you because you're a cop," she said. "To top it off, you're in crime prevention, and that means giving up evenings to talk to neighborhood groups." She touched the cleft in his chin. "One of these days, I'll be the one canceling dates with you because of a search." She smiled and skimmed a kiss across his lips. "I can't wait to see how you like it."

Gayle had been wrong to imagine she'd have an easy job. The instant the mall opened, crowds descended on the tables, and with six fingerprinting stations, she found herself dashing from one to another, tying balloon strings around little ones' wrists. She had precious little time to inflate one kid's balloon before someone called to her for another.

When Martine, Marco's twenty-year-old daughter, offered to trade places with her, Gayle jumped at the chance to help Connie take photographs. But that proved almost as stressful as chasing balloons. She played puppeteer to get the kids to smile and then had to paste the pictures in the books.

Donny whisked her away to a corner at four-thirty and slipped a Dr. Pepper into her hand.

"Having fun?" he asked.

She sank onto the bench near the potted red mums. "This is work. How can we keep this up all day?"

"Only until six," he said. "Then we'll pick up Francesca at your sister's, and I'll take both of you out to dinner."

"Six! I'll be too exhausted to eat."

Someone's pager beeped. Then another. Gayle looked toward the tables. Brenna's pager light was flashing.

She turned to Donny. "What's going on?"

The search team members turned off the beeps, only to have the alert start again. Before Brenna could get out her cell phone, her light had flashed three times.

"Donny?"

"Did you bring your phone?" he asked Gayle.

She weaved through the crowd, scooted across one of the tables, and grabbed her purse from behind the helium tanks. By the time she'd pitched it to Donny, the search team had handed off their jobs to other volunteers and clustered around Brenna.

"Where?" Donny called over to Bren.

"Office." She pushed the talk button on her phone.

"Department," he said.

"What does that mean?" Gayle asked.

He spoke as he punched in the number for police dispatch. "Whatever's going down is big and we're working it together."

Brenna had a finger in her ear and kept saying, "What?"

Donny motioned for Gayle to hand him paper and pen. Brenna squatted; the search team members bent over her, but Gayle could still hear her part of the conversation. Donny was taking notes in his own shorthand, so she got no information from him.

"Log it," Brenna said. "We're on our way." She turned off the telephone and pitched it into her bag. "Jett's picking up the dogs; he'll meet us there."

"Shut it down," Donny called out. "I'm sorry, folks, but we're calling it a day."

"What?" Gayle demanded.

Before he could answer, the team grabbed their possessions and ran through the crowd toward the exit where they'd parked their cars.

"Gayle!" Connie called over her shoulder.

"Go on," Donny said. "Tell Brenna we're giving them a police escort."

BRENNA DID NOT like this one bit. As soon as she and Connie got into her Blazer, she tuned her programmable car radio to the intracity frequency, spoke to the police dispatcher, and then tuned in the channel they'd be using for communications during this search.

"I knew something like this would happen," Connie said. "The minute my car goes down, we have a big one. Stupid fuel injection system. Steve said he'd have it fixed, but does he? Oh, no . . . my noble ex keeps putting it off until the car dies in the middle of Ferguson Avenue. Then I have to pay a tow truck–"

"Hush, Connie." Brenna pulled her handheld radio out of the glove box and tossed it into Connie's lap. "See if Marco's on the team channel yet."

Connie turned the knob and then looked at Brenna. "Gayle's with him. Should she hear everything?"

"Might as well. Either she can take it or she can't." She glanced at Connie. "I'm not sure I can take this one."

"Marco, put your ears on," Connie said. "City channel four. Our bunch will talk on the handheld, team channel."

As Brenna sped behind Donny's cruiser, they compared information from preliminary reports and the story began to take shape.

Seven-year-old Leanne Erskin had last been seen in the neighborhood park near her home. When she didn't come home for lunch, her ten-year-old brother went looking for her. He found Leanne's pink bicycle in the wooded area of the park and took it home. Mr. Erskin found a note rolled up and taped to the bicycle.

We're playing hide and seek. Want to find me? Check
out Brenna Scott. Tell her to look for a maroon van.

Mr. Erskin thought the neighborhood girls were playing a game, and he figured this Brenna was an older girl Leanne had befriended. After searching door to door in the neighborhood and finally calling his wife at work, he called the police.

A rookie named Havens took the initial call and briefly wondered if the girls were playing a game. But the note gnawed at the officer. Kids had access to computers every day; still, the wording didn't quite fit the style he'd expect of a child Leanne's age or older. A teenager wouldn't normally hang around a seven-year-old. Why would the note mention a car? He called his supervisor, a sergeant named Brummel, and described the situation. Brummel told Havens to check the neighborhood before he panicked and did something stupid. Havens went over Brummel's head and called his captain.

"Brummel," Connie said. "He knows you, doesn't he?"

"That jackass! Yes. He knows Marco, too."

"That's right; we hate him."

Brenna had to laugh; loyalty was Connie's best and worst trait. If someone mistreated a member of the team, she took it personally.

"Guess we won't be seeing much of him after this," Connie went on.

"He'll be lucky if they don't fire him."

That afternoon, a sheriff's deputy had found an abandoned maroon van in a wooded area outside Sacramento. The keys were in the ignition; no one was around. When he checked the license plate, he wasn't surprised to learn it had been reported stolen. He had it towed to the County Sheriff's automobile compound, where the tow truck driver noticed a note on a piece of pink construction paper in the cargo area. When the owner arrived to identify his property, he said he'd never seen the note before.

"Pink construction paper . . ." Brenna said.

Zoe's note had been printed on a piece of green construction paper. Brenna spoke to Donny over the radio. "What did the note say?"

"I don't know," he replied.

"I do." Mike, the dispatcher at Jett's office, spoke to them on the team channel. "Sheriff's department read it to me. One side said, 'This is a test of the emergency broadcast system.' The other side had the words 'eight hours' and 'I'll play fair. You have eight.' "

"What does that mean?" Connie asked.

Brenna's heart sank. "I hope I'm wrong. No way could that guy know about us."

"Who?"

She glanced at Connie. "I don't know. It might . . ." She shook her head. "That guy from Seattle."

"The kidnapper? It couldn't be, Bren. Unless that guy doubled back and saw the sign on Jett's Suburban, he couldn't know anything about our team."

Brenna took the handheld from Connie. "Mike, anything else?"

"A name," the dispatcher said. "Gideon."

"Who the hell is Gideon?" Connie asked.

"I don't know. I wouldn't forget a name like that." She keyed the radio. "Was there a time on it?"

"Twelve-forty-five."

Brenna sighed. "Eight hours from twelve-forty-five."

Connie glanced at her watch. "It's almost five. We've got less than four hours."

"There's more," Mike said. "Once the city and county agencies talked to each other, deputies returned to the scene and started searching for Leanne. One of the deputies tripped a wire, and an arrow with a metal tip shot into his calf."

"Perfect dog height," Brenna whispered.

Not only had this Gideon taken Leanne, he'd rigged silent

weapons to injure or kill the dogs. Four hours in a booby-trapped area.

She looked in the rearview mirror. Their caravan was getting longer. Besides Donny's lead cruiser and the team's four cars, three squad cars filed in behind Patrick's black Firebird, all lights flashing. A county sheriff's car whipped in front of Donny, and a few seconds later, Jett's Suburban kicked up dust as it veered off a side road and joined the convoy. Behind him, one of the Culpepper Services SUVs joined the line.

"Jett's here," Brenna said. "Looks like the drug-dog handlers came, too."

"Good," Connie said. "At least we'll have flankers we know."

She took the handheld from Connie again, glad this conversation would be among the team members. "Okay, y'all think long and hard about this search. The guy who took Leanne knows about the dogs. This could be a dangerous situation, not only for the dogs but for you. We're not trained for this type of possible confrontation."

"Bren . . ." Connie touched her arm.

"We don't respond to criminal chase," Brenna said into the radio, "and although they don't think this Gideon guy is hanging around, they can't be sure."

"Bren," Connie said. "No one expects you to take Feather out. You've already lost one dog. It's too soon to take a chance on losing Feather, too."

Brenna's stomach twitched. Feather. She hadn't thought of losing Feather. Instead, she'd acted on reflex. *When a callout comes, jump!* She'd jumped, and now she had to face the possibility of losing another partner.

Leanne tried to turn onto her side. Her knee hit the wall and something hard bumped her shoulder. She opened her eyes.

"Mommy?"

She raised her hand to her face and rubbed her forehead. Her head hurt. When she opened her eyes again, it was dark. Had she been asleep, was she in a dream?

"Mommy . . ." Then she yelled it: "Mom-my!"

Her fingers scraped something rough and hard. As she tried to turn again, an object slid off her stomach. She curled her fingers around it. A flashlight? She turned it on.

She aimed the light in different places. A box. She was in a box. Toby must be playing tricks on her again.

"Let me out of here," she yelled. "Toby! I'm gonna tell, let me out!"

She banged against the roof of the box.

"Toby, let me out. Mommy! Mom-my! Make Toby let me out."

There was something next to her leg. When she held it to the light, she saw a bottle with one of those plastic straws sticking out of it. She tasted it. Yuk. Orange juice.

Orange juice.

Now she remembered. The man with the dog. He'd hit her, made her drink orange juice, and locked her into a box. Was this it?

No, that one was smaller. She hadn't been able to stretch out in that one.

"Mommy. Mom-my!"

She listened.

No one was coming. She couldn't hear anyone talking. Was that man still here?

"Mister . . . let me out!" He didn't answer. "I'll tell if you don't let me out." She listened. "My daddy will get you. Let me out!" She kicked up, hard. It hurt her toe, but the top of the box moved a tiny bit.

Her leg itched. Then both legs itched. She felt with her fingers and decided she was lying on a scratchy blanket. But something else wasn't right. Then she saw that she was wearing a big white T-shirt instead of her pink one. Her vest was gone, too.

"My shirt," she said. "I want my shirt back. Mommy bought it for my birthday."

For the next few minutes, she kicked and pushed at the lid, but it wouldn't move. Then she lay there, staring at the box.

"Why did you do this?" she whispered. "I didn't hurt your dog."

Little by little, the darkness touched her. She hugged the light,

99

afraid to let go. As a tear slipped from her eye, she heard Toby teasing her.

Baby . . . Crybaby Leanne.

"I'm not a crybaby," she whispered, and wiped away the tear.

Maybe she'd done something bad. Mommy and Daddy had yelled at each other last night. This morning, too. Was it her fault?

Mommy . . . please come get me. I'll be a good girl. I promise. Please, please come get me.

She hugged the flashlight tighter.

Maybe if I sing our song, Mommy will hear it and come get me.

"Weemaway, a-weemaway, in the jun-gle, the mighty jun-gle, the lion sleeps to-night. . . ."

It wasn't the same without Mommy singing her part.

Leanne stared at the top of the box. When she kicked it before, it had moved a little. Could she kick it off?

As she studied the boards, she heard something . . . soft, whispery . . . beside her head. What was it?

No matter how hard she tried, she couldn't turn her head enough to look at whatever made that sound. She stared at the top of the box again. Bumpy white stuff was stuck between the boards. Lifting her finger, she poked a bump.

Rubbery. When she pulled, it came loose in stringy pieces.

She pinched her fingers around another bump and pulled it down. Water dripped through the tiny hole she'd made and plunked her chin.

Was it raining? She hadn't heard thunder. Mommy made them stay inside when it rained. Maybe they'd come get her when the rain stopped.

But, maybe, if she pulled all the white stuff out, the boards wouldn't stick together. Then she could kick off the top and run all the way home.

She scraped at the rubbery stuff the way she picked at the scab on her knee. It came off in little blobs. A big drop of water plunked her chin. Then another. A large white bump right above her nose looked big enough for a good hold. With her thumb and forefinger she pinched it, and she pulled.

CHAPTER

12

THE CARAVAN VEERED onto a dirt road and then turned onto another dirt road that hadn't been blazed in months. Thick broad-leafed weeds clustered like potted plants. Other spiky plants sprouted near manzanita and California lilac shrubs. Under oak, sycamore, and cedar trees, the soil was largely bare except for knee-high patches of shade-loving vegetation. In the clearings, sunflowers grew thick and tall.

Brenna shook her head. Searching the dense areas would take hours of precious time. But then, this Gideon creep wouldn't make it easy for them. That would take all the fun out of it. And what had the note said—that he'd play fair? Did he think taking Leanne was a game?

Police cars, sheriff's cruisers, two fire trucks, an ambulance, two game warden trucks, and a dozen other cars belonging to law-enforcement personnel who'd been called in lined the road. As soon as Jett opened the rear door of the Suburban, the dogs piled out. Margarita bumbled around the side of the road, sniffing the adjacent ditch until Connie called. Then she loped toward her owner, long ears flopping with each lumbering stride. Feather stopped in the center of the road until she heard Brenna. Then she barreled toward the

Blazer and skidded to a stop. Her tail wagged as she crouched and then barked.

"They always know when it's the real thing," Connie said. She nodded toward the main road. "Fire department's dive team."

A white Suburban turned the corner, two inflated rafts latched to its trailer.

"There's water?" Brenna asked. "Dandy."

"Now, now. As Aaron would say, 'Don't go looking for trouble; it'll come after you on its own, grinning like a possum eating glass.'"

Brenna laughed. Connie had been around her too long.

Someone blew a whistle to get everyone's attention; the handlers grabbed their dogs, just in case their canine partners didn't wait for the command, "Whistle."

"I wish he wouldn't do that," Connie said. "Sometimes I wonder about our whistle game."

The women put their dogs into Brenna's Blazer and then ran with everyone else toward the sawhorses on the main road. Behind them, Sheriff Whitkin had set up tables and a large portable chalkboard on which he'd taped a map of the area. Two deputies sat at another table beside a van with a huge antenna stretching fifteen feet high.

Brenna stopped beside a group of men. When one of them nudged her, she recognized Game Warden Parnell.

"You old rascal," she whispered. "What are you doing here? I thought you transferred to a smaller county."

"I did." He nodded toward the young man beside him. "Trowte's only had this county a couple of months. I spent my first nineteen years here. Figured he could use some help." He smiled. "Trowte. Darn good name for a game warden."

"Everybody listen and take notes," Sheriff Whitkin said.

She turned her attention to the tall, slender man with pewter gray hair, a weathered face, and big ears. She'd always liked Sheriff Whitkin, and he liked working with their team.

"The van was found here." Whitkin pointed to the map. "There are natural boundaries around this whole section: this main road, the dirt road where everyone parked, the river, and a ravine that cuts down from the hillside and empties into the river after a heavy rain. As you can see, the van was found relatively close to the road, not in the middle of this rectangle, so we're assuming the child will be somewhere in here." He paused. "If she isn't, we'll expand the search area, but here's where we start." He nodded to a man in a deputy's uniform. "We're passing out maps and fliers with the child's description and picture."

When the flier reached Brenna, she studied the photograph. Hair the color of cornsilk, pale blue eyes. Leanne. Brenna couldn't help it; once she knew the name of the victim, the search became a personal quest . . . not just for her, but for the team. Showing her a picture solidified her determination.

"We've got men out with metal detectors right now," Whitkin said, "trying to find whatever other booby traps might be out there. They've discovered and disarmed six so far, but if you have any kind of protective gear, wear it. Men have already walked the riverbank and they didn't find anything. And I shouldn't have to remind you to look for clues, not just the girl. We have no idea where this child is. She could be inside something, buried underground, tied high in a tree. If you see footprints, mark them. My men are wearing smooth-soled shoes, so pay particular attention if you see anything else." He pointed to Parnell and Trowte. "The game wardens are trained trackers; call in everything that seems the least bit out of place. You never know what might turn out to be important." He looked at the men and women who'd dropped everything to search for this little girl. "It's up to us to find her."

He called out a list of names, told them to meet at the command post, and then turned to Jett. "Get your team up here."

They crowded around Sheriff Whitkin and the huge map. "This entire section is a low area." He pointed to the eighty-foot rise beside the gravel road. "We've rigged a pole up there to help with communications."

Brenna glanced at Gayle. They'd leave her at base camp this

time. She could help Jett with communications and watch him mark the maps. In a way, this search was a blessing for her. She'd learn more about reading maps and coordinating a search during this one callout than in ten hours of classes.

"This whole thing's more screwed up than a Hollywood movie," Whitkin said. "That guy could have booby-trapped the whole area. I don't have canine bulletproof vests, but I brought the smallest vests I could find for the dogs. Brought some for you, too. Jett's got Velcro, super glue, and webbing. With any luck, we can tie the vests onto the dogs' backs and bellies. At least most of the major organs will be somewhat protected." He looked at the team members, gazing into each person's eyes a full two seconds before glancing at the next. "If the note is accurate, we're running out of time. The dogs are the only real chance this little girl has."

Brenna watched the team. Each nodded; she knew they would.

This was the best bunch she'd ever known. When the sheriff looked at her, she nodded, too.

"Could you show me on this map where the van was found?" she said.

Sheriff Whitkin smiled and pointed to the map. "Right here."

The team crowded around him and marked their maps.

"How far is that from here?" Brenna asked.

"About two miles."

"How far from the van to the ravine, the north boundary?"

"A little over five miles."

My God. They had less than four hours to search the seven miles between the north and south boundaries.

"What about the river?" she asked.

"It's running four to five feet deep."

"How far?"

"About a mile and a half west of the command post."

That was a lot of ground to cover in a hurry.

Three pickups stopped on the road near base camp; men who looked like farmers climbed out and walked toward Whitkin.

Jett motioned the team to a table where Wally, a drug-dog handler who often worked base camp with Jett, had assembled colored markers. Wally placed his huge copy of the map on the ground, used his compass to find true north, marked it, and taped the map to the table. Then he fastened a piece of clear, flexible plastic over the map.

"The metal from the table legs can alter the compass reading," Brenna told Gayle. "That's why he's taped it at an angle on the table. When we call in our positions, he'll know where to mark us."

"Bring the dogs here," Jett said. "Use your radios. I brought the portable base, so Whitkin can monitor his teams and ours, and you can still talk to each other without interfering with base communications."

Everyone nodded and jogged to their cars. The dogs started barking as soon as they saw their handlers running. Brooklyn tried to climb out the window of Harley's Jeep, but he caught her just in time.

When they returned to the table, Jett and Wally had already glued Velcro patches to the bulletproof vests and strips of webbing. They heaved Margarita onto the table and wrapped the vest around her, the back of the vest hugging her stomach. The Bloodhound drooled on Jett's hand and licked his neck.

"We took the plates out of the back part of the vest," Jett said. "No use in her carrying the extra weight on her belly." He tugged the front of the vest over her back but the two sides didn't meet. "This vest is almost too small for her."

"She weighs a hundred and twenty-five pounds," Connie said.

When Margarita lowered her head to sniff the table, all the loose skin around her neck and head rolled forward and created dozens of deep wrinkles.

"Isn't she cute?" Connie said. But she was biting her lip anxiously.

Connie and Brenna slipped strips of webbing around Margarita's ribcage and belly, and through the makeshift belt loops Jett had glued to the side of the vest. They then tied the strips at the top of the dog's back. Wally attached strips across the dog's chest and behind her back legs, under her tail. Then they all stepped back to look.

"Well, it looks like the rappelling harnesses," Brenna said.

Margarita shook twice, trying to dislodge the vest. Then she looked at Connie and whined, her tail barely rocking side to side.

Connie shook her head. "This isn't going to work. I have to keep a harness on her. The one I have won't fit around that thing."

"Maybe if we cut the arm holes bigger," Jett said.

"We'll rig a harness," Marco said. "There's plenty of webbing, or we can put it under the vest and run the leash out a hole."

Connie looked at Brenna a long moment, and then turned to Jett. "No, take it off. We'll run without it."

"Connie . . ." Brenna said.

"We have to move fast," she said. "Margarita can't wear this. The other dogs are smaller and they work off lead. It's different with her." She looked at Jett. "Take it off."

When the vest had been removed and the regular harness fastened, Margarita howled with delight and wagged her long tail. Connie knelt and hugged the dog, leaving her arms around the wrinkled neck a few seconds longer than usual.

"They took every shoe out of that little girl's closet," Whitkin said, "so each of you can have your own scent article." He looked at the group. "I have volunteers as flankers for you."

"We need people who know how the dogs work," Brenna said. She handed him a list of the people they'd spotted who had worked with the handlers before.

He read the names. "I can't let you have Donny and Reesa," he said. "They're team leaders."

"Yes, you can," Brenna said. "We need them more than you do."

"Now, Brenna—"

"Now, Sheriff, you just said the dogs were Leanne's best chance."

"But I need team leaders I know. I'm glad they came, but I don't know half the people out here."

"Then you know the other half. You can pick team leaders from them."

He looked at Jett.

Jett held his hands up in mock surrender and stepped back.

"All right," Whitkin said. "How soon before you're ready?"

"Right now," Connie said. "Where's transport?"

The sheriff nodded toward a blue pickup. "Over there. Howard will drive you to the spot where they found the van."

Connie picked up a sack holding one of the girl's shoes, handed it to her flanker, and then, totally out of character, hugged Brenna.

"Cross your fingers," Connie whispered.

"Don't forget your vest." Jett pitched it to her.

"These things are too heavy," she said.

"Wear it anyway," Jett said.

As Connie and Margarita climbed into the back of the pickup, Brenna took a deep breath and waved.

"Next," Jett said.

Harley placed Brooklyn on the table. The vest fit the black Lab with enough leg room for her to maneuver easily. One by one, the dogs were fitted with vests and then assigned sections. When it was Feather's turn, Brenna put her on the table.

Wally tossed a roll of flag tape to her. "You're red."

The flag tape colors matched the colored markers he would use on the map. By the time the search was over, Sheriff Whitkin would know which dog had covered what areas and whether and where they had alerted. Any clues discovered along the way would be marked with tiny stick-um arrows bearing numbers.

Brenna looked at the colored tape. Red, pink, blue, orange, and yellow. All the colors of the rainbow. The colors of wishes.

"Ready?" Donny asked Brenna.

Jett marked Brenna's sector on her map and returned it to her.

"It's the farthest from the van," she said. "You're starting me at the ravine?"

"It'll be easier to pull you from there if one of the ground teams needs verification of Leanne's scent."

She watched him a moment. "I didn't ask to be out of the action."

"If the note is a fake," Jett said, "Leanne might have walked out that way. We don't know, and if you can pick up her trail there, we can forget about this main section."

She didn't buy this for a minute. Connie had been the only one to voice what everyone must be thinking: Brenna wasn't ready to risk losing Feather so soon after Brie.

"Ready?" Donny said again.

She nodded and clipped the leash onto Feather's collar. Then she turned to Whitkin.

"Did somebody cut sign on this road we're using for transport?"

"First thing," he said. "Don't worry, Brenna. We didn't wipe out any tracks."

Tracks. Cutting sign meant more than looking for footprints. Had they noticed bent weeds, overturned pebbles, leaves stripped off twigs? Asking would imply she didn't think Whitkin's men knew how to do their jobs.

She inhaled a deep breath and then turned to Donny. "Okay, kiddo. Let's go."

The transport pickups left and returned in puffs of dust accompanied by growling engines and squealing brakes. Four men bent over a table filled with base radios and maps. One by one, the teams called in their positions and start times.

Team One. Team Six. Rescue Brooklyn.

Gayle peered over Wally's shoulder at the map. He'd outlined sectors with a brown pen. As each dog team called in, he placed an "X" at its starting point.

"What do you want me to do?" Gayle asked Jett.

"Sit here." He pulled out the chair beside him and handed her a clipboard with communication log forms attached. "Whenever a dog team calls in, you write down the time in this column and which team it is in this column. Make a note of what they say, over here." He pointed to the widest column. Then he set a twenty-four-hour clock in front of her. "Use this, not your watch."

"Do you think they'll find the little girl?"

He leaned back in his chair. "I don't know."

She put a piece of gum in her mouth and chewed so fast she bit her cheek.

Jett smiled at her. "Try not to worry."

"You're worried."

"That's different."

She watched the lines deepen on Jett's face; he glanced frequently at the woods, as if he had X-ray vision and could see through them. Twice, he wiped his palms on his jeans, and his foot tapped in quick, uneven rhythm.

He looked at one of Whitkin's deputies. "FBI coming?"

The deputy nodded. "Helicopters, too."

When Brenna and Donny called in their start location, Gayle glanced at the clock. Seventeen-sixteen. Three hours and twenty-nine minutes to go.

CHAPTER 13

BRENNA AND DONNY called in their location to Jett and studied the map. The wind was blowing from the southwest. Feather's best chance of finding a scent lay in working a zigzag pattern from the road to the river and back toward the road. Part of their area lay open with rocky ground or soil with short, green vegetation and needlegrass. The section between the road and rocks boasted trees heavy with shade.

"You're in charge of the radio and map," she said. "I spend most of my time watching Feather."

At the sound of her name, Feather turned to Brenna.

Brenna studied the ravine. Sheriff Whitkin had called it right: the draw started as a narrow crack high up on the bluff above them and widened as the land dropped. Water had carved out a ditch in the rock. At this moment, the ravine looked dry, the silt from previous mud slides clotted at the bottom. No way Leanne could have climbed up there; the silt would show her footprints, and she would have bent the vegetation or pulled it out. Still, Brenna had to check.

She opened the sack with Leanne's shoe and let the dog sniff inside.

"Feather, mark it." Then she pointed to the highest point of the ravine. "Find Leanne; check it."

The dog sniffed the ground and then, as her handler had instructed, climbed over rocks and scampered up the incline until the boulders forced her to turn around. Then she checked the bottom of the dry bed, sniffing for any hint of the child.

"If she were down there, we'd see her," Donny said.

"We're looking for clues, Donny."

He shrugged. "I know."

They started the first sweep, Feather darting in and out of the ravine and trotting through the plateau's open areas.

First out and having started at the scene, Connie and Margarita were ahead of everyone else. After Connie's flanker radioed they'd picked up Leanne's trail, Brenna kept one ear on the radio chatter while focusing most of her attention on Feather. Each time Connie called in Margarita's change of direction, Brenna stopped and had Donny plot it on her map.

Searching the open areas was quick, but whenever they entered the woods, Brenna put Feather on leash. Donny walked ahead of them, peering into shadows and thick clumps of brush for a hidden wire or a steel-jawed trap. So far, they hadn't found arrows or footprints or broken twigs. Feather had stopped twice to sniff but she never barked an alert or looked over her shoulder at Brenna. It didn't appear anyone had been through this part of the designated area, and their slow progress was tedious. They did startle a few squirrels and a pair of deer, but they didn't find any clues.

They were about to enter a clearing, so Brenna took Feather off leash. The dog trotted ahead of them and then abruptly stopped, ears up, tail frozen.

"Feather—"

Before she could finish her command, a fawn bolted from a thicket and leaped away from the dog. Feather took off after the deer, but Brenna yelled, "Down!" and the Bouvier flopped to the ground.

Swoosh-thunk. The fawn fell on its side, its legs still flailing.

"Oh, man . . ." Donny said. He jerked the radio to his mouth. "Rescue Feather to base, we got an arrow, but we're okay."

"Base to . . . anybody hit?" Jett asked.

Brenna smiled. Her boss was trying to sound calm but she could hear the quiver in his voice.

"A fawn," Donny said. "Get the game wardens out here."

The fawn struggled to its feet and limped along, dragging its right hind leg. The arrow was embedded in its hindquarter, and blood dribbled down the leg.

"Feather, stay!" Brenna spread her arms and tried to keep the injured animal from heading toward the ravine, but she was afraid to move too much. What if there were other arrows?

"That's arrow number eight," Jett said over the radio. "You should be all right for a while; they haven't found two anywhere near each other."

"Ten-four." Donny glanced at Brenna. "Just our luck we'll be the exception."

Between them, they managed to keep the fawn from the ravine and the river. But terror showed on its face; eyes wide, ears back, it frantically turned this way and that, trying to escape them.

Brenna could hear it panting, and then it fell again and uttered a small cry.

"Poor baby."

Donny was about to tackle it when it scrambled to its feet and hobbled toward Brenna. "Damn, he's quick."

"I thought it was too late for fawns."

"Apparently not." He dove for the fawn but it wheeled away from him.

Feather barked.

Brenna looked over her shoulder at the dog, who was still on her down but poised to bolt at the first hint of a command.

"Feather, crawl."

The dog belly-crawled toward Brenna until she was crouched beside her.

"Stay." She turned to Donny. "Stand still."

"What?" he panted.

"Stand still. If we stop moving, maybe it will, too."

A few seconds later, the fawn collapsed in a mass of vines, and then they heard a car stop on the road above them. Someone hollered; she recognized the game warden's voice.

"Here!" they called.

Parnell, Trowte, and another man in jeans and a white shirt slipped down the slope. When they spotted the deer, they slowed; Parnell and Trowte opened a net.

"I sure hate this," Parnell said, "but we'll take care of it. You go on."

He and Trowte gently threw the net over the fawn. It bleated again and tried to rise, but the men rushed forward and held down the net to secure it.

"Don't worry about this one," Parnell said. "Go on about your business. We'll make sure he gets to a vet and finds a good home." He smiled at Brenna. "We might even bring him back out here, if it's ever safe again. Go on, now. Go on."

She smiled back at him. Parnell was such a phoney; to the untrained ear, it must have sounded as if that entire conversation revolved around the deer, but she knew better. Every "go on" was an admonishment to stay safe, an expression of relief that one of them hadn't been hit by the arrow.

An hour later, they stopped at the river and squatted on the bank in the shade of an oak. Feather was panting too hard; she couldn't pant and sniff at the same time. When she skittered down the bank and started to drink the brownish water, Brenna called her back and offered her water from her fanny pack instead. The dog lay down, the small bowl between her paws, and lapped eagerly. Brenna silently scolded herself for not paying better attention. Not only did Feather's black coat draw heat, the dog was carrying extra weight.

She stroked the soft, black fur between the dog's perked ears. "I'm sorry, toots. Guess I've been a little forgetful today."

Feather rolled onto her side and waved her paw in the air. Brenna smiled and jiggled it.

Even in this heat, the water coursing downstream looked cold. Would all rivers and creeks give her the shivers from now on?

Donny looked at the sky. "No vultures flying. I guess nothing's dead out here . . . at least, not on top of the ground." He pointed to the gnawed remains of saplings across the river. "Beaver's been chewing. We'll probably find a dam somewhere."

The minutes were ticking by with race-car speed and there wasn't anything they could do but keep searching and hope for a break. A helicopter flew over; the pilot waved. They waved back.

"I hope he spots something," Donny said.

"Me, too."

When Connie called in Margarita's newest turn, Jett responded to the change of direction.

"Connie, you guys are going in circles. The pink lines on this map form a spiral."

"Bren . . . talk to me." Connie was panting and her voice sounded raspy.

Brenna reached for the radio and then took the map from Donny. "Go ahead."

"I'm not sure what's happening."

"Is Margarita on trail?" Brenna asked.

"Yes, no, I think so. She's been pulling really hard, but we aren't getting anywhere. She's run past the van spot three times."

"Is there a hot trail?"

"They're all hot!"

"Bren," Connie's flanker said. "All the trails seem to be the same age. None is hotter than the others. I think Margarita's as confused as we are."

Brenna could hear Connie coughing in the background.

"Are most of the trails on one side of where the van was?" she asked.

"They're all over the place," he said. "I–" His radio went silent. A moment later, he came back on. "Yes, most are between the van and base camp."

Brenna squatted and stroked Feather. She always thought better with a dog in her hands.

She turned to Donny. "What did the note say?"

"I don't remember the exact words."

"Jett, what did the note say?" she asked. "Did it mention a game?"

"Stand by." A few moments later he keyed his radio. "Negative. It said, 'I'll play fair. You have eight.' "

"Eight what?" Connie asked. "Arrows? If that's it, we've found them all."

"Irish, what are you thinking?"

She looked at Donny. "Play fair . . . play fair." She keyed the radio. "I think he's playing a game and he isn't playing fair. Have the ground searchers found anything?"

"Not much," Jett said. "Drink cans; gum and candy wrappers; cigarette butts; two men's tennis shoes, both for the left foot; plastic bottles. But no discernible tracks and no signs of digging."

Marco's voice crackled on the radio. "If Leanne were lost, wandering around, one trail would be hotter than the others, or one of the dogs would have hit pool scent."

Brenna nodded, even though Marco couldn't see her. If Leanne had stopped anywhere, her scent would have accumulated in that spot. Margarita would have hit on it the moment they got close. That there was no hot trail meant Margarita's trails must have been walked right after Gideon brought Leanne to this location . . . if she was really here.

"Are ground crews searching the area you've run?" Harley asked.

"Affirmative," Connie said, "with a fine-tooth comb. They haven't seen one of her tracks. Not one."

Someone keyed a radio, and then Brenna heard Patrick's soft baritone. "Maybe she didn't walk it."

Good point, but why would Gideon have carried her around in circles? She looked at the map.

"Connie," Bren said, "if you move a half-mile north, will you be in Harley's sector?"

"No, still mine."

"Have any of the trails run that far north?"

"Not yet."

"Irish?"

Brenna didn't answer immediately but looked at Donny and wound her fingers in Feather's beard. If they started guessing, someone might overlook a hot trail, but it didn't make sense for Gideon to hide Leanne so close to the only road in the area, the place where base camp would have to be set up.

"What if we stop zigzagging and searching for trails?" She glanced at her watch. They'd been out over two hours and hadn't found one clue. "Hasty-search it."

"Think twice," Marco said. "If he's buried her, we could miss it."

Brenna studied the map. She was on one end of the search area; Connie had the other. If this Gideon creep was anywhere near sane, he'd probably stash Leanne somewhere in the middle. Maybe that's what he meant by playing fair.

But what if she was wrong?

"Marco's right," she said into the radio. "Bad idea."

"No," Jett said, "it might work. Connie, move a half-mile north and run a straight cut from the road to the river. If you don't pick up a trail, cut sideways, back toward the van marker. Irish, do the same on your end. The rest of you keep zigzagging the middle."

Everyone agreed.

Donny's forehead wrinkled. "What are we going to do?"

She pointed to the edge of the trees. "We're going to work Feather just inside that tree line from north to south. Keep your eyes open."

They'd only been in the woods a few minutes when Feather stopped to sniff. Then she moved on. Twice she stopped to shake, as if trying to lose the vest.

Hmmm. She hadn't done that earlier, but it hadn't been quite as humid then, either.

Feather stopped and sniffed again, then headed deeper into the woods and stopped beside a sycamore. But she didn't bark, and she didn't look at Brenna.

"What's she doing?" Donny asked.

When she was working, Feather didn't get distracted easily—at least, not for long. Brenna knelt and studied the ground. Weeds, leaves, and vines covered the soil. If Leanne had left a print there, she didn't see it.

Then she spotted something white caught in a mass of vines. A cigarette butt. She picked it up and rolled it in her hand.

"This looks fresh," she said.

"I'll call it in." Donny relayed the information and described their find. "White, with a tan line at the base of the filter."

Brenna scanned the area, but she didn't see any more butts.

Feather kept her head down, sniffing, as she strolled deeper into the woods. Brenna followed. A few minutes later, the dog stopped near a thicket. Then she weaved toward the road.

"Is she trailing?" Donny asked.

"Not Leanne, but she's interested in something."

"Do we have time for her to fool around?"

No, they didn't.

"Give her one more minute," she said. *Trust your dog.*

When she reached the road, Feather circled several times and then looked at Brenna.

"What?" she asked.

The dog sat and raised her paw.

This wasn't Feather's normal routine; Brenna wasn't sure what to think. She studied the sloping earth at the road's edge. Just above the grass line, she saw a toe print in the soil. She leaned closer and stared at the wavy pattern.

"This looks . . . familiar."

"What?" Donny bent beside her.

"Reach into my fanny pack and get out those packets of gauze and a Baggie."

He did as she requested, even though, she suspected, he didn't understand why.

She tore open two packets and shook the gauze onto the print. Then she scanned the edge of the road. A couple of feet along, she found another toe print and something that looked like a skinny tire tread. But that track was only four inches long; it disappeared into the traces of this afternoon's transport.

"I thought they cut sign on this road," she said.

"They did."

"Then they missed this." She pointed, tore open another packet, and shook the gauze on the print. "Call it in."

After he returned the radio to his belt, Donny marked the prints with red flags.

"I'm going to try something," Brenna said. "Feather"—she pointed to the largest footprint—"mark it." The dog sniffed the print and wagged her tail.

"Can she take scent off a footprint?"

"It's not my favorite way to work, but I'll try anything at this point. If it's a dud, I can rescent her on Leanne's shoe." She turned to the dog. "Feather, track."

The dog sniffed the ground and then started trotting back through the woods. Halfway to the open area they'd come from, she stopped and shook. Then she looked at Brenna over her shoulder.

"The vest bothers her," Brenna said.

She watched Feather. The dog finally seemed interested in something, but the vest was distracting her.

If Brenna took it off, Feather would be vulnerable.

Tough up, Bren. You and Feather have a job to do.

She pulled the vest off and replaced it with Feather's trailing harness and long leash. Then she dumped her own bulletproof vest on the ground.

"Brenna, that might not—"

"I don't care. Feather's got somebody's trail and we're going to follow it."

When Brenna told Feather "Get on it," the dog eased into her trailing trot. They crossed the plateau at an angle and ran parallel to the river.

Were they on someone's actual trail or was the water pulling the scent closer to the river? Either way, Feather was moving at a fast clip. If Brenna hadn't attached the long line to the harness, she might not have been able to keep up.

Behind her, she heard Donny explaining to Jett the change in strategy. If her boss didn't approve, he could scold her later.

The riverbank curved and straightened; Feather stopped and started a few times, but she consistently followed a course several yards off the bank.

As they rounded another bend, Feather pulled harder. Brenna looked up to see what lay ahead. In the distance, two people wearing red shirts ran toward her.

"Feather, wait."

The dog stopped in her tracks, but snorted and whined.

Brenna turned to Donny. "Can you tell who that is?"

He squinted in the dusk. "Looks like . . . Connie."

She grabbed the radio from his belt. "Connie, are you at the river?"

"Yes," she panted. "We finally got a— Is that you down there?"

Hope and panic burst in her chest. "Jett, the river!" She looped Feather's long leash in her hand. "Feather, get on it!"

They ran behind the dog, Donny panting into the radio, the dogs charging straight for each other.

Margarita veered to the water first, pawing at the bank and throwing her head back in a mournful howl. When Feather reached them, she began to dig wildly.

Connie splashed her hands into the water. Brenna and Donny fell to their hands and knees, grabbing handfuls of dirt, digging for any sign of soft ground where someone might have dug a hole.

"She has to be here," Connie said. "Both dogs beelined to this spot."

Brenna crawled beside Connie. "See anything?"

"No!"

People and dogs burst from the trees. Marco and Chelsa, Harley and Brooklyn, Patrick and Dorsey. Officers in teams of four and five.

Feather barked and dug at a spot six feet from the water. Brenna saw a glimmer of silver under her paw.

"Something!" she called.

Donny joined her and together they uncovered a large cylinder buried under a foot of soil. From the nozzle, a black rubber tube stretched toward the river.

"What is it?" she asked.

Harley glanced at the object. "Looks like an oxygen . . ."

It *was* an oxygen tank. Donny gently lifted the black tubing connected to the nozzle. It pulled up out of the dirt and then curved over the bank into the water.

Patrick, Marco, and Donny jumped in; Harley and the women lay on their stomachs, their arms disappearing into the water. Moments later, Donny's head broke through the surface.

"Get help."

Harley jumped in. Before Brenna could get to her feet, ground searchers slid to a stop beside Connie and her. Heads surfaced for air and then disappeared. More people splashed into the river.

Then the end of a wooden box jutted from the water. A dozen hands grabbed for it . . . lifted, pulled, heaved.

Seconds later, they set the crate on the ground. Water poured out through the cracks like a sieve. One of the top slats had broken and they could see the child's leg: pale on top, dark purple on the bottom.

Lividity. The blood had settled; Leanne had been dead several hours.

Brenna slung the water off her hands, walked away from the crowd, and sat on a bare patch of ground.

"Dammit." Then she clapped her hands. "Feather, here." The dog trotted to her and lay down.

Connie fell to her knees beside Feather. "What time?"

Brenna glanced at her watch. "Eight-thirty-three."

"Twelve minutes to spare," she panted. She pulled a cup and container from her pack and offered Margarita water.

Brenna curled her arm around Feather's neck, pulled her close, and sighed. "Well . . . hell. We find her within the time limit, and he drowns her anyway."

Connie changed the leash from Margarita's harness to her collar and then patted the ground for the dog to lie next to her. "What was the oxygen tank for?"

"I don't know."

The women clapped their hands and called the other three dogs. Chelsa and Brooklyn romped to them; Dorsey looked at Patrick before strolling to Chelsa and slowly lowering himself beside her. Brenna and Connie stripped the animals of their makeshift vests and then petted and praised them. Brenna jiggled their noses; Connie ruffled their coats. Then they all watched as officers, paramedics, and sheriff's deputies headed toward the river.

The crate lay on the bank, the end of the black tube stuck between two of the slats. The unstained wood had swollen and darkened from the water. It must have been submerged quite a while.

Marco spoke to one of the deputies before joining Brenna and Connie. "They'll clear the area in a little bit," he said.

A few minutes later, the deputies herded everyone except the dog handlers toward the main road.

A female firefighter glanced at Brenna and Connie. "Why do they get to stay?" she asked.

"They're closing this search," Donny said, "rewarding the dogs for doing a good job. If they don't, the next time somebody's in trouble, the dogs might not work." He glanced at the woman. "Then who do we call for help?"

Closure. Leave it to Donny to express the perfect explanation for their actions.

After the nonessential personnel disappeared into the woods, each of the handlers praised his or her dog for finding Leanne. Brenna worked Feather last.

After she scented Feather on the shoe, the dog trotted to the crate, barked, and pawed the wooden box. Then she looked over her shoulder at Brenna, sat, and threw her head back in a long mournful howl. Margarita had whined as Connie pulled her away from her "closure," but now the dog tugged loose of Connie's grasp and lumbered to Feather. Side by side, the dogs howled a sad lament for Leanne.

The women tugged the dogs away from the scene just before one of the deputies returned with a crowbar to pry off the crate's lid.

"Bren?" Marco said.

"No," she said. "I already have too many nightmares."

She and Connie walked toward the road, their pace slow and uneven. Darkness had already claimed the shady areas; before they reached the woods, flashlights would shoot pale beams into the night.

Connie squinted at her map. "Looks like a long walk, maybe three or so miles back to base camp."

The dogs ran ahead of them, sniffing at interesting smells, playing tag. But whenever the women called, they trotted back, tails wagging. Brenna pulled a pack of cigarettes from her fanny pack and lit one.

Connie watched her and then said, "Mind if I have one of those?"

She handed Connie the pack. "When did you start smoking?"

"Today." A few minutes later, Connie said, "I wonder who this sadistic Gideon is."

As soon as Brenna had learned the details of Leanne's kidnapping, she'd known that Zoe and Leanne had been abducted by the same man. At least now she had a name.

CHAPTER 14

EVERYONE CLUSTERED IN groups or stretched out in their vehicles waiting for team debriefings. Floodlights hooked to a generator brightened the main area of the command post; flashlights and interior car lights dotted the road like fireflies.

Several people sat together in silence; others spoke into cellular telephones, and one group mechanically pitched a baseball back and forth. Patrick lay on the hood of his Firebird, playing "I'll Remember You" on his harmonica. But when the ambulance passed, everyone stopped whatever he or she was doing and watched until it was out of sight.

Connie had grabbed her camera and tagged along with one of the crime-scene photographers, leaving Margarita with Feather. Brenna sat on the tailgate of her Blazer, picking burrs out of Feather's coat, trying but failing to focus on anything other than this search. After slipping Margarita a Milk Bone, she patted Feather, picked up a burr-matter paw, and started combing.

Sheriff Whitkin had said they'd searched the river. She shouldn't have accepted that so readily. The dog team should have done it. The dogs had caught Leanne's scent on the water. If they'd searched there first . . .

"Irish!" Jett waved her to the tables.

When she arrived, he handed her two of the three Baggies containing the gauze pads she'd left on the footprints. Sheriff Whitkin had sealed, dated, and initialed them, keeping one for himself, just in case.

"Hang on," Jett said. "As soon as everyone gets here, I have something to show you."

She sat on the table and eavesdropped on Sheriff Whitkin's debriefing. For the last two hours, the Sacramento police and sheriff's departments had been comparing notes. Since Leanne had been taken from the city and ended up in the county, both agencies believed they had jurisdiction. But the physical evidence teams had been put on hold until the coroner arrived and completed her task. Now that the body had been removed, the process could continue, and Sheriff Whitkin could cut everyone else loose.

After Connie joined Brenna at the command post, Jett called the rest of the dog team and then plopped a black trash bag on the table.

"When one of the photographers crossed the river to take side shots," Jett said, "he found this stuffed behind a bush."

"In the dark?" Connie asked.

Jett smiled. "He tripped over it."

"What is it?" Brenna asked.

He looked at the five team members, and Gayle. "Don't touch." Then he opened the sack.

A small white T-shirt trimmed in pink, and a pink vest were bound together by a piece of clothesline with a very long tail. Dirt, bits of leaves, and twigs were caught in the child's clothes.

"I don't get it," Gayle said.

Connie looked at Brenna. "He dragged the clothes. That's why Margarita couldn't pick up a hot trail."

"If he put her in the water first," Marco said, "her trail to the river would be colder than the others. He dragged the clothes afterward."

"Why would he do that?" Patrick asked.

Brenna looked at Jett. "He knew about the dogs."

"We already knew—"

"No," she said. "He's learned how the dogs work. About scent trails." She shook her head. "This whole thing was a game, to see if he could fool us." She huffed. "He did."

Marco watched her and half-sat on the table. "He knew he'd won. Leanne was already dead."

"The game was not saving her," she said, "it was finding her."

"Then it wouldn't have been fun for him unless"—Marco turned to Sheriff Whitkin—"unless he watched."

Jett tensed. "Sheriff, did I hear you say you didn't know half the people who showed up to search?"

He grabbed a clipboard. "I have the name of everyone who went out with a team. I can vouch for all those who worked the command post." He dashed to the PA system in his car. "All team leaders to the command post. Repeat, all team leaders to the command post." To the search team, he said, "We'll know soon enough if someone disappeared from a group."

"He didn't have to be a team member," Harley said. He looked up at the rise behind the tables and then turned and stared at the cliffs across the river. "Did anybody ever check up there?"

No one answered. Time had been such a factor, Brenna suspected none of them wasted minutes looking for the abductor.

"Wouldn't the helicopter pilot or the men setting the radio antenna have seen him?" Patrick asked.

"Not if he hid in those trees on the cliff," Marco said. "The antenna was placed on the opposite side of base camp, on the rise."

When Donny stopped beside Gayle, she filled him in on the news.

"I know everyone who came from the station," Donny said. "Let me look at the list." Then he turned to Jett. "Do you think Leanne died right after he put her in the crate?"

They all turned to Donny.

"She didn't," he said. "Coroner said she hadn't been dead that long. Maybe seven or eight hours. She guesses Leanne died around one o'clock, but, as usual, that's not for the record. Given the water temperature and the fact Leanne was in a crate, the exact time of death will be hard to prove."

"It still fits into our scenario," Brenna said.

"One more thing," Donny said. "The crate was handmade with one-by-four, rounded fence slats nailed together. He sealed the cracks with acrylic caulk. It'd be watertight for a while, but when the wood swelled from being in the river, the slats pulled away from the caulk and let water inside."

"That's why the oxygen tank," Marco said. "He gave her air."

Brenna leaned against Marco and rested her head on his shoulder. "Tell me this is a nightmare."

Sheriff Whitkin cleared his throat and shook Jett's hand. "No need for your team to stay. We can sort out who came and left." Then he turned to the members. "Thank you for coming. I wish . . . Just . . . thanks for working so hard."

When Brenna got home, she fed Feather, dumped her clothes in the washer, and soaked in a hot bath. On her way to bed, she glanced at the photographs in the bookcase. With all that had happened, she couldn't bear to look at Brie . . . or Aaron. Carefully, she removed the double frame containing their pictures, closed it, and placed it in a drawer.

As she stretched out on the bed, she glanced at Feather, lying on the floor in her usual place on top of the blue shirt, and at the spot where Brie always lay. Even now, the house felt empty without her.

After the debriefing, she'd heard several people mention going home and hugging their children. She rolled over and dropped her hand down to touch Feather. The dog nuzzled her fingers and rested her head on her paws.

Brenna sat up and looked at her. Floor time.

From the day Aaron gave her Brie, Brenna had always spent a few minutes every day sitting on the floor to play. Since they weren't allowed on the furniture at home, floor time gave the dogs an opportunity to be on equal terms with their owner. A time for special attention and bonding.

Bewildered, Brenna realized she hadn't given Feather one minute of floor time since Brie's death.

"Come on, toots."

She grabbed a quilt and pillow, walked into the living room, and threw them on the floor. As soon as she sat, Feather jumped and wiggled, wagged her tail, and rubbed her face on Brenna's shoulder. Then the Bouvier rolled onto her back and waved all four feet in the air, a bid for Brenna to scratch her tummy. The dog's long pink tongue lolled out the side of her mouth as she squirmed back and forth on her back as if scratching an itch. When Brenna rubbed the dog's belly, Feather closed her eyes in pleasure. Then Feather rolled to her feet, sneezed, and crouched in her play position, tail wagging.

"Come here, toots."

Feather woofed, a sound between a bark and a snort, and pawed Brenna's arm.

"Oh, you want to play." She reached under the sofa and found the tennis ball she'd hidden there.

Feather barked; her front feet danced.

Brenna teased the dog by moving the ball around the floor several times before rolling it into the dining room. Feather dashed away and returned seconds later with the ball in her mouth.

"Again?"

The dog dropped the ball and barked.

She threw it over her head toward the front door. After ten minutes of fetch, she hid the ball under the sofa again.

"Enough already," she said.

Feather lay beside her and snuggled close. A night on the floor next to Feather might be just what Brenna needed to ease her sense of loss. She turned on the radio, a new ploy to see if keeping part of her mind occupied with the noise would allow the other part to sleep without nightmares. Then she wrapped her arm around the dog's neck and hugged her. That arrow could have hit Feather instead of the fawn today. What would she do if she lost Feather, too?

In the dining room, her grandmother's mantel clock chimed twelve. Midnight. It felt as if she'd been away from home for days. She combed her fingers through the strip of hair that fell over Feather's dark eyes.

"First thing tomorrow, you get a bath."

Feather's ears perked. She loved the water, even baths.

Funny, the dog hadn't tried to jump into the river today. In fact, she'd acted a bit preoccupied.

Brenna fluffed her pillow, and although Feather didn't move, she opened one eye, shutting it again once Brenna was still.

When the telephone rang, it jolted Brenna awake. A headache burst behind her eyes.

She reached up to the end table, grabbed the cord, and pulled the telephone to the floor. It pinged on the carpet. Then she yanked the receiver to her ear. "What!"

"Irish."

"Jett?" She flopped against her pillow. "What time is it?"

"After three. Is Ryan there with you?"

"No, why?"

He spoke slowly, deliberately. "Get Feather and come to the office."

"Can't this wait? I just got to sleep."

"No, Brenna, it can't. Get your dog and come here now."

She didn't like his tone.

Feather popped up and pawed her.

Bless her, this dog was ready to go twenty-four hours a day.

"What is it?" she asked.

"Just—"

"No, tell me."

He hesitated. "You have e-mail on the company address."

She flopped down again and rubbed her forehead. "And?"

"It's from Gideon."

BRENNA PARKED IN her assigned spot and jogged toward the dispatch office, Feather on her heels. Extra cars sat in the lot tonight. Maybe that new security client had signed the contract after all. He'd wanted the guards to start immediately. Marco and Jett would be happy, unless the extra cars had nothing to do with new clients.

As she slipped her key into the lock, the door opened.

"What took you so long?" Jett asked.

"Good morning to you, too."

He grasped her arm and pulled her inside. Then he stepped outside, looked around, and closed the door. "Were you followed?"

"I didn't notice."

"Haven't I trained you better than that?"

"Good grief, Jett." She pitched her purse on the table beside the time clock and waved at Mike. "You wake me up in the middle of the night, tell me I have e-mail from a murderer and to get to the office, and when I get here, you razz me about not watching for a tail. What's wrong with you?"

He shook his head and inhaled a deep breath. "Guess this whole thing has me a little jumpy."

"An e-mail?"

"I suspect there's more to it."

The lines on his face had deepened, and he kept rubbing his thumb against his fingers. That wasn't like him.

"What do you suspect?" she asked, wishing she had paid more attention during her drive.

"I don't think you're safe at home, alone. You don't have a security system or—"

"I have Feather." She scratched the dog's ears.

"She might not be enough."

So that was it. Jett wanted her at the office so she'd be around people, be safe. Gideon must have sent some e-mail to get him flustered.

"All right," she said, "where is this letter I had to come down here to read?"

"It's at the center station."

"You pulled it up on Emily? Hatch won't like that, she's his private property."

Feather trotted past them, stopped at the dispatch desk, and barked at Mike. He patted her and gave her a Milk Bone from the pile in the candy dish on his desk.

"You should have told me about him earlier," Jett said.

"Who?"

"Gideon."

She stepped back. "I don't know anything about this guy."

"Irish—"

The door opened and a young black man stuck his head into the room. "Hey-hey, everybody," Hatch said. "Something special happening?"

"Irish, the e-mail indicates you've been corresponding with him. Maybe he used another name. Have you been writing to anyone you don't know?"

"Not consistently," she said. "There's always someone who wants to know about the business or about the dogs, but . . ."

"This has to be the guy who took Zoe and Leanne; the construction paper note wasn't publicized and it doesn't seem likely a copycat would know the details of time and hours."

"I agree," she said. "Gideon must have committed both—"

"Gideon?" Hatch said. He stopped, glanced from Jett to Brenna, and smiled, nervously. "What did he do?"

Brenna and Jett stared at him.

"You know Gideon?" she asked.

He shrugged. "Yeah. Kinda. I mean, we e-mail back and forth." He grinned, but sweat beaded his forehead. "He . . . he thinks he's talking to you."

"Me?"

Jett's hands clenched but his voice remained calm. "Come into the break room."

"I—" Hatch cleared his throat. "I have a date in the car."

"We'll get her," Jett said. "You come here."

Brenna's legs felt rubbery. "I have to sit down."

Mike jumped out of his seat, rolled a desk chair under her, and ran into the kitchen. He came back with a glass of water for Brenna, then headed for the parking lot.

"Have I done something wrong?" Hatch asked.

"That depends," Jett said. "Did you save Gideon's e-mail?"

"No, after I answer, I delete everything."

Jett shook his head. "Great."

"But," Hatch said, "I've printed everything up and filed it. Would that help?"

"Yes!" Jett and Brenna said together.

"Where are they?" Jett asked.

Hatch nodded toward the living quarters above the kennel. "In my apartment."

As he dashed out the door, Brenna turned the chair to face the computer.

"When I checked the e-mail tonight," Jett said, "I didn't recognize the screen name, and I didn't understand the subject, so I opened it."

Brenna opened the e-mail.

"From Job Won," she said. "Where have I heard that?"

Mike opened the door and guided a cute little brunette in a yellow dress through the work area into the break room. Then he hurried back and stood beside Jett.

"Subject: B: today."

Hatch ran into the room, clutching a folder, and stopped beside Jett.

"Hatch, does he always call me B?"

"That started a couple of weeks ago," he said.

B:

*hour scores remaIne the same dunt Worry
leanne don't count*

untIl Next time . . .

GIDEON

" 'Leanne don't count'?" She read that line over and over. She clenched her fists.

"Bren," Hatch said, "your hand."

She turned and looked into Hatch's dark eyes. "There is no word to describe this creep."

"Be careful," Hatch said. "Don't drip blood on Emily."

Blood? She looked at her hands. The right one dripped bright red.

"You broke the water glass." Hatch held her hand away from the computer.

Someone shoved a handkerchief into her other hand. "Try this."

She looked up at a big guy with dark hair, dark eyes, and an obvious Indian heritage.

"Thanks." She dabbed at the blood. "Do I know you?"

"Not yet."

Jett came into the room. "If you haven't guessed, Simon, this is Brenna. Irish, meet Simon Blue, FBI."

Mike handed Jett a first-aid kit.

"Let me see your hand." Brenna looked away while Jett removed the handkerchief. He sighed. "We're going to the kitchen sink to wash off the blood. You might need stitches."

He tugged her into the kitchen and stuck her hand under the faucet.

A rumpled little man with white sidewall hair and gold-rimmed glasses limped through the break room and waved his pen at Brenna.

"Hello there, young lady."

She looked at Jett. "When did Owen get here?"

"About a half hour ago. He brought Agent Blue."

"Why?"

"This Gideon thing has escalated." He examined her hand. "The cuts aren't too deep. If you're careful, the bandages should be enough."

"I don't remember breaking the glass." She looked at Jett. "What's Owen doing here, and why the FBI?"

"We found another e-mail dated Friday." He started a fresh pot of coffee. "Hatch didn't work Friday, and you went home early, so we didn't know about it until tonight."

"What did that one say?"

"Come look."

As he turned to walk away, she tugged his arm again. "Why Owen and the FBI?"

"Owen's coordinating the Erskin case information for the Sacramento P.D.," he said. "Leanne. When I found the e-mail, I telephoned the department. He brought Simon with him. Come on."

She followed him into the workroom and patted Feather.

"Here's the one from yesterday," Hatch said.

She started at the top.

B:
*let's play nother game. i'Ll hidE her
And you doN't fiNe hEr.*

until next time . . .

GIDEON

"I don't like this 'next time' business," she said. "Hatch, does he always write the same way? Look at the capital letters; they're in the wrong places."

"I don't think this guy's very smart," Hatch said, "or he's a lousy typist. He misspells easy words and his games are extremely simplistic."

"What kind of games?" she asked.

"Oh, stuff like numbers or symbols representing letters. Kids' games." He leaned back. "I was doing that junk when I was eight."

Owen Winters, Jett's favorite liaison with the Sacramento police department, peeked over his glasses. "I think we should start at the beginning." He shuffled papers and then pulled one out. "Was this the first?"

Hatch nodded. Then he turned to Brenna. "Remember the day you were late to puppy class and you told me to answer your e-mail? That was the first."

"That was months ago," she said. "Have you been writing him all this time?"

Hatch nodded.

"Why didn't you tell me?"

"I-I would have, but—" He glanced at Jett. "It was never anything personal. Just games."

She leaned against the dispatcher's desk. "I can't believe I never saw any of his messages. I'm on the computer every day."

"They always come in the evening after you've left," Hatch said.

Jett took the paper from Owen. "The first one says, 'how did you fine me, dum luck or skill?' "

Hatch nodded. "I answered, 'Skill.' "

She stared at Jett. "Seattle."

Jett nodded.

"Why would he write me, and how did he find out where to send e-mail?"

Simon Blue pointed to Jett and then to Brenna. "How often have you dealt with this man?"

"I'm not sure 'dealt' is the right word," she said.

"You need to get us up to speed." He motioned to Owen. "Let's everybody sit at the table and sort this thing out. Mr. Culpepper, will you make copies of these pages for all of us?"

"Right away."

"Good." He looked at Brenna and swept his hand in the direction of the break room. "After you."

The five of them sat at the round table, which could comfortably accommodate six poker players on a Saturday night. Brenna, the only woman in the group, studied the men. All so different. Jett, with his ruddy complexion and strawberry blond hair, pretended to be tough, but since the divorce, he'd been floundering a bit, like a lost pup enjoying the company of strangers but longing for home. Hatch, never without his grandfather's Dodgers cap, was just starting his life, a little later than others in his college classes. But he had a bright future, and perhaps had found a young woman to share it.

Brenna glanced toward the sitting area. The girl in the yellow dress had curled up in the recliner and appeared to be asleep.

Mike handed a set of papers to each person at the table and then returned to his desk. Feather trotted into the kitchen, drank from the water bowl beside the refrigerator, and then lay down across Brenna's foot.

"Does the dog have to be in here?" Simon asked.

"Is she bothering you?" Brenna asked.

He looked at Feather. "Dogs and I don't get along."

"She'll be on her best behavior."

Simon Blue didn't look like the stereotypical FBI agent. She'd worked with agents before, and most of them were regular people clad in FBI windbreakers. Except rookies. Some of those young agents just out of Quantico were arrogant, opinionated, uncooperative. Simon looked a little too old to be brand-new.

"All right," Owen said. "I need to review all this, make sense of it. Start at the very beginning and tell me everything you know about this Gideon."

"It started in Seattle," Jett said.

While he talked, she watched Owen. Over sixty, he still worked as a homicide detective with the Sacramento PD, but he'd been exiled to a desk job after a car accident that claimed his right leg below the knee.

When the talking stopped, she looked up.

"Jett, have you called Garrett?" she asked.

He nodded. "He's on his way."

A cell phone rang: Owen's. He muttered briefly into it, then hung up. "Her house is clear," he said. "We left a car there, just in case."

"My house? You sent people to check out my house?" She stared at Jett. "How did they get in?"

"You know I have keys to all the team members' homes. Do you mind that they searched your place?"

She leaned back in the chair. Her phone number and address were unlisted; Jett's office wasn't. It hadn't occurred to her that Gideon might care enough to track down her personal information.

"No, I don't mind," she said. "At least I don't have to worry about going home and finding him there."

"It may seem unnecessary," Owen said, "but if this man has fixated on you, precautions need to be taken. The e-mails he sent suggest that the Erskin search might have been, in his view, a personal match between you and him."

A personal match? Had Gideon snatched and killed Leanne just to test *her*?

That darling little girl . . . lost. Because of a game. A stupid, stupid game!

Her stomach turned. "Excuse me."

A few minutes later, she sat on the tile floor in the bathroom and leaned against the shower door, a cold white washcloth pressed against her forehead. Brie, Leanne. Gideon. Maybe hunger and lack of sleep. She felt deflated and sick.

Someone knocked on the bathroom door. "Irish, you all right?"

"Dandy," she said.

"Are you coming out?"

"No."

"Do you need—"

"I'm fine," she said. "Give me a minute."

She heard him walk away; then something thumped against the door and panted.

Brenna reached up and opened the door. Feather's ears lay back as she raised her head for a pat; her tail wagged.

"Come in, toots."

With the dog inside, Brenna closed the door and lay down on the floor. Feather snuggled close, sighed, and rested her head on Brenna's foot.

"You are always on my feet. Do you have a foot fetish?"

Feather wagged her tail.

Brenna lay there, the cool tile easing the kink in her back. She often wondered if sleeping on the floor would help her chronically aching back, but tonight's experiment had proved the floor was not the answer. Maybe she needed a harder bed board.

"Bren, quick!" Jett banged on the door. "Gideon is on-line."

She sprang up and opened the door.

"He's instant-messaging with Hatch and he's discovered it isn't you. Hurry, we don't want to lose him."

She ran into the workroom. Owen stood behind Hatch, his eyes fixed on the screen. When she looked over Hatch's shoulder, the screen held a full page of *Where is she, where is she, where is she.*

Then she noticed Job Won's name on the buddy list.

"What happened?" she asked.

"What do you keep in the vegetable bin of your refrigerator?" Hatch asked.

"Veg—" She glanced at Jett. "Cigarettes."

He frowned.

"Okay, okay, I'll try again, but you're one to talk. Don't tell me cigars are that different." Hatch typed in "Cigarettes."

what kind

"B and H," Brenna said. Hatch typed that in.

The b-r-u-m sound of the instant message sang as the next message appeared.

Right. Relax, talk to me, Brenna.

She looked at Jett. "He's been in my house."

The thought made her skin crawl. She'd never feel safe in the duplex again.

Hatch turned to her. "What do you want me to say?"

She studied Gideon's request and then remembered something Aaron had often said: *Don't fret over things you can't change.* Then he'd smile and add, *But don't ever give up without a fight.*

"Get up, Hatch," she said. "I think this project is meant to be mine."

He rolled the seat away from the table and gave it to her.

Brenna sat.

"I'm here," she typed. "What do you want?"

O Brenna Brenna Brenna why did you try to fool me you no it's impossible

"I didn't."

how did you like hour game tuday

"Who are you?"

How did you like hour game

"No more conversation until you answer my question."

"Brenna," Owen said, "don't cut him off."

"I'm not playing his game again."

"It's not your choice," he said.

Jett rested his hands on her shoulders. "Yes, it is."

The b-r-u-m sounded again.

talk too me talk too me talk too me talk too me

She sat there, watching the screen fill with the same three words. Then it stopped. Several minutes passed.

"Think he's gone?" Owen asked.

"Not yet," Jett said. "His name's still on the buddy list."

"He's the one obsessed," she said. "That puts the power in my hands."

The b-r-u-m sounded.

I AM the judge, the maimer, the destroyer.

"Well, I guess that's an answer," she said.

He sent another message.

Now, how did you like our game

"I didn't."

why

"You lied."

Not true; how

"You said you'd play fair. You didn't."

what do you mean

"You gave us a time limit," she wrote, "but it was a lie."

More than a minute later, he responded.

I didn't kill leAnn; you didn't fine her in tyMe.

Job Won disappeared from the buddy list.

CHAPTER 16

BRENNA TURNED FROM the computer screen and scanned the room. "Where's Agent Blue?"

"You had the guest bathroom occupied," Jett said.

Simon Blue walked into the room; he looked at Owen and then at Brenna. "Did I miss something?"

"Yes, you did, young fella," Owen said, "but we can print it out. Where were you?"

"Checking my messages."

Jett suggested they sit at the table and try to make sense of the e-mails.

Owen pulled out a folder. "I have some of the preliminary reports from yesterday afternoon. Sheriff Whitkin faxed a few pages and Donny gave me copies of his notes."

"Anything new?" Brenna asked.

"One thing you might not know," Owen said. "One of the deputies found a pile of cigarette butts on the cliff next to the river." He gazed at Brenna. "We think he was watching. At least, someone was."

"Can't the lab get blood type or DNA or something from those butts?" she asked.

"Of course," Owen said, "but it doesn't do much good unless we have someone to compare it to." He sipped his coffee. "And that track you found belonged to a motorcycle tire. Goodyear; that narrows the possibilities."

"Maybe it belonged to someone else," Hatch said.

Simon shook his head. "If he left the van there, he had to have another way to leave the area. That place is in the middle of nowhere."

Brenna shuffled her printouts. Gideon's messages had begun in May and had come in spurts, two or three together and then nothing for weeks. Now, in August, they were starting again.

She began with the first one.

do you possess dum luck or skill

"Skill, of course."

can you dare think you or a match for me

"I play to win. What's your game?"

tri this won 154 65 285 597828 417 285 157531 3145

"Too easy. And on the eighth day the angels came."

"Hatch . . ." Brenna studied the quote hidden in numbers. "Explain this number thing to me. There are twenty-six letters in the alphabet, but he uses only numbers one through nine."

"It's similar to numerology," Hatch said. "Each number can be reduced to a single digit. Twenty-five becomes number seven: two and five equal seven. When you assign each letter a single-digit number, each number can represent two or three letters. The number five might mean letters E, N, or W."

"I see," she said. "When he gave you the numbers, you had to play with them until they formed a word."

"It didn't take long," Hatch said.

She looked at Hatch's reply to the e-mail again.

"Too easy. And on the eighth day the angels came. Who are you?"

dunt you no

Hatch hadn't replied to that one. Two days later, Gideon sent another message:

    you didn't anser

"Give me your name or this game is over."

call me Gideon want to play another game
"Hey-hey Gideon. What do you have in mind?"
a test of skill
"Give it your best shot."
iF yoU chAllEnGe me Be prepArED To lOsE wHaT mAt-
tErS MoRe

Odd, his misspelled words changed from note to note, but the challenge message was the first time he had used capital letters within the message. Was that significant? Then came the last two notes before the instant-message conversation, one before Leanne was taken, one after she was found.

B:
I'lL hidE her And you doN't fiNe hEr

until next time . . .

GIDEON

B:
hour scores remaIne the same dunt Worry
leanne don't count

untIl Next time . . .

GIDEON

If they'd read the Friday evening note earlier, might they have been able to stop Leanne's abduction? Probably not.

And these last two messages became more personal. He'd used her initial for her name, signed "until next time," and printed his name in capital letters. He'd used the capital letters only once during the instant-message conversation.

But this new information didn't ease the guilt she felt over Gideon's last comment.

I didn't kill Leanne; you didn't find her in time.

"Hatch," she said, "if you thought this guy was a kook, why did you keep copies of all the e-mails?"

He shrugged. "Jett told me to keep copies of everything I do for the office. You're part of the office."

She rested her head on the table. "Have we finished?"

"Do you have anything else to add?" Owen asked.

"I have a question," Simon said. "Brenna, how did this guy know where to reach you?"

She looked up. "I don't know."

"You have to know, or have an idea," he said.

"I don't."

Jett cleared his throat. "I've thought all along that he watched Irish in the creek with Zoe. Maybe he doubled back to the neighborhood, saw the company truck."

"That wouldn't tell him my name," she said.

"Mike," Jett called. The young man stepped into the break room. "Has anyone called asking about Brenna?" Jett asked.

Mike shook his head. Then he looked as if he remembered something. "Not Brenna," he said. "Brie."

"What?" Brenna asked.

"Brie," Mike said. "Somebody called asking if I knew where you'd bought Brie. Actually, he described her as 'that German Shepherd.' I said I didn't know."

"Did he ask for Brenna by name?" Jett asked.

Mike thought for a minute. "No, he described her as the woman who was in Seattle, and . . . I must have said Brenna." He paled. "I'm sorry; I know better than to give out any information on the employees."

"One question answered." Jett motioned Mike back into the workroom. "Anything else, anyone?"

"I want to see the note," Brenna said. "Both sides."

"Why?" Simon asked. "As of now, you're out of this."

"What?" she asked.

"This is a job for the Bureau," he said. "You've given us a good start, but—"

"You can't expect me to just stop," she said.

"You aren't law enforcement," Simon said. "Policy dictates—"

"Gideon has connected with her," Owen said. "She may be our best chance to find out something about him."

Jett looked worried. "As long as it's only e-mail contact—"

"But it hasn't been," Simon replied. "He's been to her home."

"She can stay here until this is over," Jett said.

"I wish you'd stop talking about me as though I'd left the room," she said. "I'm still here, and where I stay is my decision. Not yours."

"You can't go home," Jett said.

"I could," she said, "but I won't."

"Good," he said. "Consider the guest room yours."

More than anything else at this moment, she needed to be alone. Jett had installed an extensive security system at the office, and staying there would provide a bed and a safe haven with friends. But it wouldn't give her time by herself.

"If you'll excuse me, gentlemen, I need some air."

As she walked to the patio doors framing the fireplace, she passed Hatch's date curled up on the recliner. That girl must be able to sleep through anything.

Brenna sat down in the green glider on the patio outside the break room, Feather at her feet. Not yet sunup, the sky brightened in the east. Even in summer, this part of the night reminded her of autumn; cool, almost brisk. Everything felt fresh and uncluttered; even the air was easier to breathe.

The door opened; Hatch joined her and sat down. He patted Feather.

"I'm sorry about all this," he said. "I should have stopped writing that guy after the first letter."

"You couldn't have known—"

"But I thought he was a gamester, not a psycho." Hatch wouldn't meet her gaze. "I can't believe I got you into so much trouble. If I hadn't kept writing, maybe he wouldn't have taken that little girl. Maybe—"

"I doubt any of us can predict this guy's actions."

Hatch slapped his cap against his leg. "Man, Jett gave me a great job and a place to live. You helped me pass freshman English and taught me about dogs." He shook his head. "I was just starting to get my life together and I pull a stupid stunt like this. I wouldn't be surprised if Jett fired me."

"Don't worry about that." She patted his arm. "What would we do without you? Besides, we're learning something about this guy because of his e-mails. I suspect the FBI profilers can use all the information they can get. When all this is over, you might have helped more than you can possibly imagine now."

He smiled shyly. "Are you just trying to make me feel better?"

"Is it working?"

"A little." There was a silence. "I promise I'll make this up to you, somehow." He stood, his cap in his hand. "If there's anything I can do, anything you need, let me know."

"Right now, I'm in fair shape, but I think your date would like to go home."

He laughed. "This wasn't the night I had planned. Guess I should wake her up and get her out of here."

A few minutes later, Simon Blue stepped onto the patio. Feather raised her head but didn't wag her tail.

Brenna leaned down and scratched the dog's ears. "Are you assigned to this case?"

"Not yet."

"Then why are you here?"

"Owen is my uncle. Granduncle, actually."

"Did he call you in on this?"

He nodded. "I expect I'll be official when my boss gets to work." He turned toward the kennel at the back of the property, its floodlights illuminating the rear of the yard. "Don't the neighbors complain about the dogs?"

"No, why? The dogs are quiet."

"It's a shame," he said. "These old houses are so beautiful, there should be families living in them. If you could live anywhere in the world, where would it be?"

Poor choice of subject. The loss of the cottage still nagged at her, as if it were some kind of cosmic punishment for making mistakes during Zoe's search. She tried to switch the conversation. "Are you going to access VICAP about Gideon?" she asked.

"No, CASKU. The Child Abduction and Serial Killer Unit. It's like VICAP, but it focuses on child abductions."

"And you think information on Gideon will be somewhere in those files?"

"Maybe. If this guy has done other abductions, I expect we'll find information about him."

"Such as?"

"That depends. If we're lucky, we could find a pattern—say he operates in a particular part of the country, or he only strikes during a full moon."

"Very funny."

He grinned. "You never know what triggers some people."

"I wish I understood this guy."

"Is there any possibility you've met him or interacted with him in some way? Maybe years ago? Could he have been a classmate or a former student?"

"I don't think so," she said. "I didn't get a real look at him, but I didn't have a sense of recognition . . . from me or from him. It all happened so fast, I just remember Zoe's screaming and the rush to get her out of the water."

The sky had turned from dark gray to silver. Sunup would catch her still on the patio, and once that light shined in her eyes, she'd never get to sleep.

"Coffee keeps me awake," she said, "but it's time I started a fresh pot. The Sunday crew will be here by six." She stood, and Feather got to her feet. "Want a cup?"

He looked at the dog and then her. "Does that animal go everywhere with you?"

She smiled. "Usually."

He stood and opened the door for her. Brenna and Feather went in ahead of him.

When they reached the breakfast bar in the kitchen, she put Feather on a down beside one of the stools and started a new pot of coffee. Owen and Jett still sat at the table, which was covered with paper; Hatch and his date were gone.

Owen looked up. "Hello there, young lady."

"Is anybody hungry?" Brenna asked.

"Not if you're cooking," Owen said.

Simon glanced at Owen. "What's wrong with her cooking?"

"Everything she makes tastes like tar paper," Jett said, "including her coffee."

"Thank you," she said. "I'm making it anyway. If you don't like it, don't drink it."

When she reached the bedroom, she realized her clothes felt sticky and hot. Too much adrenaline ebbing and flowing. If she was staying a day or two, Jett would have to provide her with a change of clothes.

After a long, hot soak in the tub, Brenna wandered into Jett's bedroom and rifled through his dresser until she found the T-shirts. In her own room, she crawled under the sheet and stretched out. Feather leaned against the bed, her chin resting on the edge of the mattress. Dark eyes watched her and the dog's bushy eyebrows wiggled every time Brenna moved.

"Stop begging," Brenna said.

Feather's ears perked and then relaxed.

This was a losing battle. "Okay, toots, we're not at home. Jump up."

Feather bounded onto the bed, snuggled close, and sighed. Brenna rested her arm around the dog's neck and pretended they were alone in a safe place. She'd lived by herself so long, it was hard to sleep soundly with other people in the house. Jett's place had people in and out twenty-four hours a day. She'd never quite understood why he'd chosen to live here after his divorce. He never had time to himself.

Feather stretched onto her side and started snoring.

"Great." Brenna put a pillow over her head and pictured a sheet of white paper. If she didn't have nightmares, and if insomnia didn't raise its thorny head, she might be able to get a few hours' sleep.

CHAPTER 17

JETT LOOKED UP when someone tapped on the open door to his office.

"Simon," he said, "sit down."

Simon settled in the chair in front of Jett's desk. "Owen said you were law enforcement."

"Fifteen years."

"Do you have any influence with Brenna? I can't let her stay involved in this; she's a civilian."

Jett laughed. "You may not have a choice. Irish usually does what she thinks is right."

"I'm worried about her safety," Simon said. "She doesn't have the background for this type of situation, and I can't be responsible for her or you. We have no idea how involved this will get or how long it might last."

"Don't worry about me."

"You're her boss," Simon said. "Can't you order her to leave this alone?"

"Her job with me and her position with the search team are two separate things. I have no control over her or anyone else in that group."

"But you were at Leanne's search."

"I sometimes assist if they're shorthanded or if it's a major call-out." He opened the humidor on his desk and offered Simon a cigar. "When Brenna organized the team, the group decided to refuse criminal chase search requests. They usually respond to lost persons, building collapses, and body recoveries." He lit his cigar and handed the lighter to Simon. "I must admit, I was relieved. Sometimes, they've unknowingly been in a group where the perp posed as an innocent bystander or search volunteer, but—"

"This is different," Simon said.

"You think I don't know that?" Jett shook his head. "Half that team works for me, and I consider the rest of them good friends. I don't want them involved in this any more than you do, but if Owen's right and Gideon has fixated on Brenna, we don't have much choice. There's enough cop left in me that I want to catch this guy." He leaned forward. "You didn't see Zoe or Leanne. I did."

"All the more reason to get Brenna away from it."

Either Simon wasn't too swift, or Jett wasn't explaining himself well.

"Of course I'm afraid for Brenna," Jett said. "She'd still be a schoolteacher in Texas if I hadn't offered her a job."

Simon puffed his cigar. "Would you, at least, talk to her?"

He nodded. "And if you approve, I'd like you and Owen to consider this place as an unofficial branch office for your operations."

"Why?"

"We have good security and I can keep an eye on her."

"That's not SOP, but I'll discuss it with my boss."

After Simon left, Jett remained in his office. A few years ago, he couldn't have imagined how his life would change. He'd started his own business, failed to keep his marriage together, begun dating again, and formed close friendships with his core employees. His father would never have approved. "Business and family relationships must be totally separate," his dad had said. But Brenna, Marco, Connie, and Hatch had been Jett's strongest assets in building his professional reputation, and his best support during his divorce.

When he went upstairs, he found Brenna sitting Indian-style in the middle of the hall, talking. Feather lay beside her, the dog's ears twitching each time Brenna spoke.

"Irish?"

She didn't respond, and he realized she was asleep.

"Irish, wake up." He shook her, gently. "Brenna."

Without looking at him, she said, "I thought I locked the door."

"You're in the hall," he said. "Look. And isn't that my T-shirt?"

She opened her eyes and seemed surprised.

"My shirt?" he asked.

"I stole it." She looked around.

"Thief." His tone changed. "Are you all right?"

"What happened?"

"You were sitting here, talking."

"What did I say?"

"Something about him not being illiterate. Pretending."

"Who?"

"Gideon, I guess." He pulled her to her feet.

"Anything else?"

"Words in the letters, or something like that."

He opened the bedroom door for her and followed her inside. She sat down on the edge of the bed.

"Were you dreaming?" he asked. "What were you thinking about?"

"I don't know."

"When did you start sleepwalking again?"

"How did you know I sleepwalk?"

"I have spies everywhere."

She looked at him. "It has to be something in those e-mails." She reached for her jeans. "Let's go find out."

"Tomorrow. I'm too tired to think straight—and so are you."

Jett sat at the poker table with Brenna, Feather snoozing at her feet. Except for Mike at the dispatcher's desk, they were alone. The Sunday shift had clocked in and gone to their assignments. He glanced at the clock. Eleven-thirty.

"Where's Hatch?" she asked.

"Washing your car."

"Why?"

"I think he's trying to make amends for the Gideon thing. Here." Jett put a yellow pad, a pen, his copies of Gideon's e-mails, and the hard copy of the instant-message conversation in front of her. "What do you see?"

While she sifted through the pages and doodled on the pad, he warmed the food Leah had left in the refrigerator. Once, Sunday morning had been his day to fix breakfast for his daughters. They'd always wanted to help, accidentally spilling milk or scooping out too much batter for the pancakes. Paige loved strawberries with hers; Laurel disdained any kind of fruit. He'd spent countless hours scrubbing syrup off the kitchen table and mopping up milk. He missed every minute of it.

When the food was ready, he set a plate in front of Brenna. "Leah brought lunch."

Baked chicken, cheese rice, and broccoli.

Brenna pushed the papers aside and picked up a fork. She watched Jett move the broccoli and rice on his plate into neat piles.

"You are the only man I know who refuses to eat if your food touches."

"At least I don't talk in my sleep." He took a bite of chicken. "Find anything?"

"The easy part is the capital letters," she said. "The first time he used them, they appeared to be random, but if you take every third letter, they spell out a word. Feather."

He looked over her shoulder. "How'd you do that?"

"Hatch was right. It's an easy code to break; we just weren't looking for a secret message earlier."

He read it aloud. " 'If you challenge me, be prepared to lose what matters more.' "

"Feather," she said.

"The arrows."

She nodded. "I'm glad I didn't know."

He glanced under the table at the dog, quietly snoozing at Brenna's feet.

"But this is the interesting part," she said. "The note should have said 'most.' 'Be prepared to lose what matters most.' Instead, it says 'more.' "

"So?"

"It's his grammar."

"He doesn't have any."

"Yes, he does. 'Most' implies a comparison of three or more things. 'More' is used to compare two things. He was telling me I'd have to choose between saving Leanne and saving Feather."

"Only an English teacher would know that."

"Do you want me to continue, or am I boring you?"

"Sorry. Go on."

"In the next note," she said, "the capital letters spell Leanne. He told us her name before he took her. He *planned* it."

"Even if we'd figured it out ahead of time, we couldn't have stopped him. A first name alone doesn't help us."

"In the other note, the one in which he says Leanne doesn't count, the capital letters spell 'I win.' "

"So, he dropped using every third letter."

"More than that, he's telling us about himself. When he started using the initial 'B' to represent my name, he used a colon, as if he was writing a business letter, and he capitalizes all the letters in his name. He's showing great arrogance. And look at the sentence where he describes himself: the judge, maimer, destroyer. Not one word is misspelled; the commas are in the right places; the sentence begins with a capital letter and ends with a period."

"And you think this means something?"

"I do. In his statement about not killing Leanne, there are three capital letters: I AM. And the two separate ideas in that message—

that he didn't actively kill Leanne, and she died because we didn't . . . are joined with a semicolon. The correct punctuation."

He tapped his fork on the table. "All right, we've got a very sketchy, unofficial profile of this guy. What does that tell us?"

"I'd bet he's educated and pretending to be illiterate so we'll underestimate him." She looked at her plate and then pushed it to the center of the table. "Hoping he'll make some kind of slip on the computer is a dead end. He's too smart for that."

Leaning forward, Jett rested his arms on the table. "We can call this whole thing off," he said. "If Gideon writes and no one answers, he'll eventually give up."

"Or will he try harder? I don't want another child on my conscience."

He stared into her brown eyes. "You are not responsible for Leanne's death."

She glanced away from him, and he suspected she didn't quite believe him.

"This is Gideon's game," he said. "You're an unwilling player, and, eventually, he'll tire of you and move on."

"I know we can't control this guy," she said, "but if we can stop him, we must try."

"Are you sure? No one will blame you if you get out and leave this to the FBI. This isn't your problem, and it *is* their job."

"In a way, Gideon's made it my problem. If we don't hear from him again . . ." She shrugged. "If we do—"

"You can still walk away." He grasped her hand. "I want you to walk away."

He thought she was going to protest, but she didn't. Instead, she said, "I'll think about it."

That meant no.

BRENNA FINALLY CONVINCED Jett to let her return home long enough to grab a change of clothes. Her house felt dirty and tainted, the yellow walls less bright, shamed by the violation. On her way back to Jett's, she realized she'd have to move.

Back at the office, while the dispatcher took a break, Brenna answered telephones and was surprised to receive a call from Gayle.

"If you're testing puppies this afternoon, can I tag along?" Gayle asked.

"Sure. Meet me at the office in . . . thirty minutes?"

Feather swiped a paw at Brenna's leg.

"Great," Gayle said. "My sister has Francesca today, so I'm available all afternoon."

After Brenna hung up, she turned to Feather. "What?"

The dog sat in front of her, cocking her head and talking to her with soft *r-r-r-rrr*'s.

"Is that so?"

R-r-r-rrrr. Each time the pitch rose or fell, Feather's head lifted or dropped.

"I'm puppy testing today."

Feather swiped at Brenna's leg again. *R-r-r-rrrr*. Then she barked.

Brenna laughed. "Okay, toots, but you'll have to stay in the car."

Feather snorted and crouched in the play position: front end low, rear end high.

Brenna collected her puppy-testing supplies from the kennel, feeling relieved that Gayle was going with her to the Kelloggs'. Company would keep her from dwelling on the past.

She should have tested this litter last week, but she'd put it off. Yes, each pup had its own look and personality, but she couldn't help thinking of Brie.

Gayle was in the backyard. Brenna forced a smile.

"You brought Visa," she said.

"I hoped you'd help me with her obedience training, after the testing," Gayle said. "Do you mind?"

"Of course not. Load her into the back with Feather. After we leave Marsha's, we'll take them to the park."

They climbed into the Blazer. "How old are these pups?" Gayle asked.

"Seven weeks. Most will go to their new homes next Sunday. Marsha and Bill never let them leave the litter before they're eight weeks old."

"Why?"

"Keeping the pups with the litter helps with the dogs' socialization skills, and it allows more time to decide which one should go to which home."

"Don't people choose their own dogs?"

"Most do, but some of the out-of-state folks let Marsha and Bill decide. Those who've bought dogs from them before."

During the drive, they talked about the team, Donny, Gayle's daughter Francesca, and Christmas shopping in July. Then Gayle changed the subject.

"You know, one of the CPAs I work for just got divorced." She smiled at Brenna. "Would you like to meet him?"

"Are you trying to fix me up?"

"Absolutely. Brenna and Bob. Sounds good, don't you think?"

Brenna laughed. "Sounds like characters from a soap opera."

"Are you interested?"

"You know I see Ryan."

"You can't see more than one guy at a time?" Gayle's eyes twinkled. "Variety is the spice of life."

"I have enough spice right now." She frowned, thinking of Job Won. "Maybe later."

Visa stood, moved behind Brenna, and bumped her with her nose.

"Visa, stop," Gayle said, reaching for the dog. "Down. Visa, down."

The dog stood there, wagging her tail.

Brenna's eyes misted. Brie used to bump her with her long nose.

"What should I do?" Gayle asked. "She doesn't mind."

"Give her a break, Gayle. She's only four months old."

When Brenna spotted a 7-11, she pulled into the parking lot and stopped near the Dumpster, away from traffic and hurrying shoppers.

"Let's try this," Brenna said. In the back of the Blazer, Feather lay on top of the blue shirt. "Feather, sit."

The dog perked her ears and pushed herself into a sitting position.

"Good girl," Brenna said. "Feather, down."

The dog inched her front feet forward until she lay flat.

"Good girl," Brenna said. "Visa, down."

The Golden Child wagged her tail, looked at Feather, and then plopped into a down.

"Good girl." Brenna patted both dogs.

"How'd you do that?" Gayle asked.

"Dogs can learn from each other," she said. "That's why you wouldn't want a pup around a grown dog with lots of bad habits."

Brenna smiled. Not only had Feather adopted Brie's habit of dragging around the blue shirt, she'd recently started digging in the garbage and then lining up the items on the kitchen floor. Brenna supposed, in Brie's absence, Feather had decided some classic mischief needed to be preserved. Each time Brenna found the trash on the floor, she didn't know whether to laugh or cry.

"I can't believe Visa went down for you and she won't for me," Gayle said.

"Consistency, Gayle." She studied her a minute. "When you're at home, do you ever use the word 'down' to mean get off something as well as lie down? Or does Francesca?"

"No, I'm very . . ." Gayle trailed off and then wilted. "I don't, but Francesca does. Last night, I heard her tell Visa to get down off the bed."

Brenna laughed. "See, you have to teach Francesca along with Visa. Even if you don't use two different words to mean 'lie down' and 'get off,' the dog will eventually understand, but it makes training easier if Visa knows exactly what you want her to do."

Gayle grimaced. "I thought you were crazy."

"Which time?"

"When you said it takes longer to train the handler than the dog. I can picture Visa becoming mission ready while I'm still on the first level."

"Not a chance. In fact, we voted to let you start flanking."

"On real searches?"

Brenna nodded.

Gayle sat straight. "When?"

Brenna steered back into traffic. "Whenever we get the next search."

As Brenna drove onto Marsha and Bill Kellogg's twenty-five-acre spread, she envied the couple. They'd worked hard, invested well, and retired early to enjoy their passion of raising German Shepherd dogs. The long gravel driveway stretched to a white two-story house. The kennel area sat on two acres behind and to the left of the main residence. Behind the barn, the summer-green pasture off to the right held a half-dozen grazing sheep.

Heaven.

When Brenna parked beside the chain-link-fenced exercise area, a beautiful sable shepherd barked, wagged her long tail, and waited for Brenna at the gate.

"Hello, Gretchen." She told Feather to stay and then got out of the Blazer. As she opened the gate, the dog moved back and sat. "Are you glad to have those pups weaned?" She squatted and stroked

Gretchen's muzzle and long ears. "Have you been a good mom again?"

"Better than last time." Marsha, a brown-haired, fiftyish woman who should have spent her life as a runway model instead of a legal secretary, came out of the kennel. Dressed in jeans and rubber boots, she wiped her hands on a white towel. "I just heard two more of her children got their championships last month."

Marsha was so funny. She never called their animals dogs or puppies; they were kids, children, sons, and daughters. Like Brenna, Marsha and Bill viewed their dogs as family.

She glanced past Brenna to the Blazer. "You brought a friend."

After Brenna made the introductions, Marsha looked at the truck.

"Did you bring Feather?" When Brenna nodded, Marsha said, "Let her out. Bill's taken Batch to an agility competition and the horses are in the back pasture. She can have the run of the place."

Gayle leaned to Brenna. "Batch?"

"Sebastian, their male. He's the papa for this litter."

When Brenna lowered the tailgate, Feather jumped out of the truck and met Gretchen nose to nose at the fence. Then the two dogs raced along the fence line, happily barking and loping beside each other.

"She's missed playing with Brie," Brenna said.

"Maybe it's time you got her a roommate," Marsha said. "I've got a sweet little girl in this litter."

Brenna couldn't imagine any dog replacing Brie.

"Not just yet."

Gayle set Visa on the ground and the pup ran to keep up with Feather and Gretchen, always two lopes behind while leaping at twice the speed.

"Oh, she's a pretty little girl," Marsha said. "Looks like a ray of sunshine." She smiled at Gayle. "Mind if I hold her?"

"Be my guest." Gayle tried twice before she caught Visa and then heaved the wiggling mass into Marsha's arms. "She's getting too big to lift."

"How much does she weigh?" Marsha asked.

Gayle shrugged. "I don't know."

"Come on," Marsha said. "We'll find out." She glanced at Brenna. "You coming?"

She nodded. "How's Kneely?"

"Just bathed her. She's in the dryer."

Marsha led Brenna and Gayle inside the kennel building, which reminded Brenna of Jett's. A shepherd, more tan than black, rested in a large wire crate that had two hair dryers attached to the sides. Kneeland's Favor had rich deep colors, but her tan was really a light gold, the gentle shade of toast.

"Hello, pretty girl." Brenna stuck her fingers through the wire, and the dog nuzzled them. "Kneely wasn't pick of the litter, was she?"

"No, but there was something special about her," Marsha said. "Several people wanted to buy her, but she tugged at my heart. I couldn't let her go."

"How many points?" Brenna asked.

"Twelve. Two majors."

"Majors?" Gayle asked.

"Dog show talk," Marsha said. "It means the judges chose her as the best bitch entered in the show that hadn't won enough points to be called a champion. With the number of Shepherds entered in shows these days, that's quite a coup."

"How'd she X-ray?" Brenna asked.

"My vet says excellent, but she's got another three months before she'll be two. We'll take them again and send them to OFA. Keep your fingers crossed." Marsha set Visa on a grooming table and then tugged her to a scale they'd built into the counter. "Batch's came back 'good.' Not bad for a seven-year-old."

Like most of the breeders Brenna worked with, Marsha and Bill were considered meticulous, and, by some, overly cautious. Hip dysplasia, a debilitating condition, plagued most large breeds; it could be hereditary or environmental. Responsible breeders had their stock's hips X-rayed when the dogs turned two years old. Then the veterinarian sent copies of those X-rays to the Orthopedic Foundation Association for a rating on a dog's hips, which would spot present or probable dysplasia. The OFA report categorized the result as excellent, good, fair, or poor. If a dog received an excellent or good rating, most breeders didn't go to the trouble and expense of checking the dogs again. Since Sebastian and Gretchen were the Kelloggs' current breeding stock, they sent X rays every two years. This couple wasn't in the business to make money; they wanted to produce dogs with good conformation and stable temperaments. Maybe that's why Brenna loved the Kelloggs so much. Their ideologies were identical.

Brenna lingered in front of Kneely. Such dark eyes, and the sweetest temperament. Calm, watchful, she possessed that intelligent, ready-to-go look, suggesting she was perpetually in drive and just idling until her human companion felt the urge to tackle a new quest.

Brenna tore herself away from the crate. "How many today?"

"Three." Marsha handed her the folders with the dogs' names. "Which one do you want first?"

"Surprise me."

At Marsha's suggestion, Gayle put Visa in an outdoor run next to the litter while they tested each pup individually inside the kennel.

When Marsha pulled a three-ring binder from the shelf, Gayle looked over her shoulder.

"What are you testing for?" she asked.

"Several things," Marsha said. "See"—she pointed to a page—"each pup has his or her own sheet that shows everything from birth weight and time to how it rates on the tests."

"Why?"

"Two little ones are going out of state," Marsha said, "and the new owners are depending on me to choose the right family member for them. I'm sending two of these three, but I want Brenna's input. These children know me, and I need to see how they react to a stranger."

"What do you test for?" Gayle asked.

"Curiosity, trainability, willingness to please and to forgive," Brenna said. "We look for their instinctive reactions before they're old enough to be conditioned by any type of training. Sometimes we can tell if they have a good nose."

A minute later, Marsha set a playful black pup with tan halfway up his legs into the room. When he saw Brenna sitting cross-legged on the floor, he bounded to her and immediately crawled into her lap. Then he stretched up to lick the bottom of her chin.

"You must be Max."

The dog wiggled and played with her as long as she cooed to him, but when she sat still and silent, he left her to investigate the rest of the room. When he became interested in a squeaky toy lodged under the cabinet, she softly clapped her hands and called his name. Max looked at her and then returned to his quest, working his nose into the space. The second time she called and clapped, he left the toy and bounded to her.

Gayle peeked out the door at Visa and then stood beside Marsha.

"Are most of the pups going to be black?" she whispered.

Marsha smiled. "No, the black you see on this litter will become their saddles." She pointed to Max. "He'll have a big saddle, but the next little girl will have a small one, like Kneely's. Mattie's already showing a lot of tan."

After playing with Max a few moments, Brenna cradled him in her arms, on his back like a baby. He struggled, stopped, then kicked and struggled harder.

One by one, she led him through the rest of the puppy tests, making each one seem like a game.

After Brenna finished logging the results, she glanced at Marsha. "Anything else?"

"Let's do the stress test." Marsha squatted and gently wrestled with the pup. "You watch and I'll lift."

Carefully placing her hands under the dog's ribs and flanks, Marsha lifted him several inches off the ground.

"Front and back hang straight," Brenna said.

"Why is this a stress test?" Gayle asked.

"If the legs lean in or cross," Brenna said, "it could mean he won't respond well to stress. That might be important if the pup's going to a home with four small children—"

"Or if he's going to become a police dog," Marsha said. She cuddled Max, put him in the run with his littermates, and returned to Brenna.

"I know what I think," Marsha said. "What's your bottom line?"

Brenna handed Marsha the paper. "I marked the log sheet."

"But what do you think?" Marsha asked.

"He's a stubborn, aggressive little guy," she said. "A one-dog household might be the best place for him, one with somebody who knows what he's doing and intends to spend lots of time with him."

"I thought the same thing," Marsha said. "Charlie Ivers in Detroit has called twice about a new dog. He lost Gregor in a shooting last year. I just haven't had the right little boy until now; I thought Max might be a good match for him."

"Oh—is Charlie all right?" Brenna asked.

"He's getting better. The bastard who shot Gregor put a couple of bullets into his leg. Cathy says he isn't progressing much in his physical therapy. Seems like a good time to send him a new partner." She smiled. "As I always say, God is never late. Maybe Max is what Charlie needs to get back on track."

After Brenna tested the next two pups, Marsha placed another in her arms.

"I thought you said three," Brenna said.

"I want you to meet Maisy," Marsha said. "Doesn't she remind you of Brie? Her legs are so dark, I'll bet she turns out red and black, like Batch. I thought of you the minute she opened her eyes."

The pup wiggled out of Brenna's lap and then sat in front of her, wagging her tail and cocking her head side to side. Her big ears still flopped over at the tips, but as she grew, the ear muscles would strengthen and eventually hold those "radar dishes" up straight.

When the pup waved at her, Brenna gently jiggled the small paw. Maisy did remind her of Brie. Too much.

"Isn't she precious?" Marsha asked.

Brenna nodded and handed the pup to Marsha. "Find a good

home for her, Marsha. There's no room in my house for a pup right now. In fact, I'm not living at home, at the moment. This little girl needs someone to love her for who she is, not who you or I want her to be."

Marsha cuddled Maisy and nodded. "I had to try. When you're ready to start looking, call me first."

Feather's bark floated into the kennel building.

They stepped to the doorway. The Bouvier was circling the small cluster of sheep.

"Feather!"

Marsha laughed. "When did you teach her to herd?"

"I haven't."

The dog circled the sheep again, nudging them into a tighter knot, and then sprinted toward the kennel. When she saw Brenna, she skidded to a stop, barked, and wagged her tail as though she wanted Brenna to praise her for her accomplishment.

"Good girl, Feather," Marsha called. "Come on."

"I'm sorry," Brenna said. "I had no idea she'd bother the sheep."

"Don't be silly," Marsha said, "she didn't hurt anything. Bill trained Batch to herd; Feather comes by it naturally. Instinct, I guess. Some dogs are born with it."

Instinct. According to psychologists, people are born with it, but as they grow older, life desensitizes them to gut feelings and premonitions. Aaron had always said her instincts were still strong.

Was that true? If she'd paid more attention to her qualms the night Zoe had "gone missing," maybe Brie would still be alive, that wacko might have been caught, and Leanne would be at home with her family. As it stood now, all she could do was wonder.

CHAPTER 19

TUESDAY STARTED WITH a breakfast appointment, and Jett found himself dealing with clients back-to-back. At twelve-thirty, he finally caught a break long enough to open the manila envelope his real estate agent had left for him. Most of the listings were available on-line, if he wanted to see a larger color photograph of any of the houses.

Brenna knocked on the door. "I'm ordering a pizza. Want something?"

"No anchovies," he said.

"I never order anchovies."

"Hatch does." He shuffled the pages and discarded the information on the one-story colonial.

"He has a date," she said.

Jett glanced at the clock. "Now?"

"Lunch date," she said. "Taking after his boss."

When she turned to leave, he called her back. After she sat in the leather chair, he handed her five pages.

"Which of these do you like?" he asked.

She scanned the papers. "Lake houses? I thought you and Joanne owned lake property."

"We do, but every time I tell her I plan to spend some time there, she says she's using it."

"Didn't she hate that place?"

"Hate" was too mild a word. His ex-wife had set foot in that cabin exactly once before the divorce. Now, she couldn't stay away from it . . . or so she said.

"She rents it during her six months of possession," he said.

"Is that legal?"

"I guess—it's officially hers then. But that's about to change. She can buy me out, or we can put it on the market, but this 'sharing the house' is over."

"I can't believe your attorney didn't make you set a firm schedule with everything else during your divorce."

"Carter tried to steer me into selling it then or demanding single ownership, but I thought Joanne would be fair." He shook his head. "I never dreamed she'd sink so low."

Brenna watched him and, slowly, sat straight. "It was Saturday. I wondered why you begged off fingerprinting during the Child Fair."

Saturday. Jacob's birthday. If he'd lived, Jake would have been thirteen. But he'd been a SIDS baby. Three months, five days.

"Haven't you always spent his birthday at the lake?" she asked.

"Until this year." He pulled a cigar from the humidor, looked at it, and put it back. "Joanne said she was using the house, and I could share it with her and her new friends, if I wanted. I declined." He fingered the desk lighter. "Why did she do that?"

"Sounds like she wanted your attention. Maybe she's trying to make you jealous."

"It didn't work. In fact, I drove out there, and she wasn't there. A young couple said she'd rented it to them for two weeks."

"You cared enough to check." Brenna smiled. "You know, Joanne told me the divorce was a mistake; she wishes it hadn't happened."

"I've heard the same story."

"Would you like to start over with her, be with your family again?"

Family. Even though he and Joanne had been divorced for more than two years, she and his daughters were still his immediate family. Every time he made a personal decision, he found himself wondering how his daughters would feel about it. Maybe that was why he'd moved into the office instead of an apartment. Laurel was away at college, but Paige whimpered each time he looked into buying a house.

He leaned back in his chair and propped his foot on the open lower drawer. "I miss the girls. Paige will be a senior this year, and I want to be there taking pictures when she walks down the stairs in her prom dress, and those weekends when both of them are home." He glanced at Brenna. "I miss peeking in their rooms at night while they sleep."

"Did they know you peeked?"

He laughed. "No."

"They're young ladies now."

"They are, but they'll always be my little girls."

Brenna sat on the arm of the guest chair. "Do you miss Joanne?"

"She's part of the whole picture, part of my life."

The telephone rang, and Brenna handed him the house pictures.

"I like the top three," she said, "but it's your decision." She stopped at the door. "Want a salad with your pizza?"

"Not this time."

He stared at the door long after she'd disappeared. She usually helped him with decisions, asking leading questions that opened new avenues of thought. But when it came to Joanne, Brenna rarely expressed any opinion.

Their conversation might have started with a discussion of lake property, but it had ended with the question whether he wanted to reinstate his marriage. A decision he'd have to make alone.

At six-fifteen that evening, Brenna found herself at the office again. When she and Feather walked into the break room, Rob Garrett, Owen, Jett, and Simon Blue were at the poker table.

"Hello, String Bean." She patted the top of his head as she walked past.

Garrett laughed. "I wasn't sure you were gonna make it."

"Sorry I'm late. This was the first day I could get back into my house, and I'm up here again. Can you believe it."

"Are you living at the duplex again?" Garrett asked.

"Until I find another place," she said. "It has a brand-new security system, so it's not too bad." She grabbed a Coca-Cola from the refrigerator. "Mrs. Timmons said thanks."

He laid his pencil on the table. "I forgot. How's he doing?"

"About as well as you'd expect."

Owen looked at Jett. "Herb Timmons? I heard he'd had a stroke."

Jett nodded. "He went home from the hospital today. Bren took some food over."

"Food?" Garrett said.

"Did she cook it?" Owen asked.

"I heard that," she said.

"At least Herb has a sweet wife," Owen said. "Getting older doesn't seem quite so hard if you can share it with someone."

Brenna smiled and looked at Jett.

"Owen, can you stay for dinner after the meeting tonight?" she asked.

"Are you having something special?"

"You might say that," she said.

She slipped her chair between Jett and Garrett. "What did I miss?"

"I have two pieces of news," Garrett said. "The Hendrickses are gone."

"Gone? Where?" she asked.

"I don't know," Garrett said. "They didn't leave a forwarding address. About two weeks after the kidnapping, Mr. Hendricks telephoned his boss and quit. Gary Brown, the guy who worked with Hendricks, stopped by the house, and no one was there. We've tracked down Mrs. Hendricks's parents, and if they know where that family is hiding, they aren't telling."

"Maybe they were afraid the kidnapper would come back," she said.

"That's my second bit of news," Garrett said. "Miles Chaney is dead."

"The gambler who might have taken Zoe?" she asked.

"Car accident in Iowa the same day Zoe was taken."

"Well," Jett said, "that eliminates him as a suspect."

"Did you tell Mrs. Hendricks's parents?" she asked.

"I did," Garrett said, "but Zoe's parents were under such scrutiny after the kidnapping, I'm not surprised they disappeared."

"Why?" she asked. "Do the police think they were involved in Zoe's abduction?"

"Parents are always suspects." He placed two sets of photographs in front of her. "Take a look at these."

While the men compared details of the two incidents, she studied the pictures of the notes Gideon had left after taking Zoe and Leanne.

The paper that had been left on Leanne's bicycle looked typed. That was different from Zoe's abduction. The notes on construction paper showed the same details: numbers in the corner and the words "eight hours." Of course the messages weren't the same, but as she studied them, she noticed something else.

"He didn't use the phrase 'best served cold' on Leanne's. I still think that sounds familiar."

"It's from a quotation," Garrett said. "Revenge is a dish best served cold."

"That's it," she said. "I knew I'd heard it before."

"Did you get any information from VICAP?" Owen asked Simon.

"CASKU," Garrett said.

"Four others with practically the same MO," Simon said. "Leanne makes five, but Brenna's right; there is a difference in Leanne's note." He set his coffee cup on the table. "Are you sure the same guy abducted both Zoe and Leanne?"

"Yes," Brenna, Jett, and Garrett said together.

"The construction paper note—" Garrett said.

"Different colors," Simon said.

"The times written in the same corner," she said. "The time allotment of eight hours."

"Can you prove it's the same guy," Simon said, "in court? A

good defense attorney will argue a copycat could have committed one of these crimes. And if it turns out he's been leapfrogging all over the country, you may never pin any abductions on him. You've got to be able to prove this is the one and only man who could have committed these crimes."

She looked at Jett. "Is that right?"

"I didn't go to law school, but—"

"Simon did," Owen said.

"Isn't connecting all these tidbits and making a case the FBI's job?" she asked.

"Sometimes," Simon said. "But a criminal case requires proof beyond a reasonable doubt."

"Brenna saw Gideon in Seattle," Garrett said.

"So you've said." Simon turned to her. "Did you see him well enough to identify him?"

"No," she said. "What kind of proof would the court accept?"

"What kind do you have?" Simon asked.

She smiled at Garrett. "Hang on a minute." She stood, turned Feather loose in the yard, and then took a couple of packets of gauze from the first-aid kit in the workroom.

When Garrett realized what she was doing, he grinned. "Where are they?"

"Closet in the workroom," she said.

Owen looked at Jett. "What's going on?"

"You need to be an official representative of the Sacramento Police Department for a few minutes," Jett said.

Garrett took the case of mason jars to the table. Each jar, sealed in a plastic bag, had holes drilled into the lid and a number marked on the top.

A petite, blue-haired woman opened the patio door. "Hello, everybody." Then she turned away. "Feather, get your nose away from our dinner." She stepped into the room and pulled in a child's red wagon stacked with boxes. Then she stopped. "Oh, am I too early?"

"Just in time," Brenna said.

Owen popped up and hurried to her, his limp a bit less noticeable than usual. "May I help you with that? A young lady like you shouldn't have to unload those heavy boxes."

"Oh, go on." Leah waved her hand at him and they walked to the kitchen together.

"Now, don't you tip that box," Leah said. "Brenna said we were having special company tonight, so I made lasagna and garlic bread."

"Smells wonderful."

"And apricot cobbler," she said. "Brenna just loves my apricot cobbler, but it doesn't keep with the Italian theme of the dinner." She turned to Owen. "Do you think anyone will mind?"

"Not one bit," he said.

Brenna handed each of the men a packet and told them to open it and rub their hands on the gauze.

"You, too, Leah. I'm conducting an experiment and I need your help."

After each person had rubbed his or her hands on the gauze, Brenna started to unwrap one of the jars, but she stopped.

"What?" Garrett asked.

She looked from him to Jett.

"If we're going to do this," she said, "let's do it right."

"What's on your mind?" Jett asked.

"Let's get all the dogs here and let each one test the jars. We have lots of witnesses." She glanced over her shoulder. "Look who's here. An FBI agent and officers from two law-enforcement agencies."

"And what if the dogs don't prove Gideon committed both abductions?" Jett asked.

"Then all we've lost is a little time."

Ten minutes later, three of the team members were on their way, and Hatch had promised to bring his date by the office for dinner. None of the dogs had met her before. Patrick was out of town, so they'd have to conduct the experiment without Dorsey. Still, four out of five would be a good showing.

After Brenna realized the number of people due to arrive, she whispered to Leah, "How many will your lasagna serve?"

"About eight hearty eaters," she said. "I doubled the recipe, and I have an extra one in the freezer. Should I get it?"

"Not if you made it for yourself."

"Nonsense. I intended to bring it over here for lunch tomorrow." She smiled. "I'll go get it—if Owen will walk with me."

"I bet he'll do that," Brenna said.

As soon as Leah and Owen disappeared from the patio, Brenna dialed the local pizza parlor and ordered three large supremes.

Jett stopped beside her. "What are you doing?"

"Leah's fixed dinner for all of us and I've sprung extra people on her."

He nodded. "Good idea. I'll split the cost with you."

"A handsome, refined Southern gentleman would pay the entire bill," she said.

He grinned. "Nice try."

By the time Connie arrived, their business meeting had turned into a gathering. Marco and his wife, Ahnya, had brought tamales and makings for fajitas; Harley and his wife had brought a relish tray and assorted beverages. Gayle and Donny arrived late for the meeting, and when they realized they'd come empty-handed, Donny dashed out to Barney's Bakery and returned with napoleons and chocolate eclairs. As Connie set the pizzas on the breakfast bar, Leah popped her second lasagna into the oven with two cookie sheets filled with garlic bread.

"My," Leah said, "isn't this lovely? We have a party and a smorgasbord."

"Business first," Brenna said.

Once the dogs were secured in the kennel's indoor runs and the handlers had been exiled to the parking lot, Brenna gave new gauze packets to Jett, Owen, Garrett, Simon, Leah, and Ahnya. After each rubbed his or her hands on a pad, Brenna opened several jars and had each person drop a pad inside. Then she closed the lid tight.

"Explain this to me," Simon said.

"Hey-hey, everybody." Hatch guided his date into the break room. "This is Cheri."

"Hi, Cheri," Brenna said. This was not the girl Hatch had brought to the office a few weeks earlier. "Have we met before?"

"I don't think so," the brunette said.

"Would you help me with an experiment?"

"I will," Hatch said.

"You'll get your chance in a minute." Brenna turned to Cheri. "Are you game?"

"What do you want me to do?"

Brenna handed her and Hatch packets of gauze. "Open this and hold it in your hands for a minute."

"Is that all?" Cheri asked.

"That's it." Brenna opened one of the jars and turned to the group. "As you can see, these are ordinary mason jars, sterilized and then sealed in airtight plastic bags. Each lid has six holes, and on the inside of the lid we've glued cheesecloth to keep the future contents of the jars from being contaminated." She showed the lid to the onlookers. "Now please drop that pad into the jar."

She did and Brenna screwed on the lid.

"Okay," Brenna said. "Did I touch that pad?"

"No," Cheri said.

"Have we met before?"

"No."

"Have you ever met my dog or any of our dogs before?"

Cheri giggled. "No."

Brenna tipped the jar toward Cheri. "What is your jar number?"

"Eleven."

She set number eleven on the counter and grabbed another jar for Hatch. After he dropped his pad into the jar, she sealed it and called out the number.

"Okay," Brenna said. "Let's start."

BRENNA PICKED UP a plastic bag she'd removed from the freezer a half hour before. "Garrett, do you recognize this?"

He nodded. "That's one of the gauze pads I laid on the footprint by the creek the night Zoe was abducted." He pointed to it. "It's sealed and dated, and it bears my initials."

"Just as you gave it to me?"

He examined it. "Yes."

She opened a jar, cut the plastic bag, shook the pad from the bag into the jar, and screwed on the lid.

"You've just destroyed evidence," Simon said.

"Garrett gave me two and he has two, so we have three left." She smiled. "We taught him well."

She showed the jar to Simon. "What number is on this jar?"

"Six," he said.

Harley's wife, Liz, noted the number, as she had those of the other jars.

Brenna picked up another bag from the freezer and handed it to Simon.

"Why did you store these in the freezer?" he asked.

"To keep the scent fresh." She pointed to the bag. "Does it appear that anyone has tampered with this bag?"

He studied the seal, the date, the time, and Sheriff Whitkin's initials. "No."

"Bren . . ." Garrett said.

"Don't worry, I have two for you."

"See," he said, "I've taught you well, too."

She laughed and opened a jar. "This is the gauze pad from Saturday. We'll use it as the scent marker."

"What's that?" Simon asked.

"You'll see." She showed the jar to Harley's wife. "Number two."

"Why did you send your handlers outside?" Simon asked.

"I don't want them to know which jar has which scent."

Everyone stayed inside as Brenna carried the jars to the middle of the backyard and set them on the grass, three feet apart, in numerical order.

Then she went to the kennel, leashed Feather, and brought her to the patio. Jett, Owen, Simon, and Garrett stood outside beside the outdoor furniture. The others remained inside, their faces pressed against the patio doors. Feather tugged toward Garrett, wagging her tail, but he followed directions and kept his hands behind his back.

"Feather"—she held the scent marker for the dog to sniff—"mark it."

The dog passed her nose near it and then wagged her tail.

"She didn't smell that," Simon said.

"Oh, hush," Owen said. "Go on, young lady."

Then Brenna took Feather to the jars. "Feather, show me."

The dog walked in front of the jars, swiped her nose near the lids, and kept walking. When she hit number six, Feather knocked it over and looked at Brenna.

"Check it," she said, sweeping her arm toward the other jars.

Feather sniffed the others and then returned to jar six. This time, she barked.

"Yes!" Garrett whispered.

"Good girl, Feather," Brenna said. "Good girl!"

While she returned Feather to the kennel, Jett ran to the jars and switched the order. When Brenna came back, Connie and Margarita were with her.

Connie followed the same process, but when Margarita found a match to the scent marker, she tried to pick up the jar in her mouth.

Connie turned to Brenna. "Is it six?"

"That's it."

"Good girl, Margarita!"

Again Jett changed the order of the jars, but first he washed them all down with soap and water before Marco brought Chelsa out. Then, if someone argued that the last two dogs had alerted on jar six because they smelled Margarita on it, the experimenters would have proof that every jar had been handled exactly the same way.

Marco and Chelsa, too, hit on jar six.

Brenna turned to Simon. "All these dogs are scent discriminators and they all chose the same jar. Here's your proof."

"Impressive," he said, "but I don't know if this will stand up in court. It could lend credence to your theory, but it's still a theory."

"Good," Jett said. "Now that the experiment is complete, let's all go inside and enjoy ourselves."

Brenna stood at the patio doors, watching Visa in the backyard. Their Golden Child had just passed the gangly stage during which she appeared to have more leg than body.

Brenna had removed Gideon's jars but left the others in the grass. When Visa started nosing them, she called Gayle.

"What's she doing?" Gayle asked.

"Watch."

One by one, Visa sniffed the jars. When she sniffed one in the middle, her tail wagged, and she looked up, as if to see whether the person was near.

"She recognizes that scent," Brenna said.

"But she wasn't part of the experiment," Gayle said.

"This has nothing to do with Gideon," Brenna said. "Visa doesn't realize it, but she's scent discriminating. Go see which number is on the jar."

It was the number nine.

Brenna looked at the list. Hatch. Visa should indeed have recognized his scent; she'd been around him more than the other "testers."

She pulled Hatch away from Cheri and walked with him into the backyard. Visa trotted to them, her golden coat rippling with each stride.

Then, per Brenna's instructions, Gayle called her back and rolled the jar on the ground. Visa sniffed it, as if Gayle were teasing her with a ball. Then Gayle said, "Show me." The dog's tail wagged; she looked at Hatch and trotted to him. He knelt, praised her, and ruffled her coat.

"Come praise her, Gayle," Brenna said. "Bring the jar. This is a good exercise in giving Visa positive reinforcement."

While Hatch and Gayle played with the dog, Brenna let the others out of the kennel. They romped into the yard and nuzzled the pair with Visa. Then they trotted off in different directions, willing and able to entertain themselves.

Brenna collected the remaining jars and took them into the house. Everyone had started eating, buffet-style.

"Bren," Harley called, "got your Jive Bunny tape? Let's make this a real party."

They started the tape and moved furniture to clear a spot for dancing. Few could resist the first song, an "In the Mood" compilation with cuts from Elvis songs. Toes tapped, feet moved, shoulders wiggled in time with the intoxicating beat. Whenever the Elvis clips came on, Harley, Donny, and Hatch mimicked the King's famous movements. Leah and Owen held hands and swayed in perfect harmony.

Brenna had just eased into a gray chair and set her plate on an end table when Simon stopped in front of her and extended his hand.

"May I?" he asked.

She hid a smile. "Can you dance?"

He grasped her fingers. "On your feet, woman."

As he pulled her up, his left hand grasped hers, and before she realized they'd started, he twirled her.

To her surprise, Simon was an excellent dancer. Most men his size were clumsy or self-conscious, but he moved with the grace of a dance instructor. Once, she heard herself squealing as he twirled her in an extended spin. Embarrassed, she tried to sit down, but he tugged her back to the center of the "dance floor."

"Do I pass the dancing test?" he asked.

"I suppose your toes tap pretty well, for an agent's."

"A toe-tapping agent." He smiled. "I like that."

Soon the glass doors were opened, and people spilled onto the patio. As the song "Sentimental Journey" began, she realized she and Simon were the only couple still dancing outside.

"You're smiling," he said. Then he smiled. "What were you thinking?"

She glanced away from him and her gaze stalled on the dogs. Feather and Margarita were lying down, facing each other, playing Trap the Paw. Feather's paw would flop on top of Margarita's, and then the Bloodhound would pull it loose and plop her paw on top of Feather's. Chelsa, Brooklyn, and Visa were tugging a rubber ring, each trying to pull it away from the others.

Simon tapped her chin with his finger. "You know, that's the first time I've seen you smile. Really smile."

"Is there more than one way to smile?"

"Absolutely." He danced her a few steps backward, pulled her closer, and made two turns in a couple "spin."

"Boy," she said, "I need to take a break."

Feather shifted onto her back, squirmed back and forth like a sidewinder, rolled to her feet, and snorted. She barked at Brenna, wagged her tail, and trotted toward her.

Simon stepped back. "I think you're right; it's time we take a break. Are you ready to go inside?"

"You go on," she said. When Feather stopped in front of her, Brenna knelt and ruffled the dog's coat. "Have you had fun with Margarita?"

The dog wagged her tail and rubbed her face up and down on Brenna's leg. When she looked up, Feather's visor—Connie said "bangs"—fanned out in all directions. She looked like a cartoon character who'd stuck her finger in a light socket.

Connie walked out onto the patio and squatted beside Brenna.

"Simon seems nice," she said. "He's kept you occupied for a while."

"He's a good dancer." Brenna wasn't sure what to think about Simon. She liked him, but she was involved with Ryan. Unless that relationship ended, she felt bound to honor it.

"You look a little flushed." Connie leaned toward Brenna and whispered, "Do we like him?"

She smiled. "We might, if he weren't afraid of dogs and Ryan wasn't coming back into town tomorrow."

"Too bad." Connie glanced into the break room. "When he finishes dancing with Gayle, can I have a crack at him?"

Brenna turned to look at the dancers. Simon was guiding Gayle around the floor with the same attentiveness he'd shown her.

"Sure," she said. "Give him your best shot." After Connie left, she stroked Feather's ears. "We have our hands full with Ryan, don't we?"

Feather cocked her head side to side and then made her r-r-r-rrrr sound.

"Exactly." She ran her finger along Feather's muzzle.

Back in the break room, she passed Simon and Gayle and heard her laugh.

Brenna's untouched plate had disappeared, and when she reached the breakfast bar, she searched for the apricot cobbler. The pan was empty.

"No fair," she said. "Leah made the cobbler for me, and I didn't get any."

Owen stopped beside her. "Sure was good." He leaned toward her and whispered in her ear. "Thank you, young lady."

Hatch called and waved at her. "Bren, I put your plate in the oven. Want me to warm it up for you?"

"Thanks, Hatch, but I can manage."

He joined her in the kitchen. "What about salad? I can throw lettuce and tomatoes together."

"I don't need salad, but thanks for—"

"What about something to drink?" Hatch dashed to the refrigerator and yanked it open. "We have—"

"Hatch, go back to your date. Have fun."

He slumped, the refrigerator door still open.

"All right," she said. "A glass of water with two cubes of ice."

He brightened, handed her the water, and grinned.

"Now, go dance with Cheri. If I need anything, I'll call you first."

The party went on, happy people enjoying good company. The only disruption occurred between Donny and Gayle. Since the Leanne search, he'd had second thoughts about Gayle working with the team, but she had her own ideas. He might have maneuvered her into becoming interested in the group, but she made it clear that staying or leaving would be her choice. Not his.

Jett stopped at the door to the hallway and motioned to her. "Where's Simon?"

She looked around. "I don't know."

"Get Garrett and Owen. Come to my office."

"Why?"

"Gideon's on-line again. Says he has a message for you, just you."

The men huddled around Brenna as she sat at Jett's desk.

"Why didn't you pull it up in the workroom?" Garrett asked.

"I was checking for e-mail from Lauren," Jett said. "He came on after I was already on-line."

Brenna typed, "I'm here. What do you want?"

That picture in your bedroom . . . is the man your father?

She looked at Jett. "Has he been in my house again?"

"I don't know how," Jett said. "Maybe he's using something he saw the first time."

"Yes," she typed.

What color is the shirt he's wearing in that picture?

"Blue-and-white stripe."

Hello Brenna. Having a good night?

She thought of their experiment.

"Not too bad," she typed.

Good.

They waited for him to respond again. Six minutes later he sent her another instant message.

Wanted to let you know I won't be in touch for a while, but you'll never be far from my thoughts.

"Why?"

I'm taking a trip.

"No, why are you."

She stopped. "Should I use the word 'obsessed'?"

"No," Owen said. "We have to find out something about this man. See if he'll talk to you."

"Okay."

She typed, "No, why are you writing me at all?"

I like you. If you had been there, maybe things would be different.

"Been where?"

There. You saved Zoe so I let her go. A fair game. Maybe you could have helped Jorge.

"Jorge who?"

Chavez. He tried.

"Tried what?"

You know.

"No, I don't. Where is Jorge?"

Gideon stayed silent a few minutes.

"Well, we have a name," Jett said.

"But no city or state," Garrett said. "Do you know how many men named Jorge Chavez must live in this country?"

"I'll bet we find out," Owen said.

"What makes you think it's a man?" Brenna asked. "Maybe Jorge is a little boy."

"Maybe," Garrett said, "but he hasn't told us anything we can really use."

"He's not sending code with capital letters out of place or misspelling words," she said. "That's different."

The instant message sound b-r-u-m-m-e-d again.

Still there?

"Yes."

Have any questions?

She looked at the men. "This is a switch." She typed, "Will you answer them?"

Try me.

She looked at the group around her. "What do you want me to ask?"

"Don't waste your time asking his name," Owen said, "or where he is. He won't give you straight answers on those."

"Ask him why," Garrett said. "If there's anything that ties these two cases together, it might give us a lead we can use."

"Why did you take Zoe and Leanne?"

It's my job.

"What job?"

You'll figure it out one day.

"Tell me."

No.

"Why are you talking to me at all?"

I told you; I like you. You care . . . And you're a good competitor.

"What if I won't play your games anymore?"

You will.

"Why should I?"

Our score. Five for me, one for you, one for her. Leanne doesn't count.

"I wish he'd stop saying that," she said.

"Keep going, Bren," Garrett said. "If he's willing to talk, take advantage of it."

"Who else doesn't count?"

Gideon didn't answer.

"Okay, who has another idea?" she asked the men.

"Look at the last message," Jett said. " 'One for her.' "

"Who's her?" she typed.

Who?

"One for me, one for her. Who's her?"

one to go unlless naturee flexxes hiis poweer.

"I spoke too soon," Brenna said. "At least this one is easy."

"What do you mean?" Owen asked.

"The double letters," she said. "L-E-X-I-E."

"Who is Lexie?" she typed.

OlD Sol risEs iN the east; you lIve in the weSt. We'll meEt again at noon.

"Old Sol?" Garrett asked.

"The sun," Owen said.

"I don't understand," she typed.

When he didn't answer, she wrote again.

"Where are you going?"

Gotcha! Now you'll play my game. Until next time . . . Gideon

"Well, shoot." She leaned back in Jett's chair. "I jumped too soon. If I hadn't asked the second question, he might not feel he has the upper hand now."

"It doesn't matter, Irish. We know more now than we did before." Jett turned to Garrett. "Five for him. What do you make of that?"

"Well, the four we know about—five, if you count Leanne, were all girls."

"But," Owen said, "he said Leanne didn't count."

"We're missing one," Garrett said.

"Maybe one of the agencies didn't turn in a report to CASKU," Brenna said.

"We might be getting ahead of ourselves," Owen said. "We've found four cases similar to Zoe's and Leanne's, but that doesn't mean Gideon was responsible for them."

"What if he was?" Garrett said. "The numbers almost match."

"They're close, but this isn't a game of horseshoes," Owen said.

"I think he's leaving the West Coast," Jett said. "That message sounded straightforward. The sun rises in the east, Irish lives in the west. That noon business sounds like the country's midsection."

"Then he can't expect me to challenge him," she said. "What's the point?" She turned the chair to face Garrett. "Is there any way you can warn agencies?"

"Where? That description's so vague, we have no place to start."

"Yes, we do," Owen said. "Gideon said 'five' for him. Brenna saved Zoe, so if we assume no one saved the others, he's killed five times. Those people had to have something in common."

"Well, in the message about Sol, the capital letters spell out 'Denise.'"

"His next victim," Garrett said.

"That doesn't help much, does it?" Brenna asked.

"No," Owen said. "We could send an alert to every law-enforcement agency in the country and tell them to notify us if someone named Denise turns up missing, but that's a real long shot. We'd be chasing our tails from now until the next millennium."

"That's probably why he gave it to us," Jett said. "We can't do anything with it." He pushed the printout of the conversation in front of her and pointed to the next coded message. "What jumps out in this one?"

She glanced at it. "I told you before. The double letters spell 'Lexie.'"

"Anything else?" Garrett asked.

"It's wrong," she said. "Nature is a her. You know, Mother Nature." She shook her head. "You guys are looking so hard for secret messages, you're missing the obvious."

"Anything else seem obvious to you?" Jett asked.

As she studied the line, her stomach twitched. "One to go." She glanced at the men. "He's targeted one more."

"We know that," Garrett said. "Denise."

"What if there's only one more?" she asked.

"So if there's one more," Jett said, "is it Denise or Lexie?"

"I'd guess the 'Lexie' has already happened," Garrett said. "He spelled Denise in the line that targets the next victim."

Owen looked at his copy of the conversation. "Gideon said, 'Five for me, one for you, one for her.' Question: Who's 'her'? Answer: Lexie." He eased into the leather chair in front of Jett's desk. "Well, at least he answered." He looked at the trio still behind the desk. "If we knew who Lexie is or was, we might have something to go on."

CHAPTER 21

A FEW DAYS LATER, Brenna made a stop at a cemetery before going home. She parked the Blazer in the shade of a tree and told Feather to stay. Farther down the path, two men were dusting off a headstone. After they left, she walked to the grave; it was still covered with flowers.

No one lingered in the cemetery at this time of evening. She knelt and laid a pink rose next to the blanket of pink carnations.

"I'm sorry, little one," she said.

She wanted to say more, but the words wouldn't come. What could make the slightest difference now?

After staring at the tombstone and the inscription—"Leanne Nicole Erskin, Our Precious Daughter"—she rose and returned to the Blazer. Feather stuck her head out the window and wagged her tail.

She stroked the soft fur between the dog's ears. "Bad idea, toots. We shouldn't have come."

By the time Brenna parked in her driveway, her head was pounding. She gave Feather a shorter-than-usual daily brushing, fed her, and soaked in a hot bath. But the night felt endless and empty. Every two hours, she awoke. At first, she wondered if Feather had bumped the bed or made a strange sound; the dog raised her head each time Brenna stirred, but Feather didn't stand or show any signs that a stranger might be near.

Before the sun rose, Brenna wandered into the kitchen. Two stainless-steel bowls sat on the floor next to Feather's water bowl. One was empty; the other held kibble mixed with canned dog food.

Closing her eyes, she leaned against the refrigerator.

Brie's bowl. And Feather, a walking garbage disposal, hadn't touched it.

In swift movements, she dumped the food in the trash, washed the bowl, and stashed it in the cabinet above the built-in oven.

Shadows moved in every room; she felt as though someone was watching.

"Damn you, Gideon."

Feather stood in the doorway, cocking her head this way and that. Brenna knelt and combed her fingers through the dog's thick coat.

"We can't let him win, can we, toots?"

R-r-r-rrr.

"This is our place, at least for now."

"Woof!"

Brenna dressed for work; Jett had two meetings with prospective clients that day, and even though she had the documents ready for his presentations, double-checking never hurt. As she slipped on her watch, she glanced at the pictures on the bookcase. On impulse, she collected the photographs and Brie's ashes and tucked them into her car.

Just before lunch, Jett stopped at her desk. "Do I have anything important this afternoon?"

She checked her copy of his agenda. "Dr. McKenna at one. Look, you wrote the notation yourself."

He tapped his fingers on the desk.

"What's wrong?" she asked.

"Joanne wants to have lunch, and I'm not sure how long that will take."

"About the lake house?"

"Among other things."

"Go on," she said. "I'll keep McKenna entertained until you get back." She straightened the papers on her desk. "Should I prepare anything special for your presentation?"

"No, he didn't ask for this meeting," Jett said. "I did."

As he walked out the front door, she grasped the folders that needed to be filed. Dr. Wesley McKenna was a well-known psychologist who occasionally umpired for the city league baseball teams. He looked like a sandy-haired Pillsbury Doughboy, and all the players called him Spud. She tried not to speculate why Jett had made an appointment with him; it wasn't her business. But the lunch with his ex-wife suggested a connection. Joanne's telephone calls had become more frequent the past few days.

McKenna arrived a little early. "Jett's been detained," Brenna said, rising. "May I offer you coffee or a cold drink?"

"No need to be so formal. I've seen you slide into home base."

"And you called me out." She leaned toward him and whispered, "You know I was safe."

He laughed. "A cold drink sounds good. Iced tea?"

"Right away."

He followed her into the kitchen and suggested they wait for Jett on the patio. Connie agreed to cover the telephones until Jett arrived.

As they sat in the gliders, she asked, "Would you like a brownie, Dr. McKenna? Our neighbor brought us a treat for lunch."

"None of this Dr. McKenna; we know each other better than that. Call me Spud."

She smiled. "Who nicknamed you Spud?"

He patted his basketball-like stomach. "Started in high school. I could eat more potatoes than anybody." He leaned toward her. "Actually, I come from a farming family, and my dad grew potatoes. I suppose it was a combination of my background and my eating habits."

"Brownie?"

"No, I'd rather visit with you." He glided back and forth a few times. "I haven't seen you lately. How have you been?"

"Fine."

"Really? You look tired."

"I haven't been sleeping well."

She watched McKenna a moment, thinking of him more as a friend than a business client. Everyone knew he volunteered his time as a psychologist for the fire, police, and sheriff's departments, and during debriefings after traumatic searches.

"Nightmares?" he asked.

She nodded.

"Several people who were involved in the search for that little girl have come to see me." He turned toward her. "Would you like to talk about it?"

To her surprise, the sadness of the past few months spilled out in one big gush.

"Logically, I know Gideon took Leanne's life," she said, finally, "but I feel partly responsible. If Brie hadn't found Zoe and him, he might not have considered the possibility that dogs could help find the children he hides. He used Leanne to see if he could fool the dogs."

Spud shook his head. "That was his choice. You had nothing to do with it." He took her hand. "You cannot be responsible for other people's decisions or actions. The only person you can control is you."

"I haven't done a good job with that, either. I feel as if I've punished Feather for Brie's death. I pulled away from her and didn't realize it."

"Grief is a dark companion," he said. "Most people either close up or put a death grip on the loved ones who remain. It takes time to work through all that. But I think you're on the right road." He paused. "Tell me about Brie."

She still couldn't talk about it, even though the image of that river and the memory of helpless panic haunted her sleep.

"Many clients have told me that nature gives us animals to show us the true meaning of love," he said. "Some people feel their animal friends are the only things in this world that truly love them; no matter how many mistakes we humans make, they forgive us and love us anyway. Our animal companions ask for little and shower us with a priceless gift."

Her eyes misted. "Brie must have been so scared," she said, "and I couldn't help her."

"You didn't fail her, Brenna."

"I feel the same way about Leanne," she said. "I couldn't get to her, either." She crossed her legs and then uncrossed them. "I don't know why these two deaths have hit me so hard."

He rubbed his chin, as if considering something.

"What about other personal losses?" he asked.

"My dad," she said, "and Aaron."

"What happened to them?"

"A drunk driver smashed into Dad's car," she said, "and a heart attack took Aaron."

"There's your answer," he said. "You couldn't control either of those situations. There must be a part of you that still thinks you could have saved both Brie and Leanne."

Maybe he was right. Maybe not.

"You know," he said, "most people in my profession let their clients do all the talking, but I tend to say what I think. Do you mind?"

She wasn't sure she wanted to hear this, but she nodded for him to continue.

"First," he said, "be careful of this Gideon character. You're right; you can't walk around being afraid, but you must be aware. Don't let your feelings of helplessness push you into taking unnecessary risks." He held up two fingers. "Second, let me know how your experiment with sleeping with a radio on works out. If it helps end your nightmares, I might suggest it to some of my clients."

"Just call me Guinea Pig Scott," she said.

He grinned and held up three fingers. "Third, your concern that you've lost your compassion is nothing but fear talk. A person's reaction to loss is usually dictated by his view of death. If he believes that death is the end, it's more difficult to accept. If he believes death is a stepping stone to the next . . . whatever, then the loss is only a temporary separation."

He leaned toward her and grasped her hand between both of his. "Brenna, you have the ability to see man's cruelty to man and file those images away into a dark, numb pit somewhere inside you. That's a good thing for you, and for paramedics, firefighters, police, and emergency room doctors and nurses. All of you must be able to put aside grief and fear in order to do your jobs as well as you can. You must place Leanne and Brie's loss in that pit. If the day comes that sad memories interfere with your job, it's time to make a change." He watched her a moment. "I see fidgeting fingers. What's wrong?"

"I feel a little silly," she said.

"No need. We all have to talk things out once in a while; humans are complicated beings. I'll bet you're never too busy to listen to a friend's troubles." He leaned back and patted his stomach. "Does that offer of a brownie still hold?"

"How about two?" When she stood, she saw Jett in the kitchen. "Jett's back. I'll refill your glass and bring the brownies to you in his office."

Ten minutes later, Spud left. When Jett passed through the break room, he waved but didn't look directly at her.

That was the tipoff. She didn't know whether to be furious or grateful; Jett had asked Spud to the office to see her. She wouldn't have consulted Spud on her own, but talking with him had made her feel better.

Even though he wasn't in the room, she lifted her tea glass in a silent toast to her boss . . . and friend.

At the end of the business day, Brenna changed into her favorite attire: jeans, a big shirt, and no shoes. She sat on the floor in one of Jett's bedrooms, Feather lying beside her, a squeak toy in the dog's mouth. A framed bulletin board was providing her with a sturdy and inexpensive base for her jigsaw puzzle, colorful tulips in front of a windmill. When she heard footsteps, she looked up. Simon Blue walked along the upstairs hall, going in and out of rooms, a sketch pad in his hands.

When he came into Brenna's room, Feather dropped the toy and barked once. Startled, Simon stopped.

"Sorry," he said. "I didn't know anyone was up here." He glanced at Feather and smiled at Brenna. "Jigsaw puzzle?"

"I started it when I was staying here, and I want to finish it."

"Isn't that a bit tedious?"

She shrugged. "It's one of the few occasions in life when you have all the pieces and can make them fit." She glanced at his sketches. "What are you doing?"

"Did you know, when this house was built, the entire upstairs was one big room?" He squatted in front of her and pointed to his sketch pad. "Over the years, the owners added walls, modernized here and there. Did you know, originally, there was a fireplace in every room downstairs and two up here?"

She smiled at his enthusiasm. "How do you know that?"

"The attic. The old flues are up there, and when this house was built, everybody used fireplaces for warmth." He grinned. "It doesn't hurt that Jett found the blueprints, either."

Feather held her rubber newspaper in her teeth, turned her head, and grasped the toy between her paws. Then she chewed it, the squeaks eee-eeking over their conversation.

"Why are you so interested in this house?" she asked.

"Not just this house, although it's structurally sound. I love all the old houses. They had big rooms—"

"And no closets. And no indoor bathrooms."

He grinned. "Newer houses do have advantages." He picked up a red piece of the puzzle and clicked it into its slot. "Why didn't you take the jigsaw home and finish it there?"

"I might lose a piece."

He laid his sketchbook aside and settled on the floor across from her. When he picked up another red piece, she playfully slapped his hand.

"If you're going to help, work on the sky. That's on your side." After a few minutes, she said, "If you like houses so much, why do you live in an apartment?"

"We had a house, before the divorce," he said. "Actually, I've bought a house in Shreveport. It's a rundown two-story in an old neighborhood; but they're revitalizing that entire area."

"Does it have all the charm and character of the Old South?"

"Not yet. It's what my mother would have called a 'Plain Jane' house. It was built because someone needed a place to live, but it has a good foundation and structure. When I get through with it, a buyer will think I've restored a mansion."

"You plan to fix it up and sell it?"

"Maybe. One day, that will be yuppie territory—or whatever they'll call the up-and-comers." He dropped the puzzle pieces in his hand and leaned toward her. "It's a big lot, so I can add a covered front porch and a screened garden room in the back. I'm going to replace the small windows and open up some of the rooms."

"What about stained glass?"

"That's an idea, if I can find the right piece. I found a hand-carved frame fireplace mantel at a salvage shop—you know, the kind of mantel that goes around three sides of the fireplace opening—and I found a woman who hand paints tiles. Her business is just getting started, but she does beautiful work. We have a deal that she'll paint for me at a discount and use the pictures in her portfolio."

"Do you like cutting deals?"

"Not on the job."

There was a silence while they worked on the puzzle. Finally Brenna looked up. "Have you learned anything else?"

"Not much. Like most killers, Gideon seems invisible when he isn't making his move. I suspect he's planning. So far, he's been very organized, and I don't expect that to change."

"Isn't there anything we can do?"

"Get out of this, Brenna. If Gideon contacts you again, let the Bureau handle it. Go on vacation, visit friends. Disappear for a while."

"Will that stop him?"

He watched her a moment. "Probably not."

She nodded, smiled, and wrapped her arms around her bent knees. "What's my second choice?"

He smiled. "Finish the puzzle."

CHAPTER

22

THE AUGUST HEAT spread into September and threatened to broil autumn's first weeks. Brenna had helped Connie with a freelance photo shoot after a morning presentation of Hug-A-Tree for a first-grade class. Then Brenna had visited with the emergency management liaison for the county. If the team wanted to keep working, they had to maintain friendly relations with their contacts.

When she returned to the office, she was carrying a gumball machine under her arm.

"Why are you dragging that in here?" Hatch asked.

"It ate my quarter." She set it next to Hatch's computer.

"Isn't that Mrs. Voranik's, from the cleaners?"

She nodded. "I told her you'd try to fix it. Do you mind?"

He laughed. "For you, anything. Besides, I like taking stuff apart and trying to put it together again." He started off and then turned back. "Oh. You got another e-mail from Gideon. About an hour ago." He handed her a hard copy of the note. "This one's short. Jett faxed a copy to Owen and Garrett."

Brenna read the note. *If I could find them, I'd send you forget-me-nots. I know she'll never forget me.*

She looked at Hatch. "Is this it?"

He nodded.

"Old Gideon is losing his touch. This almost borders on boring."

An hour later, the call came.

"An eight-year-old didn't come home from school," a deputy from Wills Point said. "The game warden gave us your number."

Connie slipped the initial callout form under Brenna's pen.

"Her name?" Brenna asked.

"Peter Willis, sandy hair—"

"Peter?"

"Yes," the officer said.

She glanced at Connie. "It's a boy this time."

"Wearing a red-and-blue-striped shirt, jeans, green-and-white tennis shoes. Last seen riding a silver bike."

Brenna took the rest of the information while Connie collected the dogs from the backyard and filled gallon jugs with water.

"Should I call Jett?" Hatch asked.

"Not until we know what we've got."

Too often, they arrived on scene and found different circumstances than those described to them in the initial callout.

Less than four minutes later, both women were dressed in search team uniforms. As team members called in, Hatch gave them preliminary information and directions.

Brenna and Connie dashed out past Hatch. Brenna said, "Tell Jett we'll call when we get there."

When they climbed into the Blazer, Connie said, "Thanks for letting Margarita and me hitch a ride."

"Flash never minds extra passengers." She backed out and opened the automatic gates.

"Flash?" Connie asked. "You named your car?"

"She's part of the family. Didn't you name yours?"

"No."

"Maybe that's why you're having so much car trouble." She drove out of the parking lot and turned left.

"Do you know where this place is?" Connie asked.

"I hoped you would."

Connie looked at the directions and then opened the county map. Feather hung her head over the back of the seat and tickled Brenna's ear. Margarita propped herself against the searchers' backpacks and thumped her tail.

"Old Stony Road," Connie said. "Wouldn't you know Marco would leave early?"

"Ahnya got promoted to nurse supervisor today. Her friends gave her a party."

"Hope it's over," Connie said.

"It is for Marco." She glanced at her friend. "Did Hatch call Gayle?"

Connie nodded. "She's catching a ride with Harley."

They crawled amid drive-time traffic until the highway stretched through a rural area. Brenna's heart always pounded a bit on her way to a search; this afternoon, it drummed.

If Gideon had taken this child, his pattern had changed. Unless boys had been part of Gideon's game all along, and they just hadn't found all the pieces yet. Maybe this boy had nothing to do with Gideon. They'd had searches before Gideon showed up; they'd have them after he was gone.

"Bren, you just ran a stop sign."

"I did?" She looked in the rearview mirror. "Was anybody coming?"

Connie laughed. "I don't think it matters at this point."

They drove forty-five minutes, taking the cops' shortcuts.

When they came to a railroad track, Brenna pulled to the side of the road. "Did he—"

"Yes, we've come too far."

She looked at Connie. "Did you see Old Stony Road?"

"No."

They turned around and drove all the way back to the convenience store at a four-way stop. More than a dozen cars filled the lot.

"Busy," Connie said.

"It's the only thing out here. Radio the others, tell them where we are." Brenna hurried inside.

Six people stood in line at the counter, the young male clerk talking on the phone instead of waiting on them. Each time he hung up, the phone rang again.

Brenna walked to the counter. "Excuse me, but—"

The young man held up his finger and answered the phone. Everyone groaned and shifted from one foot to the other.

"Excuse me, but I need—"

He spoke into the receiver. "Yes, ma'am, that video came in today. You're welcome." He hung up and turned to Brenna. "Ma'am, you'll have to stand in line."

"We're lost," she said. "Do you know—"

The phone rang. He held up his finger and reached for the receiver.

Brenna leaned over the counter and slammed her hand on top of the telephone. "Answer that call and you're dog food!"

He stepped back.

"We're looking for a missing child, and we're lost," she said. "Do you live around here? Do you know Old Stony Road?"

The young man shook his head.

"I do," a woman said. "It's back that direction. I think the sign's down, but it's a dirt road off to the right. There's a barbed-wire fence on one side and a pipe fence on the other. You can't miss it."

"Thank you." Brenna dashed outside. Marco's and Harley's cars were stopped behind hers. As she climbed into the Blazer, Patrick's Firebird came into view.

"We're all here," Connie said.

They sped along the highway, turned onto the dirt road the woman had described, and raced to the PLS—place last seen. Peter had been at a friend's house before he disappeared.

Farmland stretched to the left of the road, and a huge, deep pit cratered the land on the right. A backhoe, arm raised, stood frozen next to the chasm.

"What's that hole?" Connie asked.

"A quarry, I think. Looks like they're mining for sand and gravel."

"They're what?"

"Mining. They dig the rock out of the ground and haul it to a blending plant. That's where they separate it into gravel, rock, sand."

"I thought gravel was pebbles."

"With sand."

They crossed a bridge, and Brenna glanced at the river. She shivered. Then she saw a movement in the bushes ahead. She put on her flashers and slowed.

"What was Peter wearing?" she asked.

"Red-and-blue-striped shirt—"

"Found him."

For the first time in an hour, her heartbeat slowed to a normal rhythm.

Before she could open her door, Marco stopped at her window. She pointed; he smiled. Then he sauntered toward the boy.

"Are you Peter Willis?" he called.

The boy stopped, took a step back, and then nodded. He had bloody arms and torn jeans, but he was in one piece.

Connie radioed Hatch and told him to call the police and tell them where they were.

Marco squatted and spoke to the boy. After a few minutes of conversation, Marco and the boy headed toward the caravan. The rest of the team got out of their cars.

"Peter had a little problem," Marco said.

"My mom's gonna kill me," Peter said.

"What happened?" Brenna asked.

The boy shuffled his foot in the dirt. "I was riding the dirt hills around the quarry. Guess I slipped. I ended up in the gravel pit and I couldn't get out."

"It's not easy climbing gravel," Marco said. "Every time you take a step, it rolls out from under your feet."

"Don't I know it," Peter said.

"Where's your bike?" Marco asked.

"Still in the hole." He looked at Marco. "I couldn't get it out."

"Where?" Harley asked.

The boy pointed. "Over there."

"Well, I guess a search-and-rescue team can save a bike."

"It's a little bent."

"Fixable?" Harley asked.

"I dunno."

"Let's go see."

As the men and Gayle followed the boy, Brenna and Connie stayed with the cars until the police cruiser arrived. Then they picked their way to the quarry.

Peter stood beside his bent bicycle. Harley and Marco worked a rope, hauling Patrick up the side of the crater. Marco had been right; every time Patrick took a step, the gravel rolled out from under his feet, creating a small avalanche below. Pebbles and rocks binged and bounced down the side of the hole to the bottom.

"Boy . . ." Gayle looked at Brenna and Connie. "Do you usually have to search places like this?"

"Only if the police think somebody's buried in it," Connie said.

Gayle shook her head. "I thought rope work was just for high-angle stuff."

"It's the same principle," Connie said.

Patrick finally reached the top. He took off his hat and swiped his arm across his forehead. "Man, that's a hard climb. Can't get footholds." He patted Peter's shoulder. "You did a good job getting out of there."

"Jackie said a guy got crushed here last year," Peter said, excitedly. "The rocks fell and trapped him."

"And you came out here anyway?" Brenna asked.

Peter frowned. "You sound just like my mom."

The police officer picked up the bike. "Let's go, Peter. You can tell me all about this adventure while I drive you home." Then he turned to the team. "The game warden was right; you folks do work fast. Thanks for coming."

As they trekked back to the cars, Connie said, "We've got him fooled."

Brenna nodded. "I wish they were all this easy."

Some searches were easier than others; some defined the word *disaster*. Still, happy endings were so rare, she should enjoy this one. And to think, she'd suspected Gideon had taken another child. The forget-me-not note had birthed that suspicion.

This time, she was happy to be wrong.

CHAPTER 23

HALLOWEEN FOUND THE team at the mall again, finger-printing tiny witches and Frankenstein monsters. Brenna kept an eye on her pager, superstitiously fearing a repetition of the last finger-printing session. Each time her stomach twitched, she checked to see if her pager had accidentally slipped to "vibrate." To her relief, nothing eventful occurred.

As they were packing up at the end of the night, a man stopped behind her. "Need help?"

She turned. "Garrett! What are you doing here?"

"I'm staying with Jett for a few days."

"Why?" She leaned on a table. "More news on Gideon?"

He shook his head. "I've been suspended without pay for insubordination. Since I can't afford to keep my apartment, I'm mooching off Jett."

"The sheriff found out you were still working with Simon on the Gideon case?"

He nodded. "He told me to drop it, and I didn't. If he loses the election, I get my job back for the new sheriff. If he wins, I'm unemployed."

"Hi, Garrett." Simon Blue stopped and held out his hand. "When did you get in town?"

"A few minutes ago. Did you help fingerprint?"

"No, I came to pick up Connie."

Brenna turned her back to the men and filled a box with leftover booklets for parents. There weren't many left. Donny would have to order more before the next session.

Connie set a box of limp balloons next to Brenna. "Will you pack these for me? Simon's taking me dancing."

"You've been going out with him quite a bit."

"Not as much as Owen and Leah have been seeing each other," she said. "You're a pretty good matchmaker, Bren."

"Oh, right. That's why Ryan's never around."

"Isn't he due in tonight?" Connie asked. "Meet us later." She brightened. "We found this club where they play forties music and dance swing. Or sometimes twenties stuff, and we Charleston or tango. It's so much fun, you and Ryan should come."

Brenna shrugged. "Maybe. We're due for a big talk, and I'm not quite sure how it will turn out. Besides, Ryan can be a real flirt."

"So is Simon," Connie said, "but nothing happens—not with other women, not with me." She leaned closer. "In fact, nothing has happened so often, it's almost insulting. I know I'm twice twenty, but . . . jeez. You'd think I'd get a real kiss or something."

Brenna smiled. "What's a real kiss?"

"You know, one where lips actually touch. He'll kiss my hand or my cheek, but that's all."

While Connie got her purse, Simon leaned over the table toward Brenna.

"I took your advice," he said, "and I found a large stained-glass window with a rounded top. It'll be perfect for the breakfast room, and it's given me the idea to arch all the doorways."

"Where'd you find it?" Brenna asked.

"In the attic of an antique store in Texas," he said. "Some of the small panes are broken and the solder has to be repaired, but it'll be beautiful."

Connie joined Simon and slipped her arm through his.

"It even set the colors for the house," he said. "I wish you could see it."

"Send me a picture," Brenna said.

Simon patted Connie's hand and turned to Brenna. "Why don't you come with us tonight?"

Connie tensed. "She and Ryan have plans this evening."

"Can't you change them?" Simon asked.

Brenna glanced at Connie. "Not tonight. Maybe another time."

She watched as Connie and Simon left arm in arm.

"Need some help?" Garrett asked.

"Sure."

Back at the office, Brenna found a note from Jett instructing whoever was present to give Garrett a key to the workroom door.

While he unpacked, she rolled up a chair beside Hatch. "If I wanted to find the source of a quote, how would I go about it?"

"Isn't Simon's office working on that?" Hatch asked.

"I guess. He never tells us anything," she said.

"Have you tried a search engine?"

She nodded. "What are my other options?"

"You could post it on a bulletin board," Hatch said.

"Where?"

"That depends. Does it relate to science, or books, or–"

"I'm not sure. Is there a nonspecific area?"

"Sure, but you might not get what you want there." He watched her a moment. "What do you want to know?"

"Remember that phrase Gideon sent you to decode? 'And on the eighth day, the angels came.' " She rolled toward him. "I want to know where that came from, if anyone's ever seen it."

He looked at the computer screen and then at her. "You could sponsor a contest, offer a prize."

"A prize? Money, I guess."

"How much?" he asked.

"Ten dollars." When he shook his head, she said, "Fifty?"

"Not worth the trouble." He smiled at her. "I'll put up one hundred. The whole Gideon thing is my fault anyway."

"No, Hatch. You can't control him; no one can."

"But if I hadn't—"

"One hundred it is." She laid her hand on his shoulder. "Out of my pocket, if you'll help me post it." She turned his chair toward the computer. "How would I—we—go about this contest?"

"I could post it on bulletin and message boards, but you'd get hundreds of e-mails. Some people will make up anything to win cash." He rubbed his chin. "You could be real strict. Tell people you're looking for the one original source of this quote. The first one who guesses right, wins the money."

"That's a thought."

"How will we know when it's right?" Hatch asked.

"We'll check the work cited," she said.

"I guess we can ask Gideon, if we hear from him again."

When Garrett came downstairs, Brenna joined him at the poker table.

"You look like you could use a friend," she said.

"So do you." He rested his elbows on the table. "Aren't you supposed to meet Ryan?"

"He's stuck at the Chicago airport, so we talked on the telephone."

"Not good news?"

She shook her head. "Since he's out of town so often, he wants to cancel the lease on his apartment, move all his stuff into my place, and just stay with me when he's in the area. Can you believe it?"

"You don't want to do that?"

"No, that's a step I'm not ready to take," she said. "He thinks I'm totally unreasonable, and I think he's being cheap and wormy."

Garrett laughed. "Wormy?"

"He's already asked to live together, and I've already said no. I think he sees this as a way to wriggle into my life on a more permanent basis." She glanced at Garrett. "He makes three times as much as I do; let him keep his own place or rent a storage room."

"Sounds like you're not committed to this relationship."

"I'm not," she said. "In the beginning, I thought it had possibilities, but after a while, the friendship deepens or it becomes habit. We hit habit." She shrugged. "It's time we both moved on." Garrett's expression made her smile. "Want something to eat?"

"Whatcha got?"

She went into the kitchen, hoping Leah had made a stop this afternoon, and opened the refrigerator. "Cold cuts, fried chicken, and . . . spaghetti."

"Chicken?"

"It's safe," she said. "I didn't cook it."

He smiled. "It wouldn't matter if you had. I haven't had much appetite lately."

"This will tease your hunger. Leah made potato salad and baked beans, too."

After they shared dinner, she propped her elbow on the table. "No news from Yvonne?"

"Not much. It kills me not to see Reggie every day. I can't understand why she did this."

"She's mad at you. Taking Reggie is her way of getting even."

He looked into her eyes. "What did I do?"

"I don't know, Garrett. Yvonne is the only one who can answer that question."

She told him about her plan to post a contest.

"If it works," he said, "I'll split the hundred with you."

Brenna leaned back. "Odd: a man we don't know has taken over our lives. Every time we get a search call, I wonder if he's grabbed someone again. Even old people. We got a callout for a missing nursing home resident, and I immediately wondered if Gideon had switched to snatching old folks. I think he's in the back of my mind twenty-four hours a day."

Garrett nodded. "I'm obsessed with this guy, too."

"How thick is his folder now?"

"Two folders."

She pulled a yellow pad in front of her and picked up a pen. "Jett's filled me in on each new piece of information you sent him, but would you summarize for me? It's gotten so complicated, I feel like I've lost all sense of it."

" 'Summarize'? That'll be a good trick." He cleared his throat. "Gideon said his score was five, plus one for you, one for her. We've found four child abductions that match in every detail. St. Louis, Richmond, New Orleans, and Denver. Last week, a report from Boston arrived. Two years ago last July, a little girl disappeared. Construction paper note, twenty-four-hour clock notation, message. Everything the same, but they found Katya sitting on a park bench. He hadn't touched her."

"Did she tell the police anything?"

"Not much—she was only four, and they had to work through an interpreter besides. A professor and his wife had adopted her from Russia, and she'd only been in the country a few weeks. All they got was that the kidnapper was a big man with dark hair."

"What was the message on her note?"

" 'A lesson well learned.' "

"Did you say the father was a professor?"

Garrett nodded. "The police checked students past and current, everything." He left the room and returned with two folders. After digging in the thinner one, he slipped two pieces of paper in front of her. "I've made notes of the messages, and when and where the girls were taken. See if I've missed something."

Jen-Jen Abbott. Stolen from front yard. Oct. '93. Denver. 16:39

Found: bound in stolen car; carbon monoxide poisoning (exhaust hose fed into vehicle)

Message: You reap what you sow.

Jenny Shotke. Stolen from her bedroom. Feb. '94. New Orleans. 23:51

Found: bound in vacant apt; carbon monoxide poisoning due to defective kerosene heater

Message: Live with this.

She looked up. "What did Jenny's father do?"

"Owned real estate, a landlord."

"I suppose they checked unhappy tenants."

"First thing," he said.

"What about Jen-Jen's dad?"

"Died from a drug overdose when she was two. Keep reading."

Megan McCauley. Stolen from her backyard. Sept. '96. Richmond. 10:12

Found: inside garage; cause of death, smoke inhalation due to fire

Message: All's fair in love and war.

"Megan's parents?" she asked.

"Divorced. Mother remarried, to a postal carrier. The father's a private eye, specializes in background checks. The police already had an open investigation on him. They suspect he accepted large bribes to change facts on clients' credit and criminal reports."

"Well, plenty of folks could be mad at him for changing information, or not changing it." She looked at the page. "Have the police charged him with anything?"

"Not yet. The biggest problem is that he doesn't connect, in any way, to the other parents."

"Do any of the parents or kids connect to each other?"

"Not that anybody's found."

She read the next entry.

Katya York. Stolen from backyard. July '98. Boston. 15:32

Found: park bench, unharmed

Message: A lesson well learned.

Amy Guinn. Stolen from bedroom. Sept. '98. St. Louis. 14:20

Found: in a box in a drainage ditch; drowned when the city opened spillway to lower reservoir

Message: Et tu, Darla?

She stopped reading. She knew Zoe and Leanne's stories by heart.

"Boy, he really has leapfrogged all over the country," she said.

Leapfrog. Why had she used that word, because Simon had used it?

She considered the penciled dates on the chart.

"This thing started eight years ago."

Garrett nodded. "I'm beginning to wonder if it will ever end." Neither of them said anything for a moment. "There are four commonalities in the girls' deaths," Garrett went on. "They all asphyxiated; no weapon was used; the juice he left them was loaded with Restoril; and none was sexually assaulted."

"So he doesn't appear to be a pedophile." She glanced at him. "Why did he take them?"

"If 'best served cold' is a clue, revenge. I wish we knew what these parents had done."

"Why the Restoril?" she asked.

He leaned back. "The lab reports stated all the girls were dead, or at least heavily sedated, before the gas, fire . . . whatever."

"It looks like he didn't want them to be scared."

"Except Leanne," Garrett said. "She didn't drink the juice, so—"

"She was awake when she drowned."

Brenna looked at the chart again. Gas, exhaust, drowning, smoke.

"Where were these girls found?" she asked.

"It says—"

"No, I mean—in the middle of a city, on a farm, in a park near home? And how far from the place of abduction, or the place where they found the construction paper note? Distance."

"I don't remember that being in the CASKU reports. Is it important?"

"I don't know. The construction paper note for Leanne wasn't with her bicycle, it was in the stolen car."

"But Gideon put her in the woods to test the dogs."

"Probably, but as a searcher, I'd like to know where he left the others. So far, his pattern hasn't changed, except for Katya. Maybe there's a pattern here, too."

Garrett looked toward the workroom. "Is there an open computer in there?"

"Take your choice."

Within two days, Garrett had the information Brenna had requested. When the Monday morning phone rush slowed, she browsed through the report.

Jen-Jen Abbott had disappeared from the playhouse in her backyard and was found in a stolen maroon Cutlass parked under a rural bridge 7.8 miles from the note.

Jenny Shotke was found in a vacant apartment, inside a cedar chest in which someone had drilled twenty-four holes. The apartment was in a condemned building, .8 mile from her bedroom.

Megan McCauley, stuffed into a car trunk, was found after a garage exactly 8 miles from her backyard burned to the ground. Her body had been protected from the fire, but the holes drilled in the trunk allowed the smoke to claim her life.

Katya York's family received two notes. The typed one, like the one taped to Leanne's bicycle, had been taped to their back door. It directed them to the construction paper note, which was nailed to a tree beside a convenience store eight blocks away. But Katya was found unharmed in a park twenty-six blocks from the store.

Amy Guinn drowned, trapped in a homemade crate like Leanne's, in a rural area 6.8 miles from her bedroom.

Zoe would have died in a fire, lying in a crate in a smokehouse, 4.8 miles from her bedroom. Leanne was found 3.8 miles from the maroon van.

Brenna left her desk and found Garrett in the workroom. "They were all double-sacked," she said.

"What?"

She rolled a chair next to his. "Inside the car parked under the bridge, inside crates in a garage or in the water, a trunk inside an apartment."

He nodded. "But there's no consistency in final destination. If you count Zoe and Leanne, three were found in the city, four in rural areas. No obvious pattern."

"Did you think about the distance?"

"Couldn't come up with anything specific. The farthest was eight miles; the closet was eight-tenths of a mile."

"The number eight keeps popping up." She leaned back and slowly turned the chair side to side. "Is Simon still your FBI contact?" Garrett nodded. "Has he added any information lately?"

Garrett logged off and turned to face her. "The FBI is very active when someone is missing. Kidnapping, abduction, whatever. But once the person is found, the race slows down. They don't stop working, but more immediate problems come to the top." He tipped his coffee cup before he realized it was empty. "It's the same way in our department . . . my former department. When you've done all you can do, it's time to move on and try to help someone else. But, for some of us, those open cases hover like storm clouds."

"Thank goodness," she said.

"Nothing we've done really helps. We could have blood type, hair fragments, handwriting analysis, profiles, even fingerprints—but if this guy doesn't have some kind of record, then without his real name or a photograph we're looking for the invisible man."

"I suppose you or somebody checked every person named Gideon everywhere."

He nodded. "That's not his real name. He chose it because it symbolizes something to him. I looked it up; 'Gideon' means warrior, destroyer, maimer. The judge."

"That's what he said in his e-mail," she said. "Speaking of e-mail, did anyone trace those notes?"

"I've heard nothing about tracing e-mail from Simon," Garrett said, "but my computer whiz friend in Seattle said if Gideon was using a dial-up service, the authorities could trace him to the city, but not necessarily to an exact address. There are too many gateways he could use. Unfortunately, we didn't have tracing equipment available when you've instant messaged him."

"Could you have found him then?"

"I don't know. Maybe. Right now, we don't have many answers."

She smiled. "In the search business, we rarely have all the answers. Sometimes we'll get summaries of final reports so we'll know why someone ran or where a person was eventually found if we didn't find him. But sometimes we don't hear anything." She touched Garrett's arm. "It's like you said, we do what we can and then move on."

"Easy to say," he said, "but you can't do it."

"What does that mean?"

He grinned. "Do you know what Jett says about you? Your greatest asset is your worst fault: you care too much."

She laughed. "He's teasing you, String Bean. Ever notice whenever Jett can't do something, he blames me or says I can't do it? I can walk away from unanswered questions much easier than he can."

"He also says you're stubborn and entirely too independent." He stood. "And he couldn't run this place without you."

"Are those your words or his?"

"Both." He refilled his coffee mug and sat beside her again. "Have you and Jett ever . . ." He tilted his hand from side to side. ". . . well, *dated*?"

"No, we have not."

"Why? I can picture you two together."

"That's because you see us together all the time."

He shook his head. "More than that. I see the way he looks at you."

"You're imagining things," she said. "When I first came to work for Jett, we made a pact, of sorts. His wife suspected hanky-panky, so we set out to prove that a man and a woman could be good friends without sexual . . . interaction. Look at us; you and I are friends and there's nothing sparking between us."

"But Jett isn't married now."

"No, he isn't, but if we started dating and it didn't work out, I'd have to quit this job. Right now, this is the perfect place for me; I can bring Feather to work and go on searches without penalty." She shook her head. "I'd never find another job with the perks I have here."

"Bren, we have a hit," Hatch said. He turned toward them and then stopped. "Oh, did I interrupt something?"

"What kind of hit?" She rose and moved behind him.

"E-mail on that quote. Some guy named John in Mississippi says he saw it on an underpass near the college in Jackson."

She turned to Garrett. "Should we call Owen?"

"Immediately," he said. "I'm unofficial these days."

After she made the phone call, they waited at the table. Brenna tapped her feet and hoped this lead would turn up something. Anything. When she looked at Garrett, he was smiling.

"What?"

"You're humming again," he said. " 'Moonlight Bay.' What were you thinking?"

"I'm trying not to think at all."

When Hatch told her she had a telephone call, she glanced at Garrett. "Boy, Owen was quick."

But the caller was a woman—her real estate agent. "Guess what? The people who own the cottage can't wait any longer and they want to know if you're still interested."

"You're kidding."

"They've already moved, and they're ready to unload it."

Brenna didn't know what to say. A few months ago, she had been dreaming of that cottage as a home for her and the dogs, but so much had changed since then. Privately, she'd debated leaving her job and the team, even though she'd just defended her position to Garrett. No matter what Spud had said or how she'd tried to rationalize the situation, she felt she was losing her edge.

"Do you want to make an offer?" the agent asked.

"Let me think about it," Brenna said. "I'll let you know."

She returned to the table and sat beside Garrett.

"Problem?" he asked.

Leaning back in her chair, she sighed. "Not anymore." She poked at Garrett's folders. "Have you or anyone talked with the girls' parents lately?"

"Not that I know of; why?"

"We have more information now."

"I don't know if CASKU does that," Garrett said, "but I'd be willing. It'd give me something to do instead of missing my daughter." He started shuffling papers. "If nothing else, I'll ask the officers who worked the abductions to give it another shot."

Each minute felt like an hour until Owen telephoned. The quote had indeed been spray-painted on an underpass wall in Jackson, but the investigating officer said the blue paint looked fresh. John, or someone, probably wanted the contest prize money.

"Well," Garrett said, "we knew it was a long shot."

"Get ready," Hatch said. "We might get a hundred cranks before we find the source of that quote."

"If there *is* a source," she said. "Maybe Gideon made it up."

HATCH SAT IN front of Emily on Saturday morning, studying the fifty-second e-mail entry to the contest. Owen occupied the corner workstation, where they had removed the computer and plugged in an extra phone line. Folders and papers lay in heaps around him.

"Anything?" Owen asked.

"Not yet," Hatch said. "This is the umpteenth time someone has said the quote came from the Bible, but no one can cite chapter and verse." He scrolled through the next four entries.

"There has to be something we're missing," Owen said. "If we could just get a name or a picture. A name." He turned to Hatch, watched him a moment, and then noticed his own empty coffee cup. "You want something from the kitchen?"

"No, thanks."

A few minutes later, he heard the patio doors open and Leah's happy voice in the break room. "Hello, everybody!"

"Hello there, young lady," Owen said. "What are you doing here?"

"I brought apricot cobbler."

"You're spoiling me," Owen said.

Hatch smiled. Owen had been splitting his evenings and weekends between Leah and Gideon. He had complained his job kept him from committing the time he thought the case deserved, so Jett had offered him a workstation next to Hatch's.

"I came by to keep you and Hatch company and answer the telephone," Leah said. "Since Mike's on vacation, I get to work an entire shift." She moved behind Hatch and patted his shoulder. "And how's my favorite computer genius?"

Hatch laughed. "Fine." He glanced up at her. "Can I have some of that cobbler?"

"Only if you beat me to the kitchen," Owen said.

Leah had seemed so happy lately, Hatch thought. At least one good thing had happened because of Gideon. If only he hadn't answered that e-mail from him the first day Gideon had written. Why had he continued to exchange e-mail? Why had he let Gideon think he'd been writing to Brenna?

He opened the next entry, number 59, and logged the screen name, Calliope.

I don't know if this is right, but I've seen that exact phrase on a tombstone near my father's grave in Rose Hill Cemetery. Detroit. Is that what you're looking for? Why would you want to know about a tombstone?

A tombstone. That might fit. He added Calliope to his buddy list to see if she was on-line, but the name didn't appear. As he typed a response to her note asking for a location of the grave, he hollered for Owen.

The man limped into the room and stopped behind him. "This looks good. Let's get the cemetery's phone number, and we'll see if they keep a record of tombstones."

"What can I do?" Leah asked.

"Hand me the telephone," he said. "I'll call the Detroit PD."

Hatch talked to the cemetery's business office. They didn't keep records of epitaphs, but the manager gave Hatch the name and number of the tombstone engravers they used if a family member purchased a headstone from them. She didn't give him much hope; without a name, the company probably wouldn't be able to help him.

Meanwhile, Owen convinced a Detroit detective to send someone to the cemetery to look for the inscription. The detective promised to contact him the instant he found a name.

Owen grabbed the telephone when it rang. Detroit.

"Did you find it?" he asked.

"Yes," the detective said. "It's engraved on a headstone for an Alexandra Renee Merrick. Four years old. Died ten years ago. Nov. 1991."

Owen made notes. "What about the parents?"

"I don't know."

He drew tight circles on the notepad. "Who was responsible for the burial?"

"The cemetery billed an Ellen Hanson. Her address is listed as Detroit, but she's moved since then, and we haven't found out where yet. We'll keep looking."

"Give me her old address." Owen hung up and turned toward Hatch and Leah. "We may have found our Lexie. Alexandra."

"We have to tell Jett and Brenna," Hatch said.

"Not yet." He tried to sound calm. "This could have nothing to do with Gideon. It's a possible lead, that's all."

Hatch's fingers twitched and his foot bounced.

"Keep reading the e-mails," Owen said. "You may find something else."

Hatch stared at him instead of turning back to Emily.

"On the other hand," Owen said, "we might do a little research. If I wanted to find somebody but I didn't know where she lived, could I do it?"

"Do you have an old address?" Hatch asked.

Owen held up the paper. "Right here."

"This shouldn't take long." A few minutes later, Hatch leaned back in his chair. "I tracked her to Denver. After that, she's blank. No utilities in her name, no action with her social security number. No death certificate. Nothing."

"Keep trying," Owen said. "We have to find her."

Three hours passed before the fax machine rang and hummed in Marco's office. Owen had started toward the break room when his phone rang. Asking Leah to get the fax, he picked up the receiver.

"A former neighbor of Ellen Hanson's gave me a lead," the detective from Detroit said. "I've tracked her to Denver and then Lake Tahoe, but there's no answer at the number we have for her. I also found a tiny mention of that child's death in the newspaper files. You should be getting the fax about now." Leah brought the Fax, and Owen scanned it. "Leah, see if you can find the number for the police department in Lake Tahoe."

Then he turned to Hatch. "We need to find a birth certificate for this child. Start calling county vital statistics offices. Begin with Detroit. Lexie died there."

Lexie. He'd used her name as if he knew her, as if she were a personal friend.

"Owen," Hatch said, "it's Saturday. Those offices are closed."

He stared at Hatch. Saturday. This one new lead had gotten his adrenaline pumping, and he hated sitting instead of following up on every possibility.

"Owen," Hatch said, "we wouldn't have to wait until Monday if the Vital Statistics systems are connected to the Internet. I could . . ." He shrugged. "Of course, hacking could be considered–"

Owen brightened. "You might not want to tell me how you do it, but . . . see if you can find something."

Officer Tara George was parked, watching for someone to come home to the white frame house across the street. The inspector who'd telephoned from Sacramento seemed desperate to talk to Mrs. Hanson.

When a blue station wagon pulled into the driveway, Tara jumped out of her squad car and approached the woman.

"Mrs. Hanson?"

The fiftyish woman stopped and squinted at her.

"Are you Mrs. Hanson?" Tara asked.

"Do I know you?"

"No, ma'am. I'm looking for Ellen Hanson. Do you know where I might find her?"

"Ellen is my niece," the woman said, "named after me. I'm Ellen Young."

"Is Mrs. Hanson here?"

"Oh, no. Ellen's been institutionalized for the past six years."

CHAPTER 25

THE DOOR TO the workroom opened and the crew strolled in, all in their baseball uniforms with "Culpepper Investigations" printed on the front. Owen had hoped to have more information by the time they returned.

"Who won?" Hatch asked.

Seven dogs trotted inside behind their owners, all wagging their tails at Hatch and Owen but not stopping until they reached the dispatcher's desk. Leah gave each a pat and a Milk Bone.

Connie opened the door to one of the storage rooms and piled the bats and gloves into their boxes. "I'm glad this was our last game," she said.

"We lost?" Hatch asked.

"It's my fault." Brenna stopped behind Hatch. "If you want to do something for me, take my place on the team next year."

"Please," Marco said.

"I told you I can't hit the ball," Brenna said. "I've told you all season I can't hit the stupid ball, and you make me play anyway."

"You're a great catcher," Jett said.

Laughing, Gayle said, "Every time she came up to bat, the whole outfield moved in so close, I could see their freckles."

"Psychological warfare," Brenna said.

"It worked."

"At least my dog didn't slip her leash and race onto the field to chase a grounder," Brenna said.

"She's just a puppy." Gayle clapped her hands and Visa bounded to her. "And anyway, she *is* a retriever."

When the telephone rang, Owen grabbed it and barked "What?"

"Tara George here," a woman said. "Lake Tahoe police."

"Yes, yes. Did you find her?"

"Not exactly," Tara said. "Ellen Hanson had a breakdown after her daughter, Jen-Jen, was abducted and murdered in October of 'ninety-three in Denver."

Jen-Jen. Wasn't that one of the girls on the list?

"She'd recently married Mike Abbott," Tara said, "and—"

"Abbott!" Owen said. "Jen-Jen Abbott." He grabbed Garrett's chart. "Go on, Officer George."

"She and her new husband were expecting their first child, but after Jen-Jen died, they divorced and Ellen moved to Lake Tahoe to live with her aunt. When she broke down, her husband took custody of the baby."

"Did you talk to her?" Owen asked.

"No, her aunt says she's completely withdrawn; she doesn't communicate at all."

"What about Lexie?" Owen asked.

"Ellen Abbott's niece," Tara said. "Mrs. Young—that's Ellen Abbott's aunt—told me the whole story."

Owen slid his notepad in front of him.

"Patricia Hanson, Ellen Hanson Abbott's sister, married a man named Merrick while he was still in the service, stationed in Virginia. They had a child, Alexandra, and later moved to Chicago. But Patricia left him and moved into a trailer in Detroit that her sister owned, while she saved money for a divorce.

"Ellen had moved into a house and had planned to sell the trailer."

"I see," Owen said. "Go on."

"Eight days later, while Patricia sat in a car with her new boyfriend, the trailer caught fire, and the little girl died. Patricia collapsed, so Ellen Abbott made the arrangements for the child's funeral. Eight months later, Patricia committed suicide."

"What about Alexandra's father?"

"Mrs. Young said she thinks he must be dead. He didn't go to the funeral, and no one has seen or heard from him since."

"Who had the tombstone inscribed?"

"She supposed Ellen Abbott did, but she isn't sure."

"What else did she know about Merrick? Does she know his first name or middle initial—anything?"

"She doesn't know, sir. Said she'd never met him, and she and Patricia weren't close. When Ellen Abbott moved to Lake Tahoe, most of her mind was gone."

Owen thanked her and asked for her pager number in case he needed to speak with her again. Then he studied his notes. Eight days and then the fire . . . eight months and then the suicide. A bit too coincidental. Eight hours to find a child.

If Officer George's information was right, Lexie and Jen-Jen were cousins. Lexie had suffocated in a fire; Jen-Jen had been killed by carbon monoxide poisoning. The note connected to Jen-Jen's abduction stated, "You reap what you sow."

Could Merrick have blamed Patricia's sister Ellen for Lexie's death? Her trailer had been his daughter's death chamber.

But how were all these other children connected to Merrick? Surely, they weren't random choices.

Was Lexie's father alive?

"Owen?" Brenna said. "What is it?"

"We might have a lead on Gideon," he said.

The noise stopped; everyone stood statue still.

"How?" Jett asked.

"Good old-fashioned legwork," Owen said.

Brenna moved first.

"What did you find out? Tell us!"

By the time Owen finished repeating what he'd discovered, everyone had crowded around him. Brenna wasn't sure whether to hug him or burst into tears. Now, it seemed, they were on to something.

"Our phantom has a name. Merrick," Garrett said.

"Maybe." Owen held his hand up. Can't get too excited just yet. A last name only gives us a start."

"Call Simon," Jett said. "This is right up VICAP's alley. Those FBI analysts will have information and a profile on Merrick in no time."

"CASKU will probably take this one." Garrett looked at Owen. "Where are your notes?"

Owen handed the papers to Garrett, looking, Brenna thought, like a five-year-old who'd expected to get a pony for Christmas and found a tricycle under the tree instead.

"Great job, Owen," Brenna said, draping her arm over his shoulder and giving him a gentle hug.

"Anybody hungry?" Leah asked. "If someone will watch the telephone, I'll make meatball sandwiches."

"I'll play dispatcher," Gayle said.

Everyone but Owen and Hatch followed Leah into the break room. Brenna motioned for Jett to meet her in his office.

"What?" Jett asked.

"I know we have to send this information to the FBI," she said, "but does that mean we have to rest on our laurels and let them handle everything?"

He sat on the corner of his desk. "What's on your mind?"

"Can't Owen and Hatch keep working on their own?"

"Why? The FBI has more resources than we do. Besides, it's their job."

"Do these analysts work during the weekend?" she asked.

"I don't know."

"How fast will somebody research this new information?"

"I don't know."

She closed the door. "I think Owen and Hatch need to feel that they're doing something."

"They did. Without them, we wouldn't have a possible name."

"So now you expect them to stop in their tracks and hand everything off to someone else?" She leaned against the door. "Just this little bit of information makes me want to dash in there and help them dig for more, and you and Garrett dismissed them like they were diggers who'd just finished a big ditch."

He removed the lid from the humidor on his desk and pulled out a cigar. "What do you want, Irish?"

"First of all, I want to know what's wrong with you. You've been preoccupied all day, and that grounder went right past you."

"You got it."

"But you didn't. What's on your mind?"

He sighed and lit his cigar. "Joanne and I had dinner last night. Every time an attractive woman passed, she asked whether that was one of my girlfriends. She's so jealous," he said, "I can't stand to be around her."

"Well, one night doesn't—"

"It isn't only one night," he said. "We've been getting together two or three times a week, just to see how we feel about . . . things. Her jealousy's getting worse, not better."

"Is there anything I can do?"

He puffed his cigar, staring into space, and then he looked at her. "You're right about Owen and Hatch. If the FBI people trip over us, they can get up and brush themselves off."

She went into the workroom and found Owen winding the cord from the telephone at his station.

He smiled at her. "Things can get back to normal now."

"Plug in your phone," she said. "You get to keep your workstation for a while."

"Why?" Owen asked. "The FBI is in charge."

Hatch stopped typing and turned toward her.

"That doesn't mean you have to stop looking . . . unless you're ready to hand off this whole thing."

Owen glanced at Hatch and then smiled at Brenna. "There is one more thing I'd like to try."

* * *

Owen had telephoned the officers who'd worked the abduction cases, in hopes they could interview the parents one more time. Two had been available. One of the officers had already called back; the other was still in the field.

Owen sat beside the telephone, Hatch and Brenna beside him. Every time the computer voice announced Hatch had mail, he checked it, but nothing came in about the quote or Gideon.

"It may be a false start," Owen said. "Jenny Shotke's parents didn't recognize the name 'Merrick.' "

"But Mr. Shotke said he didn't know who his tenants had been," Hatch said. "He's been out of the business more than five years. His apartment manager might have recognized the name."

"But the manager's dead." Brenna turned to Owen. "Isn't that a little too convenient?"

"He died seven years ago," Owen said. "Sometimes people die; it doesn't mean there's a conspiracy."

Hatch leaned back in his chair. "Do you believe that?"

"I don't know what to believe right now." Owen stared at the telephone.

It *was* suspicious that Zoe's parents, the Hendrickses, had sneaked out of town. If only they'd had the name "Merrick" before the family disappeared.

The telephone rang and Owen snatched it to his ear. Professor York.

"I hear from the police that you need to talk to me," the professor said.

"Yes, sir. Does the name "Merrick" mean anything to you? A man you might have known years ago."

"What's his first name?"

"We don't know, sir. We hoped you could tell us."

"Merrick . . ." York paused. "I've been teaching for over twenty-five years. Unless you can give me something more specific, I don't know how I can help you."

Owen glanced at Hatch and Brenna. They were staring at him so intensely, he could feel the hope radiating from them.

"Professor, does the name 'Lexie' jog your memory?"

"Lexie Merrick. The officer said you were looking for a man."

"We are, but Lexie might—"

"Lexie. Of course," the professor said. "Allen Merrick. Now I remember. He was my teaching assistant at Chicago. Lexie was his daughter. She died . . . in a fire, I think."

Owen tried to keep his voice calm. "What did you teach?"

"Computer science."

Owen wrote "Allen" on his pad and showed it to Hatch and Brenna.

"I remember that poor young man," Professor York said. "He tried so hard to climb out of the gutter. He'd started a new life, had a family, and earned a scholarship to work on his master's. But after his daughter died, I never saw him again."

"And you're sure his first name was Allen?"

"His middle name. His first name was Ivan, but he never used it."

THE ANALYSTS AT the FBI provided information and promising links much faster than Brenna had anticipated. Simon had arrived in time for dinner, the reports tucked under his arm. But no one ate the casserole Leah had prepared. Instead, Garrett, Simon, and Jett joined Brenna and Owen at the table, passing around papers and trying to make sense of Gideon's targets.

Owen handed everyone an enlarged photograph.

"Is this Merrick?" Brenna asked.

The picture must have come from a driver's license. It showed a man with a receding hairline and brown hair, a mole in front of his left ear. And gray eyes. Dull gray eyes. The creases on his face made him look older than she'd expected.

"Looks like a mug shot," Garrett said.

"Have you ever seen a driver's license photo that didn't?" Jett asked.

"Let's start at the beginning," Simon said.

"Or what we think is the beginning." Owen looked at Brenna. "Ivan Allen Merrick. His initials spell, I AM. He answered you truthfully that day on the computer. We just didn't understand him."

She scanned the information for the third time and then looked up at Owen. "You know, in an odd way, Gideon's . . . Merrick's hit list . . ." She glanced around. "Do you mind if I keep calling him Gideon? The name Merrick doesn't feel right."

No one cared.

"Gideon's hit list almost makes sense," she said.

"For a wacko," Garrett said.

Jett glanced at Garrett. "You've been around Irish too much. You're starting to talk like her."

Simon took the lead, explaining everything the analysts had uncovered.

Ivan Allen Merrick met Patricia Hanson in Virginia, while he was in the military. After they married, he finished college and they had a daughter, Alexandra. Lexie. Then they moved into an apartment building owned by William Shotke in Chicago, and Merrick became Professor York's teaching assistant at the university.

While working on his master's degree in computer science, Merrick created a computer game. Darla Guinn, one of the students in Professor York's class, learned of the game, helped Merrick test it, and then suggested that her boyfriend, Miles Chaney, and his friend Tom Hendricks might be able to help Merrick perfect it. Unfortunately, Chaney and Hendricks had gambling debts and weren't interested in helping Merrick. They stole a copy of the almost perfected game and sold it to Progressive Software, owned by Ross and Kathryn Weston. When Merrick realized what had happened, he approached the software company. But the Westons had bought the game in good faith; they denied Merrick's claim.

Merrick used his family's savings and borrowed money to hire an attorney to sue the company. He lost. Darla Guinn refused to testify and implicate her boyfriend Chaney. When the manager of the apartment building evicted the Merricks, Patricia left Allen and took their daughter to Detroit. Her sister, Ellen, had just moved out of her trailer into a house in preparation for her marriage to Mike Abbott. Patricia and Lexie moved into the trailer. Eight days later, while Patricia sat in a car with her new boyfriend, the trailer caught fire, and Lexie died. Merrick disappeared.

"That's quite a story," Brenna said.

"I visited with Professor York on the telephone again this morning," Owen said. "He knew about the game, but he never saw it. He'd let Merrick keep his notes in the file cabinet, and one morning they found his office ransacked. The cabinet had been pried open; Merrick's notes, as well as many of Professor York's papers, had been burned. Their computer had been stolen, and the only remaining copy of the game was on a computer in the tech lab." Owen shook his head. "Apparently, Professor York indirectly blamed Merrick for the robbery and admonished him for trusting people he didn't know well."

Garrett laid his copy of the report on the table. "Progressive Software made big bucks off that game."

"That must have made Gideon so angry," Brenna said. "Can you imagine how it must have felt to watch your dreams come true for the people you believed robbed you?"

"But the software company didn't commit a crime," Simon said.

"Irish, are you beginning to see this guy as a victim?"

She could understand Gideon's anger, but she couldn't accept his vengeance. "Of course not."

"Then explain how you think Gideon's targets make sense," Jett said.

"Miles Chaney and Tom Hendricks stole the program and sold it," she said. "Zoe was taken, and Gideon's note to the Hendrickses said, 'Don't bet what you can't afford to lose.' According to the report, Chaney didn't have a child."

"I get it," Garrett said. "Kathryn and Ross Weston owned Progressive Software, but their children were grown, so—"

"Gideon took their granddaughter, Jennifer," Brenna said. "That note stated, 'Now it's your problem.'" She looked at Garrett. "I don't understand that one."

"It must have meant something to Gideon," Owen said.

"Megan McCauley's dad worked for Progressive," Simon said. "This report says he's credited with perfecting Gideon's game."

"How would Gideon know that?" she asked.

"Sometimes the software creator's name is on the box," Simon said.

"His note stated, 'All's fair in love and war,' " Garrett said.

"Darla Guinn wouldn't testify for him so she lost her daughter, Amy."

Owen shuffled papers. "*Et tu*, Darla." He sighed. "Well, she did betray him, for Miles Chaney."

"William Shotke owned the apartment building," Simon said.

Garrett looked at his notes. "That note stated, 'Live with this.' " He looked at Brenna. "No wonder Shotke didn't understand it. Unless you know the whole story, it doesn't make sense."

"If Gideon's family hadn't been evicted," Brenna said, "Patricia wouldn't have taken Lexie to Ellen's trailer."

"Ellen's daughter was an obvious payback," Jett said.

"Obvious now," Garrett said.

Jett read the note left after Jen-Jen's abduction. " 'You reap what you sow.' " He leaned back in his chair. "A child for a child."

"But that's his motivation," she said. "A child for a child. He lost Lexie, and he's taking children from the people he believes contributed to Lexie's death."

"Then why didn't he kill Katya York?" Owen asked. "Gideon took her, but he let her go."

"What did her note say?" Simon asked.

Brenna read, " 'A lesson well learned.' "

"Know what else I find interesting?" Simon said. "He sets the girls up to die, but he doesn't kill them directly. Serial killers usually get their kicks from the kill."

Serial killer. Brenna hadn't attached that tag to Gideon until Simon said it.

Garrett nodded. "That's what we found with Zoe. She would have been all right until the candles burned down and set the charcoal and stuffing on fire."

"This might have been easier to connect if the girls had been taken closer together," Simon said. "These abductions are spread out over eight-plus years."

"Is that normal?" Brenna asked. "I mean, you see movies and read newspaper articles about serial killers, but those guys aren't portrayed with the kind of patience Gideon has shown."

"He's atypical, definitely," Simon said. "That's one of the reasons he's been so hard to identify. In fact, serial killer might not be the right term for him; his victims aren't random."

"Well . . ." Owen removed his glasses and laid them on the table. "That's five. Brenna saved Zoe, and he let Katya go. If he's telling the truth in his e-mails, he's targeted one more child."

"Whose?" Brenna asked.

No one had an answer.

"Who's left?" Owen looked at Simon. "Did one of those analysts have an idea?"

Simon nodded and held up two pages of names.

"You're kidding," she said. "How do those names connect to the scenario we have?"

"When you're reaching for straws," Simon said, "you must consider everything. Our scenario might be wrong."

"It makes sense," she said.

"To us," Jett said. "Gideon may see things differently."

She pointed to the list. "Is somebody trying to locate all those people?"

"We do have one lead," Garrett said. "Denise."

"Of course," she said. "How many of those families have a daughter named Denise?"

"You can't count on that name being a clue," Jett said. "If Gideon thinks we're getting close, he'll lie to throw us off track."

"You can't discount it, either," she said. "It might be the truth."

Sunset came, but the air felt hot and sticky. Brenna turned Feather loose in Jett's backyard; instead of playing, the dog trotted to the kennel runs and nosed a new yellow Labrador Retriever named Jazz, whom Marco had acquired that afternoon. The dogs sniffed each other, wagged their tails, and assumed play positions.

Back inside, Brenna passed Jett's office and heard him talking on the telephone.

"We agreed—" He paused, as if he'd been interrupted. "Dammit, Joanne, you've upset her with your spiteful games." He paused again. "I said I would, but you can't expect me to turn my life upside down on one of your whims. I won't do that to Paige, and I won't do it to my employees. They depend on me and this business for—"

Brenna started humming "Cuddle Up a Little Closer" to block out his conversation while she dug through her desk for Sparks's telephone number in Santa Fe. Her friend had fallen for an Australian named Kevin, and they were spending a few days visiting the art and antique shops there. With the number tucked into her pocket, she tiptoed past Jett's office and joined Simon on the patio.

He pointed to the kennel. "Is that Garrett's dog?"

Garrett knelt beside the run, one hand on Feather, the other pressed against the chain link. Then he stood, went into the building, and came out inside the run with the dog.

"Marco got Jazz today," she said. "His daughter Martine adopted Sophia, the pup he was training for search work, so he's been looking for a replacement." She watched Garrett sit on the ground and play with the dog. "I think he'll have to keep looking."

"Isn't that dog too big to be a puppy?" Simon asked.

"She's about eight months old," she said. "Marco's neighbor got the dog as a companion, but Jazz is one of those hyper Labs that needs something to do. When the woman decided to find Jazz a good home, she called Marco."

"Will she be a search dog?"

"I don't know. Labs are good drug dogs, too."

Feather loped to Brenna, nuzzled her owner, and looked at Simon. Instead of soliciting a pat from him, she snorted and lay in front of Brenna's feet.

"How's your house coming?" she asked.

He moved papers, uncovered his sketch pad, and pointed to a floor plan. "This is my idea for the upstairs. Change this bedroom into a bath with a large walk-in closet. Then enlarge the present bathroom between these two bedrooms and build closets across the inside wall." He wrinkled his forehead. "The house has a full attic, so it wouldn't be difficult to open the largest bedroom to two levels. Have stairs and a loft area in the master suite. A study. Might even put a fireplace up there." He looked at her. "What do you think?"

"Bedroom fireplaces can be romantic, but I'm not crazy about them. Hauling wood up and ashes down can be a pain."

"Not if you have one of those new electric ones," Jett said.

She hadn't heard him come outside. As he sat across from Simon, she asked, "Everything okay?"

"No," Jett said. "It's a long way from okay." He watched Garrett playing with Jazz. "I suspect Marco's lost another dog."

"What kind of people are on the 'Gideon's Next Victim' list?" Brenna asked Simon.

"Creditors, mostly," Simon said. "People in the neighborhood who had contact with him. Pawnbrokers, bankers."

"Bankers?" she asked.

"He applied for a loan and didn't get it," Simon said.

"There are other places to get loans."

"Yes," Simon said, "and they all turned him down. We have a list of everyone who filed for his credit report."

"What about illegal businesses?" she asked.

"Loan sharks?" Simon asked. "They aren't likely to tell us if someone ran off with their money."

"Who else is there?"

Simon turned the list facedown and smiled at her. "Who would you expect to be on the list?"

"Think back." Jett had a cat-that-ate-the-canary look on his face.

"What do you know that I don't?" she asked.

"Think," Jett said.

Think back? How far back?

"Parents sometimes loan money to children," she said.

"His and hers, both gone before Lexie died," Simon said.

She leaned over and scratched Feather's ears.

Gideon and Patricia married, he finished school and his military tour, moved to Chicago, started his master's degree. The boys stole his program and sold it. They went to court—

"Attorneys!" she said. "His attorney took all his money and lost the case." She leaned back. "I might have gone after him first."

"He didn't have a strong case," Simon said.

"Did anything happen to that guy's family?" she asked.

"Not yet," Simon said.

"Does he—"

"No daughter named Denise," Simon said. "He has a twelve-year-old son and the three girls are teenagers."

"What about the software company's attorney?" Jett asked.

"E. D. Williams," Simon said.

"Ed?" she asked.

"We aren't sure if it's Ed or E. D.," Simon said. "The old contracts are signed with a capital 'E' and a small 'd.' "

"Has he disappeared?" Jett asked.

"Not the way you mean," Simon said. "He quit the company soon after the suit and moved to Ohio. They just started running the names on the list this afternoon. We'll find him."

Jett shifted in his chair. "Are they focusing on the attorneys?"

"Not necessarily," Simon said. "Even if we had all this information at the beginning, there's no way of predicting whom Gideon might target next."

"There is," Jett said. "People with daughters in that age group."

"If he keeps to his pattern," Simon said.

Brenna looked at the papers lying facedown. "What do you say to the people on that list? 'Excuse us, but we thought you'd like to know there's a wacko out there that may be stalking your child.' " She shook her head. "I think he's after another female who betrayed him."

"Who?" Jett asked.

"I don't know," she said, "but Gideon's last note, about the forget-me-nots, said something about a woman not forgetting him. It can't be the child; he kills her. It has to be the mother."

Simon looked at her as if she were someone else. "What would you do if you married me?"

She stared at him a moment. "Huh?"

"If you married me," Simon stood, "or Jett or Garrett, how would you write your name?"

"Brenna Scott Whoever," she said.

"What if E. D. Williams is a woman?" Simon asked. "She could have gotten her law degree under her maiden name and later married."

"Wouldn't there be a record of that?" she asked.

"Not if she married outside the United States," Jett said.

"Interesting." Simon scanned the papers. "How many women are on this list?"

THE NEXT MORNING, at twelve minutes after eleven, the "You've got mail" voice announced Gideon's next message.

> B:
> *I wish things had been different. We would have made a good match, you and I.*
> *Ready for another game? I'll play fare this time. You have four hours to be notified and arrive before the countdown begins. Be prepared to lose. I always win.*
>
> GIDEON

Brenna stared at the computer screen, stunned.

"Brenna . . ." Hatch said something but she didn't understand him.

Four hours to be notified and arrive. Four hours.

Someone touched her shoulder. "Bren . . . he's on-line. Look."

Job Won was on the buddy list.

Maybe, if she refused to participate in the game, he'd leave the next little girl alone.

She hit the instant-message button and typed, "No, I won't play. You're on your own."

Minutes passed before he answered.

Yes, you will. It won't be fun without you.

"Then don't play. I'm through."

She logged off and shut down the computer.

"Brenna . . ." Hatch stood behind her, panting. "W-what are you doing?"

"Playing poker," she said. "Everybody stay off the computers," she yelled. "Hatch, tell Jett and Marco, then close off all phone lines but the main number. Disengage call waiting, plug in Caller ID Box, and turn on the tape machine."

"Brenna, we can't—"

"Do it," she said.

Seconds later, Jett, Marco, and Connie stood beside her. Garrett's heavy footsteps thudded on the stairs.

"I've got to call Owen," Jett said.

"Cell phones!" she said. "Turn them off, everybody." She looked at Jett. "You, too."

"He can't call me if I'm talking on it."

"Yes, he can," Hatch said. "He can leave a voice mail message."

"He could," Jett said, "but I don't think he will. He wants to talk to Brenna."

Connie rummaged through her purse, found her own cell phone, and beeped the Off button. "Why am I turning off my phone?"

"We can't take the chance he'll call on a phone without Caller ID," Brenna said.

"He could have everybody's number," Garrett said. "Gideon believes in being prepared."

"But he hasn't telephoned here before," Hatch said.

Jett covered the receiver. "He didn't have to. Irish talked to him over the computer. It kept him safe."

"What if he blocks the number he's calling from?" Connie asked.

Marco smiled. "Hatch won't answer it. If Gideon wants his message to get through, he'll have to risk our getting his phone number."

"Stand by with the area codes booklet," Brenna said.

"What makes you think he's out of the area?" Hatch asked.

"His note," Garrett said. "The only word he misspelled was 'fair.' He spelled it f-a-r-e, as in paying a fare to travel."

"One of the last notes mentioned meeting at noon," Jett said. "We're guessing he meant somewhere in the middle of the country."

They all pulled chairs in a semicircle around the dispatch desk and stared at the telephone. Each time it rang, they jumped, but all of the callers were employees making their usual hourly check-ins.

"Bren, what possessed you to take this kind of chance?" Connie asked.

"If Gideon wants to play hardball," she said, "he'll have to play my game this time." She glanced at Garrett. "This may be our last chance to get evidence."

"Evidence?" Connie asked.

"If this works," Garrett said, "we'll have his voice on tape."

"Does that voice pattern stuff really work?" Connie asked.

Everyone looked at Garrett.

"It's helped in the past," he said.

"Is taping his voice legal?" Hatch asked.

"Taping a call coming into my business is legal," Jett said. "Of course, we're supposed to tell him we're recording the conversation. When Owen gets here, he can determine if it might be usable in court."

"If we get anything," Garrett said.

"Okay, everybody," Connie said, "cross your fingers."

When Jett pulled up a chair next to Brenna's, she asked, "Is Owen coming?"

"On his way."

"What about Simon?" Connie asked.

"He's gone again," Jett said. "Shreveport, I think."

The telephone rang again; the message "unavailable" appeared on the Caller ID box.

Jett looked at Hatch and shook his head. "Don't answer."

The ringer sounded thirteen times before the phone fell silent.

Brenna glanced at Jett. "What do you think?"

"We'll see."

Three minutes later, the same message appeared on the box. This time, they counted twenty-two rings.

"My, my, my," Garrett said. "I'd bet he's getting a little testy about now."

"What if he doesn't call back?" Hatch asked.

"We're no worse off than before," Jett said. "As it stands, we have to wait for someone to contact us. If an agency telephones, the number will show on the box; they wouldn't block it."

"Do you think Gideon knows we're not answering because he's blocking the number?" Connie asked.

"I bet he'll figure it out," Garrett said. "He's not stupid. And if he does call, we'll have his voice and an area code. If we're right, and he likes to watch the searches, he'll still be in the area where he's hidden the child."

They all stared at the telephone again.

When Connie coughed, Brenna jumped.

Twelve minutes later, the telephone rang and a phone number appeared in area code 972. Hatch pushed record on the tape machine and watched Brenna.

"If it's him," Garrett said, "try to get him to give his name."

"Why?" Connie asked.

"Just one more connection to the e-mails," Garrett said.

Brenna took a deep breath, picked up the receiver, and hit the button for speakerphone. Her hand shook.

"Culpepper Investigations," she said.

It was Gideon, in a rage. "You can't cut me off!" he yelled. "You can't refuse to play, it's my game, my rules, and you can't change them."

"I beg your pardon, sir," she said, calmly, "I believe you have the wrong number."

"I don't and you know it, you come, you play, or I'll kill her now, do you hear me, now!"

She looked at Garrett.

"I'm sorry, sir," she said, "I don't know what you mean. How may I direct your call?"

He remained silent a few moments, but she could hear him breathing.

"Oh, Brenna Brenna Brenna . . ."

"Yes, this is Brenna. Have we met?"

"Have we . . ." He laughed. "Trace all you want; you'll never find me."

"To whom am I speaking?"

He laughed again. "I'm like Job, the director of your destiny."

Job? Not job, like go to a job every day. Job! From the Bible. The most patient man in history.

"And your name, sir?"

"Gideon," he said. "Call me Gideon."

"Yes!" Garrett whispered.

"Oh, my dear Brenna," he said, calmly, "you've learned the game well. I'll be waiting for you."

"I meant what I said. I won't play this time."

"Yes, you—"

"No, the agency in charge wherever you've stashed her may not call me, and even if I did know where you are, I will not respond to a search uninvited. No matter what you say or what you do, there are some people you cannot control."

"You'll come, or Denise dies before the eight-hour countdown begins. Don't try to fool me, I'll know if you board that plane. I'll know." He hung up.

"How will he know?" Connie asked.

Brenna looked at Hatch.

"Dallas," he said.

"Aren't you going to trace him?" Connie asked. "Can't you telephone Dallas and have them find that number or something?"

"We'll tell them," Garrett said. "But he'll be long gone before they could find the location."

"He had to know we were doing something to try to find him," Hatch protested. "Why would he give his name and mention Denise? Wouldn't that be damning evidence?"

Jett nodded. "If it ever goes to court. Somebody has to catch him first."

Catch him, Brenna thought. What if no one ever caught him? What if Gideon had lied and this wasn't the last one? What if it was the last, and they never had another chance?

"At least we have a starting point." Brenna turned to Garrett. "If you fax everything to Dallas, maybe they can get a jump on him."

"What are you going to do if the Dallas police call?" Connie asked.

"I don't know."

As Brenna walked into the kitchen, she heard Jett behind her.

"Irish . . ." He tugged her arm. "I understand your wanting to go, but you can't control what Gideon does. Stay or go, his plan is already in motion."

"We may be worrying about nothing. The police might not call us."

"And if they do?" he asked.

She didn't know what to say.

"Let the FBI take this one," he said.

They stood in the kitchen, looking at each other for several minutes. She didn't need to hear his words to know what was on his mind, and she suspected he didn't need to hear hers.

"Brenna . . ." Hatch stuck his head in. "Do you know someone named John T. Remig?"

"From McEntyre County?"

He nodded.

"Oh, my gosh." Her heart sank. McEntyre County, Texas.

Gideon was bringing her home. She ran to the telephone and grabbed the receiver. "John T.?"

"Brenna-Honey," the familiar voice said.

She smiled. John T. always attached "Honey" to her name, as if it were hyphenated.

"What the hell is going on?" he asked.

She had to be sure. "What do you mean?"

"We found a note with your name on it," he said, "about someone named Denise."

"My name?"

"A small, typewritten note glued in one corner," he said. " 'If you want to find Denise, send for Brenna Scott in Sacramento.' It has your phone number."

So, it was true. Gideon had stashed Denise in John T.'s territory.

Covering the mouthpiece, she nodded at Jett and said, "McEntyre County."

"Where?" Garrett said. "I thought the area code matched Dallas."

"Brenna learned to train dogs with Aaron in Windsor, Texas," Jett said. "McEntyre County. It's a little north of Dallas and Fort Worth and almost halfway between them. John T. Remig is the sheriff there."

While she gave Remig a brief synopsis of the situation, Garrett ran to Marco's office and started faxing everything pertinent to the sheriff's office; someone at John T.'s office faxed their information to Jett. Gideon had added one other twist to Denise's note, a message to John T.: "She's somewhere in McEntyre County."

"Good Lord, Brenna-Honey," John T. said, "we may be one of the smallest counties in the state, but that means searching dumpsters, construction sites–"

"I know," she said.

"In eight hours?" John T. said. "We can't do it."

Eight hours.

"What time is on the construction paper note?" she asked.

He paused. "Seventeen-twelve."

She calculated in her head. Subtract twelve hours: 5:12. She looked at her watch: 11:43.

"What time is it there?" she asked.

"Almost one-forty-five."

"The countdown doesn't start until five-twelve your time. You've got three extra hours."

"That doesn't help much," he said. "How many dogs can you bring?"

She covered the mouthpiece and looked into Jett's moss green eyes. "I have to go," she whispered.

He studied her a moment and skimmed his thumb across her chin. "I know."

Speaking into the receiver, she said, "One, John T. Feather and I can be on a plane within the hour."

Marco tapped her shoulder. "Put him on hold for a minute."

"Why?"

"Just do it." When she laid the receiver down, he said, "You and Feather, alone? I'm part of this team."

"This isn't a team callout," she said. "Gideon wants *me* there."

"Then he wants us," Marco said.

Marco had a family; she didn't. All the team members had children or parents or siblings who needed them. Gideon had rigged arrows for the dogs last time. What might he do now?

The team would go with her, if for no other reason than loyalty. But this wasn't their problem; Gideon had made it hers. More than that, theirs was a volunteer team. No one got paid; searching wasn't anyone's livelihood, anyone's job.

"No matter your reason," she said, "I'll feel responsible if you go and something happens."

In his soft but authoritative voice, Marco said, "Tell me you wouldn't come with me if this situation were reversed."

"That's different, I don't have—"

"Yes, it is different," Marco said, "but we knew this day would come. I've already discussed it with Ahnya, and the decision's been made. Harley and Patrick are going, too," he said. "So is Gayle. We discussed this weeks ago, and we decided that if and when this call came, we'd all be ready."

"Count me in," Connie said. "I've talked to my sister and taken care of business"—she threw her arm over Brenna's shoulders—"not that I'm ready to cash in my chips. But you know what else? It's time we gave old Gideon a run for his money."

"You're not leaving me here," Garrett said. "I started this investigation and I'm going to finish it."

She wanted to argue. She wanted to hug them.

"You know I'm going," Jett said, "but we do have one problem. Adam took the plane to Hartford; we don't have wings."

"Why did he do that?" Connie snapped.

"It's his plane," Jett said. "He's closing a merger, and although he flies us when he can, he isn't on call."

"Oh, well, if you want to get technical," Connie said.

Marco nodded toward the telephone. "Get back on the line with your sheriff and tell him we're bringing five dogs."

She picked up the telephone. "John T.? Correction, we've got five dogs ready to go."

"I've got three," John T. said.

"Only three dogs?" Brenna asked. "What—"

"Can you get us more reinforcements?" John T. asked. "Only dogs and handlers you know. No strangers."

"I'll try, but transportation—"

"We'll call Scott Air Force Base and get a federal I.D. number," John T. said. "They'll arrange transport if they can. See who you can line up and get back to me. Twenty minutes?"

"I'll do my best." She hung up and leaned on the desk.

"What else is bothering you?" Marco asked.

"We've never been involved in criminal chase searches," Brenna said. "We don't carry weapons, we're not trained to confront—"

"We're not searching for a criminal," Connie said. "We—"

Marco stood straight. "Maybe we should. Brenna and Connie both found Leanne, but they were following different trails. Maybe some of us should use the scent pads Brenna made from Gideon's footprints and have the dogs look for Gideon's trail."

"It might give us a break," Garrett said.

"Can I go?" Hatch asked.

"No," Jett said.

Hatch wilted.

"We need you here," Brenna said.

"Owen will want to be kept informed," Jett said. "I'm depending on you to hold down the fort while we're gone. You're in charge."

Hatch brightened. "Hey-hey, I'm boss for a day."

Brenna motioned to Connie and turned to Hatch. "Come on, boss; we've got calls to make."

They ran to the kennel room and jerked open the storage cabinets.

"Who are we looking for?" Connie asked.

"Dogs and handlers that Aaron or I trained," Brenna said. "They're spread out all over the country."

Hatch rifled through files and called out names; Brenna said yes or no, depending on the pair's skills and whether the handlers were connected to law enforcement. Her team might not be trained to handle felons, but most of their reinforcements would be.

The dogs knew something special was happening. Feather and Margarita followed them into the kennel, dancing in anticipation. Feather barked and paced around Brenna's legs; Margarita slobbered on Connie, her tail wagging.

"Feather, down."

The dog looked at Brenna and barked.

"Okay," she said. "Don't."

Each time Brenna said yes, Hatch yanked the folder and handed it to one of the women, who had both kennel phone lines and their own cell phones engaged at the same time. When the trio raced back to the office, nine handlers had agreed to stand by with their dogs for final callout.

Jett, receiver braced between his shoulder and ear, was sitting at Hatch's computer station; he beckoned to Brenna. They traded papers as he handed her the telephone.

"Phillips," he whispered.

"Who?"

"The computer company's attorney; E. D. Williams Phillips."

Dammit. They'd been so close. If they'd just had more time. A little more time.

On screen was a child's picture. Denise Phillips was African American.

"How many?" John T. asked.

"Fourteen, total," she said, "counting Denby in Dallas. You should hear from him any minute." Jett vacated the chair and Brenna sat on it. "I've got messages out to more, but I don't know when I'll hear from them."

"We'll take what we can get," he said. "See you soon."

She couldn't help but wonder if soon would be soon enough for Denise.

C H A P T E R

28

McCLELLAN AIR FORCE BASE gave the team special permission to park near an airstrip. Jett went to talk with the base commander, a Colonel Steiner, while the others unloaded their gear.

Brenna put Feather on leash and led her to a patch of grass.

"Hurry up," she said, Feather's command to relieve herself.

The dog's ears drooped, and she gave Brenna a look of disgust. Apparently, she didn't feel the urge.

"Hurry up," she repeated. "We don't have the option of stopping if the spirit moves you later."

Feather snorted and then squatted; a few drops trickled onto the grass. She scraped her back feet against the grass and kicked her rear legs out: finished.

"Good girl." They jogged back to the Blazer.

While Brenna loaded up her fanny pack and search vest pockets, Feather lay next to the backpack. She cocked her head this way and that. Her tail wagged. *R-r-r-rrrr.*

"I know." Brenna dug into a gallon-size plastic bag, pulled out a handful of kibble, and placed it in front of the dog. "This will have to hold you until later."

Instead of scarfing the food as usual, Feather nosed it. *R-r-r-rrrr.*

"I just gave you water."

This time, Feather barked.

"What?" Brenna stopped and looked at Feather. "If you could talk, you'd drive me crazy."

R-r-r-rrrr.

She leaned forward and held the hairy black head between her hands. "We're going to Texas, to look for a little girl named Denise. It's still hot there, even in November, and you'll find all kinds of new smells and a few new friends. But we've got to find this little girl before we do anything else." She kissed the dog's nose. "No fooling around, toots. This is serious, and we've got to work fast."

Feather barked and wagged her tail. Then she looked over Brenna's shoulder and stood.

Brenna turned.

"Excuse me, ma'am," a young man in uniform said. "Are you Brenna Scott?"

She nodded.

"Colonel Steiner said don't unload your cars. You're taking them."

"What?"

He pointed to the huge green plane on the runway. "In the C-141. As soon as they open the gate and lower the ramp, you can drive into the plane."

"All of them?"

"Colonel Steiner said four, ma'am. With the center row of seats out, they'll fit."

Brenna had worked through Scott Air Force Base, the headquarters for Inland Search and Rescue, among other things. Even though the base was in Illinois, they coordinated transport for emergency situations all over the country once the requesting agency received a federal I.D. number. She'd hitched rides on all kinds of Air Force helicopters and planes, but never one this large. Well, it made sense to take the cars if the plane was large enough. Getting personnel to the site of an emergency had priority; getting them home afterward didn't. Once, she and Aaron had been stranded in Missouri for three days after a search was suspended. At least now, they'd be able to drive home.

The group gathered at the Suburban's tailgate. Marco had bought topographical maps of the area they'd be searching.

"It shouldn't be too bad," Harley said. "I heard this part of Texas is flat."

"You heard wrong," she said. "It's not the Rocky Mountains, but it's hilly in places. There are bluffs, ravines, high ground, low ground, and an occasional cave, but most of those are farther south. Be prepared for thick vegetation, fire ants, mosquitoes the size of Rhode Island, all kinds of snakes, and some of the best people you'll ever meet."

"Sounds like a regular run to me," Connie said.

Gayle looked toward the plane. "Are you sure that thing can fly?"

"The Air Force has bigger planes than that." Donny smiled at her. When Gayle told him she was participating in this search, he asked if he could tag along as flanker, both to keep an eye on his honey and to help the team.

"Boy," Gayle said, "my first out-of-state search." She glanced at Brenna. "I wish Visa were mission ready."

"She will be," Brenna said. "Now, John T. said they've had a lot of rain, so it'll be humid."

Marco pointed to the map and they discussed possibilities, but they were only guessing. John T. Remig was in charge of this search, and by the time the team arrived, work would be well under way.

Jett jogged toward them and waved his hand in circles, indicating the plane was ready. Garrett climbed into the Blazer with Brenna; Marco and Patrick loaded Chelsa and Dorsey into his car; Gayle rode with Connie; and Harley shifted Brooklyn and his gear into the car with Donny and Jett. Then a young soldier drove Harley's car away.

One by one, the SUVs backed up the C-141's ramp, and the team members prepared for takeoff. They unloaded the dogs and placed each beside its owner on the bench-type seats that lined the aircraft. They unwrapped tampons and worked them gently into the dogs' ears to protect their sensitive hearing. Then they stuck earplugs into their own ears and fastened the orange straps around their waists, the Air Force version of seat belts.

The navigator poked his head out of the cockpit and smiled. He looked so young, and so did the pilots. Not one line on any of those faces. Brenna shook her head and thought, as she always did on military flights, that their lives were in the hands of children.

Then the engine roared, and the beast whined and shivered as it came to life.

Jett sat beside Brenna and wrote her a note on his clipboard. The Air Force would deliver the two dogs and handlers from Colorado; Alabama had wheedled a ride from American Airlines. Jett had reached Adam, who'd pick up Virginia, Kentucky, and Tennessee. Arkansas had his own transportation. John T. would have escorts waiting at NAS Fort Worth Joint Reserve Base.

Where? she wrote.

West Fort Worth. Used to be Carswell when it was a SAC base.

She didn't know they'd changed the name. At least she knew where it was. If they could avoid drive-time traffic, it shouldn't take too long to get to the search site.

As the plane tilted and rose, everyone held onto the dogs and then glanced at their watches. Nine different people with the same thought.

When the plane leveled and one of the pilots signaled they could move around if necessary, Jett weaved to the Suburban, removed the magnetic navy-and-white "Search Dogs" signs from the cargo area, and smoothed them onto the cars. Then he pitched jackets to everyone. At their flying altitude, it could get cold before they arrived at their destination.

Garrett pulled Gideon's files from a briefcase and handed several to Donny. Connie and Gayle dealt cards for a game of gin rummy, and Patrick played his harmonica, even though no one could hear it. Marco turned sideways, stretched out, and pulled his cap over his eyes. Brenna did the same.

Feather wiggled between Brenna's legs, making her owner shift one foot to the floor, and rested her head on Brenna's thigh. The dog sighed contentedly.

Brenna loved Windsor, McEntyre's seat and one of the two towns in that small county. In the 1800s, the entire county had been a ranch owned by the McEntyre family. Windsor, built where the main ranch house had once stood, still bore Mrs. McEntyre's influence. Enamored of British architecture, the matriarch insisted that Windsor's houses resemble English cottages or include Tudor or Georgian details.

A bedroom community within reasonable driving distance of Dallas and Fort Worth, Windsor had two unique qualities: no apartment complexes within the city limits, and no malls. In this community of 25,000, no one seemed to mind.

In the center of the town square stood a huge gazebo like the one in the movie version of *The Music Man*. Bands played there on some Sunday afternoons while listeners sat on park benches or admired the colorful flowers. The courthouse and municipal offices filled the entire north end of the square; specialty shops decorated the other three sides.

Brenna had wanted to see Windsor and John T. again, but not like this. No wonder Gideon had said she'd come. And he'd picked particularly difficult terrain for this search. The maroon pickup with his construction paper note had been standing in a no-parking slot off the town square. John T.'s crew would have to check every Dumpster, construction site, drainage ditch, sewer pipe, abandoned or condemned building, and toolshed . . . even every backyard that showed signs of recent digging. All that would take countless hours, hundreds of people, and a meticulously coordinated command post. Scouring unimproved county property might be a shade quicker, but John T. would need people to organize and oversee that segment who knew what to look for. To make matters worse, night would fall within an hour of their landing at Fort Worth. Darkness didn't affect the dogs as it did people; they'd work tirelessly until the job was over, their noses and ears unhampered. Most volunteer ground searchers, however, would be stumbling along.

She smiled. John T. Remig had his own way of doing things, but if anyone could manage this search with the slightest hope of a happy ending, he could.

Evangeline and Henry Phillips rode in the back of a Dallas police car, holding each other's trembling hands. A grocery sack filled with every shoe Denise had worn more than once sat in Eva's lap. She couldn't believe all this was happening.

Their housekeeper, Marie, had picked up Denise from half-day kindergarten as usual and prepared lunch for her. Then she'd cleaned the kitchen and started the laundry. Denise had been in their fenced backyard, playing on the swings one minute. The next minute she was gone. How could this have happened? Who would take their daughter from her own backyard?

Here in Texas, they'd become members of the symphony league; Henry joined the chamber of commerce; she'd taken a position with a loan company because she loved the job. They'd bought a beautiful house; for once, they could buy luxuries without looking at the price tag first. Their pastor was a wonderful man, and Evangeline loved singing in the choir. Their son, Darren, excelled in school, and Denise had made a dozen new friends.

Now, their daughter had been stolen. The police suggested they wait at home, in case the kidnapper tried to contact them, but after Detective Claudia O'Neil explained who might have taken Denise and why, Eva couldn't wait at home. Marie would wait by their home telephone. Eva had to be where they'd found the truck and the note, had to be as close as possible to her daughter.

As they drove along the highway toward a town she'd never heard of, they found themselves in heavy traffic. In fact, the officer driving the cruiser stopped behind a long line of cars. Then she heard a deep-pitched siren wail one long tone somewhere in the distance.

"What is that?"

Claudia said, "It's John T.'s version of the Amber Alert."

The Amber Alert. Several years earlier, a nine-year-old girl named Amber had been yanked off her bicycle and then found near a creek with her throat cut. The Dallas–Fort Worth metroplex later set up a warning system to alert the entire area when a child had been abducted. Television and radio stations interrupted their programming to broadcast all the information available—the time and place of the kidnapping, a description of the child, and, if possible, details of the getaway car and culprit. Eva had never dreamed for one fleeting moment that the alert might one day be sounded for her daughter.

The officer driving the car swerved onto the grassy median and passed the parked traffic. Half a mile north, they saw a roadblock.

Claudia motioned toward the police cars and sawhorse barriers. "This is part of the alert," she said. "Windsor's a small community, and it rallies like an extended family. When the sheriff here, Remig's his name, found out Denise might be hidden in his county, he put up roadblocks. No one leaves until your daughter is found."

"Can he do that?" Mr. Phillips asked.

"He's doing it," Claudia said.

Eva looked at the line of cars. "These cars are going into Windsor. Why have they been stopped?"

"If someone doesn't live in Windsor, he's asked to take a detour back to the main highway," Claudia said. "It doesn't sound believable, but when there's a big search, some people come just to sit on their cars and watch."

Henry squeezed Eva's hand. "What was that siren?"

"His callout," Claudia said. "Sheriff Remig works closely with the emergency management coordinator for this county. They have mock disaster drills every summer, with everyone who wants to participate. That siren was first call; team leaders are running to the courthouse right now."

"I don't understand," Henry said.

"Don't worry. John T. Remig knows what he's doing."

Eva gripped Henry's hand tighter. *Don't worry.* Such easy words to say when your daughter wasn't the missing child.

BRENNA GLANCED AT her watch. Less than an hour before they'd land. She looked toward the cooler in Jett's car, but the thought of drinking anything made her queasy.

She stood and made her way to the Blazer. Before she crawled into the back with Feather, she glanced at the tinted window. Jett was watching her, and for a moment, they stared at each other in the reflection.

She turned away and lay next to Feather. The dog snuggled against her and then rolled onto her back so Brenna could scratch her stomach.

Running her fingers through the black coat, she smiled. Feather was such a good girl—when she wasn't nosing open cabinets or digging holes in the yard. Well, no dog was perfect. Neither were people.

Brenna had tried to catch a nap, but she'd forgotten her Walkman. Leaving the radio on at night blocked her nightmares and had become a habit.

Feather sat and began one of her dog/person conversations. Brenna couldn't hear her, but she watched the dog's head go side to side and her beard wiggle with each r-r-r-rrrr.

She stretched out and pulled Feather close. This day had felt like a lifetime, and it was just beginning. Gideon said he'd play fair this time. Dare she believe him? She was reminded of victims who believed their assailants when they said, "Do what I tell you, and no one will get hurt." The assailants always lied. Still, if it was the only chance, one had to take it.

That was how she felt now. She didn't trust Gideon, but the hope that he might play fair this time burned inside her.

Eva and Henry Phillips followed Claudia up the steps to the stone courthouse. The siren wailed three long blasts. They covered their ears, and Eva watched as shop doors opened and people hastily place "Closed" signs in their windows and dashed toward the gazebo in the center of the park. People came from all directions, gathering near posters held high by deputies. They were obviously street names: "Tudor Lane," "Cottage Row." Inside the gazebo, a cluster of people wearing orange vests ripped open stacks of boxes.

Eva grasped Henry's arm. "Look! How wonderful of everyone."

A short man with more salt than pepper in his hair rushed past, arguing with a balding man.

"Sheriff Remig," Claudia called.

Salt-and-Pepper turned toward her.

"These are Eva and Henry Phillips," Claudia said.

"Don't lose hope," he told them, shaking hands. "Are those the shoes?"

She nodded and handed him the bag.

"Thanks." He glanced at Claudia. "Ask for McClain; he's got a room all set up."

He and the other man resumed their argument as they jogged toward the gazebo.

Eva and Henry followed Claudia inside the courthouse to the wing that housed the sheriff's department, met Captain McClain, and followed him into a conference room. A blond man and a woman, both in dark suits, stood as the couple entered.

"Mr. and Mrs. Phillips," the man said, "I'm Agent Carlisle and this is Agent Ashford. FBI." Then he pointed to Simon, in muddy boots and jeans, sitting in the corner. "This is Agent Blue."

Eva sat down and grasped the edge of the table to keep her hands from trembling. "Is there news of Denise?"

"No, ma'am," Agent Carlisle said.

Agent Blue came over to them. "Did you ever know, or know of, a man named Ivan Allen Merrick?" he asked.

"Does this man have my daughter?" Henry asked.

"We think so," Blue said. "Did you live in Chicago?"

"Yes, I was a stockbroker there before we married," Henry said.

"Mrs. Phillips," Blue said, "you were the attorney for Progressive Software, weren't you?"

"Yes, I . . ." Eva stopped. "Merrick." She stared at Blue. "He sued the company. I remember now. After Mr. Weston died, his wife took over and she bought a software program, a game, from a couple of college boys. It still had a few glitches. Then this man, Merrick, sued Weston. He said the boys had stolen his program."

"Tell us what you remember about him," Claudia put in.

Eva thought a moment. "The entire situation was so sad. Merrick begged Mrs. Weston to be fair, let him prove he'd created the game by programming it on one of her computers. She refused and told him his difficulties were not her problem. As far as she was concerned, she'd bought the program in good faith and he didn't have a claim." She looked at Claudia and then Blue. "I believed him, and I tried to tell him he'd lose in court." She shook her head. "He lost everything. I heard his wife left him and moved away."

"Why would he take our daughter?" Henry asked. "That was years ago, and Eva quit that job right after the lawsuit."

Blue handed her a picture. "Is this the man?"

She put on her glasses and studied the picture. Her hand shook. "Oh, he looks so much older than I remember." She glanced at Blue. "Why did he take Denise?"

"We have a theory," Blue said, "but until we catch him, we'll never know the truth."

John T. Remig stood in the gazebo, people buzzing around him. He'd thought twice about the mock disaster drill last summer, but David Ballentine, the county's emergency management coordinator, had insisted. He and David had been friends since grade school, and he remembered not one conversation with him that didn't include an argument, but when David was right, he was right.

Every off-duty deputy and firefighter had been called in, including volunteer law-enforcement personnel from neighboring counties. Team leaders had their assignments; the head of supply stood ready to distribute Cyalume lights to color-coordinate the ground search teams. Communication lines and small-scale maps of the streets, roads, easements, power lines, water systems—every inch of the county—were in place; deputies, armed with blue markers, scoured drainage ditches and sewer pipes, flagging each searched and cleared; street leaders checked every backyard, toolshed, and freshly dug patch in their assigned areas; groups on horseback, led by mounted patrols from the Fort Worth police and the Tarrant County sheriff, were scrutinizing remote areas.

Remig had planned this exacting search, starting where they'd found the truck and working out. Since the child's shoes had arrived, Remig's dog teams were finally sniffing for Denise's trail. Brenna had warned him about Gideon's last trick, dragging the little girl's clothes to establish false scent trails for the dogs. He couldn't take the chance that this insidious madman would try that again. Any lead, no matter how weak, must be investigated.

"John T.," David said, "who do you have working in Tattersall?"

This was the other city in the small county. Seventeen miles away, it could have been in another country. Tattersall residents were like those in most other towns; good and bad, strong and weak, oblivious to their neighbors' troubles, yet always in someone else's business. The people of Windsor had spoiled Remig, and he sometimes felt they were a world unto themselves.

"Tattersall? We've got the deputies normally assigned to that area," he said, "the chamber of commerce, and anybody who volunteers at the substation."

"You need a more deliberate search pattern up there," David said, "like you have here."

"We don't have the resources," he barked.

"Why have you focused everyone here?"

"You know why." He found the fax with Brenna's notes. "Look. Every child was found within eight miles of the note. We have to pray he's done the same thing this time."

"What if he didn't? This note says the kid's somewhere in McEntyre County. Did the others say that? Were they that specific? Do you know how many square miles this county—"

"Yes, I know." He slapped the folder against his leg.

"Maybe he's trying to throw us off, maybe—"

"What do you want me to do, David?"

"Expand our resources. Let me call the National Guard Reserve in Fort Worth, and the one in Dallas, too. You coordinate the search from the county line north up through Windsor, and I'll have the military work from our northern border south through Tattersall. Eventually, we'll meet in the middle."

John T. glanced at his watch. He hadn't wanted to use strangers in this search; too often, criminals stayed around to watch the commotion they'd created. But they'd lose daylight in a few hours and the life of this child lay in his hands.

He nodded at David. "But don't turn those soldiers loose without specific directions and mandatory communications. I want to know every move they make, every bent blade of grass they find."

David turned to walk away, but then stopped. "Do you think the man who snatched this child is still here, somewhere?"

"I don't know," he said. "That's why no one joins the search unless someone we know vouches for them. That goes for the military, too. Make sure their team leaders personally know each member of their squads."

* * *

Denise Phillips sat on a scratchy mat in a corner of a small room with a bumpy wood floor. Three piles of dirt on the floor looked like anthills, but there weren't any ants.

She'd been awake for a while, and her head and mouth still felt yucky.

A big yellow lantern flashlight was glowing from its middle instead of the glass at the end, and when she picked it up, her fingers couldn't reach all the way around it. But the light had begun to blink. If it went out, she'd be in the dark, the kind of dark that happened when all the lights went out at home and Daddy let her sit in his lap while he told her a story. When she was little, the lights going out had scared her, but she'd learned there wasn't anything in the dark that wasn't there in the light.

A small table and chair, like the ones at school, were in the middle of the room. A glass and two bottles of juice—one apple, one orange—sat on the table next to a tall yellow candle stuck in a silver holder. Five stick matches lay beside the candle. Mommy told her not to play with matches, but if the flashlight went out, it might be okay to light the candle. Wouldn't it? Maybe Mommy wouldn't get mad this one time.

She looked around and tried to remember how she'd gotten into this room. Her chest was sore, and she remembered playing in the backyard, swinging higher and higher. Then someone called her name, said he had a surprise. She didn't remember anything else.

"Something stinks." She wiggled her nose and then pinched it closed with her fingers. The smell made her eyes burn, too.

She looked at the door. When she'd turned the knob and yanked on it, nothing happened. It was just like the time she got locked in the bathroom.

Maybe she should look for another way out. Above her, way up, she saw three windows with wooden strips across them. Was it dark outside? She couldn't see anything.

Pushing herself to her feet, she walked to the door and jerked it again. It didn't move at all. Then she looked at the windows and the chair. If she could open a window, she could climb out. It looked easier than climbing the monkey bars at school and the big tree in the park. And if she couldn't get out, with the window open at least the smell might go away.

She moved the chair and stood on it, but she wasn't tall enough to reach the window. She picked up one of the flat wood strips that had fallen off the window, but that didn't reach the opening either. Determined, she cleared off the table and shoved and pulled it under the window. She climbed onto the chair and stepped onto the table.

Almost.

With all her strength, she heaved the chair onto the table, set it straight, and then climbed up on it. Now, with the flat stick, she could reach the window, but there wasn't any glass in it. Dirt. Just dirt.

She poked and poked and poked. Each time she pulled out the stick, crumbs of dirt refilled the hole and trickled onto her toes. After a few minutes, she could smell fresh air, but she still couldn't see outside.

As she climbed down, she decided the stink had gotten worse. She pulled off her sweater and the T-shirt underneath. Then she tied the T-shirt over her face like a bandit and wiggled into her sweater. That helped, some. But her eyes still burned.

The flashlight flickered.

She looked at the candle and then at another window. Maybe that one would be better.

EVA STARED OUT the window at the gazebo. Large groups of people clustered together, some standing, others kneeling, while someone in an orange vest spoke to them.

"It looks like chaos," Claudia stopped behind her, "but everyone down there knows what to do."

"There must be five hundred people."

"Still others are meeting at the elementary school, dropping off their kids and picking up assignments. The teachers will stay there with the children until the search is over." She smiled. "Kinda like a twenty-four-hour day-care center."

"What are those people in orange passing out?"

"Cyalume sticks," Claudia said. "When you shake them, they light up, like those green rings they sell at the circus. They come in assorted colors, and they'll glow for up to six hours." She looked at the door. "Wait a minute; I'll show you."

Henry moved beside Eva and slipped his arm around her waist.

"Look at them," she said. "They don't know us or Denise, but they're here anyway." She dotted her eyes with a tissue. "I feel so helpless, so . . . worthless just staying in here." She turned and gazed into the soft, brown eyes that had hypnotized her the first time she'd met Henry. Denise had her father's eyes. "Isn't there something we can do? She's our child; we should be down there with them."

Claudia returned with a four-inch-long orange plastic cylinder. "This is a Cyalume Lightstick. Shake it up, bend it, and the liquid inside glows." She made it into a wristband with a strap to hold it in place. "John T. color-codes the teams. The team leaders and mobile runners, those checking out specific locations, wear these." She handed them another wristband with a large silver circle sewn onto it. "These dots are reflective. They're cut from those silver emergency blankets that fold up to four inches square. Everyone involved with this search wears a Cyalume light or one of these."

"How do you know all these details?" Henry asked. "I thought you worked for the Dallas police department."

"I do," Claudia said, "but my sister lives here and teaches at the elementary school. If I could make a lateral transfer so as to keep the rank I have and John T. had an opening, I'd work for him in a minute."

"Does anyone have news?" Henry asked. "Have you talked to Marie, is Darren all right?"

"The agents at your home are taking good care of Darren," Claudia said. "Don't worry about him."

Eva turned back to the window. "Isn't there something we can do?"

Claudia perched on the edge of the table. "I'm afraid all you can do is wait."

Jett glanced at his watch. They'd land soon. The dog handlers clustered beside the Suburban, still as statues, each wearing the team uniform: red shirt, khaki pants and search vest, red gaiters up to their knees, red fanny pack. He wished he had Connie's camera, but if he asked, everyone would move, and he'd lose the picture of that moment. The dogs sported their identification, too: red back patches with a white cross on each side. In a large search like this, the command post appreciated being able to identify people by their uniforms.

The more Jett watched everyone there, the more he realized how much he enjoyed their friendship. He and Joanne were going to counseling sessions but not making much progress. She insisted he sell the business and take an investigative job with her father's law firm in San Francisco. He couldn't do it; he couldn't abandon the thriving business he'd built and toss his coworkers into the unemployment line because of his wife's unreasonable jealousy. She refused to consider his position, and she'd encouraged Paige to beg for the move and a reconciliation.

Although he loved his daughters, the people in the C-141 were more than his friends and employees. Each was a combination of hopes and dreams, generosity and stubbornness, loyalty and independence. They freely shared their lives with him; Joanne expected him to exist in her little black box of suspicion and minute-by-minute accountability. He still cared for her, but he could no longer tolerate the scheming, possessive woman she'd become.

People began milling around the cars. He nudged Garrett, indicating it was time for them to change into their red shirts, too. Although he'd met John T. twice, years before, most of what he knew about the sheriff came from Brenna. Jett hoped John T. would let him run communications for the team, but this search was not his show. Still, he knew the team members' habits almost as well as they themselves did, and he'd feel more secure if he could keep tabs on them.

When he and Garrett returned to their seats for landing, everyone else was already buckled in, holding their dogs across their laps or close to their sides. He turned to Marco and held up four fingers. Marco responded in kind. Connie acknowledged three and Brenna, two. He'd lead the caravan, and if everyone's timetables matched, a sheriff's escort should be waiting for them.

An instant after the plane stopped on the runway, everyone had jumped out of their seats and dashed for the cars. Engines purred, dogs barked and wagged their tails. Every driver stared at the ramp, anxiously waiting for it to lower.

The plane's navigator ran to Jett's window. "You've got company," he said. "Colorado just beat us here. The sheriff's got them."

Then he pointed. "When the ramp lowers, drive straight out, go down to the gate, and turn left. They're waiting for you." He smiled and slapped the side of the truck. "Good luck."

As soon as the ramp dropped and stopped humming, Jett shot down, the three other vehicles following him like the tail of a kite toward a uniformed man motioning toward a gate.

"There," Garrett said, pointing to the far side of a parking lot. "The sheriff's unit."

Before Jett reached it, the unit's lights flashed and it raced toward the entrance of the base. Another sheriff's car fell in behind Marco's.

"Nothing like being the meat in a sheriff-bread sandwich," Harley said.

Garrett turned to face the backseat. "Have you got everything? Do you have the kidnapper's scent article?"

Harley nodded. "Brenna gave one to each of us on the plane." He held up a plastic bag with a gauze pad inside. "I hope this sheriff lets us look for Gideon instead of Denise. Oh—I didn't mean that the way it sounded."

"I know," Garrett said.

Jett knew, too. On the chance John T. would let them search for Gideon's trail instead of Denise's, Brenna had placed six more pads into the Baggie with the two she'd used to prove the same person was involved in Zoe's and Leanne's abductions. Then she divided them among the members, giving each a sample. Garrett had the extras in his pocket.

They hit heavy traffic on the highway that circled the Fort Worth area. Even with lights flashing and sirens blasting, they slowed to a crawl several times and had to drive on the shoulder. But the real surprise came when they veered onto the highway leading to McEntyre County. It looked like a parking lot. Cars and trucks and vans stood idle, their drivers pacing on the shoulders and waving their arms in frustration. Some vehicles drove across the grassy median of the divided highway and headed in the opposite direction.

The lead sheriff's car pulled onto the median and kept going. A few miles later, they passed a roadblock of sawhorses and black-

and-white Department of Public Safety cars. Then the lead car veered back onto the highway. From that point, the road into town was clear.

"DPS?" Harley asked.

"I think it's their state police," Garrett said. Then he grinned. "Don't you watch *Walker, Texas Ranger* on television?"

"Oh, yeah. The Rangers are part of DPS." Harley craned his neck to look out the back window. "They film around here, don't they? I wonder if we'll see them."

Jett laughed. He'd never suspected Harley of being a groupie.

But his laughter soon faded. If the rest of the county looked like this, the searchers were in for a battle. Everything was still a weak shade of green. Windsor would have a late winter this year, if it had one at all. Matted vegetation nibbled barbed-wire fences; weeds and bullneedle stretched knee high; saplings were braided with brush. Two construction projects faced one another across the highway, one with several trenches and with stacks of lumber. The other plot of ground looked smooth and pale, as if it had just been skinned.

Then they drove through a section of woods, crossed over a creek, and passed a quarry where earth-moving machines stood idle, some with their dishes half raised as though the drivers had abandoned them in the middle of a shift.

Closer to Windsor, the scenery changed. A stock pond sported ducks floating on its glassy surface. Black Angus cattle grazed near mounds of hay and swatted at flies with their skinny tails. White rail fences took the place of barbed wire. They sped over stone bridges like touches of New England.

When they traveled over a metal bridge spanning a river, Jett caught a glimpse of police officers on horseback at the bottom of the draw. For an instant, he'd forgotten why the team was there.

The terrain grew rocky, with bluffs, ravines, and stands of trees. At least they didn't have mountains in this part of the state. More than the others, Brenna hated climbing.

"He's slowing," Garrett said.

The lead sheriff's car braked around a hairpin curve, and Jett saw the Windsor City Limits sign. Someone was tying blue flag tape around a street sign; a cluster of people jogged toward a baseball field, something green shining from their wrists. In front of a white church, a woman in a bright yellow shirt was kneeling beside a Doberman wearing a back patch like those their dogs wore. She waved to them.

Jett had seen her before.

"National Park Service," Garrett said.

"Right. That's Cecile," Jett said. "Adam must have gotten them here fast."

"How'd he beat us?" Harley asked.

"I don't know," Jett said, "but I'm glad they made it."

At the town square, the lead car stopped. As fast as the handlers and dogs piled out of cars, someone in a uniform slid behind the wheel and drove their vehicles around behind the courthouse. Brenna went swiftly to the gazebo, where Marco and Connie saw her hugging a man with salt-and-pepper hair.

"Brenna-Honey." John T. hugged her. "The clock's ticking, and I've assigned your team to these areas." He handed her folders filled with maps, a shoe print, Denise's picture and a description of her clothes. He looked up. "Where are they?"

She waved them over. Good old John T. He never changed.

"This is—" she said.

"No time for introductions," he said. "If you trust them, that's all I need to know." He passed out the folders. "Program your radios to the frequency beside your names." He glanced at Jett. "Don't I know you?"

"Jett Culpepper."

John T. shook his head. "Forgive my bad manners. Do you need flankers?"

"Four," Brenna said. "Gayle marks the maps."

"We've got mappers upstairs," John T. said. "Take Gayle with you."

Donny glanced at Gayle, but she elbowed him, a sign to him to keep quiet, and smiled at Brenna.

"Is this radio frequency just for the dog teams?" Jett asked.

John T. nodded. "Need something special?"

"Do you have another channel available, just for this team?" Jett asked.

"Why?" John T. looked from Jett to Brenna.

"We have an idea," she said.

"Brenna-Honey, I don't have time for ideas."

"Give us thirty seconds," she said, "and then we'll do whatever you want . . . without question."

When she finished their proposal, he stared at the ground a few moments. "Who's going to run communications for your team?"

"I will," Jett said.

John T. looked at Garrett. "Who's this?"

"Rob Garrett, Seattle," Garrett said.

John T. nodded. "I read your reports." He studied all of them a few seconds. "You got any more of those gauze pads?"

"Yes, sir." Garrett pulled the plastic bag from his pocket and handed it to the sheriff.

John T. looked at the folders and then the team. "Your areas remain the same, but we'll have to put another dog in the sector with you unless you want to switch them off and on."

Brenna didn't like switching scents on dogs during a search, although she had done it when necessary. She'd switched Feather from Leanne's shoe to Gideon's footprint during that search, and the dog had worked well. But having the dogs mark a specific scent and then giving them another person's scent article before they found the original victim made her nervous.

"Right now," he said, "I've got most of the dogs working within an eight-mile radius. David thinks I'm crazy, but the reports you sent make me think our best chance of finding this child is within that circle."

"How many scent articles do you have?" she asked.

"Enough."

"We'll take five."

He looked at Garrett. "And what do you plan to do?"

"Whatever you want."

John T. smiled at Brenna. "I like him. Now, you-all get your tails moving." He looked at his watch. "You've got three minutes before transport picks you up over there in front of the art supply store." He glanced at Garrett and Jett. "You two come with me. We've moved communications to the top floor of the courthouse; I'm sure we'll find a spot for you."

Jett turned to Brenna, looking as if he wanted to say something. Instead, he smiled and followed John T. and Garrett. She gave him a thumbs-up.

As the group walked to the art store, Brenna checked everyone's folder. Each handler had been assigned a specific area.

Connie tugged her sleeve. "Do you want to switch scents?"

She looked at Marco. "What do you think?"

"If Denise and Gideon are together," he said, "it won't matter. But if the trails split, there might be a problem if this goes to court. How can we prove the dogs didn't switch scents on their own and start following the wrong person?"

"We know who we're looking for," Patrick said.

Harley shook his head. "Maybe, when this thing is over, we should include switching scents in our training. Then we'd know better next time."

Next time. Surely there wouldn't be another search like this.

"Everybody ready?" Brenna asked. Then she noticed Gayle twitching. "Gayle, are you all right?"

She nodded. "Excited, nervous." She shrugged.

"You should stay here," Donny said. "I don't like the—"

"I don't care what you like," Gayle said. "I've been flanking with Connie and I can do it." Then she kissed his cheek.

"Calm down, Gayle," said Brenna. "Don't let Margarita pick up on your anxiety. We need her to be steady and on the money." She glanced at the team members. Gayle was the only one without goggles already hanging around her neck. "Safety glasses are required for night searches," she said, "especially in wooded areas."

Gayle smiled, weakly. "I forgot them."

"Never fear," Connie said. "Brenna brings two of everything."

Brenna turned so Connie could get the spare pair from her fanny pack.

"Now," Brenna said, "as soon as you reach your location, put them on."

Gayle nodded.

The three flankers and pickups arrived, and the searchers showed them the maps. The drivers nodded. To run transport, John T. had picked old-timers, men who knew every inch of the county.

"That's part of the old Foster place," Brenna's driver said of her location. "I know right where it is." He glanced at Feather. "Mighty fine-looking dog. She a crossbreed?"

"Bouvier," she said. "Herding dogs, originally."

He drove along the main street toward the highway and then made two turns. After crossing a stream, he pulled to the shoulder of a dirt road.

Brenna kept Feather on leash while she and Donny listened to their driver.

The old man pointed. "Down yonder is a leg of the old creek. Dry most of the time. Never did have much of a name, but it's your boundary on the south side. This piece stretches back almost a mile. When you reach here"—he pointed to the map—"you'll hit a stand of timber. Has a few mesquite scattered through, so be careful of the thorns, but most of it's pecan trees. The back side of the grove, at the stream, is your east boundary."

"Stream?" She tensed. "How deep?"

"Maybe three feet," he said. "Some goldarn fool planted bamboo out here once, and there's patches all over the place. Be careful, the broken shafts can sure cut up a dog's feet." He pointed to the map again. "This here fence—mainly mesquite limbs but it still has some barbed wire—is both your north and south boundary . . . north on this section, south on your next one."

"Are there any houses out here?" she asked.

"A few, but most of this land is up for sale right now. The owners are hoping for some big developer to offer them a million dollars." He shook his head. "Ain't gonna happen." He flashed Brenna a toothless smile. "When you finish your second section, radio. I'll pick you up at the old windmill. You'll see it."

After he drove away, Brenna let Feather sniff the area while she studied her folder. Someone had taken the trouble to include a larger map showing which dogs had been assigned to which areas. Bless him. Or her.

Then she looked at the preliminary report on Denise. Last seen wearing black jeans, red-and-white tennis shoes, and a black print sweater. Personality: precocious and daring. Five years old.

"Five?" she said.

"What?" Donny asked.

She looked at him. "Denise is five. That's not right; all the others were four."

"What do you mean, it's not right?"

For the first time since the callout, doubt crept into her thoughts. If Gideon had changed his pattern with the child's age, might it indicate other changes? Maybe all their cogitations had been for nothing.

"Feather, here."

The dog trotted over; Brenna placed the tracking harness on her but didn't attach the twenty-five-foot leash. Then she opened the small plastic bag with the gauze pad and held it next to Denise's black Mary Jane shoe.

"Mark it." Feather's ears perked and she swiped her nose across the items. "Find 'em. Get on it." She swung her arm in the direction of the pecan grove they didn't see but which the old-timer had said was there.

The wind blew from the north, a lucky break, considering their assigned area. They'd zigzag through their sector until Feather picked up a trail. Then, Brenna would attach the long line and put the dog on a track command . . . if they found a trail at all.

CHAPTER 31

THE HOURS PASSED too quickly; the humidity and dark clouds made the night feel thick and heavy. Brenna gave Feather a short break every thirty minutes, letting the dog lap water and cool down. Then they hit the sector again.

The pecan grove sloped to the riverbank, unharvested pecans crunching under their feet. Raccoons made their bubbling noises as they watched the searchers weave between the tree trunks. An otter swam in the river, dipping and floating as if performing a private acrobatic show. No sign of its mate or family. No sign of Denise.

They'd scared up an owl, who screeched a warning that strangers were in the area, and an armadillo, which Feather wanted to sniff. But the dog minded her manners and stayed on the job. All kinds of critters were around, everything except the child they were looking for.

On their last break, Donny, unusually silent, put his hand over hers.

"You can't slow time by looking at your watch," he said.

He was right, but it didn't make her feel better.

"Rescue Margarita to base camp," the radio squawked.

"Go ahead," Jett said.

"We have a problem," Connie said. She sounded tired and disgusted. "A skunk got Margarita square in the face. Someone else needs to finish this sector."

Brenna didn't know whether to laugh or scream.

"Stand by," Jett said. "Base camp to Rescue Feather."

"Go ahead," Brenna said.

"Did you copy?"

"Ten-four," she said.

"Where are you?"

"Our sector two."

"Can you take over Margarita's assignment? You're the closest."

"Will do. We should finish here in about ten minutes."

After Connie radioed her location, Brenna and Donny studied their map. If they went back to the road and followed it north, they would reach a curve, and there they could cut straight through some woods into Connie's area.

She clipped Feather's leash to her collar and started jogging. Beyond the woods, they crossed a pasture dotted with mesquite. A wisp of blue light flickered to their left, and she spotted a group of ground searchers spread ten feet apart in a straight line, kneeling. The one in front, probably the team leader, waved his light side to side to alert her to their presence. Bless John T.; he'd trained them well. When dogs were in the area, everyone stopped until the animals had passed through. This allowed the dogs to continue their jobs with less distraction and provided easier access if the dogs wanted to sniff the ground searchers to eliminate them as their victim. Tonight, Brenna didn't let Feather check out the searchers.

They found Connie, Margarita, and Gayle in a clearing framed with post oaks and carpeted with vines and leaves. Twenty-five feet upwind of the dog, Connie wore mud up to her knees and on both arms; Gayle held Margarita's long leash with one hand and pinched her nose closed with the other. The Bloodhound, her face and neck caked in drying tomato juice, lay in a clear spot, pawing at her nose and violently shaking her head. Her eyes watered and she sneezed every few seconds.

"Are you all right?" Brenna asked.

"We're fine, I guess," Connie said. "Our cans of juice didn't go very far."

Brenna removed the two cans of tomato juice from her fanny pack and pitched them to Gayle. "Add these to the red coating. And put your goggles back on," she said. "They'll help keep your eyes from burning.

"They bug me," Gayle said.

"Wear them anyway."

Feather wagged her tail and woofed at Margarita, but she kept her distance. Brenna patted her partner and handed the leash to Donny.

"Are you sure we aren't in the mountains?" Connie said. "We've been over and around hills, through a boulder garden, up and down banks, across the creek twice—a creek, I might add, that had water moccasins playing tag right in the middle—and ended up here in this sumac patch." Margarita sneezed and pawed her nose again. "But I haven't seen any indication of a trail, exactly."

Brenna tensed. "What does 'exactly' mean?"

"Cigarette butts." She walked to the far side of the clearing, Brenna beside her. "We found one, and then others either leading into this clearing or out of it. We never got the chance to find out. Just as Margarita started into the brush, the skunk got her. But Margarita had just started wagging her tail. I think we might have been onto something."

"Where?"

She pointed to a thick growth of sumac bushes. "We must have found a den. Every time I get close, the odor intensifies. I think the skunk's still in there."

"What about footprints?" Brenna asked.

"Too many leaves for me, but a tracker might see something if we haven't destroyed every trace. When the skunk got Margarita, we were jumping around trying to grab her and not get sprayed. I'd bet we trashed whatever was here."

"Maybe not." Brenna hollered for Donny to put Feather on a down and bring the radio. She used it to reach Jett. "Is Grady Stone still around?"

"Stand by," Jett said. A few moments later, John T. spoke to her. "Have you got something, Brenna-Honey?"

"We're not sure."

She told John T. what they'd found. Meanwhile, Donny shinnied up a tree several feet beyond the skunk-inhabited brush and shone his light down into the bushes.

"Brenna," he said excitedly, "it's not a den. You've got three skunks in cages."

"Cages?"

"Looks like cat traps," he said. "Those wire things shaped like boxes."

"John T.," she said, "have you heard of anybody trapping skunk?"

"No," he said. "You may be on to something. I'll get Grady out there right away. Where are you?"

Donny climbed down from the tree to give John T. their exact coordinates.

"Who's Grady?" Connie asked.

"He used to be the game warden for this area," Brenna said. "He retired just before I moved to California, but he knows everything that goes on in this county. And he can track a flea across a sow's belly."

She smiled. That was one of Aaron's sayings.

"Where were you going from here?" Brenna asked.

Connie motioned toward a section cattycorner to where they were. "We've cleared everything to here. That was our next area."

"Okay." Brenna looked at her watch. Three minutes after eleven. Deadline: 1:12 A.M. But the skunk traps bothered her. Three together. With every passing second, she felt she was in a trap. "Connie . . . do you think–"

"Yes." She looked west. "This feels just like Leanne's search. I'd bet the road is the west boundary and the river, the east."

Brenna took the radio from Donny. "Rescue Feather to base camp." After Jett answered, she said, "Connie and I think we may be in the right area. Could we get more dogs in here?"

"Negative," Jett said. "Most are shifting north, close to Tattersall."

"Why?"

"They found Denise's trail up there near a construction site. Gideon's, too."

Connie looked at Brenna. "Why didn't we hear about that?"

"Jett put us on a different channel, remember? We only hear what our team's doing." She keyed the radio. "Jett, are you pulling us out, too?"

"Negative. Tattersall is out of the eight-mile radius. John T. doesn't want to chance missing anything."

"Stand by." She turned to Connie and motioned for Donny and Gayle to join them. Feather barked, and then Margarita howled. "Hang on, girls. We'll be there in a minute."

The group squatted, sitting on their heels instead of the ground to avoid becoming a fire-ant meal.

"What do we know about Gideon?" she asked.

"He's full of tricks," Connie said.

"But who's being tricked?" Donny asked. "Us, with the skunks, or them, with the trails?"

"I sat next to Wally when he worked the map for Leanne's search," Gayle said. "Gideon had everybody going around in circles, and he rigged those eight arrows approximately a mile apart."

"But Gideon's changed his pattern," Brenna said. "This child is five. The others had just turned four."

"Would he change everything?" Donny asked. "He said he'd play fair this time."

"We can't trust him." Connie looked at Brenna. "What if these skunks really are an illegal trapper's catch?" She shook her head. "Bren, what do you think? Gideon said you've learned the game."

They all looked at her, as if she had a crystal ball.

She shook her head. "I don't know."

"You have to know, Bren," Gayle said.

"But I don't."

"Then give us your best guess," Connie said. "Your instincts have been right about him all along. What does that little voice inside say?"

Little voice? She hadn't heard her little voice for the past few months, but she could still hear Aaron's. She knew what he'd say.

Brenna keyed the radio. "Jett, keep us posted on everything."

"Ten-four. Does Connie want transport to pick them up?"

Connie took the radio. "Negative. We'll follow Rescue Feather."

Brenna walked to the tree where Feather had been resting. The dog rose and wagged her tail.

"Ready to work?" she asked.

Feather barked and her front feet danced.

She unclipped the leash, opened the bag with Gideon's scent pad, and held it for Feather to sniff. "Mark it."

"Only Gideon's?" Connie asked.

"We have to know if he's been here."

She put Feather on the "Find" command, and turned her loose. The dog circled, sniffing both in the air and on the ground. She wandered around the clearing, approached the skunks three times, and then veered south. A few minutes later, she stopped between two cottonwood trees, looked at Brenna over her shoulder, and barked.

Connie touched Brenna's arm. "He's been here."

She nodded and then clipped the leash to Feather's harness. Gayle trotted behind them with Margarita on leash.

They weaved through the woods, crossed another clearing, and then stopped at the stream. Leanne had been found in a river very much like this one, but Feather wasn't interested in the water. She sniffed, stopped, trotted, and circled. Before long, they entered the woods again.

"Base camp to Rescue Feather."

"Go ahead." Brenna was glad for a break.

"They found a blanket, a pair of socks, and one tennis shoe at the construction site near Tattersall."

"Tied with clothesline?" she asked.

"Affirmative."

She looked at Connie. "He's tricked them."

"A Bloodhound hit on the socks and shoe," Jett said. "They're Denise's."

"You know," Gayle said, "he left Leanne's clothes at the opposite side of the search area from where you found her."

"Jett," Brenna said, "we think he's tricked them. We've found his scent here, too. Can you get the dogs back here, between the river and the road?"

"Stand by." A minute later he came back on the radio. "Negative. They have to scour the area where the physical evidence is located."

She wanted to protest, but they were only guessing.

"What about our team? Can the guys meet us?"

"Patrick's in Tattersall, but Marco and Harley are still south of town." He paused. "Irish, are you *sure*?"

The word reverberated in her head.

"No," she said. "It's a hunch, and we do have a trail, but he's fooled us before."

"Have Grady and Simon arrived yet?"

"Simon?" Connie smiled. "Hey, my dancing buddy showed up."

"When did Simon get here?" Brenna asked.

Jett didn't answer, but Grady's voice crackled over the air.

"How-do, Brenna," he said. "Simon's got Intercity on his radio; I have your team on mine. Now, don't go getting nervous if you hear three shots in a minute. We're going to tranquilize these little fellows so we can get them out of here and see what's left. We're close, if you need us."

"Thanks, Grady."

"Call if you find a track. I'm anxious to catch this guy, too."

"FEATHER, GET ON IT," Brenna said.

The dog trotted at a not-fresh-but-been-here speed, leading them to a spot that was once a clearing; nature had reclaimed man's neglect. Off to one side, a grass-covered mound rose four feet high and covered a swatch of ground twelve feet wide.

"What is that?" Connie asked.

"I don't know."

"I have a blister on my foot that looks just like that," Donny said.

"Green?" Gayle asked.

"It might be by now," he said.

Brenna watched her partner. Feather's ears perked. She sniffed the ground, raised her head, looked at the earth blister, and then sniffed the ground again. She meandered along an animal path into the woods and then looked toward the bubble.

"What is it, Feather?" Brenna knelt beside her. "What?"

Feather sat. *R-r-r-rrrr.*

She'd seen the dog do this before, at Leanne's search. Feather acted as if she were torn between two actions. If it was the same scent, the dog would follow the freshest trail, but if there were two separate scents and they split. . . .

"How's Margarita?" she called.

"She's stopped sneezing," Connie said. When she looked at Brenna, she straightened. "What is it?"

"Bring her." When Connie, Donny, Gayle, and Margarita joined her, she said, "Scent her on Denise's shoe."

"But—"

"Feather's on Gideon," she said, "and she's . . . divided."

Connie did as Brenna requested. Then they put both dogs on the track command. They both headed south into the woods, but when a gust of wind filtered through, both dogs wheeled and gained speed. Feather veered to the left, but Margarita loped straight for the bubble and started sniffing around its base. Then Feather stopped and pawed a mass of vines. Brenna pulled her away and dug, her leather glove protecting her hand from the thorns.

A shoe. A child's red-and-white tennis shoe.

"Connie!" Afraid to change scents on Feather, Brenna wanted Margarita to verify the scent.

When Connie brought her dog, Margarita sniffed it and wagged her tail. All of them looked at the bubble, the blister on the earth. Then Brenna held the shoe under Feather's nose.

"Mark it."

After the dog sniffed it, she jerked Brenna toward the mound. Donny yelled into the radio, telling Jett what they might have found. The four of them circled the bubble, scratching at the soil, scouring every inch for a hint of digging, an airhole, anything. The dogs stopped on opposite sides of the blister, digging at weeds and dirt.

This didn't make sense. No loose soil. Weeds fully rooted. Wild grass thick and strong. Vines matted together by years of neglect. Gideon had taken Denise this morning; how could he have stashed her here without leaving some sign?

"Here!" Donny called. "Plats."

"What?" she asked.

"Some of this grass is in plats . . . like you buy at a nursery. There's a two-foot-wide row from the ground up."

Gayle joined Donny and pulled her goggles down around her neck to get a better look. "They *are* plats." She walked to the side where Margarita pawed the grass. "I'll check over here."

"Bren," Connie said, "should I pull Margarita?"

"No," she said, "I'll have Feather check for Gideon's scent. Feath–"

The explosion shot smoke and blinding fire out three sides of the bubble and peeled back a small piece of the blister's top. The dogs yelped, thudded to the ground several feet from the blast. The force of the explosion threw the searchers onto their backs. White smoke shot upward like a giant flare.

Brenna couldn't breathe. She couldn't hear clearly. When the night stopped spinning, she forced a deep breath. Muffled sounds reached her ears; smoke clouded her vision.

Feather. Where was Feather?

She pushed herself into a sitting position and ripped off her goggles. Donny lay on his back, his chest heaving between coughs. Connie was crawling toward Gayle; the young blonde rolled on the ground, her hands clamped over her eyes.

"Donny?" she called.

"Okay," he choked.

"Connie!"

"Gayle's hurt," Connie yelled, "and I can't find Margarita."

Brenna crawled through the smoke until she found Feather lying on her side, whimpering.

"Are you okay, toots?"

The explosion and flash had crinkled the hair on one side of the dog's face; the other side was singed. One eye bled.

Brenna found her flashlight. A splinter of wood pierced the skin on the outside of the eyeball. She gently pulled it out, and Feather nuzzled her hand.

"Stay here, sweet girl." She kissed the dog's nose. "Stay."

Brenna pushed herself to her feet and glanced at the bubble, which now resembled a tin can with a bent lid. Smoke gushed from the top and three sides in thick plumes. No way they could see inside until help came.

But she struggled to the opening and called into the smoke. "Denise! Denise!" Bitter smoke filled her mouth and burned her eyes. "Denise!"

Nothing.

She fought the smoke and finally found Margarita curled around an oak trunk; it looked as if the dog had been thrown against the tree. She panted and trembled but didn't respond when Brenna cooed to her. Her eyes had a glazed look, and one side of her face had already begun to blister. Feather's thick coat had protected her; Margarita's was short and left her open to more damage.

"Hang on, Margarita," Brenna whispered. "Your mom isn't ready to let you go. None of us are." When something nudged her, she jumped. "Feather! I told you to stay."

The dog wagged her tail, slowly, and then lay beside Margarita. Brenna had forgotten what good friends they were.

"Okay, toots, you stay here with her." Brenna took off her vest and fanny pack. After offering the dogs a drink, she left her gear with them and crawled to Connie and Gayle. "How is she?"

"She won't let me look," Connie said. "The girls?"

"Over there." She studied the expression on Connie's face. "I'll stay here. You go." She didn't have to say more.

Donny scrambled to them. "Gayle, let me see."

"No," she moaned, rolling side to side.

He glanced at Brenna. "My radio's gone."

She found Gayle's still on her belt and handed it to Donny. Jett and the others were talking so much, asking for teams to report in, wanting to know what happened, where it happened, Donny had to try three times with "Emergency" to get everybody quiet.

"Hang on, Gayle," she said.

"I can't see," she cried. "I can't see."

"We're right here; help is on the way."

While Donny spoke into the radio, Brenna looked at the bubble. Nothing but smoke, but she felt sure Denise was inside. She glanced at her watch. Twelve-ten. They'd found her before the time limit, and Gideon had killed her anyway, just like Leanne. But this time, he'd tried to send all of them to heaven with her.

Pattern. He'd hung around to watch Leanne's search. This was his biggest moment, would have been his greatest triumph. He couldn't have known when they'd find the mound; he had to be near.

She touched Donny's arm. "I'd bet money he's around here, watching."

Donny radioed her suspicion in the middle of telling them where they were. Then Jett said something, and in the background, she could hear John T. telling all ground searchers to hold their positions; the suspect could be in the area. The sound of his words on the radio made her shiver.

Connie called to them. "I got Margarita to drink a little water."

Past the shock of the explosion, Brenna looked at her teammates and thought of the dogs. None of them had ever hurt anyone. She moved beside Connie.

"Wouldn't you like to get your hands on Gideon for five minutes?" Connie asked.

"No," Brenna said, "I'm not strong enough. I'd like someone bigger and meaner and downright dirty to work on him for an hour or two. It'd thrill me to lock them into a room together."

An owl screeched somewhere in the woods near the road. Maybe it was warning them about Grady and Simon. They were closer than anyone else, and they could get Gayle to Grady's truck and out of here before the fire trucks with EMS personnel could find them.

"I'm going to the road," Brenna said. "If I leave a marker, help will find us faster."

Donny looked at the bubble. "That smoke is hard to see at night." Then he glanced at her. "Just smoke, now. You go on, mark the path from the road. I'll send up flares and then go down into the hole."

She took the radio and two rolls of yellow flag tape and jogged into the woods. Her legs were still weak, but without her vest and fanny pack, she felt twenty pounds lighter. At the first tree, she tied a piece of the thin plastic to a limb and slipped the roll onto a twig. As she jogged, she left a bright yellow trail. When she reached the road, she hung several strands from a limb; then she turned and took a deep breath before heading back.

Halfway through the woods, she heard something off to her right. The ground searchers they'd passed earlier had been in that area. The team leader would have more first aid equipment.

"Hey," she called. "We're over here."

"I'm over here," a male voice said.

She wheeled toward the voice, but when she saw him in the night's shadows, the hair on the back of her neck prickled. She stepped back.

"Where's your group?" she asked.

"I got ahead of them," he said.

She still couldn't see him, only the silhouette of a man.

Slipping her hand onto the radio, she said, "Where's your light?"

He held up a dark flashlight. "Here."

"That's not it." She jerked the radio to her mouth. "Jett! He's here, he's—"

As he leaped toward her, she pivoted and bolted, trying to alert everyone as she ran.

"He's . . . woods . . . between . . . road and . . ."

He grabbed her collar and jerked her backward. An arm curled around her throat, fingers wrenched the radio from her grasp. Then he threw her into a stand of bamboo, broke the antenna off the radio, and flung it into the darkness.

He pointed at her. "My war is not with you."

The bamboo poked and cut her, but she pushed herself to her feet and backed away. She saw a long, heavy beard and a nose with a huge bump. This wasn't the man in the picture.

"You son-of-a-bitch! Why did you kill Denise?"

"I didn't make her strike that match. Why did they let Lexie die?" He stepped out of the shadows; she grabbed a broken shaft of bamboo with a sharp point and aimed it at him.

"So you get back at everyone by killing children and trying to kill us?"

He stepped forward; she stepped back.

"I didn't kill them; no one found them in time. I gave those parents a chance; that's more than they gave me."

She wanted to call him by name, surprise him.

"Stay out of this, Brenna; leave me alone."

"Stay out . . . ! You dragged me into this!"

He pointed at her. "Our game is over. Let's hope I never have to put the words 'best served cold' on a note for you or one of your friends. Let's see—Garrett has a daughter in Pennsylvania, doesn't he?" He turned and jogged deeper into the woods.

She stood there, the bamboo still in her gloved hand. Garrett's daughter. Reggie.

Blackmail.

She couldn't let Gideon go, not like this, not with a threat to Reggie hanging over her head. But she had no weapon except the piece of bamboo, and she was no physical match for him. Five seconds in his grasp had convinced her of that. Still, she couldn't just stand there and watch him run away.

"You son-of-a-bitch."

Her feet were moving before she made the conscious decision to run after him. He hadn't expected her to follow; when he heard her footsteps, he turned.

"Stay away," he said. He ran again.

Different. What was different?

The beard. His beard was gone. No wonder he'd chanced facing her. He'd been in disguise.

She had to stop him. Her hands curled around the bamboo shaft. Then she remembered the whistle. As she ran, she placed the whistle between her teeth and blew short loud blasts with each stride.

Thirty yards ahead of her, he wheeled. "Stop blowing that whistle."

She kept blowing, backing up when he moved toward her.

"Stop!"

Blow, blow, blow. She could picture the scene in her mind. Wherever they were, people and dogs would dash toward the sound.

What if Gideon had a weapon he hadn't shown her? What if this rash action caused someone else to be hurt or killed? Could she live with that?

Could she live with letting him escape?

"Stop blowing that damn whistle!"

He charged her and she ducked under low limbs and around trunks, keeping an ear tuned to the sound of footsteps behind her.

The woods grew thicker. She found a worn animal path and streaked along it. It made easier running . . . for him, too. Twice she could feel his heat; fear fed her speed. Then the woods ended. Wide, if not deep, the stream lay before her, a steep bluff on its other side.

When she veered left, he cut left, too. If she didn't cross, he'd catch her. At least the water would act like an amplifier. The more she blew, the farther the sound would carry.

She reached the stream.

Jump, just jump! It's only water.

Closing her eyes, she splashed into the stream. Gideon bellydove into the water, grabbing for her foot. He caught her ankle but she jabbed the bamboo shoot into his elbow. He grunted; she kicked free.

The bluff was rocky and steep. She wouldn't be able to climb it fast enough to get away from him. She dashed to the right.

The moon slipped behind another mass of dark clouds. In the darkness, she might elude his sight, but the whistle would mark her trail. If she stopped now . . .

At the side of the bluff, the ground had been cleared for a rock quarry. She glanced behind her to see if he still followed, but she didn't see him. She stopped, bent, braced her hands on her knees. Her chest pounded and she couldn't catch her breath, but she kept her ears open, straining to hear any sound that might indicate he was near.

Silence.

Had he given up, had she lost him?

Well . . . hell. All that for nothing.

Relieved and furious, she hoped someone else might see him.

She straightened, inhaled deeply, and looked around. An enormous hole held water like a near-empty cup; rain and water from the stream must have leaked into the pit. Piles of sand, gravel, and rock rose over forty feet toward the sky. Bulldozers, a black-and-yellow conveyor belt, and one gravel truck stood like monster sentinels. Two top-loaders sat near a backhoe.

Maybe it was a good thing he hadn't followed her here. She stood in a hole created by the bluff and mountains of stone. The whistle wouldn't carry far unless she could climb onto a high point. Across the stream, lights dotted the darkness.

Dammit, she'd lost him.

She slapped the bamboo against her leg, and then wished she hadn't. It stung.

Time to go back.

As she stepped forward, her feet crunched on a mass of pebbles. Too late, she wondered if he might be waiting for a sound from her.

He charged around the side of the bluff, wailing a bone-chilling cry, his arms stretching for her.

She ducked and with both hands swung the bamboo shaft at his throat. It struck the side of his neck. He grabbed her arm, spun her around.

"I told you to stop," he said. "I let you go, and this is how you thank me?"

She kicked the back of his leg; her foot caught the crease of his knee. When his left side buckled, she yanked free, lost the shaft, and ran toward the pit, blowing her whistle.

Gideon must have seen the lights; he knew people were coming. And he still chased her?

The game had changed.

She ran, and realized she was headed toward the pit. Curving away from the edge, she scrambled over a low place between heaps of small stone. His footsteps crunched behind her.

Thunder rolled. She glanced toward the black-and-yellow conveyor belt and wondered if she could climb out of his reach.

Too far.

The sky spat bits of rain. She circled right, found herself headed for the crater, and pivoted to the left, around the top-loader. Gideon jumped from behind it. She whirled and realized she was trapped between him, the pit, and two mounds of gravel that formed an "M." The only way out was up.

She scrambled onto a pile of gravel, each step sending her back toward the base. Pebbles rolled under her feet and tumbled down. When she tried to kick footholds into the mound, she slipped farther. She inched upward, clawing; if she got high enough, he couldn't grab her without climbing up himself. Then she spread herself flat like a spider. He tried twice to reach her, but she slithered sideways, skipped one foot across the surface, and sent pebbles bouncing onto his head. He stepped back and disappeared into the darkness.

Was he giving up? Not likely. She blew the whistle again.

The rain grew heavier, plunked against the rocks. She looked down. In her effort to avoid him, she'd moved too near the crater. If she fell now, she'd land in the water.

Then an engine coughed and chugged. A yellow top-loader with a deep dish rumbled toward the mound. He was going to scoop her off the pile.

She looked up. If she could get to the crest of this heap, she might be able to reach the conveyor belt. Gideon's monster didn't reach that high. She scrambled, slipped down, pressed herself against the mound. Inch by inch, she rose higher. But the shovel scooped stones from beneath her, and the top section of the hill folded in on itself. She tumbled to the ground, pelted by pebbles. Then the top-loader backed up and churned toward her, its dish skimming the earth.

Rolling to her feet, she tried to run around the pile, but it grew tall and wide at the pit's rim. Gravel above, a crater below.

She shinnied up the pile a few feet and then hugged the mound with open arms. She looked up, looked down. There wasn't enough room for the monster to crawl between the rim and the heap. If she could inch her way around the hill's belly, the machine couldn't follow. At least she'd have a running start before Gideon got back on foot and chased her again.

The monster rumbled toward her and raised its mouth, swinging out before it turned to scrape her off the pile.

But the yellow beast rolled too near the edge. As the dish skimmed the belly of the mound, its left tires slipped off the rim and the machine tilted. It tumbled down the side of the pit, splashed into the water, and grumbled a few seconds before the engine died. The pile of stone crumbled where the dish had hit, cascading into the pit on top of the machine. The hill shifted; Brenna lost her footing and spilled to the ground, over the edge of the crater. Her fingers gouged at the rocks.

Her legs dangled into the hole. If she fell now, she'd land on the machine, and more than that, she'd be in the pit with Gideon.

The rain paused and then burped a short deluge. Someone grabbed her wrist and hauled her across the rocks and into strong arms.

"Simon," she whispered.

Someone said something over his radio, but she didn't understand it or the reply.

"W-where . . ." She stuttered and realized she was trembling. "D-did Gideon get away?"

"He's down there." He nodded toward the pit.

She turned and looked at the crowd of people and dogs gathered at the crater's edge, their flashlights aimed at the machine in the water. Even through the rain, she could see the monster on its side, part of it hidden beneath rocks. Gideon must have jumped or fallen from the driver's seat; the lower half of his body was trapped beneath the machine's weight and his arms were splashing the water.

Simon hugged her tighter. "You maneuvered him to that edge perfectly. I couldn't believe he fell for it."

"You were watching?"

"We all were," he said. "We just couldn't get here fast enough. Gideon must have been so focused on you, he didn't watch where he was going."

A deputy slid down a rope into the pit. Up to his thighs in water, he waded around the machine and looped his arms beneath Gideon's to keep his head and shoulders from disappearing into the water.

She stared at the man who'd caused so much fear and grief. "Let him drown. It'd be poetic justice."

Feather bounded to her and pawed her leg.

"Hey, toots." She hugged the dog. When she looked at the crinkled hair on the side of Feather's face, her eyes misted. Too close.

Then Brenna looked at Simon. "What's she doing here?"

"When she heard the whistle, Grady couldn't hold her back."

"How're Gayle and Margarita?"

"John T. sent a vet, and he gave Connie salve for Margarita's burns. He predicts she'll be fine."

A helicopter chop-chopped overhead. She looked into Simon's eyes. "For Gayle?"

"And Denise."

"Denise? She's alive?"

"The blast went out through the windows and the top. It threw her against the wall. Her hands and forehead are burned, she has a concussion, but they think she'll make it."

"What about the smoke?"

"She'd tied a T-shirt around her face; it probably saved her life. We'll have to ask her why she did that."

She sat straighter. "What caused the explosion?"

"They found a leaking butane container in the shelter."

She glanced toward the pit. "So that's what he meant. Strike the match or breathe the fumes. Either way, Denise had little chance to survive."

"But she did," he said.

Then she thought about what Simon had said. "What windows?"

"What?"

"You said the blast went out the windows."

"Merrick hid her in an old fallout shelter," he said. "You know, back in the fifties, people buried them in their backyards. He found one."

"But this wasn't completely underground."

"Over the years, it had started inching up."

"Double sacked." She took one more look at Gideon. "Can we get out of here?"

"Come with me, darlin', I'll lead the way."

BRENNA PITCHED HER backpack into the cargo area of the Blazer.

John T. had arranged for the out-of-towners to stay at the local Holiday Inn. After spending the rest of the first night at the hospital waiting for word about Gayle and Denise, all the dog handlers met in the hotel's conference room, renewing old friendships and creating new ones.

By the third day, Brenna's team was the only group still in town. They'd arrived together and all agreed they were leaving together. Gayle's doctor had removed the bandages from her eyes that morning; her sight had returned, and, although the skin around her eyes was red and swollen, the doctor predicted a full recovery. Denise had suffered a mild concussion, and the explosion had damaged her hearing, at least temporarily, but her burns weren't too bad.

The team members took turns staying with Gayle at the hospital whenever they could pry Donny away from her bedside.

"Surprise." Simon stepped from between Marco's Bronco and Jett's Suburban. "I haven't seen much of you lately."

"Really?" She tried to sound nonchalant, but she'd done her

best to avoid him the last three days. He'd been openly amorous toward her, and she knew Connie had a real crush on him.

"Can you spare a minute?" He leaned against the Blazer. "What would you say about our going out after we get home?"

"Aren't you moving to Shreveport?"

"Not for another month." He grinned. "We could squeeze in a few dates before I leave. I'd really like to get to know you better."

"Maybe the entire team will go out dancing one night."

"What about just you and me?"

"I thought Connie was your favorite dancing partner," she said.

"You were involved with someone else. Connie and I had fun, but nothing happened." He tugged a strand of her hair. "I wanted to ask you out the night we met, when you cut your hand."

"Is that why you acted like a jackass those first few weeks?"

"I don't warm up to people easily," he said.

She'd wondered what it would be like to date Simon. If Ryan hadn't been in the picture when they first met, she might have given Connie a run for her money. But Connie was her friend, and Simon was on his way to another state.

"It's just a date, Bren. We're not running off to get married."

"I know, but it doesn't feel right. Think what you want, Simon. I can't do it now."

He watched her a moment. "Another time?"

"That might be fun."

"Bren!" Garrett stood outside the hotel's side door, waving at her. "You coming?"

"On my way." She slammed the tailgate closed and called Feather. This time, when the Bouvier neared Simon, she wagged her tail.

Brenna joined Jett and Garrett in the hotel's coffee shop. As she scooted in beside Garrett, Feather crawled under the table and lay down. The waitress smiled and then closed that section to whoever might pop in during the slow period between lunch and happy hour.

"We're almost finished," Garrett said, "and we just about had it right."

Gideon had survived his fall and dousing, but he wasn't talking . . . to anyone. Even though the police were holding him in Dallas, several other agencies were vying to have him extradited to their cities.

Gideon's laptop had been found in the floorboard of a maroon pickup; Garrett and John T. had little trouble piecing together the man's recent history before passing along the laptop as evidence to the FBI. Ivan Allen Merrick kept the details of his life logged in the little black box. He'd tracked everyone he felt betrayed him. Katya lived because she looked so much like Lexie: he couldn't bear to hurt her. After Ellen Hanson Abbott moved to Denver, he bought a new tombstone for Lexie's grave.

"Who was Jorge Chavez?" she asked.

"Ellen Hanson's neighbor, who tried to pull Lexie out of the burning trailer," Jett said. "John T. found him yesterday in Miami Springs. Every year in November—"

"The month Lexie died," Garrett said.

"Jorge gets cash in the mail," Jett said. "He never knew why or how this anonymous benefactor found him. His family moved around a lot, but the money started coming the year after Lexie died."

"Gosh," she said, "that's strange, even for Gideon. What did Jorge say when they told him where the money came from?"

"Not much," Garrett said. "How would you respond to something like that?"

"Creepy," she said. "Was there anything about Denise on his laptop, something we didn't know?"

"Like what?" Jett asked.

"Why he waited until she was five for instance," she said.

Garrett nodded. "One notation. 'First and last the same. Bookends.' He took Weston's granddaughter first. She was five."

"And Denise was the last on his list," she said, "so he waited until she was five."

"I suppose that fits with his warped sense of logic," Jett said.

"Any news on the Hendrickses?" she asked.

"I talked to Mrs. Hendricks's parents," Garrett said. "They don't know where the family is, but they do get a weekly phone call."

"Did they think Miles Chaney had taken Zoe?"

Garrett nodded. "When they found out Miles Chaney wasn't Zoe's kidnapper, it spooked them more. They were afraid the police really would think they were involved in the kidnapping, so they stayed underground."

She looked at Garrett. "Did Gideon's log say anything about the skunks?"

He nodded. "He trapped, tranquilized, and left them there specifically for the search. He thought it was a big joke."

"Well, I guess this adventure's over." She scooted out of the booth and called Feather.

"Where are you going?" Jett asked. "We're picking up Gayle at five and heading home."

"Not me," Garrett said. "I'm taking a flight to Pennsylvania. After all this, I have to see Reggie. Maybe Yvonne and I can sit down and work something out."

"I wish you better luck than I had," Jett said.

Brenna leaned on the booth. "You've made a decision about Joanne?"

He nodded. "Both of us have changed too much. When I lived at home, I didn't notice. Most of our time was spent with the girls. But now"—he shook his head—"we can't spend ten minutes together without fighting. That's no way to live."

"I'm sorry," she said.

"So am I." As she walked away, he called after her. "Don't forget, five o'clock."

"I'll be back before then."

Brenna knelt beside Feather, in front of a gray tombstone.

"I've missed you, Aaron. If you haven't seen her yet, Brie's up there with you. Take care of Funny Face for me. Feather and I miss her so much.

"There's another little girl named Leanne who needs a hug, too. I'll rest a bit easier if I know you're watching out for her . . . for all the little ones Gideon sent your way."

She sat on the ground and touched the engraving. Feather lay beside her and rested her head on Brenna's knee.

"This is Feather."

At the mention of her name, Feather raised her head and looked at Brenna.

"We had a tough one, Aaron. It ended all right, but I can't help but wonder if I could have done something different, better. Everybody thinks I lured Gideon to the edge of that crater on purpose. I was just trying to get away."

She combed her fingers through Feather's coat.

"I wish you could talk to me for a few minutes. Five, just five minutes."

"Will I do?" a woman said.

She twisted and saw Connie.

"I'm not Aaron," she said, "but I'm willing to listen." She smiled. "You're not good at losing a tail, Bren. I followed you from the hotel."

"Why?"

"In your effort to avoid Simon the last few days, you've avoided me, too." She squatted next to Brenna. "I appreciate your loyalty, but I'm not really interested in Simon Blue."

"Neither am I."

"I wish you were. Since Brie died, we've watched you hit emotional shutdown, and you've been slow in coming back."

Brenna shook her head. "These past few months have been one big blur."

Connie touched Brenna's shoulder. "If Aaron could talk to you, he'd tell you to get on with life. You've done the best you can, and no one can ask for more."

Odd, the voice was Connie's, but the words sounded like Aaron's. Brenna smiled.

"What?" Connie asked.

"I was wondering if a particular stone cottage might still be available."

"That's the Bren I know." Connie stood. "On the way home, let's spend some road time together and cook up a scandalous scheme. I met a man last month I'd like to know better. What if we throw a huge party and invite every person we know?"

"To celebrate what?"

Connie tilted her head as if she was thinking. "The end of a nightmare and the beginning of happier days."

Feather woofed and wagged her tail. Brenna kissed the dog's nose and looked at Connie.

"Sounds good to me. I just happen to have the perfect dress to lure an unsuspecting man into a fabulous fling."

Brenna rose, skimmed her fingers across Aaron's marker, and moved beside Connie.

Maybe the cottage was still waiting for her. Roots . . . and a fresh start. Marsha would breed Kneely next year; maybe there'd be a sweet little girl in that litter who'd like living with her and a black, headstrong roommate who'd teach her to dig in the garbage and sneak onto the bed.

"Come on, Feather. It's time to go home."